MW01489223

THE BILLION-AIRE'S SHAMAN

A BWWM Romantic Suspense Thriller

Mia Caldwell

Mia Caldwell

California, United States

The Billionaire's Shaman / Mia Caldwell   2nd ed.
ISBN 978-1539859116

Dedicated to Nicholas

PROLOGUE

-Sabrina-

The Law Note Daily Review – Ten Years Ago

The ten-year-old girl a key witness in the Fourth of July Kidnapping case, created a work of art last summer which ultimately led police to save two of three kidnapped children. The child, dubbed the 'psychic artist,' by the press used her remarkable artistic skills to create a mural on the wall of her bedroom, made entirely of torn bits of paper and glue, after having an alleged "psychic vision."

The mural depicted, in remarkable detail, each of the three kidnapped children who had been taken only the day before. The art work also showed three men, presumably the kidnappers. Only two of the men's images were completed, but the third man's image had no facial details. After conferring with the parents and learning that the child artist had depicted the clothing worn by the children when they were kidnapped, police decided to release photographs of the mural to the public. The two men who's faces were shown were almost immediately identified. Shortly, thereafter, police recovered two of the stolen children, safe and unharmed.

The press went nuts, wanting to proclaim the marvels of the young mystery artist. She was a hero, but of course, her identity was to remain confidential, known only to a few police. However, during a press conference, one of the grateful mothers, let slip, "Thank you, Sabrina, thank you for saving my baby." Obvious, that the police department hadn't been careful enough in protecting the identity of the child witness, a judge stepped in and slapped a gag order against the Washington State police, all parents and parties involved and against the press, reminding them to not reference the name Sabrina, and to give the child the privacy and anonymity which was her right.

But, as the days went on and two-year-old Scott Jenson remained at large, his parents, broke the gag order and held a press conference demanding that the Washington Police question the child again and compel her to finish her mural. Threatened by actions from the courts, they backed down on their public pressuring of the police. However, per the complaint, they took matters into their own hands and conspired to influence two unidentified Washington State Police officers to illegally detain and question the minor witness without the knowledge or presence of her parents. Per the complaint, the ten-year-old girl was allegedly severely traumatized by the unlawful interrogation and remains hospitalized pending mental evaluation, thus adding child endangerment to the list of charges.

"We are very disturbed that this has occurred," stated Jolene Hoffman, director of Child Services for the DHAHS, "we are already making plans to relocate the child to another state and hope that the media refrains from trying to learn the identity of this child or her family. They've suffered enough."

CALEB

Somewhere in Northern Washington State
The child Sabrina didn't save... ten years later

Caleb was a wild child, with long hair that had never been cut.

By day they let him run free in the woods because his captors knew he wouldn't run. There was nowhere to go. They told him that if he tried, he'd die. Either from starvation or by eating a poisonous plant, or by being sucked into the raging stream and drowned, but most likely he'd perish as soon as the sun went down when the wolves came out in the forest to hunt for an easy dinner.

Caleb had seen wolves, sometimes long before sunset. He knew to stay close to the cabin, where the sounds of the humans and the noises inside the house frightened the wolves and kept them at bay.

When he became old enough to explore far and wide, Caleb kept an eye on the sun. When it reached the apex of the sky he turned around and headed back, always returning to the safety of the cabin before dusk fell over the deep forest.

He'd grown up, from a small child to gangly pre-teen, and saw the seasons change ten times. He watched the moon wax then wane into another month over a hundred times. The cabin, despite all its mysteries and horrors, was his home for better or worse.

Two ugly sisters from Bulgaria, with identical hearts of stone, were his captors, or his "caretakers," as they preferred to be called. They did Sir's bidding, whatever that might be. Every month they'd take turns. One would appear in a car, spend the night, and then the next morning he'd have a new sister in charge of keeping him alive.

Olga was by far the worst of the two, always quick to beat him if he got out of line. But Babette, who enjoyed giving him a good beating, was too lazy most of the time to lift a finger. Because she liked to drink and do other things when she didn't know Caleb was watching—things that would get her into trouble if Sir ever found out—Caleb liked it best when it was Babette's turn to keep an eye on him.

Sir never showed his face. That was his thing.

Sir did stop by, often when he least expected a visit. Sometimes one time per season, sometimes only once or twice the whole year.

Caleb feared Sir most of all, but he also looked forward to the visits.

Sir was interested in Caleb. Sir broke the monotony of his world. Sir was cruel, but he wasn't indifferent like the twins.

When Sir came, he'd stay for several days, his face always obscured behind his mask. He'd spend hours talking at him, explaining how the world worked. Sir was his teacher. Sir taught him how to read and how to write. Sir brought him books. Sir gave him his name. Sir told him that he was important—a special child, a child whose purpose in life was to accomplish an important task.

Sir refused to explain what that task was, or when Caleb would be sent out to complete the task, but as Caleb grew older and wiser with each passing day, so did his understanding.

SABRINA

I stared through the dirt-encrusted window, beyond the wrought iron bars, and into the street, willing Jeanette's car to appear. I checked my phone to see if she'd called back. Nothing.

I stamped my foot on the ground and crossed my arms in frustration.

I needed to go, but I continued to stall my departure. My suitcase sat by the door and I'd even had some success taming my wild hair. I was good to go. And yet I stood there with not-quite-ready-to-leave-yet cold feet, sabotaging my best chance of earning enough money to start fixing my biggest mistake thus far. But it was all on the pretext that I couldn't go unless Jeanette got there first.

Huh!

I knew that was a load of BS. I knew she and her two boys would arrive soon enough. I also knew that even though Ellis wasn't well, he wasn't that much of an invalid and he'd survive just fine if he had to spend a few hours on his own. I checked my phone for the time and then to see if Jeanette had called me back, and my stomach tightened. I was running out of time. I had to decide.

I was stalling, not due to any anxiety over my chances at being hired by some billionaire, or if I had the skills and talent to get the job done. I stalled out of a deep-rooted phobia, fear. I hated leaving people I'd grown close to. For good reason.

After my mother died when I was just a little girl, I'd learned that people that claim to care about you can disappear forever. And as I grew older, it kept happening to me repeatedly. A new foster family would take me in and I'd feel like one of theirs, and then pow—I'd be sent off to live somewhere else. Granted, there were several foster families I was thrilled never to lay eyes on again, but I'd had a few that were awesome. But when someone in the "system" decided that I should move on, it was always the same. No matter how much they promised to stay in touch with me, or I promised to stay in touch with them, once I walked out that door it was over.

The phone rang, startling me.

"Hello, Jeannette? How close are you?"

"Sabrina, is that you? You all set and at the ferry, I hope?"

THE BILLIONAIRE'S SHAMAN

"Uh..." I said, suddenly wishing I hadn't answered the phone.

A noise erupted from her car.

"Hang on a minute, Sabrina," she said. A second later I had to jerk the phone away from my ear as Jeannette yelled at her kids. "Tyler Samuel Hawkins, what have I told you about not torturing your brother? Give Jerrod's turtle back right now!"

A second later Jeannette came back on the phone. She seemed almost calm, but my heart was thumping. "You already on the boat, then?" she pressed.

I gulped, knowing she could turn that temper on me. I tried to put her in the hot seat. "How long till you get here?" I asked, with a little more snot in my voice than I'd intended.

"What do you mean, till I get there? Sabrina?"

I didn't respond. Her voice rose a notch. "Sabrina, don't tell me you're still at the damn house."

She had no right to yell at me. I tightened up. "You said you'd be here before I had to go—"

She cut me off. "I said I might be there before you left. What the hell? I can't believe you're screwing this up, after everything I did to get you this gig."

Now that was going too far. Even for Jeannette. My jaws clenched and I scrunched my shoulders around my neck while heat rushed into my face. "I interviewed with the lady, I got the gig. All you did was take a message."

"Yeah, and if I hadn't," Jeanette retorted, "Cerise would have taken the damn message and then thrown it straight into the trash."

I let out a breath.

"You don't know that."

"And you don't know Cerise."

We let our tempers cool for a few moments, then Jeannette said in a diplomatic, pleading tone, "Sabrina, look, it's not too late. You still have time if you leave right now and if you don't drive like an old lady."

"All right," I said. I was about to hang up and get going when I heard her voice.

"Wait, Sabrina, wait."

"What?"

"It's a long drive to Diversion," she reminded me, as if the last of my money for a full tank of gas hadn't sunk that bit of news right into my brain. She continued. "Promise me you'll call after you get there, before you go to bed."

"I promise."

Instead of just taking off right then and there, I went back into the kitchen to say goodbye and check on Ellis again, just in case he'd heard me talking at the front door. He was in the same spot at the kitchen table.

Ellis had been a jazz musician apparently, and though he hadn't told me the whole story yet for some reason, it was his music career that had caused him to meet my mother. Furthermore, it was their brief encounter roughly twenty-three years and nine months ago, that was the reason I existed.

THE BILLIONAIRE'S SHAMAN

He had his eyes closed while he listed to music on his headphones, and even though I couldn't hear the music he was listening to, the whole kitchen was filled with a rhythmic and disturbing group of sounds. Once again it made me reconsider the wisdom of leaving, especially for as long as two weeks.

Ellis suffered from lung cancer and COPD, double trouble in the breathing and long-life department. Each breath he took, every inhale and exhale, created a tortured kind of music, a kind of prelude to death which was coming sooner rather than later. As his chest rose and fell, there was a symphonic ocean of noises, waves that seemed to be filled with gravel which crashed then receded on a shore made of tin. But despite his poor health and the scary noises he was making, Ellis gave no indications that he was suffering in any way. His face was relaxed, his eyes closed and soft, a picture of contentment, serenity, and bliss.

I envied him.

I thought about just leaving since he obviously didn't know I was still there, but as soon as I turned around he spoke. "Ah, daughter, so glad you're still here."

He had his eyes open, and he was smiling at me in that way that made my heart melt every time.

As he rested the headphones around his skinny neck and onto his bony shoulders, he looked at me as if I were the most precious thing he'd ever seen. He waved me over and I stepped closer toward him. "There's something I meant to give you for the trip."

I was close enough to him to catch faint sounds of a Charlie Parker riff under the wheezing. I waited to hear more, even though in the back of my mind I was thinking about the long trip to the ferry and how Jeannette would be royally pissed if I missed it. "Uh, Ellis, I actually need to get going—"

"This will only take a second," he said.

I shrugged. "All right, what is it?"

"See that cabinet over there?" He pointed to some cabinets to the right of the stove. "Inside, there's a box. Bring it here."

In a place where most people would have pots and pans, I found a cardboard box. I brought it to Ellis, who opened the lid and spent a few moments digging around inside. Finally, he pulled out an object and handed it to me.

I drew my hand back as an unexpected static shock went through my fingers. "Ouch." I shook out my fingers as my eyes open wide. Ellis's pupils dilated with glee like a mischievous child. "What is it?" I asked, still getting over the painful shock.

"Try again," he said.

I rubbed my feet back and forth to ground myself and made another attempt to take the bag. I didn't get a shock that time, but my breath quickened.

"What is it?" I asked as I turned it over in my hand. The fabric was old and faded, but there were places where some of the bolder colors remained, mostly hidden under some beads. Deep oranges, greens, and reds were dyed onto the animal skin cloth as bold designs which look vaguely African zigzagged around it. Macraméd into the embroidery were stunning beads, some made of metal, or bone, or stone. But it was the fringe at the bottom of the bag that intrigued me almost as much as what was hiding inside it. Tiny brass bells in the shapes of human skulls hung from each strip of leather fringe, and as I moved the bag they seemed to sing to me.

"Wow, it's beautiful," I said, at last, remembering that Ellis was sitting there, as I pulled hard with my fingers trying to undo the knot that kept the mysterious contents out of my reach.

A cool hand grasped my wrist, pulling my fingers away from the drawstring. "Don't open it now, Sabrina," Ellis said. "Wait till you got time to appreciate what's inside." I saw him glance over my head at the clock. "You best be going."

Turning around, I grabbed at my stomach when I saw the time. Crap.

I clutched the bag close to my chest and started to head out, but then I had second thoughts. "Ellis, can you at least tell me what it is and where it came from? I'm dying to know." I had my body aimed at the exit, ready to race to the car the moment he finished telling me.

"Why, daughter, it's a shaman's medicine bag. I thought your mother would have shown you one of these. This one belonged to your grandmother, your Mamago."

"Huh?" I said, then took another look at the clock. "Whatever, we'll talk about it when I get back. I better bolt, or Jeanette will never let me hear the end of it."

Ellis's face split into a huge grin and he nodded agreement. I ran over to him and kissed him on the forehead. "I love you, Daddy," I said.

Then I hurried outside. So, that I wouldn't be tempted to try and look inside before I'd made it to my appointment, I placed the shaman bag carefully into the side of the trunk out of harm's reach from dusty, dirty bags of grout and cement that I used to create my mosaics. I drove like a crazy woman to make up lost time, while at the same time keeping my eye peeled for kids playing in the street.

2 HARCOURT

The moment Harcourt caught a glimpse of Sharon's cottage, the constant pain in his gut sharpened. He stood there for a moment, staring up at it, while gulping back an urge to cry out. He'd done enough fist-shaking and cursing at God, and it hadn't changed anything. It hadn't brought them back. The crippling guilt and sorrow passed as he moved closer and more pleasant memories entered his thoughts. His mind flashed back to the construction of the cottage, and he could picture it with just framework. He almost smiled as he recalled how the cottage had come to be. He'd built it for his wife, Sharon.

Sharon adored the big ten-bedroom mansion that he'd bought and restored for them. The building had historical significance, having originally been built in the Seventies by a famous Canadian rock star as a retreat for other celebrities of the time. It had been the site of many parties, but it had eventually become vacant and fell into disrepair.

She loved everything he'd had done to it, but since he was rarely home she complained that it sometimes felt too big. He offered to build her another house, whatever she wanted, in any town or country in the world. She laughed and said that she didn't want a new house anywhere else— she just wanted a cottage right there in Diversion.

He said that her wish was his command, and it was.

The next month when he'd had his next opportunity to come home for a visit, Sharon had a picture for him. She'd drawn it herself, admitting that it was something she'd envisioned from a fairy tale. Harcourt took it to Vancouver to the best architectural firm in town, and soon he had plans drawn up, ready for Sharon's approval.

He was back in New York and flying around the world making his company as big as he could for his baby boy when the cottage was built. Cedric and Sharon continued to live in the big house mostly without his presence.

Whenever Harcourt came home—which was less frequently as Cedric grew older—he'd always find his wife and son at the cottage instead of in the big house. Sharon confessed that they'd moved into it, citing its size and their loneliness without him there. Harcourt felt bad, but his company needed him now. Soon, he promised. In the meantime, he pressed her to hire servants and a nanny, anyone so there would be other people around. But Sharon refused.

"No butlers, no boarding schools." Those were her rules. Sharon and Cedric loved to garden. In her letters, she'd send pictures of her and Cedric planting beds of flowers and working in a vegetable garden ripe with sweet peas and tomatoes and watermelon. And when he visited home, Cedric couldn't wait to show him his little garden and the flowers and vegetables his mother had helped him plant. He'd even created a little miniature village in the garden, complete with tiny little people and thatched homes with bridges and carts.

In the two months before Cedric and Sharon died, Harcourt hadn't been able to get away once. But he missed his wife and child, and so he insisted they fly to meet him while he was conducting business in Seattle.

If he'd have just told them to stay, to wait until he could get back home, they'd still be in his life.

This time when the flood of anger came he directed it not at the heavens, but at his own selfish, stupid heart. How could he have been so blind? He had paradise already and he wasted it, trying to get more money, when he already had more than enough.

Harcourt had to brace himself again before stepping up to the cottage he'd become obsessed with. Every day after his morning six-mile run, he'd shower, then visit the site. He was obsessed with his plans for it.

He let the garden and the flowers go to seed. Even Cedric's little garden had turned back into the land.

He pulled the key out of his pocket and unlocked the front door.

The cottage had bleached pine floors and white walls. After they died, he had all the furniture, household goods, and all personal items removed. No one would ever live in the house again. And he never stayed overnight inside. That would be far too painful to consider.

He intended to make it into a shrine. The only furniture was the window seat and a folding chair and table.

His plan was to take every rare picture he found of his wife and son and have them recreated as mosaic art and plastered over every wall and useable surface in the cabin. Then he would spend hours in the cottage every day and he'd never forget them. Ever. But despite multiple attempts to hire an artist, none of them would accept the job, or if they wanted it, none had the talent to capture the essence of Sharon or Cedric. It frustrated the hell out of him because he was running out of time before he had to go back to work. He'd managed to get a year off to deal with the tragedy, but he'd already begun his final month.

Italian Smalti and other expensive mosaic tiles, which he'd ordered from around the world, lay in pallets and boxes about the main room. When the last mosaic artist totally embarrassed himself when he submitted his sample of the picture he gave them all to try and recreate, Harcourt considered flying to Italy. He wanted to find a master craftsman, or hire a firm to conduct a contest in which they would offer the winning artist some huge cash prize just for getting the gig.

But he hadn't left his home in Canada since returning there after the funeral, so the idea of going to Italy was hard to stomach. Risking publicity about something so important, so private, so tragic... That wasn't an option, either.

As he did every day, Harcourt moved to the window seat, which was Sharon and Cedric's favorite place in the house. It was a bench with a cushioned seat, and inside he kept his most prized possessions. On top of a soft, neatly folded blanket lay Sharon's hand-crocheted wool scarf and Cedric's favorite toy, and underneath it all, the heavy wooden box which contained the only photographic evidence that he'd ever been happy, the pictures of his wife and son.

He lifted the blanket first, smelling it, then put Sharon's scarf to his face as he tried to inhale her scent. Almost a year had passed since the accident, but he imagined that he could still sense the whisper of his son's young boy smell in the blanket and his wife's flowery sent in the scarf.

He set the scarf and the blanket onto the floor, then picked up Cedric's red fireman's hat, what was left of it. Ignoring the part of the hat where the plastic had melted from the heat of the crash before the plane succumbed to the sea, he thought again about how special that hat was to his boy. It was plastic and cheap, something he'd bought on a whim while on a rare non-working weekend when he'd taken his son to downtown Diversion. He took him into Hammond's general store, and he said, "get anything you want, son." All Cedric wanted was that cheap, plastic toy. So, he bought it. And Cedric loved it that fireman's helmet. Never went anywhere without it. Slept with it. Cried when his mother took it away from him for his bath. Cedric wanted to be a fireman when he grew up, but thanks to Harcourt, Cedric would never get that chance.

Harcourt squeezed his eyes closed. The box sat there, waiting for him to open it. But he wouldn't open the box that day. He hadn't opened it in a long time. "I'm sorry," he said to the box and the people inside he couldn't face. He slumped to the floor, holding the box in his lap, as his shoulders bounced and his heart shattered again.

An hour or so later, Harcourt headed back to the mansion, his heart heavy and spirits dipping as he took the footpath to the house. He was surprised to see Molly McCarthy's old truck at the back of his house. He'd given her the day off since she planned to go to Victoria for the weekend.

Molly was one of those senior citizens that could run rings around people half her age. She lived down the hill, about a mile away at the bottom of Dogwood Canyon Road. She was his only close neighbor. There was another house up the hill even closer, but it was a vacation rental cabin that never seemed to be rented. Just seeing her car lifted his spirits somewhat. After the funeral, after he'd come back to stay in Diversion to get away from everyone and grieve in private, he'd had zero intentions of meeting any neighbors. He planned to spend his year of grieving, speaking to no one, and becoming a hermit and growing a beard. He planned to stay locked up in the big place, until the emptiness of it all killed him dead, and he stopped hurting so bad. But it hadn't worked out that way. Only three days after he'd moved back in, that very same truck rolled up to his house.

He met her in the driveway, hoping to get her to leave, but she'd heard about the tragedy and she'd been a close friend of his wife. She'd taken care of Cedric, and helped with things whenever Sharon needed a break or needed to drive herself to Port Hardy for something.

The tragedy hit Molly hard. When she expressed her condolences, for the first time it didn't seem fake or full of pity like everyone else. She too was in real pain and it comforted him to know he wasn't alone. After the initial condolences were over, however, Harcourt expected her to leave. Instead, she went to her car and pulled out a sack of groceries and motioned for him to come over and take it from her.

"What's this?" he remembered asking her.

"Food," she said.

Without invitation, she lumbered into the house and made herself at home in his kitchen. Over the next few hours, she recounted her memories of Sharon and little Cedric as she placed a casserole in the oven, washed the dirty dishes piled up in the sink, and made room for the groceries inside the refrigerator.

She sat with him as he ate his first proper meal since leaving New York, and over the next week, Molly McCarthy was the only speck of light that broke through the morass of pain and grief that clung to Harcourt's soul like hot tar clings to a roof.

She stopped by every few days to cook and make sure he ate something. She cleaned and did laundry and even picked up his mail from the post office in town. She distracted him with bits of news and gossip, and never stopped looking for

MIA CALDWELL

ways to help. After almost a month of her continual kindness, Harcourt came out of his bubble of pain long enough to realize that he couldn't tolerate her kindness and charity another minute.

"You aren't welcome on this property again, Molly, unless you agree to accept a salaried position."

The arrangement turned out better than either might have expected. Molly came and went as she pleased, squeezing her visits between her busy life as a grandmother and president of the Diversion Gardening Club. Yet, despite the loose schedule, Harcourt was never left wanting for anything. She handled everything, including household cooking and cleaning, but she also hired and dealt with any handymen and landscapers so Harcourt didn't have to. When a wicked storm blew over their side of the island two days before Thanksgiving, Molly arranged to have the fallen tree cut into pieces and hauled away. When a dead squirrel plugged up the septic system, Molly contacted the plumbers and watched as the men got it out.

There could be a million reasons why Molly hadn't gone to Victoria yet. She probably wanted to make him dinner. She was such a momma hen when it came to food. But she wasn't in the kitchen.

He moved past the kitchen, into the formal dining room, then into the hallway and called out into the big house, "Molly, where are you?"

"In your office."

Sure enough, Molly was in his office, knees bent on the floor as she crouched behind his desk trying to do something

• 22 •

with a plastic object in her outstretched arms. She groaned with the effort, then lost her balance, and the plastic object clattered to the floor. "Cheese and rice!" she said.

Worried that she might have hurt herself, Harcourt rushed over. "Can I give you a hand? Here. Please, take my arm. And by the way, what the heck are you trying to do?"

Molly recovered and her cheery round face beamed at him. She stayed behind his desk and picked up the plastic object. She handed it to him. He could see it was a computer camera. "Hold this right on top of the screen while I plug it in."

Harcourt did as he was told, while Molly grunted and groaned until she managed to get back into the kneeling position and plug the cables into his company's desktop computer. He reached over and helped her to her feet. She smiled, clearly satisfied with her work, then dusted her hands off on her skirt before pushing an errant gray curl out of her face.

"Are you going to tell me what this is all about?" Harcourt asked, unable to stop a lopsided grin from forming on his face.

Molly was always doing something unpredictable around his house. Instead of answering him, Molly's eyes narrowed in concentration and she shuffled past him, then moved to his desk and sat in his chair. She turned on his computer and began to toy with the camera and the keyboard, typing in commands. Soon, a red light glowed on the camera and Molly's live image appeared on the screen.

"Oh," she said, apparently surprised to see her face so close up. She backed up a little, then spoke. "Testing, testing, one two three." A little voice graph pulsed up and down indicating that the sound was working. "All set," she said, beaming with her accomplishment as she spun the chair around and let Harcourt help her to her feet. She picked a piece of paper and handed it to him. "Follow these instructions, and you should be all set for your call. Just remember that it's going to start exactly at twelve o'clock our time, which, in case you've forgotten, is going to be three New York time." Molly stopped talking long enough to give Harcourt an appraising look. "You should probably change clothes, maybe a shave as well."

"Molly!"

"What?"

"What are you talking about? What meeting? I didn't agree to any meeting. It's not time yet. I've got—" Harcourt glanced at his watch, and his eyes moved to the ceiling as he calculated his remaining days.

Molly waved her chubby arm to get his attention. "Thirty-two days, I know. That's what I told Bianca."

"Who's that?"

"Peter's new assistant. Apparently, Beatrice Rhodes left the company."

Harcourt's eyebrow lifted at that news. Beatrice Rhodes had been his executive assistant for over seven years, and she was the best on the planet. When he'd left Peter Talbert in charge of his company until he got back, he thought Beatrice would stay with him. Then when he got back, Peter would go back to his old position and find a new admin.

Harcourt rubbed his hand over his growing stubble, wondering what had caused her to leave. Had it been her idea to go, or Peter's? He had a sudden pang of guilt for pushing away everyone that had been a part of his life. He thought that perhaps she might have become ill, and he didn't even know about it. Harcourt shook away the thought. He wasn't supposed to worry about these things. He wasn't supposed to even know about them.

Harcourt took a steadying breath. "What is the purpose of this meeting?"

"I'd tell you, but Bianca wouldn't say much. Something about getting you prepared, I think."

Harcourt wanted to tell Molly to call back this "Bianca" woman back and have her pass along a message to Peter Talbert that he had no intention of doing any work before the sun set on his last day, and if they didn't like his position on the matter, then they could kindly go fuck themselves. But he held back, partly because Molly didn't seem like the kind of woman who would appreciate such colorful language, and partly because as he considered it a little longer, it made sense that he'd need some time to prepare for his return.

His old friend Peter had flown in from wherever he'd been to stand with him during those darkest first days. Peter kept the press and other people away when Harcourt could barely inhale, let alone think about the company he was supposed to run. In the week after he buried his wife and only son, Peter hammered out the details, allowing Harcourt the opportunity to have an extended sabbatical from the firm. Peter took over as acting president and CEO so that Harcourt could go back to his home in Canada and have a chance to grieve without any business distractions. The board only wanted to give Harcourt six months, but Peter convinced them to give him a year—six months for each family member lost.

For just under eleven months Harcourt had done exactly that—stayed out of the world of his company and tried to heal. And not once during his time off did he have to deal with anything related to his company. He'd not been inclined, nor compelled to give a single shit about anything going on in his company. It was a complete 180-degree turnaround from the way it used to be, when the drive to keep growing his company bigger and bigger seemed to consume his every waking thought.

As much as he wanted to refuse this meeting—and to make them hold to every hour of his full one-year off—Harcourt understood that they wouldn't just allow him to saunter into his office on the first day of August and hand over the helm to the mighty ship. Not when he couldn't state the ship's current position, or its bearing. Not when he had no sense whatsoever of any dangers lurking beneath the waves.

And it wasn't just company details he'd blocked from his mind in the last eleven months. He'd also deliberately completely ignored and remained blissfully unaware of what was happening in the world. He read no newspapers, nor watched the television news nor listened to the radio. Other than to pop in a DVD of a movie occasionally, or to use the internet to order mosaic materials for the cottage project, Harcourt had avoided technology and the media as much as possible.

And when he did use his computer, which wasn't very often, he averted his eyes at the first glimmer of a headline. For all he knew, the President of the United States could have been impeached in the last eleven months and replaced by a communist cross-dresser from Austin, Texas.

Other than the occasional accidental slip-up made by Molly when she came to do his laundry or cook his meals and she'd mention something she'd heard in the news, he was in the dark, even about the most basic details regarding his company.

Per the terms of the bereavement leave agreement approved by the Board, Harcourt's only commitments to the company were a two-minute phone call with Peter at the beginning of each quarter. The primary purpose of the call was to assure the board that Harcourt was still alive. The calls never lasted more than two minutes, and Peter's short report regarding the company, rarely varied, the same one sentence summary, always along the lines of "The company is doing great." No specifics, no numbers, no details of any kind. Just like Harcourt had wanted.

But that was before, and this was now. They needed to prep him, so he wouldn't fight it. Most likely, this would be the first of many such meetings to come.

After Molly left to get ready for her trip, he presumed, Harcourt went upstairs to take her advice and get presentable for the conference call. As he decided on a suit, shirt, and tie, he imagined how the meeting would go. In a large conference room at corporate headquarters, Peter and the rest of his executive staff would be seated in a room waiting for him to come online. The minute they saw him, they'd probably clap, maybe even give him a standing ovation. After that, Peter would probably express their sincere condolences for his loss on behalf of everyone in the room.

Harcourt would nod somberly and then they'd get down to business. Peter would start by presenting charts and graphs, highlighting the numbers of the company's great success in the year he was off. Then the others would take turns, presenting their various divisions and regions, and drill down how each had contributed to the company's continued success. They'd be touting their personal contributions, gathering brownie points for his return, making sure that he noticed them.

Harcourt stepped into his shower, allowing the water to fall over his head and face as he bent his neck back. As the water showered over the tense muscles in his neck, a melancholy grew up in the steam, thickening the water and darkening his mood. His time off and leave-of-absence would soon be over, and something had been nagging at him, doubts lingering in the recesses at the bottom of the closet in his mind. He hadn't been able to put his finger on what was troubling him, but as he finished soaping himself off and went in for another rinse, it suddenly became clear.

He was worried about going back to work. Worried that people would expect too much from him. Worried that they'd expect him to come back as if he were good as new, or perhaps even better than before—as if the horrible tragedy had toughened him and made him stronger. As if being stripped of his emotional ties in the world would make him an unstoppable force in the business arena.

He tried to picture himself back in the saddle, the nobleman of business improving the country's global position as he manipulated and reshaped commerce and industry again. He snorted at the absurdity of it. "Yeah, like that's going to happen," he said to himself as he stepped out of the shower, then reached for a towel.

Did they just expect him to walk into the office in thirty-two days with the same spit and vinegar he'd had before? To have the same drive and tenacity that had helped him to turn the modest multi-million-dollar company he'd inherited from his father into the multi-billion-dollar juggernaut it was today?

Well, if they were counting on that kind of performance, they were in for a rude awakening.

Harcourt wouldn't hesitate to work hard and with dedication and do his best to be a competent leader, but that was as far as he could go. He could never be the man he was before. He couldn't let himself be that man again.

How could he?

He brushed his teeth and spit into the sink, scowling into the mirror.

He'd never be the kind of man who put his drive for wealth and power ahead of his family ever again. That man had destroyed everything he held dear. How could he even think of walking in those shoes again?

Everyone said that the plane crash was a tragic accident—that it wasn't his fault. But Harcourt knew better. It was his blind ambition that had sent them to their graves. He was responsible for what happened and he would never forgive himself. Never.

And no one was ever going to change his mind on that subject.

Taking a deep breath, and after giving himself another dirty look in the mirror, Harcourt decided to take Molly's advice and shave off his beard. The least he could do was look the part.

He ran water in the sink until the water began to warm up. He splashed his face and applied shaving cream with a brush to his beard. Sweat trickled down the back of his neck. He turned off the water and walked over to the French doors, opening them wide to let some fresh air into the room. His eyes traveled over the trees that surrounded his property and up into the sky. It had been a long, dry summer, but there was humidity in the air and clouds forming out in the east. He hoped there would be some rain. They could certainly use it.

The call of an osprey in the distance pierced the silence of the day. He loved the grand birds. He scanned the sky and the tree tops on the ridge where ospreys and bald eagles often perched, but he didn't see it.

His watched beeped at the quarter hour, reminding him that he didn't have much time. Leaving the doors open to continue to cool off the room, he went back to the sink and picked up the razor.

Outside the osprey called again, sounding much closer, as if right outside his window. Intrigued, Harcourt put down the razor and walked back to the balcony, spotting the magnificent bird of prey almost immediately. It was perched on a stripped branch near the top of the tallest pine growing in the center of his circular driveway. The osprey turned its head and seemed to be looking directly at him.

The osprey expanded his white chest, opened its beak and called out to the sky. Too-ooh, too-ooh, toooo-ooh. With the mournful bursts of sound, a chill ran through Harcourt, raising hairs on the back of his arms. Was that supposed to be a sign? Harcourt shook his head in disbelief. He didn't need to worry if he could do the job. He didn't need to worry about returning to work in thirty-two days. He didn't need to return to work ever.

"Thank you," Harcourt said as he applauded the great bird. The osprey cocked its head in Harcourt's direction, scoping him out with his beady eye. Unimpressed, the bird lifted his great black wings and soared effortlessly away, over the trees and towards the sea.

Harcourt returned to the sink with a skip in his stride, his head up, and eyes sparkling with newfound purpose. He stared at his face as he picked up the razor. He'd not shaved for several weeks and he had the start of a fine-looking beard. He'd intended to shave it all off for the conference call, but why bother? He didn't need to impress anyone, and he'd always wanted to grow a beard. After rinsing away the previous application of shaving cream, he swirled the brush back in and this time applied his shaving ritual to cleaning up the areas where he didn't want to grow his beard, specifically his neck.

He pondered his new plan, liking it more and more with each cleaning swipe of the blade. It was so simple. He'd announce that he was stepping down, that he'd decided to retire from business, because why the hell not? He certainly didn't need the money. His success had been so spectacular that even if he never worked another day in his life, or never invested a penny of the billions he'd accumulated, and he'd still have more money than he could ever hope to spend in his lifetime.

But working will help you forget, will help you occupy your thoughts, will help you move on from the tragedy.

"Shit," Harcourt said as his razor nicked a spot near his Adam's apple. He let the razor fall into the sink and grabbed a towel to stop the bleeding. Cursing again, he waited for the bleeding to stop. He finished his shaving and put a piece of tissue on his wound while he considered the cons against retiring, casting doubts on his new plan.

Perhaps going back to work would make sense. Perhaps going back to my old life will be the only chance I have to put the past behind me.

Stronger voices inside Harcourt's head began to drown out the idea that he had any right or deserved in any way to move on. Like a preacher knows that someday a parishioner will steal from the collection plate, Harcourt knew with a certainty that if he ever became "that man" again, the kind of man who could abandon and ignore his family the way that he'd done—then it would be no different than betraying Sharon and Cedric all over again.

He'd made up his mind.

Harcourt finished his ablutions and dressed quickly into his business attire. Then he sat down at his desk in the bedroom, pulled out a notepad, and wrote down the key bullet points for his resignation announcement, which he intended to give to Peter Talbert as soon as the video conference call was over.

Eyes wide and glowing, Harcourt hurried downstairs and settled himself in his chair in front of the computer as he reached for Molly's instructions. His whole body hummed with anticipation, as if he couldn't believe that he was going to go through with the new plan. He wasn't sure he'd be able to sit through the whole meeting with a straight face. In less than an hour, he'd be done with Raymondson Industries forever, and done with being "that man." Good riddance.

3 SABRINA

I broke every speed limit on the way to the ferry, but managed to arrive just in the nick of time. After following the attendant's directions to the bottom of the ship, I parked my car, turned off the engine, then put on the emergency brake as instructed by all the signs.

I locked my car and leaving everything inside except my purse, I went up to the top deck and straight to the bow of the ship. It was already underway, heading out into the Georgia Strait toward Vancouver Island. I'd never been on a boat before and I was excited, telling myself that I should stay out there the whole time and not miss anything.

But visibility was crap, and the wind relentless, so I gave up and headed down into the ship. I walked around until I found a seat far away from yelling children. I dug through my big, white purse looking for my phone.

"We're here," announced the text from Jeannette.

I let out a small sigh of relief, and started to reply, "I made the ferry," but when I tried to send, it wouldn't go through. Not enough bars.

Frustrated, I was about to put my phone away when I noticed there was a voicemail pending. "Oh, shit," I blurted as soon as I saw that it was from an unknown number. My first thought was that it had to be my client, the billionaire dude who kept his cell number private, calling to tell me not to come...

"Dang it," I muttered and tugged at my collar. This was all I needed. I'd pushed past my reservations about leaving Ellis and Jeannette and the boys for a few weeks, and now I was already on the ferry and on my way. Well, it just rubbed me raw that I'd now have to turn around and go back, having wasted both time and money.

"No," I said to out loud as I stomped my foot and crossed my arms over my chest. He wasn't going to get rid of me that easily. The person nearest me gave me a doubtful stare, then gathered his umbrella off the floor and moved to another seat.

My thoughts raced as I tried to think what to do. I wasn't giving up without a fight. I wanted this gig. No, I needed this gig.

Coming to a decision, I gritted my teeth and held onto the button until my phone powered off.

"There," I said to myself, keeping my voice down so as not to tip the ship by number of people exiting my location, "if I didn't actually hear the message telling me not to come, then when I got there I could just say, 'I'm sorry, I didn't get the message. Let me show you my portfolio, seeing as how I've come all this way.'"

Yes. That might just work. He couldn't just send me away... not after I'd driven so far. Not when I hadn't received the message not to come.

So I wouldn't be tempted to pull out my phone, I hid it deep in the bowels of my purse and tried to put it out of my mind. I stared out the window at the sea as we sailed toward Vancouver Island. There was wind on the water, and white caps that looked like whipped cream appeared and disappeared on the surface like they were playing a game of whack-a-mole. After fifteen minutes of doing that, my leg was bouncing and my fingers were going a mile a minute on the hard-wooden bench. I tried to think of something, anything but that damn unheard voicemail. The more I tried not to think about it, the more alternative scenarios raced in my head.

What if the message wasn't what I thought it was? What if it wasn't anything bad at all? What if it was just the client telling me to come in the morning, instead of tonight? Could I risk ignoring it? Would I blow my chances for certain because I showed up at the wrong time?

At that point, the back of my teeth started to make a racket as I ground them together. My jaw ached from the stress. "Screw it," I blurted as I dug through my purse for my phone. I turned it back on, and found the message.

"Here goes nothing," I said. Immediately, a man's voice came on the phone and for a split second my hopes fell, thinking that I was right and it was the billionaire telling me not to come.

"...I'm in Vancouver. I got on a plane as soon as I heard about the article. I want you back. I miss you, Sabrina...." Blood seemed to drain out of my face as I froze in my chair, my hand seizing up as I gaped at my phone. My leg muscles tightened and I jerked up from my seat, sucking in short gasps of air as the voice on the phone continued, "...please, Sabrina. I need you. Come back with me. It wasn't my fault. I love—"

I pitched the phone away from me as fast as I could, as if it were made of live spiders crawling all over my hand. It bounced off the metal support beam, then clattered to the floor with a sickening crunch. The room swayed as I stumbled, scooping up my purse and my phone, then, clutching them to my bosom, I jerked around, eyes darting as if I expected him to be standing there on the passenger deck, watching me.

Lunging towards the hall to the bathrooms, I pushed past startled passengers, as sweat poured down my neck. I made it into a stall just in time, then doubled over. The nausea and the dizziness passed, as I held onto the walls of the stall for support. When it felt safe to move again, I slumped onto the toilet, fully clothed and hugged myself, and rocked, until my body stopped shaking.

"No, no, no, no, it's not possible," I repeated to myself again and again, as I stayed in that stall for the rest of the voyage. I couldn't make sense of how he'd tracked me down. I'd left the country for pity's sake, and he didn't know anything about Jeannette and Ellis, I was sure of that.

The horn blew, and the ferry jerked, forcing me to brace myself in the stall. As the anchor chain clanked down the side of the hull, I remembered what Jack had said in his voicemail... "I'm in Vancouver," he'd said. "I got on a plane as soon as I heard about the article."

That's how he found me. That stupid article.

Feature Article in the Piedmont Gazette

Valuable Art Work from Mysterious Talent Found Selling for Peanuts at Vancouver Coffee House

An artist whose identity had been shrouded in anonymity and mystery since first coming to light while she was just ten years old, has allegedly been selling her valuable and distinctive mosaic artwork at a Vancouver coffeehouse at coffee house prices for the last several months.

"Needless to say, discovering her artwork in Vancouver, at a coffee shop no less, was a huge surprise." Local art collector, Lee Thibodaux told the Gazette. He brought in the 2-foot by 3-foot mosaic he purchased at the Piedmont Coffee House in Piedmont, last Thursday, and showed us examples

from the internet and a brochure he'd received at a recent showing of her work in San Francisco, to help show that the artistic styles were the same.

Citing a desire to keep his lucky find to himself, he refused to allow us to photograph his piece for this article, but we brought in our local art critic and everyone agreed, there was no doubt that the artwork had the same look and feel.

For those that aren't familiar with the story of Sabrina, Child Psychic Artist, the following is a summary.

In 2001 on the 4th of July, three children from three prominent and wealthy Seattle families were kidnapped while watching fireworks at a fancy party at a private estate in Beacon Hill. During the first twenty-four hours, while the police negotiated with the kidnappers, the public was not informed of the event. But, after the ransom was paid and the three children were not delivered as promised, police went on the offensive and the public was notified. When the story broke on the night of the fifth of July, images of the three missing children, and the heart-wrenching pleas of the devastated parents, filled every television screen both in Seattle and across the country, including here in Canada.

Police and the parents asked anyone with any information to call a hotline. Rewards were established, but despite hundreds of calls, police had nothing to help them find the missing children. That was until a hotline volunteer received a call from a parent who claimed that her daughter had created a picture of the kidnappers. "My daughter knows who the kidnappers are," the hotline volunteer remembers hearing. He told her to bring the picture to the police station, but when the caller claimed that he couldn't because the child had done the image on her bedroom wall, the volunteer passed the information along to the police who dispatched a patrol to the caller's home to take a photograph of the image.

Police were stunned to find on the bedroom wall of a ten-year-old girl the images of not only the three missing children but also of three men. Since the artwork had been made painstakingly with scissors and paper and glue, and could not have been completed after the pictures of the girls were broadcast, and because the parents identified the clothing being worn as clothing the children owned, yet not shown in the public photographs, it was determined this child might be onto something.

The entire image was photographed and plastered on television. Two of the men in the image were depicted with full and exacting facial details, but the third man's face had no features, as if the child artist couldn't see him clearly enough in her mind's eye.

Within, hours of broadcasting the images, citizens called in with reports, and police had the identity of the two men, brothers with a long history of trouble with the law. A few hours later, they located a possible hiding place, and found two of the children. They were frightened, and tied up, scared, and dehydrated, but otherwise unharmed.

The two relieved families thanked authorities and praised the young artist who led police to their children. One of them even let slip her name, "Thank you, Sabrina."

The media wanted to know about this child artist, but the police declined to comment, including declining to confirm if her first name was Sabrina or not. They had more important things to do, because while two of the kidnapped children had been returned, the third was still missing and the two brothers, although identified, were still in the wind.

Since they had no idea who the third man was, Police concentrated their efforts on finding the two known culprits, hoping the third child would be found with them. They did find the men; at a warehouse, they'd been known to use. But, they'd been killed, execution style, and there were no signs of the still missing child.

The media began to speculate, fueled by interviews and demands from the parents of the still missing child. They insisted on having the police bring in the child artist to see if she could recall the third man's face. It was now the operating theory that it was the third man with the missing face in the child's image, had probably killed the other two accomplices, and ran off with the money. It was hoped also, that he ran off with the third child.

Publicly, the police declined to acquiesce to the parent's pressures, citing safety concerns for the child. But, somehow, probably through a series of bribes, the parents of the missing child managed to convince the police to interview the girl, privately, at a hotel with a police officer present. Unfortunately, after meeting with the parents, the young girl had a severe mental breakdown, and had to be hospitalized.

After that incident, the courts put a gag order on the parents and gave them a restraining order, which forbade them to contact the child or her parents again. The Seattle Police Department was fined for endangering a child, and *the mystery girl was taken off the grid, and her records and her full legal name sealed from the public.*

Six months later, after the story had died down, and the public forgot about the still missing three-year-old-boy, the boy's father was found dead of an apparent suicide.

Six months after that on the fourth of July, the mother who'd now lost a child and a husband, gave a news conference where she begged, Sabrina, to come forth and help her find her child and the third man.

It was ironic, that when the young woman finally did come forward and admitted that she was the Child Psychic Artist it was 10 years later, and the woman who'd never stopped pleading for her help every year on the fourth of July, had only weeks before succumbed to Ovarian Cancer.

Sabrina's admission which was held at a press conference in front of a Hollywood studio on July Fourth 2014, hit the wires and garnered international media attention. Requests for an interview and on-camera appearances flooded the studio, but Merge Right Productions refused to give the media access to their golden girl. They were making a movie about her story, and if people wanted to know more they could wait for the film. Sabrina, who still only went by her first name, appeared very shy and uncomfortable on camera and read from a statement.

And while the studio was reluctant to grant her interviews, they weren't reluctant to promote that she was creating and selling her art. Her showing at art galleries around the West Coast, were sold out, her art selling for more and more each time. But, her handlers kept her off camera, and when they let her on camera, they did all the speaking for her.

And then after the initial media interest seemed to die down, the film studio had another press conference. Sabrina was now considering other kidnappings and crimes, and he put out a request for people to send letters with pictures of missing loved ones, to Sabrina, care of the studio. This announcement put Sabrina and the movie back in the forefront of media attention and per the unnamed source at the studio, letters and calls requesting Sabrina's help flooded the studio.

It wasn't long after this, apparently, that Sabrina, allegedly went AWOL. Art gallery appearances were canceled, and the studio stopped promoting the film. Our unnamed source close to the project said that the future of the film was now contingent on the return of the Sabrina. Our requests from Merge Right Studios for comment on this story were declined.

Some people the Gazette spoke to, suspected that the young psychic artist might have had another mental breakdown after reading some of the letters. It was possible that the studio was denying her admission to a mental hospital or similar, concerned that it might destroy the likeability of the woman featured in their film.

So, for now, all we can do is speculate. Sabrina, if you're out there in Vancouver somewhere, come forth and let us tell your tale. And for any of you lucky enough to have purchased her art from the coffee shop wall, before you knew

THE BILLIONAIRE'S SHAMAN

who made it, the Gazette would like to get a picture and interview you for a follow-up story.

Send inquiries to ScottCarmen@PiedmontGazette.com

* 45 *

4 HARCOURT

After punching in the right set of codes, Harcourt pulled back as he saw text rather than a group of people on his screen. Instead of the room full of people eagerly awaiting to see him for the first time in almost a year, there was just a graphic with the words Waiting for Conference Room Leader written on it. Harcourt scratched under his ear, pondering the meaning. With important video conference calls, usually the conference room leader—often an administrative assistant—would be there a good thirty minutes prior to the start-time.

Before he could think of who to complain to about the lax business protocol, the graphic went away and the screen showed live video. He relaxed, and readied himself for the last business meeting before his official retirement, until he took the unexpected scene. He'd expected to see: one of his company's large, familiar conference rooms, and a roomful of faces he recognized, like Peter's and others from the executive team.

Instead, the conference room was small by corporate standards, and instead of a dozen or more people in the room, he only saw three. The three men sat staring back at him, poker-faced. Harcourt did not recognize these men; he was sure of that. He must have transposed a number or something, dialed into the wrong conference call by mistake. Harcourt reached for Molly's instructions to check the conference room ID number when the man in the middle spoke.

"Harcourt Raymondson?" he asked.

"Yes."

The man who'd addressed him was in his late sixties, wearing a well-tailored gray suit. He pushed a pair of gold-rimmed reading glasses down his nose and stared at Harcourt.

Harcourt tensed up, but forced his voice to sound relaxed and unconcerned. "Where is everyone? Are we early?"

The man in the middle lifted an eyebrow then glanced at the other two men, then they all started staring at him again. Harcourt had the uncomfortable feeling that they were observing him like he was a rat in a cage.

"We're exactly on time, sir, and everyone who's coming is present," said the man in the middle.

"All right," Harcourt said, surprised, but eager to move things along. Once the meeting was over, he'd just make his call and give Peter his resignation. "I take it you're my preppers?"

"My name is David Gooding," said the man in the middle after giving Harcourt a pained look. "This is my associate Jason Petrovich, and this is Garner Forestdale, who is representing the stockholders in this matter."

Harcourt held up a hand, then leaned forward. "I'm sorry, what do you mean by 'this matter,' and what do the stockholders have to do with prepping me for my return?"

"Sir, if you'd let me continue, it will all become clear," said Gooding.

Harcourt had heard enough. He sat forward in his chair and spoke, his voice clear in its seriousness and need for a straight answer. "Where's Peter?"

"Mr. Talbert isn't present per my suggestion," Gooding said. "Now, if you don't mind, we'd like to get started. I have a plane to catch."

Harcourt's jaw clenched and his lips pressed together as he held back a biting retort. *One hour, just put up with these assholes for one hour and then it will all be over.* Apparently satisfied that he was going to be allowed to continue without further interruptions, Gooding nodded to the man on his left, the man he'd called Petrovich, and the young attorney started digging through a thick file. Harcourt noticed that his hands shook as he struggled to find what he was looking for.

"Give me that," Gooding snapped as he yanked the file out of the younger man's hands.

Petrovich sat back in his seat, and Harcourt saw color rise in the young man's cheeks.

Gooding wasn't having any better luck finding whatever they were looking for. As the seconds ticked past, Harcourt felt an urge to turn off the computer and go for a run. But he didn't want to give the press anything to talk about, such as his aberrant behavior, nor was he interested in doing anything else that might compromise his new plan.

He straightened the notepad and pen on his desk as he waited for them to get their act together. A smile flitted at the edge of his mouth, and he felt the tension in his neck lessen. That was it. That's all it was. *They need lawyers to prep me, because Raymondson Industries is in the middle of a major acquisition.* He went on to confirm that postulation.

While on leave of absence, he technically wasn't a member of the firm; he was just another member of the public until he came back to his official capacity. Anything they told him now had to be carefully vetted to make sure he didn't receive any details which would give him insider information when he wasn't an insider.

Lawyers would be far more suited to that task than a roomful of old friends and colleagues—the executive team of Raymondson Industries—men and woman who in their enthusiasm to share with Harcourt all the amazing business milestones they'd reached in the last year might accidentally let something slip that he shouldn't yet know about.

Yes, it made sense that lawyers would handle this, if for no other reason than to keep the SEC from galloping up the company's butt.

Patting the piece of paper in his pocket, Harcourt reminded himself that he didn't care. The crinkling sound comforted him. He looked at his watch. Only five minutes had gone by. It seemed like an hour already. He breathed in. All he had to do was get through the next hour.

"Yes," Gooding said as he found what he was looking for. He smoothed the single sheet of paper on the table in front of him and pushed his glasses up his nose and read the document.

Harcourt's fingers drummed on the table. "What's on the agenda first, gentlemen? International acquisitions? Next quarter's revenue projections?" he said, hoping to move things along.

They looked up at him, and Harcourt added, "I have a plane to catch as well, gentlemen," he said, and looked at his watch. These pretentious slackers were wasting his time.

The man to the right of Gooding, the one introduced as Forestdale, spoke for the first time. He was a rotund man with sharp black eyes and a fleshy, doughy face dripping with oatmeal-colored skin. He smoothed his thin comb-over and looked down his nose at Harcourt as he spoke. His voice was nasal and his tone condescending. "We're not here to discuss business affairs, Mr. Raymondson."

"Then what are we here to discuss?" Harcourt said through gritted teeth, as his fingers rounded into fists on the desk. Forestdale gave Gooding a meaningful stare and Gooding handed over the document. Forestdale's multiple chins bounced as he reread the paper, and Harcourt's whole body tensed as if he knew it wasn't going to be good news.

"This meeting is to inform you that the board of directors will be voting to rescind your upcoming reinstatement."

His jaw dropped open and he felt a boulder land in the pit of his stomach, taking the breath out of him. He shook his head, sucking in air. "What? What the fuck are you talking about?"

"I'll read it again," said Forestdale, as if he were explaining something to a four-year-old child.

Harcourt put out his hand. "No, don't. I'm not saying another word, or listening to another word from you. I demand to speak with Peter Talbert, right now!"

Forestdale's black eyes gleamed in the crevasse behind all that flesh. He held up his hands to his two colleagues as if to say that he would handle this, then said, "Mr. Raymondson, you have no authority to demand anything."

He sat back, a smug smile forming on his face. Harcourt wanted to reach through the screen and tear the smug expression right off his face. He couldn't control the volume in his voice. "What do you mean, I have no authority? It's my company. I built it with my own two hands!"

"That may be the case," said Forestdale, clearly unperturbed by his outburst. He had his elbows on the table and he looked at Harcourt through the upside down V made by his templed fingers. Continuing to speak to Harcourt as if he were talking to a person with limited mental abilities, he said in a slow and well-enunciated voice, "It's true, you did build the company, Mr. Raymondson, but then you had an IPO, remember? And that made Raymondson Industries a public company, which means it belongs to the shareholders, who I represent. Are you with me so far? And due to the recent catastrophic drop in value, you are no longer a majority stockholder, which means you have virtually no authority. The board of directors, which is tasked to look after shareholders' interest in case you've forgotten, has tasked us with giving you this notice. They've been forced—with reluctance—to instigate this action to stop the bleeding before the company is irreparably harmed. Has this explanation helped you at all?"

Harcourt's eyes went wide. He'd stopped listening after he heard the words catastrophic decline in value. His heart thumped like a cat trapped in a bag, beating so hard and hurting so bad he feared he might be having a heart attack. He pressed his palm against it to stop the thrum. He gasped for air. Nothing made any sense. Peter had assured him the company was doing great all this time. He shook his head, feeling the floodwaters of doubt sinking his hopes. When he finally managed to speak, his voice cracked. "Ca...catastrophic decline in value?" he asked, shaking his head again as if the concept was too absurd to contemplate.

Petrovich let out a laugh. He turned toward the others and spoke like Harcourt wasn't there. His voice was high-pitched and his hand motions effeminate as he squealed almost with delight. "It's true, then. I thought it was just a rumor. He has no idea what's been going on with his company. Powerful evidence if you ask me."

Gooding and Forestdale nodded, like they agreed with the little runt.

"Evidence of what?" Harcourt shouted. He wanted to jump through the screen and pound all three men into a fucking pulp, starting with the little runt.

Gooding took off his glasses and leaned in, enjoying himself as he spoke. "You've made a series of decisions recently which have been devastating to the company. As Petrovich says, the fact that you appear to be unaware of what you've done only supports the rumors that you've lost your nut. No offense, sir."

Harcourt's throat tightened and his mouth felt dry. "But I've been on a leave of absence. I haven't been making any decisions. I don't know what you people are talking about. I left Peter in charge. I signed over all authority to him. You should be having this conversation with him, not me."

Forestdale hoisted himself up after pushing his chair way back to clear his enormous gut. He stood up and leaned forward, pointing his chubby finger at Harcourt. His fleshy oatmeal-colored face had turned red as he almost shouted his response. "No, sir. That is not true. You did not sign anything away. The truth is, you've made countless decisions regarding the company, you've refused to account for missing funds, and you've refused to set foot in New York or respond to our numerous demands for your attention."

Harcourt wanted to correct them, to set them straight, but the wind had been knocked out of his sails. Whatever was going on, he wasn't going to get any help from the men in the room. He slumped into his chair, unable to respond. He closed his eyes. He'd been manipulated. Played like a fucking fool. Trying to explain that to these men would be pointless, futile. He didn't think they were part of the plot, but he was starting to understand who was.

He tugged at his tie. He needed to get off the call, get out of his suit. He needed to get ahold of Peter and confront him. He needed to find out what the fuck was going on.

"Sir?"

When Harcourt spoke again, his voice was calm and even, defying the boiling turmoil inside. "Thank you, gentlemen, for your communication. Is there anything else you need to tell me?"

Before letting him go, the lawyers gave Harcourt the details of the date, time, and location of the emergency board of directors meeting. Upon hearing that it was going to take place the following Wednesday in New York, Harcourt's fake confidence slipped another notch. They explained that he would have a chance to state his case at this meeting and that if he wanted to keep his position, it would be his only chance before the board put his removal to a vote.

As soon as the call disconnected, Harcourt had one last burst of anger. He tore the video camera away from the monitor and fast-pitched it into the far wall. It broke and clattered to the floor, and he staggered down the hallway, through the kitchen, and out into the back of his house.

"Fuck!" he screamed into the sky, as the trees surrounding his property seemed to close in around him.

There was an old-fashioned porch swing on the deck behind the kitchen and he sat on it, slumping forward. He put his hands on his head and shook it, still not able to believe what had just happened. Then his shoulders began to shake. Not from crying, but from laughter.

"You idiot, what did you expect?" he yelled, as his laughing broached hysterical. "You've had your head in the fucking sand for a year and you handed over your company to a man that once coveted your wife, you fucking moron. Could you have been more of a fool? Not likely!"

He hadn't had a drink since giving it up after Molly came on board, but he sure as hell wanted one now. As he gathered himself up to go get good and drunk, he felt for the note in his pocket with his bullet points on why he felt it was best for him to resign, and pulled it out.

No. He wouldn't get drunk like some beaten weakling. He was going to fight, and he sure as hell wasn't going to resign. He held out the paper in front of him in two hands and tore the note into tiny pieces, then went back inside, ready to start making calls to the men and women in his company he trusted to find out what the fuck was going on.

Despite spending the next few hours diligently attempting to get to the bottom of things, Harcourt could not get any useful information because he couldn't get through to anyone that knew anything. He'd started by calling Peter Talbert, and was ready to rip him a good one sideways and up and down his ass. Peter wasn't unavailable to take his calls according to his new executive assistant, a snotty woman named Bianca. She wouldn't tell him anything, not where he was, or when he might be able to call him back.

He had no better luck with the executive staff, or even the members of the board that he was acquainted with. After an hour of burning up the company switchboard to no avail, the receptionist—who'd been the only supportive person he'd spoken with the whole time—said with much regret in her voice, "I'm so sorry, sir, but I've been told not to put you through to anyone anymore. They asked me to tell you to call Gooding and Associates instead. I'm so sorry."

"That's all right, Abagail, thank you for your help," he said, not wanting to take his frustrations out on her. When he hung up, he pounded his fist so hard on the desk that pain shot through his arm and he bit his tongue.

"Fuck," he said as he thought about what else he could do. It had been almost a year since he'd tried to log onto the company intranet. No surprise, his old password no longer worked, and he doubted he'd be getting any support from IT under the current circumstances.

He sat back and tried to think things through. His situation was more precarious than he'd first imagined. He'd need to be close and he'd need help to deal with the crisis. He called Molly and hoped she was still in Diversion, and that she hadn't started her weekend trip to Victoria to visit the grandkids early.

When Molly didn't pick up, Harcourt cleared his throat. "Molly, it's me," Harcourt began. "If you're still in town, I need your help with some urgent business, mostly travel arrangements. Call me as soon as you get this message."

He hung up. Molly would handle his travel arrangements and get him a flight to New York out of Vancouver as early as tomorrow. For the rest of the day, he'd go to plan B, gathering troops—lawyers mostly—to help him fight this upcoming vote.

The only attorneys he knew all had dealings with his company, so he spent an hour researching law firms and left messages with his top choices. He'd have Molly book a floor at the fanciest hotel nearest his headquarters, and if necessary he'd pay to have an entire law firm set up a room in that hotel with the sole purpose of helping him get to the bottom of whatever was going on and keep him in power. He hoped that they'd figure out a way to stall the vote, to give him more time to prepare a response and dig into what kind of shenanigans Peter had been up to.

But after an hour of doing internet research and reading dry CVs about the partners of New York's top law firms, Harcourt's head was pounding. Wanting to talk to someone in his camp, he tried Molly again, but got voicemail. This time he just hung up and considered grabbing his keys and driving down to her house to check if she was still there.

He felt out of sorts and decided against it. He needed to clear his head. He needed to go for another run.

A few minutes later, he breathed in the scent of pine when dried-needles crunched under his feet as he ran. Along with the scent of pine, there was also the smell of the ocean, and what he hoped was the scent of a coming rain. Through the tall trees he saw clouds forming. He hoped a storm was coming. The drought which the entire island and most of the Pacific Northwest had suffered was getting out of hand. Certain species of trees had weakened and become diseased, making them matchsticks for any forest fire, and the streams and creeks which he passed as he ran were the lowest he'd ever seen.

He picked up his pace, finding that the harder he sucked in air and the hotter his muscles felt, the less he suffered from the day's events. Switching his thoughts to the video conference call and all that he'd heard, he was certain that Peter Talbert was behind everything. Why else would Peter have lied to him during those quarterly mandatory calls, telling him that the company was doing great, when it wasn't? What other explanation could there be for the abrupt departure of an executive assistant as loyal and talented as Beatrice, unless she'd got wind of what was going on and resigned?

Or maybe, he thought, breathing hard as he ran, maybe Beatrice no longer worked for Peter because she'd seen something improper coming out of his office, and Peter got rid of her so she wouldn't spill the beans?

The more Harcourt thought about what Peter had done to him, the angrier Harcourt became, but also the more determined he was to fight it. Swearing to himself that he wouldn't rest until he proved that Peter was behind everything, including the company's apparent decline, Harcourt finished his run. He leaned over, hands on his knees, breathing hard.

"I'm not going to rest, Peter, you son of a bitch, until everyone knows what a rat bastard you are," he spat after he caught his breath.

Just saying it empowered Harcourt. He stretched with vigor, his face relaxed yet determined to win. He'd find a way to prove that Peter had manipulated the board, and had orchestrated an elaborate con to fool them all. And when he did, he'd make sure Peter paid for his treachery. Because no one fucked with Harcourt Raymondson. No one.

After completing his stretches, he walked back toward the house at a fast pace, eager to get through to Molly and continue implementing his plan. When he saw a bit of Sharon's cottage peeking through the trees, it stopped him in his tracks.

Sharon and Cedric. He hadn't thought about Sharon and Cedric once since getting on that call... nor had he felt that constant thrum of pain and sorrow throughout his body.

He recalled the voice in the back of his head which had been so weak only hours before—the voice that told him walking away from his company was a bad idea. He understood that returning to work meant having something to fight for again, and it was exactly what he needed to do. Working, reclaiming his position would cure him. It would give him purpose again. It would make him whole. It would help him move on, help him rid himself of the guilt.

His natural competitive zeal had been doused by the cold waters of grief and self-hatred, but now they were bubbling and heating up inside his belly like lava in a volcano. Harcourt began to jog, eager to get in his car and drive down to Molly's. If she wasn't there, he'd come back and book the travel himself. But as Harcourt came upon the mansion, he remembered something that had totally slipped his mind.

"Damn it," he said, as he snapped his fingers with frustration. "I forgot about that mosaic artist."

Deciding he wouldn't have time to deal with her, he raced into the house and found his keys. He'd have Molly call the woman and get her not to come, and then he'd tell her all about what had happened and enlist her help. He was dripping with sweat, so he took the stairs two at a time to change into a dry T-shirt. He was coming back down the stairs when another thought hit him. Why cancel the artist at all?

He stopped on the steps and tried to recall the picture of the young artist that had been in the article Molly had shown him. He'd not bothered to read it, and given his sullen state of being at the time, hadn't noticed her picture in any significant way. In retrospect, he was trying to remember what she looked like. She'd been in some evening dress. Definitely attractive, now that he could almost recall. Young, too, probably single. And she was due to arrive at his house in just a few hours. What was he thinking? Why send her away?

Maybe he should fuck her.

He felt his pulse quicken at the thought and felt his Adam's apple bob in his throat.

Why the hell not? Fuck her, fuck her good and hard, he told himself.

His body hummed with the idea, and a comforting warmth seemed to radiate through his body. It made total and absolute sense. He was about to go into battle with a foe that had all the advantage. Shouldn't he rally for every ounce of support he could find? During his initial rise to the top, before he'd settled down and married Sharon, he'd sought the pleasure of many attractive women. They'd found his skills in the bedroom as worthy as his skills in the boardroom. Having sex whenever he wanted it kept his confidence up and his energy sharp. If he truly wanted to get his company back, it was clear.

He needed to start thinking with his dick again.

5 JACK BRESSLER

When Jack Bressler strode into the Piedmont Coffee House, Cerise Ferris, who worked the counter most days, noticed him straight off. She nudged Michael Souderman, who was loading beans into the espresso machine and said, "Check him out. Whoo-hoo, what a looker, drink bet?"

Michael peered over his glasses at the man as he made his way through the crowded coffee house, stopping to examine the art for sale on the walls.

"Frappe, for sure, he's a frappe kind of guy, he orders a Frappe I win," Michael said.

Cerise whispered, "He won't. I agree he probably wants a chocolaty, frozen Frappe with extra whipped cream, but, he'll order a coffee with a couple of shots, to look extra macho."

"You're on," Michael said, then moved back to his position in front of the espresso machine to await the results of his bet.

The man finally stepped to the counter. Cerise covered her mouth with her hand, pretended to cough, then muttering under her breath, said, "Tall coffee two add shots, tall coffee two add shots."

It had worked before, like a witch casting a secret spell, she'd send them a subliminal message, and suddenly whatever they'd intended to get would change. Each time her little trick words, Michael owed her a dollar.

"I'm sorry?" said the man. His perfectly white teeth sparkled like the Canadian Mountie Dudley Do-Right. He leaned forward, his voice barely audible. "I'm looking for Sabrina. Is she here?" he asked, as he craned his neck to look towards the office in the back.

"No one by that name works here."

"Is that so. But, she was selling art?"

"So. We get a lot of artists selling art. Look buddy, you're holding up the line. You want something to drink or not?"

The man looked behind him. There was no one in line. He raised his eyebrow, and gave Cerise an appraising look. It made her tingle a little, and she stuck out her chest and flipped the side of her head that had hair. The man studied the board, as if trying to decide what to get, then discreetly pulled a money clip out of pocket, bulging with a thick wad of American cash. He pulled one twenty off, placed it on the counter, then after giving Cerise a meaningful wink, pulled off another twenty and then another.

His voice was low as he leaned close and spoke quietly so no one else could here. "It's very important that I find her as soon as possible. I'd be very grateful for anything you could tell me."

Cerise couldn't take her eyes off the money, the way a person about to be killed can't stop looking down the barrel of a gun. "Well?" he prodded.

"You've got an order over there, yet?" shouted Michael. "You want a Frappe, right man?"

Cerise darted a disapproving glance at her co-worker. The suggestion strategy was her cheat, not his.

Realizing that she had an edge, since the man wanted something from her, Cherise, pocketed the money and whispered. "Order a tall coffee with two add shots, and I'll see what I can do for you."

After collecting her winnings from Michael, she said grabbed her smokes and announced she was taking a break.

As she carried the man's drink order to him and motioned him to follow her towards the door, she started singing, "Love you Baby, Baby, Baby, we love you Baby Adalyn...," as the hit song from Canada's favorite celebrity couple blasted through the speakers overhead.

The slick, good-looking American followed her across the street, accepted his drink, took one sip, then grimaced and tossed it into a nearby trashcan.

Cerise tapped out a cigarette, then started looking for her lighter. The man stepped in close, flicking a Zippo to life. It sparkled like it was made from platinum.

Cerise leaned in close to light her cigarette and got a whiff of the man himself. He even smelled rich. After she got her cigarette going, she offered him her pack. He pulled one out with his lips, lit it, then after sucking in a deep drag, blew it close to her face, his eyes never leaving hers.

"So, can you tell me where I can find Sabrina?"

"I'm not sure, I should, I mean. You could be a serial killer, for all I know."

The man's deep blue eyes flashed dark and Cerise felt a sudden urge to bolt.

But, he was looking her up and down, his movie-star smile turning slightly predatory, and not in a bad way. Her knees buckled.

"I heard about her talent, from the article. I want to buy some of her art. You appeared to have sold out."

"Whoa 'kay, that makes sense. Her stuff sold out, and I don't know if or when she'll come back."

"Oh," said the man. "In that case..." He held out his hand.

Thinking about all the pot she could buy with that sixty dollars, Cerise said. "But, I might still be able to help."

"Oh?"

"I don't know where she, exactly, but I know that she's living with her Dad in Skenet City."

"Skenet City, where's that?"

"About a half-hour out of the city, to the southeast."

"Can you get me an address?"

"I could, but from what I hear, she's not going to be there. Her sister said she'd going to be on Vancouver Island for a week or so, to work for a billionaire. He's supposedly got a mansion in Diversion, if you can believe that."

"Why is having a mansion in Diversion such a hard thing to believe?"

"Because it's at the end of the world, a place for Indians and loggers and tourists who don't mind roughing it. Not a place for billionaires."

"Cerise... may I call you Cerise?" the man asked as he eyed her nametag again. "I appreciate your information, but I'm afraid none of it will help me locate her soon. I'm in a rush. How about you get me her telephone number?"

"Uh, I can't do that. I mean, I could get into a lot of trouble." Cerise felt empowered, and gave him a look that she hoped told him that there would be more information if he was willing to fork over more dough.

"What if I make it worth your while?" he said, catching on fast.

"You come back with her number and I'll have two more twenties for you."

"Make it sixty, and you've got a deal."

"You drive a hard bargain, Cerise," he said, his voice turning husky. "Makes me want to drive something even harder into you."

Cerise was wet with desire as she hurried back to the coffee shop.

Fifteen minutes later, she was back, and carrying another cup of coffee as if making a delivery.

After he took his coffee, took a sip of the Frappe, then took another.

Then he handed her the promised three twenties and waited, his hand out.

Cerise couldn't help smiling at her cleverness. "I wrote it on the bottom of the cup, along with my number. Nice doing business with you."

She turned and started to head back to the coffee shop, tucking the new money deep into her apron pocket when she was pulled back, as he spun her around, his fingers digging painfully into her forearm. It thrilled her. This guy was dangerous. She liked that in her men. She'd been with bad boys before, but this would be her first rich one.

"I'm sure you understand that I expect you to keep our little conversation to yourself?"

"Sure thing. Call me," Cerise said, with a wink. He let her go, and Cerise hurried across the street, making sure to shake her tiny ass with each step.

6 PETER TALBERT

Peter Talbert sat at his desk in his thousand dollar Herman Miller executive chair, and admired the view of the Manhattan skyline. He leaned back in his chair and rolled it back a little to give her more space, since she'd had to struggle to get under his desk in her tight skirt and high heels. She put her hand on the arms of his chair and positioned her head over his crotch. Keeping her eyes on his, she slowly unclasped his trousers. When she pulled her fingers away and bent her head in, he loosened his tie and lifted his hips, giving her better access.

This was one of the things she liked to do, one of her skills he would miss. His head fell back and he closed his eyes, keeping his hips still as she took the zipper between her teeth. Once the zipper was down, he felt her hot tongue on his lower abdomen, and forced himself not to react. A moment later he felt the tug of her fingers on his pants, so

MIA CALDWELL

he lifted his hips to help her slide his pants and boxer shorts
down to his ankles.

Weaving his fingers together behind his head for support,
he smiled as she got to work. The woman under his desk
was good with her mouth, but nothing compared to the success of a long-term plan. He let her do her thing as he gloated
inwardly over his accomplishments. His day had been excep-
tional, starting with the video conference. He hadn't attended it, of course, but Petrovich had sent a replay as
agreed. He couldn't have been happier with the way that
idiot had taken the bait, after showing that he had no idea
that he'd been conned when he'd opened his mouth like a
fish.

His assistant continued to tease him with her tongue, as
she held onto his hips for support. Instead of looking at her,
he admired his view of the city lights outside, knowing it
might be the last time he saw them from that position. For
just a moment, something like regret tightened in his chest.
He'd miss the life he'd been leading and the trappings of
wealth and power, but he shook his head at the thought that
it was better than what he'd soon have. His cock jerked
when she finally took it into her mouth, and he imagined
how it would feel when the world finally knew it was him,
when he finally got credit for all his true accomplishments
in life.

Everything was going to plan except for one unfortunate
wrinkle. He'd planned too long and too hard to delay his
biggest crime to date because of some vain little news reporter. He tried not to think about Jack and the missing

Sabrina as his assistant began to slide his dick in and out of her throat.

Before Jack had screwed everything up, everything had been going to plan.

It had taken him close to ten years to track down the brat who knew too much. Her name was Sabrina Cane and she was an orphan, who'd lived with foster parents when she'd made her stupid mural, which nearly put him behind bars. She obviously had some kind of gift. He was lucky, that he'd been smart enough to have worn a mask when he kidnapped those kids, or she would have put his face on that mural, for sure, and he wouldn't be up in a private jet thinking about her, ten years later

At first, when he'd been trying to locate her, he'd intended to eliminate her, because he considered her to be a threat. But, when he finally tracked her down, he was no longer concerned about her exposing him. In fact, he was counting on it.

He was tired of his crimes staying under the radar. He craved the limelight, his moment in the sun. Which is why he wanted that film, highlighting his first major crime, turned into a major motion picture. And Sabrina Cane was critical in helping that dream come to fruition.

And now that he'd embezzled and had earned through his kidnapping enterprise enough money to disappear, comfortably, he was ready to go out with a bang. But, first he needed Sabrina back in LA and Jack Bressler there with her to make sure she went back to getting that film completed.

In his spare time, he'd worked on the movie script, the movie that would make him famous, someday. He worked on it secretly, never telling a soul, aware that he could never pitch it to Hollywood himself, but also knowing the timing wasn't right. But, after he found Sabrina Cane, it occurred to him that if she was a consultant to the film, then the studios would be more intrigued with the idea.

Which is why he recruited Jack Bressler to become the so-called writer of the script and he recruited Jack Bressler to seduce Sabrina Cane.

The vain, disgraced news broadcaster, was down on his luck when Peter made his offer, through a surrogate, of course, Jack had no idea who was pulling the string. Nor, did he care once the money had cleared his account. Jack was hungry and blackballed from working in journalism, so he'd tried acting, but hadn't gotten a break. Jack was about consider going into adult films, when he'd received a far more attractive offer.

He brought Jack to Los Angeles, set him up in a fine home with an allowance for clothing, and sent him off to woo Sabrina Cane.

He even gave Jack the script, telling him to act as if he was the writer. He told him which studio to pitch it to, then set up a shell company to act as executive producer, funding the film with his own money.

When the studio heard that Jack was dating Sabrina Cane, and they got the promise of funds from the mystery producer, they bought it. But, then Sabrina was getting cold feet, according to Jack, talking about wanting to date other people. So, he gave Jack and incentive to make sure that didn't happen. And Jack had carried it off.

With Sabrina under his control in those first months, the production was the talk of the town. Sabrina had even started attending art gallery events and other public appearances, all part of the studio's marketing campaign to promote the movie. His movie.

But in the three months since the stupid idiot had driven her away, Sabrina wasn't available to assist the movie studio, on making the movie about the Fourth of July Kidnappings, and her part in it. They'd insisted on filming her for the documentary part of the film, even though Sabrina was reluctant to get in front of a camera.

With Sabrina missing, there was even some talk that the studio was considering tabling the film until she came back. That would be regrettable, and he hoped that it would not happen. But unless Jack could get to Sabrina and bring her back into the fold soon, his hopes of getting credit where credit was due sooner rather than later would be dashed. After he'd been on the lam for a few years, maybe he could fund another studio to create the film.

His assistant was getting his blood pumping now, and he started breathing hard as she took him deep into the back of her throat.

His balls tightened, as he pondered the potentially good news. Per his last communication from Jack, he'd had a lead, and he was going to Vancouver, Canada to see if that's where Sabrina was hiding out. There was a FedEx envelope which he had locked in his briefcase he intended to read later during his flight to Washington state. But knowing Jack Bressler, it was a bad lead.

He felt the orgasm simmering at the back of his spine and had a sudden idea that would fix his problem, even if the movie was put on the back burner for a few years. "Yes," he said out loud, not about the way his cock felt in his assistant's mouth, but at the genius of his new plan. She looked up at him, eyes hopeful for his approval. He gave her an indulgent smile since she still wasn't done. Then he made a note to himself to grab some extra magazines for the note he'd planned for later. He'd always wanted to make one of those notes made from letters cut out of different sources, instead of using giveaway handwriting or an identifiable typewriter. The note he had in his mind would put Sabrina back in the spotlight – and help focus the world back to him, even if they, currently, had no idea who he was.

It was brilliant.

"Ugh," he groaned as he got close. She was growing tired and tried to pull off him. But she hadn't finished her damn job yet. He gripped her head like a vice and shoved her mouth over his cock, pushing himself deep into the back of her throat. She tried to protest, but her cries were masked by his dick and he felt a rush of power as her eyes began to bulge. She pounded her fist against his abs, as a sense of serenity washed over him while enjoying the fear in her eyes. Then his orgasm let loose and he released her ears, giving her just enough space to gag herself off of his cock.

She sucked in air, gasping, staring at him with undisguised horror, but then she pulled herself together and forced a submissive smile.

She was about to stand up when his buzzing burner phone startled the girl, forcing her to slam her head against the underside of his glass-topped desk.

Peter pulled up his pants and grabbed for the phone. "Wait," he said. He put the phone down and zipped up his pants, and watched as his assistant buttoned her bodice and smoothed her skirt.

He laughed inwardly at how easy women were to manipulate. He loved it when they let him treat them like crap, thinking all the while that they were playing him, instead of the other way around. As so many others had been, she was under the mistaken illusion that he gave a shit about her, or that he might someday agree to marry her. They'd put up with unbelievable humiliation if it meant a ticket to the land of fancy homes, and society pages, and endless summers in the Hamptons. But he had no intentions of settling down, with Bianca or any other woman, or with any man for that matter.

"About fucking time," he said into the phone. He was about to continue his conversation with the moron, when he sensed that his assistant was still in the room, leaning over him, as if trying to read the caller ID.

"Get out!"

She huffed and slammed the door behind her.

"Jack, don't waste my time. Do you have her or not?"

HARCOURT

Once he'd decided on a new strategy regarding the mosaic artist, Harcourt decided to skip seeing Molly, and wait until later and deal with the travel himself. Best if she just went along to Victoria and had no idea of his plans to turn the interview into a twenty-four-hour fuck-fest.

Guilt tugged at Harcourt's chest, restricting his air. How could even think like that? Twenty-four-hour-fuck-fest, what was wrong with him? Is that how he planned to honor his dead wife? Appalled at where his head had been going, he tried to rationalize his abnormal behavior. Deprivation, was a key factor, no doubt, but it was having his balls cut off by Peter Talbert.

Harcourt's hand balled into a fist. That's why he couldn't stop thinking about having sex. It was his body's way of telling him that he had to get back in the game, and fast

He blew out a breath, then put his head in his hand and thought back to his playboy years, when he'd had a healthy and active sex life. Even in the height of his sowing his wild oats years, he'd never allowed himself to be an asshole. He'd always been a gentleman.

Maybe this was a bad idea. Maybe it was too soon to reclaim his sexual mojo. Maybe he should just forget about this crazy plan. That's not who he was. He wasn't some pussy crazed frat boy. He was a Raymondson.

Harcourt showered and dressed into everyday clothes. Then, after making the decision to have a drink, he found the file Molly had put together with the CV's or details, on all the mosaic artists that were being considered for the project.

He'd just have the meeting as he'd planned. No monkey business. If she had the talent, and was right for the job, she could work on it while he was away, or start after he got back from saving his company.

After locating the file on Sabrina, he took the file and a bottle of scotch into the living room. He started a fire in the grate, then poured himself a drink and settled into an overstuffed chair, to scan the article for highlights. When he turned to the inside page and saw her picture again, he sucked in a breath. "Damn!"

She was more beautiful than he'd remembered. He stared at her picture, fantasizing about how she'd look without her fancy, designer ball gown, how she'd look in that glistening russet skin and those pouty full lips as he came inside her.

Harcourt's mind flipped flopped again.

He would try to seduce her.

How could he not?

And besides, like he'd told himself before. Having sex again, would be the best way to stop feeling sorry for himself. He needed to do this to get out of his funk.

Of course, she might not be willing, in which case, he'd graciously shut down his plans to seduce – but if she was willing, he wouldn't hold back.

"Yeah, don't hold back," he said, and he thrust his hips out of the chair. Then laughed at himself, for being a total ass again.

"Sometimes, you have to be an ass to get ahead," came his father's voice in his head.

Harcourt eventually finished his drink, and put aside the article. He'd been too wired, too turned-on by her picture that he'd barely read a word about her. He yawned and his eyes drooped.

It had been a long, fucking day. Not only had he done his six-mile run twice in the same day, he'd endured that bull-shit conference call, then wasted hours of his life trying to reach people, to no avail. His let his eyes close for a bit.

He jolted awake, in the chair. The fire had burned down to coals and he knew he'd been asleep for a little while.

The room had become gloomy, as if the day was coming to an end. He picked up the article off the floor, folded it and put it into the file. He'd read it about her later, and as his stomach grumbled reminding him that he needed to eat something, he headed towards the kitchen. Molly was in the kitchen, wearing her red floral apron, as if it was just any other day.

"What are you doing here?" Harcourt asked.

She whipped around, and thrust her hand onto her chest. "Oh, hi, Mr. Raymondson, you shouldn't creep up on a person like that."

"Sorry."

She collected herself and went back to stirring the pot. The smell made Harcourt's mouth water.

"Did you have a nice nap?" She asked, glancing at him over her shoulder.

"Yes, I did, thank you for asking Molly. What are you doing here? I thought you were headed to Victoria."

"Oh, I am, but I wanted to make sure you didn't forget to feed your guest." Molly opened the oven door and wearing an oven mitt adjusted something inside.

"What's in there?" Harcourt asked as the smell of garlic washed over him.

"It's garlic bread. It's already done. Just heat it up a few seconds before you serve."

"All right," Harcourt laughed, wondering why she hadn't brought up his calls, or the trips he wanted her to book. Maybe, she never got his messages.

"Molly, where's your cell phone?"

"Huh?"

"You're cell phone?"

"Oh, it's back at the cottage, somewhere…"

That answered his question. Glad, in a way, since he wanted her to go so he could focus on the night to come, he went to the refrigerator and pulled out the pitcher Molly always kept filled with spring water and fresh mint leaves from the garden, and poured himself a glass.

As he drank, he watched Molly. Apparently done with her preparations, she removed her apron and hung it on a hook by the door. It occurred to Harcourt that he could use a stalwart and competent person like Molly McCarthy back in New York. "Have you ever considered going back to work?"

She gave him a curious look. "What do you think I've been doing for you?"

"I mean for real."

She nodded as if she understood. "Mr. Raymondson, I have no desire to give up my life. I only work for you a few hours a day because you obviously can't get by without me."

Harcourt laughed. "Exactly, I can't get by without you, which is why I was hoping you'd come back with me to New York."

Molly hooted, grinning. "Oh, Mr. Raymondson, you are too funny. You know I'd never leave Diversion. This is my home. And just so you know, I was just kidding. I'm sure you can get by just fine without me."

Harcourt shrugged, disappointed, but not surprised at her reaction.

"Listen, Mr. Raymondson, the dining room table is already set. When she gets here, after you've shown her the project, do yourselves a favor and enjoy this dinner I've been slaving over. There's a fresh garden salad ready to go in the fridge, plus some of my homemade ranch dressing in the Mason jar. Shake it up a bit before you serve it, and don't forget to make the garlic bread."

"I won't. Only broil for a few seconds…"

"Very good. I'll make a chef out of you yet, Mr. Raymondson."

"Highly unlikely."

"Oh yes, one more thing. I'm afraid you're going to have to do the dishes yourself. I'm not planning on coming back until Sunday night."

Knowing that Molly wouldn't be around the next morning, banging pots and pans in the kitchen like she did most days was a good thing, especially if he had Sabrina Cane naked in his bed. He chuckled at the decadent thought without thinking.

"Mr. Raymondson?" Molly said. "Is everything alright with you. You seem, well, different?"

"I was just thinking," Harcourt said, unable to stop the grin from spreading on his face. "All this wining and dining... it's like you're trying to set me up."

She put her hands on her ample hips. "It's not wining or dining, just common courtesy. You can't expect someone to come this far out into the wilderness, especially during the dinner hour, without offering them something to eat."

"Whatever you say, Molly," he said, chuckling. It felt good to smile. It felt so good to laugh. And Molly was right. His property and the little community of Diversion was literally at the end of the road.

After making sure everything was turned off, Molly said. "Look, I better get going. Storm's a coming."

JACK BRESSLER

Jack Bressler regretted calling Sabrina and leaving her that stupid voicemail message. What had he been thinking? He also regretted calling 'the boss,' with an update, before he had her in his possession. The dude was a dick as usual.

He'd decided to go straight over to Vancouver Island and drive out to Diversion that night. It was a pity that Cerise hadn't known the billionaire's name and address, but if the place was as Podunk, as Cerise had indicated, it probably wouldn't be hard to find a billionaire, or his mansion. He'd followed the directions to the ferry, but had to stop when he saw that it was closed. He sat in his rental car staring at the metal sign, flapping wildly in the wind, which hung from the chain blocking access to the ferry.

Closed Due to Inclement Weather.

"Fuck!"

Jack was to go back to the city and check into his hotel, when he noticed a man sitting in what looked like a ticket booth on the other side of the chain. Jack left his car running, got out, hopped the metal chain, then sprinted to the booth. Inside, the employee paid no attention to him, running his fingers over an adding machine. Jack banged his fist against the window until the pencil-pusher acknowledged his presence.

He rolled his chair around, slid the ticket window a crack. "We're closed."

"When's the next ferry?" Jack asked.

The man sighed like he'd been asked to carry a pregnant moose up three flights of stairs. "Not till five-thirty tomorrow morning."

Jack wasn't a morning person. "How about the next one?"

"Ferry runs five-thirty, six-thirty and every thirty thereafter till eight-thirty every night, weather permitting, except on holidays," rattled off the man like he'd said it a million times before.

"Can I buy my ticket now?"

"Not from me. I'm closed." The man slammed the window shut and turned his back on Jack, then returned to his 10-key.

Jack indulged in a fantasy involving a tire iron, if there was one in the trunk, and what he could do to the man's disrespectful head... But as much as the idea appealed, Jack had more important business to attend to.

By the time Jack reversed his Mitsubishi out of the entrance and was on his way back towards the heart of Vancouver, he'd already forgotten about the man in the booth, having moved his thoughts to more important things. For one thing, he was hungry, not having eaten anything but a small packet of peanuts all day. He'd booked the first flight to Vancouver the moment he heard Sabrina might in town.

He thought about checking in at the hotel, but it was too early. Since he was stuck in Vancouver, he needed to do something other than twiddle his thumbs in his room until morning. Jack Bressler considered himself a man of action, a man who knew what he wanted and wasn't afraid to go after it. What he wanted was a good meal and an even better fuck.

He thought about Cerise, the young woman from the coffee shop. His lip curled into a smile as he remembered the way she'd swayed her hips at him during their last encounter. She wanted him to call her back. She wanted him to fuck her. He thought about what she'd said about where Sabrina was staying—no living—with her father. He wondered about that.

Before Sabrina had gotten suspicious of him, while he still had her under his thumb, before he'd lost his temper for the first time, —she'd told him everything about her life.

Or at least, he thought she had.

But she'd never mentioned a father. He shook his head, trying to remember those conversations. No, she'd said more than once that she was an orphan. So this father thing had to be a ruse.

Wishing he knew the address where Sabrina was living, he regretting not pressing the barista for that bit of intel, when he'd had the chance. Then he remembered. There were two phone numbers on the bottom of the paper cup.

After pulling off the road, he searched for the cup, and found it behind the passenger seat.

"Hello?" said a young woman's voice when the call connected.

"Cerise, it's me," Jack said.

"Tall coffee, two add shots?"

Jack chuckled at her joke. "Yeah." He let the word linger, stringing her along. "Hey, Cerise, my little boat trip was canceled, so I'm free for the night. Can I take you to dinner?"

"Sure."

She prattled on, explaining that she'd just gotten off work and that she needed at least an hour to get ready. She gave him a time and a place where he could pick her up, a bar called The Pit, two blocks south of the coffee shop.

After Googling the address for The Pit and putting it into his navigation app on his cell phone, he got back into the flow of traffic and headed toward Piedmont.

He thought about the call as he drove, liking that she needed time to "get ready," before their dinner. He hoped she'd doll herself up good, in something that screamed, I'm ready to get fucked.

When he saw the exit that would take him back to his hotel, he made a fast decision. Jerking the wheel, he flew across three lanes, garnering angry brake screeches and honking of horns in his wake. He could care the fuck less. He parked in a Handicapped spot at the front and checked into his hotel. In his room, he showered fast and put on fresh clothes, then rushed back to his car. Since time was tight, he justified driving hard, speeding around slow-moving cars, and keeping his hand on the horn as he went.

By the time he made it to Piedmont and to the location of The Pit, the rain had begun in earnest. Cerise was waiting for him, leaning against the brick wall under a protective awning, smoking a cigarette in her tight miniskirt. Jack's eyes followed her long legs up to her ass and sucked in oxygen. He could almost see her butt cheeks poking out under that strip of fabric. Other young people joined Cerise, hunkered in the doorway, out of the rain, smoking and talking.

He tapped his horn and Cerise looked up, smiled, then tossed her cigarette towards the gutter than bolted toward the car. She didn't have an umbrella, and when she plopped herself into his car, droplets of water flew sprayed onto his arm.

"Hi," Cerise said.

Jack kept his eyes straight ahead, ignoring her as he moved back into traffic. He'd learned from years of experience that the best way to seduce any women was never to appear very interested in them.

Cerise tittered, her wet hands stroking his rental car as if she'd never been in one so fine. She was a ball of energy, bouncing in her seat, like she was going somewhere exciting. Or maybe she was high. He shot her a glance, and caught the dilated pupils.

High, definitely high. He'd have to find out what she was on and maybe get some from her.

She touched his arm quickly, then drew her fingers back just as fast after getting his attention. "Got a name, hot shot, or should I just call you tall coffee two added shots all night?" She snorted, laughing at her own joke.

Jack ducked his head, and looked out the window to hide the cringe at her uncouth behavior. He couldn't risk pissing her off, not until he got what he wanted. He reached a hand on her bare thigh, gave her his charming smile, and remembering his favorite name from his date-rape days, said, "Paul. I'm Paul Peterson."

7 HARCOURT

Despite having made up his mind to get down and dirty with the mosaic artist if she was willing, Harcourt's couldn't stop the needling thoughts that threatened to make him give up his plan. Most prominent of those thoughts was how wrong it would be to seduce a woman, and then make love to her in the same home he'd shared with Sharon.

But, each time his guilt and better sense tried to steer him away from the plan, he'd see the snide faces of Gooding, Petrovich, and Forestdale, and imagine Peter Talbert's face and how satisfied he had to be about his little scheme, and he'd forget the guilt and think again about the worthiness of his plan.

No more Mr. Nice Guy.

No more Mr. Sad Widower.

He needed to fuck a woman, so he could then fuck up Peter's plans – or whoever was behind this bullshit campaign to shove him into the dirt.

If things didn't work out with Sabrina Cane, so what? He'd be in New York soon enough and he'd find someone else. Sex and plenty of it, would be the best and fastest way to snap his brain back into another way of thinking, to break out of his grieving funk. He needed to get himself laid as soon as fucking possible, ideally with the beauty already closing in on his cock – even if she didn't know it.

Pushing the guilt thoughts aside whenever they came up, Harcourt focused on getting ready. He changed the sheets on his bed, scrubbed down the toilet, and generally tidied up his bedroom. Finally, he did the one thing he'd been dreading. Bracing himself, he unlocked the door to the master bedroom he'd shared with his wife. Expelling a breath, he pushed the door open and ignoring the lump rising in his throat, kept his eyes straight ahead as he moved to his dresser beside the bed.

He found, then took out, the box of condoms. Carried them back into the hallway and locked the door behind him.

"There," he said, relieved to have made it in and out of that room without succumbing to the grief and memories that lived in it, he walked back to the room he'd moved into. He sat at the table by the French door windows and checked inside the box. "Yes," he said, as he counted six condoms in the back, but then he read the expiration date. "Shit."

They'd only expired a few months before, and Harcourt tried to convince himself that there was nothing to worry about, that the manufacturers were overly-cautious, and that there wouldn't be any problem.

But, then he had a flash of fathering an unwanted child with the first meaningless fling out of the gate. He rubbed at his temple which had started to throb. Then checked his watch. He still had time to go to the store.

He grabbed his wallet and keys, then bolted downstairs and out the kitchen door, not bothering to lock the house and got into his G-class Mercedes SUV, praying that it would start. He couldn't remember the last time he drove it anywhere.

It fired right up. When he drove past Molly's house at the bottom of Dogwood Canyon Road, he made a point of not looking her way, in case she was still there, in case she knew what he was up to, in case she tried to stall or stop him from his very important mission.

He exceeded the speed limit on the windy, forested road, determined to get what he needed and return to his house in plenty of time to greet his important guest.

By the time Harcourt skidded to a parking spot outside Hammond's General Store in downtown Diversion, it was five o'clock. He bolted out of his car, and bounded up the steps, fearful that they might close at five. He had to get inside. He pushed open the door, activating a bell. He paused in the doorway, blinking as his eyes adjusted to the gloom. The store was part of a log building, and the walls, ceilings, and floors were all stained wood. It had been built in 1950 a few years after the Hudson's Bay Company founded the town to trade with the Talhkahaw'ka people.

Moving past a display of touristy souvenirs and a stack of books about the history of Hammond's General Store, Harcourt walked toward the front counter, where the proprietor was busy ringing up another customer's purchases.

He stood shifting his weight from foot to foot. The older lady took her bag and when she walked past Harcourt, she gave him a curious stare. Harcourt moved to the counter. The man, who looked somewhat familiar, looked up and smiled broadly. "Well, this is a surprise. Mr. Raymondson, right?"

Harcourt's spirits lifted. The man knew his name. Of course, in a town as small as Diversion, that's just how things were. You could be a billionaire or a bum, it didn't matter. If you lived there year round—meaning you weren't a damn tourist—then people knew your name and most likely your business as well.

Even when you hadn't visited downtown for over a year. Even when you tried to live like a hermit and had your neighbor do all your shopping.

"I'm Fred Hammond," said the man behind the counter and he extended his hand. Harcourt shook it. Fred Hammond was lean and well-built in his late forties, with an extravagant mustache worthy of a barber-shop quartet. As soon as he released Harcourt's hand, he put two fingers on one tip of his mustache and twirled the bit of waxed hair, shaping the end into a point.

"We met, a while back," Hammond said, as if trying to help Harcourt remember their last encounter. But then his amiable smile faded. "Sorry," he muttered.

He got busy straightening his display.

Harcourt understood the reason for the man's discomfort. He'd been referring to the hastily put-together memorial service which had taken place at his mansion a few days after his return.

Molly had organized the service and hundreds of Diversion's residents had come out to pay their respects. Harcourt couldn't remember much of it, but he'd endured it, because it was obvious that the townspeople who'd known Sharon and Cedric needed their chance to say goodbye and grieve.

And even though Harcourt assumed Bill Hammond had been at the event, he couldn't recall any part of it. That day and much of the first month after the tragedy, Harcourt seemed to be walking through the dark in someone else's body.

"It's all right," Harcourt said and forced a smile. Then he added, "Call me Hark."

Hammond blew out a breath and smiled broadly. "Right then, Hark. What can I do you for?"

Harcourt scratched the back of his neck, then looked up at the ceiling. There was a massive cobweb on the deer antler chandelier.

"Uh," he muttered, unsure if he could come right out and say what he wanted. His eyes darted around the store. There were a few other customers, all of them women, and they seemed to have stopped their browsing. He wasn't sure, but he thought they might be eavesdropping.

"Harcourt? I mean Hark?" said Hammond.

A display of cigarettes caught his eye.

"A pack of Marlboros," Harcourt said, pleased to have come up with something. He glanced over his shoulder, relieved to see that other shoppers had gone back to their shopping. He didn't smoke, but maybe he should start. If just for the night…

Hammond reached to his display and asked, "Hard pack or soft?"

Harcourt pictured James Dean with the pack rolled up into his sleeve and tried to recall if that was a hard pack or a soft pack. "Hard?" he said, wishing it hadn't come out like a question.

Hammond chuckled, and slapped the hard pack onto the counter as he reached underneath for a small paper bag. "Let me give you some matches, too," he said, as he threw a few packs inside the bag. "Will there be anything else?"

Harcourt scanned the store again, relieved to see that the women who'd been closest to him had moved to a display of T-shirts near the far end of the store. Still, he didn't want to be overheard. He leaned forward, motioning Hammond to do the same.

"I need a couple of boxes of condoms," Harcourt whispered.

Before leaving Hammond's General Store with his cigarettes and condoms, Harcourt decided to buy some candles, which Hammond added to his purchases. They were the kinds of candles that were inside jars, which Harcourt thought would add to the ambiance and would be safe in case passions got out of control.

As Harcourt got into his car, ready to speed back up the hill with his purchases, there was a knock on his driver's side window.

Harcourt turned the key in the ignition, so he could roll down the window as he wondered if he'd done something wrong.

"Hey ya, Hark," Mark said amiably. "Long time, no see buddy. What brings you to town?"

Harcourt relaxed. Mark just wanted to shoot the breeze. Harcourt was about to give him a quick answer and then tell him he had to run, but before he could open his mouth, the radio on Mark's belt let out a squawk. Mark wasn't wearing his policeman's uniform, but when you're the only law in town, you carry your radio with you 24/7.

Mark's smile faded as he reached for his radio and held it in front of his face. "Don't go, I'll need to talk to you," he mouthed, before moving away to answer the radio.

Rain misted through his open window, so Harcourt rolled it up. He checked his watch, already 5:20 p.m. He thought about the attractive mosaic artist on her way to his home, and the condoms in the paper bag on his seat. He didn't have all day to hang around, in fact, if anyone else had asked him to wait, he'd have put his SUV in reverse and just split, with plans to apologize later for running off. But, he couldn't do that to Mark Pearson. He owed him. He turned off his engine.

He'd met Mark Pearson for the first time, not long after the funeral and only a few days after he'd moved back to his Canadian home. He gave his colleague, Peter Talbert, all powers and authority to run his company so that he could go on a year-long leave of absence to deal with the horrific tragedy. With the worries and responsibilities of running a multi-billion-dollar company off his chest, Harcourt returned to Diversion and moved into the mansion where his wife and son had lived and where he'd spent so little time. Now that it was too late, he was finally spending time at the house, but there was no other place he'd rather be.

He couldn't bear the sad looks from his colleagues and well-meaning acquaintances that were part of his world in New York. He couldn't bear the intrusive questions from the press. All he wanted was to be left alone, closest to the memories of his wife and son.

Hunkered down in the ten-bedroom house, Harcourt set out to do some serious drinking. He'd been three or four days into his bender when someone knocked at his back door.

"Am I being arrested?" Harcourt said as he stared bleary-eyed at the man in uniform standing on his back porch. Harcourt's tongue was thick, and his words slurred from alcohol, even though it was only nine in the morning. He'd just woken up and he was just getting started on his drinking.

"Not today," said the officer in reply to his question.

After introducing himself, Constable Mark Pearson of the Royal Canadian Mounted Police explained that he was the sole officer in Diversion and that he was there on official business.

"May I come in?"

"Sssuit self," Harcourt said, waving the man inside.

"I wanted to give you a heads up that some agents are on their way to ask you some questions."

"Agents?"

"Yes, FBI and some representatives from the JCAAITF."

"Huh?"

"Joint Canadian and American Aviation Investigations Task Force. They want to talk to you about the crash."

"All right," Harcourt said as he went to his bottle and poured out another drink. "You want some?"

Mark came over and picked up the glass and the bottle and moved them to the sink, pouring the contents in the glass down the drain.

"Hey, what'dya do that for?"

Mark ignored him and came over to Harcourt.

"Look, this is serious. If they want to talk to you then they think you had something to do with the crash. Do you want to be drunk, or will you go take a shower and put on some clean clothes and get back here so I can sober you up with some coffee before they get here?"

Harcourt might have been drunk that day, but he wasn't stupid. Not quite comprehending what was going on, he went ahead and showered, changed into clean clothes, and shaved before the agents arrived. He had three cups of coffee in his system when they knocked on the front door.

"Stay here, I'll get them," Mark said.

"No, it's my house. I'll answer the door."

Constable Mark Pearson stayed right behind Harcourt as he made his way to the front of the grand mansion and opened the large main door, where three grim-faced men in suits stood waiting. One of the men stepped forward, flashing his badge. "FBI," he said, then after lifting his eyebrow at the sight of the Canadian Mountie, he turned to Harcourt and said, "Harcourt Raymondson? We'd like you to come with us. I want to bring you to the Seattle FBI offices for questioning about the plane crash." He stepped forward as if to take Harcourt's arm. Harcourt just froze, not comprehending what was happening. Was he being arrested?

Mark pulled Harcourt back into the house and stepped in front of him, and put out his palm. "Now hold your horses, bud. Can I see the court order from my government authorizing you to extract a citizen from Canadian soil?"

The FBI agent gave a wan smile, then reached into his breast pocket. "He's an American citizen, constable. Now if you'd please step out of the way."

Mark didn't move. He put his hand on the butt of his gun.

"That may be true, but he's also a citizen of the great country of Canada. If you want to force him to go with you anywhere, I'm going to need to see the court order from a Canadian judge."

Harcourt was surprised that Mark knew about his dual citizenship. He'd been born Canadian, but after his family had moved to the United States to live with his American father, the paperwork had been put through granting him dual citizenship. Harcourt had spent the bulk of his life growing up in the US, had made his fortune running a US-based company, and he'd thought of himself as primarily an American most of his life. But at that moment, when Mark Pearson had come to his aid, he'd never felt prouder about his Canadian heritage.

The two representatives from the Joint Task Force tried to ease the tension by explaining that they just had some questions. The FBI agent backed down and Harcourt agreed to let them question him in his house. Mark wanted him to wait until he could have an attorney present, but Harcourt wasn't worried. He knew he had nothing to do with the accident. And besides, the sooner these people were out of his hair, the sooner he could get back to his drinking.

During the interview, he learned that authorities now believed that the plane might have been sabotaged due to recently received reports from witnesses on a fishing boat that a small plane had apparently exploded in the sky.

The news shattered Harcourt. He couldn't accept it. They had to be mistaken. Why would anyone deliberately try and kill his wife and son? For the next several hours they grilled Harcourt, asking him question after question about where he'd been in the days and hours leading up to the crash.

He'd recalled enough to convince them that he hadn't been anywhere near the Port Hardy airfield where his wife and son had met a private pilot for their flight to Seattle, flying the most expensive and safe twin engine commuter plane available for private travel. He'd purchased it and kept it at the nearest airport, because it was the fastest and easiest way to get flights on and off the island without having to take the long drive to Victoria.

In the end they left, the FBI agent reminding Harcourt not to take any long trips to parts unknown.

After the questioning was over, Harcourt just wanted to return to the comfort of his bottle. He did for several more days before Molly came to his aid as well, reminding him that there were still good people in the world, and he didn't have to go through his trials completely alone.

He couldn't recall if he'd bothered to thank Mark at the time for looking out for him the way he had, but he sure as hell hadn't forgotten what the man had done for him.

Harcourt opened his eyes and peered out the window. Mark was still talking on the radio. He stared at his watch. It had only been a few minutes. Slumping back into his seat, Harcourt thought about another time when Mark had been there for him. He could wait a few more minutes.

Several weeks later, after Harcourt had Molly helping him out and he gave up drinking in favor of running, Mark showed up at his front door instead of his back door. He was dressed in his uniform, a grim expression on his face. He held an official-looking cataloged-sized envelope in his hand.

"What's that? Am I'm being subpoenaed?" Hark asked.

"No," Mark said with a small laugh. "Remember a while back, when you had your chat with the FBI and the Aviation Task Force people?"

"Vaguely," Harcourt replied, moving his fingers in the air. Truth was, he'd recalled more of it than he wanted to. And the memory made his jaw tighten. "Why, what is this, Mark?"

"Can I come in? I guess those guys didn't want to make the trip again, so they decided that I should show you some pictures."

"What pictures?"

"Why don't we sit down?"

After they sat in the living room, Mark continued. "They found some debris from the probable wreckage site. They wanted me to ask you if you could identify any of these items as possibly belonging to, well, to your wife or son."

Harcourt couldn't breathe, as his throat seemed to close. "Of course," he said, gritting his teeth. He didn't want to let go of the possibility that their plane had been taken by aliens, that someday Sharon and Cedric would show up at his front door, not having aged a day, but alive.

They sat down on the large couch in front of a massive mahogany coffee table positioned in front of the grand fireplace. Harcourt didn't spend any time in the large room, preferring to live in his office and in the kitchen. Mark glanced longingly at the fireplace several times, as if he wanted to throw some logs into the grate and strike a match and get a fire blazing against the spring chill, but Harcourt wanted to get it over with.

"All right, what do you have to show me?"

Mark took off his gloves and unraveled the thread securing the flap of the envelope. He tipped it upside down. Several glossy photos fell out, face-down. Harcourt's pulse raced. He didn't want to see the pictures, whatever they showed.

Mark picked up the photos, then spread them out facing Harcourt like they were tarot cards. Fearful of what he might see in the photographs, Harcourt's eyes went to the envelope, where he saw the word Evidence stamped in red across the top.

Forcing himself to look, he started with the first 8 x 10 photograph on his left, looking at it carefully before moving to the next picture. The first few pictures were taken at the crash site and showed debris floating in an ocean, as a helicopter with its searchlight beamed onto the obvious night scene, whipping up the seas. The only thing he could make out were chunks of foam.

The next picture was easier to decipher. Various items were laid out on a table in a dry and well-lit room. Small squares of white paper were placed next to each item, and they were labeled with alphanumeric codes that meant nothing to Harcourt.

"This is what they found at the crash site?" he asked, as he accepted the magnifying glass offered to him from Mark and examined the photograph with the chunks of what looked like airplane seats. His chest tightened as he recognized the upholstery fabric. Then he told himself that was probably used in a lot of planes and not just his.

When his eyes traveled to the last picture, he sucked in a breath.

"What is it?" Mark said.

Harcourt turned his head away, not wanting to believe it.

"Harcourt, do you recognize something?"

Harcourt fought back tears and braced himself to look at the photo again. There right in front of him was proof that his son was dead.

"The hat, the fireman's hat," Harcourt said, pointing to the plastic child's toy, with the Diversion Fire Department logo still visible. "It was Cedric's. That belonged to Cedric."

Harcourt opened his eyes, not wanting to think about that memory any longer, and jumped when Mark banged on the window. "Finally," he said, hurrying to switch on the power again so he could roll down the window.

He checked his watch. "Look, Mark, I've got company coming, I've got to go. What is it?" he blurted before the window was halfway down.

"It's just really good to see you in town, Harcourt. I heard Molly was heading out for the weekend and Maggie and I thought we'd invite ourselves over, maybe make dinner in that fancy kitchen of yours."

"Uh, not this weekend. I have some things to do for work."

Mark lifted his eyebrow. "I thought you didn't have to go back to work until the first of next month."

"I don't, but I've got to do some homework. In fact, I'll probably leave next week and do some meetings in preparation for my return."

"Well, it's good to see you out and about."

"Is that all you wanted?" Harcourt asked.

Mark paused. "There was something else, but I guess that's not important."

"What?"

"Don't worry about it. You better run along, and I'll talk to you later."

Harcourt started the car.

"Wait," Mark said. "You hear about the super storm?"

Since Harcourt had returned to Diversion, he hadn't heard about much. He didn't listen to the radio, watch television, or even look up news on the internet. That included the weather report. He just took each day as it came, resigned that he had no more control over it than he had over the tragic turn of events his life had taken. But perhaps he should find out about the current weather news, especially if the storm might last for days. He thought about Sabrina and him being stuck up there, and his mind wandered as a smile formed. Maybe he should go back into Hammond's and pick up more condoms.

He felt a tap on his shoulder. "Hark? You all right there, buddy? Looked like you went on a short trip."

"No, I'm fine. What's the news on the storm?" Harcourt asked.

"I hear it's going to be intense. Of course with the drought, we could certainly use as much rain as we can get.

I just hope there isn't much lightning. Those trees are tinder at the moment."

As if on cue, a flash brightened the sky behind Mark, toward the direction of the Talhkahaw'ka reservation and Shipwreck Cove. A short while later, they heard the rumble of distant thunder.

"Well, that's my cue. Better go," Harcourt said as he fired up the engine.

Mark reached his hand inside and squeezed Harcourt's shoulder. "Good to see you, buddy. Seriously, good to see you out and about. Be safe."

8 HARCOURT

At six o'clock, Harcourt turned on the stove and stirred the pot as he attempted to reheat the pasta sauce. Outside, a steady rain fell against the house, and he wondered if the mosaic artist would decide not to come. He was glad it had started raining, because that would make it easier not to show her the project tonight. Despite his determination to get laid, he wasn't sure if he could follow through with his plans to have sex with the woman after having to spend time in Sharon's cottage and explain to the artist how important it was to keep their memories alive.

"Talk about a cock-blocking moment," he muttered to himself.

So, rain was a good thing. He'd keep her at the mansion, invite her to dinner, ask her about herself, and get more details on her interesting past. Then depending on how things went, he could show her the project after another round in the sack after breakfast. What was the rush?

And even if it turned out that she wasn't game for sex that night, he'd insist on having her stay in the guest room instead of going all the way into Diversion to stay in the only motel. He could take another stab at getting her into bed in the morning. If he had sex with her before looking at the cottage and the pictures, all would be well. And once he got his powerful urge to fuck another human being out of his system, he'd be able to get his head on straight and go to New York and take back what was rightfully his.

At 6:15 p.m., everything was ready, but there was still no sign of her. The light rain had become heavy and a strong wind buffeted the trees. At six thirty the hail came, so strong he feared that windows all over the mansion would break. Worried that she might not be coming, or maybe got stuck in an overflowing stream, he went back to the living room and found the file with the article, hoping to spot a cell phone number for the young woman. But the only number in the file was the number for the Piedmont Coffee House.

He took the file back to the kitchen and pulled his cell phone off the charger. He tried to call, but there was no reception. That didn't surprise him, since the reception was spotty even during good weather. He headed to his office to try the land-line, and had just picked up the receiver when a crack of lightning lit up the whole house, followed almost immediately by an ear-splitting boom. There was a creaking, whining noise, and then there was a deafening bang and he was thrown onto his knees.

"Shit!" Harcourt covered his ears as lay on the floor on hands and knees as something massive tore into his house. When the sound of splintering wood and breaking glass stopped, Harcourt scrambled to his feet and bolted towards the front of the house. As he rounded the corner into the great living room, he pulled up short.

Where there had once been a giant series of floor-to-ceiling windows which looked out into his impressive view of the woods and the sloping tree-lined vistas of Dogwood Canyon, there was now a massive pine tree piercing all the way to the back of his living room. His designer interior items were flung as if swept aside by a giant, and everything was annihilated.

He ran his hand across his forehead as another stroke of lightning illuminated the scene.

He started into the living room, watching his step, and getting wet as the rain flew into his home at a sideways slant. The farther into the living room he walked, the more it felt like he was outside in the storm. Hail the size of jawbreakers bounced off the strewn furniture, and the walls. He covered his head and ducked his head. The clamor made his ears hurt. Adrenaline rushed through every cell, as he tried to come up with a plan, a what to do next. But all he did was gape at the disaster, which had once been the grandest feature of the entire mansion.

A sound different from the cacophony of storm noises echoed into his brain. He froze. What was that?

He heard it again, and froze, ear's cocked towards the sound. It was a horn honking! A fucking car horn. Heart thumping, Harcourt bolted towards the front of his house, dodging debris and keeping his arm in front of his face to protect his eyes from the pine needles slapping out from branches of the fallen tree. He made it to the front door, and pushed to open it, but it wouldn't budge. From outside he heard the scream of a woman. "Help," followed by more desperate bursts of the horn. Gathering his strength, Harcourt heaved his shoulder into the door and it gave way, just enough. He squeezed himself through the opening and searched for the source of the screams.

The sun was hours from setting, but thick storm clouds and the relentless rain, made it hard to see. He moved away from the tree and stopped in his tracks at the sight. Two beams of light lit up the rain, beams of light coming from somewhere under that tree.

"Holy shit!" Where was the car?

Shoving aside branches Harcourt followed the beams of light into the cover until he managed to get close to the car. A flash of lightning illuminated her frightened face. The young woman was on her knees, both hands pushing against the door, as the rest of her body sprawled behind her.

She jumped when she noticed him standing there. But, then her face changed from fright to relief. "Help, I can't open the door. It's stuck!"

Harcourt shouted over the raging wind and pouring rain, "Don't worry, I'm going to get you out of there."

Scrambling to position himself under a tree and next to the car door, he grabbed for the handle with his left hand and felt around for the edge of the door frame with his right. The bent frame had pushed the door open an inch and his fingertips burned as he squeezed them around it.

"When I say go, push with all your might," he said.

"One, two, three, GO!"

He yanked hard on the outside and she grunted her efforts inside the car, but nothing happened, the door didn't budge. Another flash lit the darkening sky and Harcourt caught a look in the girl's eyes, a look of hopelessness as if she knew he wouldn't be able to save her. Overhead the tree groaned and Harcourt understood. It was seconds from shifting its position, seconds from crushing them both. Harcourt thought of Cedric, of how he'd let him down. Determination surged through his body. He wouldn't, couldn't fail someone who counted on him, again.

"I'm getting you out," Harcourt shouted. "Push, again, now!"

A string of curses rang into the night as they each put everything they had into the task. A flash cracked overhead, splintering wood behind him. The door gave, and the next thing he knew, the door came off its hinges, and Harcourt fell back, as the woman inside shot out of the car.

The tree gave way, and out of the corner of his eyes, Harcourt saw death crashing down. He pulled her into his arms and flung them both out of the way. The giant limb crashed against the car, crushing the area they'd been in only seconds before. He embraced her tight and rolled her away from the splintering wood and flying glass, protecting her by lying on top of her, and shielding her body with his.

"Hey, what are you doing? Get off me."

But he didn't dare. As the tree crushed into the car, the sound of the metal twisting and screeching filled the air. The girl screamed. Instinctively, he covered her with his body and tucked his face as he tried to protect them both from flying glass.

"Let go of me," she said again, just as another flash of lightning lit struck on the ground nearby.

He disentangled himself off her body and got to his feet. She propped herself up on her elbows and he offered her his hand. She didn't take it. She glared at him instead.

What the fuck?

"Are you injured, can you get up?"

She continued to glare at him like he was scum.

"Look, lady, I wasn't trying to cop a feel just then, in case you hadn't noticed I just saved your life."

Rain flooded over her face. She put up a hand to protect her eyes, then narrowed them at Harcourt, and then relaxed a little. She offered him her hand. "Sorry," she muttered as he helped her to her feet.

"Follow me," he said and guided her back towards the house, his hand gripping her elbow.

Thunder cracked and then the clouds broke loose, pelting them with jawbreaker-sized balls of hail.

"Ouch," shouted the woman, and she pulled her arm out of Harcourt's grasp as she tried to cover her head.

"This way!" Harcourt shouted. He grabbed her hand and yanked her towards the house.

She was laughing hysterically when they reached what was left of his front door. The awning partially crushed by the tree offered only a slight amount of shelter. He let go of the young woman's hands and stooped down to heave a giant piece of broken tree limb out of the way of the door. He opened it and was about to pull her inside to some shelter, when she let out a scream.

He spun around, fearful that something had hit her. But, she was just standing there, pointing out into his front yard. "My car, look at my car!"

From the position of the front of his house, he could see the scene, as more lightning flashed around them. Beneath the giant fallen tree, he could see glimpses of yellow metal. Her car, was almost completely crushed by the tree. The wind whipped up hail into their faces and splattered them with sideways flying rain that cut like metal into their skin. Harcourt pulled open the door.

"Let's get inside," he said. Then he pulled her into his house.

"Whoa, what happened in here?" she asked, eyes wide, as her pulled her away from the front of the house, guiding them through the debris field.

"Where are we going?"

"To the basement," he said, "It' the safest place."

Outside the storm raged on, the lighting and thunder directly overhead.

When he made it to the basement door, he opened it. "Go down there."

"No way. It's dark down there."

Harcourt reached for the light, but it didn't come on. "Electricity's out. It's still the safest place, come on."

He tried to pull her down the steps, but she put down her foot and braced her arms against the door frame. "No, way, I'm not going down there. Are you nuts? It's pitch black."

"What, are you afraid of the dark?"

"Damn straight. And you're not?"

"Okay, I might be a little afraid," Harcourt said. "Wait here, then, I'll find a flashlight or something. I'll be right back."

Harcourt left her by the entrance to the basement then headed to the hallway that led to the back of the house and the kitchen where he hoped to find a flashlight. In a junk drawer, he got lucky. But, when he turned on the flashlight, the batteries were weak. Still, it was better than nothing. He dug around the drawer for extra batteries, and found a pack of matches instead.

Recalling the romantic dinner in the dining room, he went to it and grabbed the two candlesticks with the tapers and taking care not to drop them, returned quickly to his guest waiting at the top of the basement steps.

She hadn't moved from the spot where he'd left her, but her expression had moved. Her eyes were wide with fear as she stared at the chaos, the rain and wind blasting through the holes in his house and stirring up his living room.

The wind was strong and the whole mansion groaned and creaked, making Harcourt think of a great wood ship caught in a monster squall. "You alright?" he asked.

A bolt of lightning tore through the gaping hole at the side of his house and struck his mahogany coffee table. It flew off the floor and spun as it came right for them.

"Watch out!" Harcourt yelled, as he threw himself between her and the hurtling object and pushed them both into the stairwell, and slammed them against the closed door. The coffee table pounded into the wall's just where they'd been standing. And the woman screamed and threw her arms around him, then buried her head in his chest, as she burst into tears.

"It's alright," he said.

He'd left his flashlight and the candles on the other side of the door and it was pitch black where they stood. "Don't move, I'll get the lights," he said.

"Don't leave me, I'm afraid of the dark," she said.

"So, am I. I'll be right back, I promise."

Harcourt opened the door, grateful that nothing blocked it, and ambient light flooded into the top of the basement stairs. He heard the young woman let out a breath of relief. Quickly, he found the candles and the flashlight, and deciding to come back for the candles, picked up the flashlight.

"Here, you hold onto this," he said, "go downstairs and wait for me while I get the candles."

He heard her walking down the stairs as he scanned his living room, looking for signs that a fire might have been started. He sniffed the air. No smoke. That was good.

She was leaning against a wall when he returned with the unlit candles.

The dim light was aimed at him, and even though he could barely see her, it was obvious that she was shaking.

He walked over to her and took the flashlight out of her trembling hands. Her knees buckle, and he almost didn't catch her in time. She started to sob.

He pulled her into his arms. "There, there," he said, stroking her hair as she leaned her face into his chest. He turned her around in his arms so he was behind her, then he leaned against the nearest wall, and settled himself down so that she could rest in his lap.

"Shush now, you're safe now, everything's going to be okay," he said as he continued to hold her close, to try and make her feel safe.

After a few moments, she stopped crying. A few minutes later, her body stopped shaking. He knew he should get out from under her and light those candles, but he didn't let go. He continued to hold her close and stroke her arms, and lean his face into her hair, breathing her in.

She let out a sigh, relaxing in his arms. She leaned her weight against him. Trusting him.

He wrapped his arms around her and cupped her hands with his. She responded by snuggling deeper into his protective embrace. His chest filled, as a sense of peace washed over him. He liked protecting this woman. "It's going to be okay, everything is going to be fine. I promise."

Then he let his face drop on top of her head and he buried into her wild, sweet-smelling hair. He left it there for a long moment, losing himself in her intoxicating scent.

Then he felt her body go stiff. He lifted his head and hurried to disengage his arms from her soft curves. He stood up. "Uh, let me fix that bench over there," he said, pointing to the weightlifting bench which was set at an extreme angle.

He picked up the flashlight, aimed it at the bench, then got to work. A moment later, the bench was parallel to the floor. He glanced over at the girl by the wall and realized that his heart was thumping.

"Is it ready?" She pulled herself to her feet. Her legs looked a little wobbly, so he held out his hand to her.

"I can walk," she said.

He got her onto the bench, and he got the candles. After lighting them with the matches, he placed one on top of a metal file cabinet next to the wine cellar, and the other on the first stair.

The young woman watched and appeared to have gotten over her fright. She kept dropping her head and not looking at him.

"You all right?" he asked after he'd finished lighting up the room.

She avoided eye contact again. "I'm sorry, I guess I'm still a little freaked out. Have you ever seen a storm like that?" She laughed.

And then they both fell silent.

Finally, Harcourt spoke. "I take it you're Sabrina Cane, the artist?"

For the first time since he'd held her in his arms, she looked him in the eye. Her eyes were dark brown, deep and mysterious. Then he saw her lip move as a smile tugged at the corner of her mouth. Something tugged in Harcourt's chest. She stared right at him, fluttering her eyelids, as she turned her mouth into the most perfect little pout. Then she put her shaking hands on her hips and said, with a flip of her wild hair, "And I take it you're Harcourt Raymondson, the billionaire?"

It was too much. They both burst into laughter. And didn't stop laughing until they felt the rush and relief of tears running down their faces.

"Ahh, ahh," Harcourt said putting his arm out in front of him as he tried to get ahold of his laughing fit. He hadn't laughed like that for years. It felt good.

Sabrina pulled her arms around her body and her expression changed. She started to shiver. He reached for her hand, grasping it with two of his. "Oh, shit, Sabrina, you're trembling."

"You poor thing, are you cold?" he asked, then he smacked his head. "Of course you're cold, you're soaking wet." He let go of her hands and jumped to his feet as his eyes darted around the room looking for something to cover her up.

"Don't poor thing me, Mr. Billionaire, you're soaking wet too," Sabrina said, and then they both started laughing again, even though she was now rattling her teeth she was

THE BILLIONAIRE'S SHAMAN

so cold. Harcourt felt a sudden urge to rip off her clothes and warm her up from the inside out, but he thought better of it.

Deciding to take charge, he announced, "You need to get out of those wet clothes or you'll get sick. I'll get some dry clothes for both of us to change into. Wait right here."

Her face lost color and her eyes went wide with alarm.

She reached out and grasped onto his arm. "No, please don't go. I don't want to be left alone down here."

She went from spunky and cocky and self-reliant to needy and frightened in an instant. What was up with this woman? Harcourt tried to laugh off her sudden change of mood, but her nails dug into his arms.

He took a deep breath, knowing that his strength would help her. In his confident and calm voice, he said, "Now, Sabrina, you have nothing to be afraid of. We both need to get out of these wet clothes or we'll both get sick. We don't want that, do we? Just be patient. I promise I'll be back real soon. Okay?"

"Okay," she said. Harcourt saw her bite her lower lip. It was the juiciest, plumpest, most kissable piece of mouth candy he'd ever seen.

"Promise you'll come right back?" she said, biting harder on that luscious lip. He wanted to take her bottom lip into his mouth and suck on it long and slow. His cock jerked.

"I promise," he said, but his voice cracked a little as he spoke. Fearing he was about to get a boner in her presence, he hurried up the stairs.

JACK BRESSLER

About three hours after picking up Cerise in front of The Pit, Jack Bressler sat in his car considering what to do next. The alcohol and the sex and the meal had taken its toll. He wanted to return to his room and get some sleep before he had to hop on an early ferry, but he knew he should check in with his boss.

He contemplated what to tell him, as he reflected on how well the night with Cerise had gone.

He'd taken her out for dinner in a swanky little restaurant, the kind of place where they weren't surprised to see a little hand and footsie action under the table. The lobster was good, and so was the view of her body in her slutty attire. Cerise clearly had no love for Sabrina or any of her other co-workers. She was a shameless gossip, and told him everything she knew. Sabrina never knew she had a sister or a father alive until Jeanette tracked her down. Sabrina was working or something and couldn't get away, so Jeanette was saving her pennies to go visit her sister. "And then one day she just shows up in the coffee shop, and there was all this hugging and crying. It was totally gross."

"So, Jeannette is her sister?"

"Half-sister, I'm pretty sure. They share the same father, but different mothers."

"Jeannette works at the coffee shop as well?"

"Sometimes. She's got a couple of kids, so she's busy. Maybe, two, three days a week."

Jack pushed his chair closer to hers and put his hand under the table and onto her leg. She wore a very tight, very short skirt and it wasn't hard to reach inside and discover that she wasn't wearing any underwear. He caressed her with his fingertips, and she let out a moan into her champagne.

"After dinner, will you take me to the coffee shop? I've always wanted to go down on a barista."

She'd not only let him into the coffee shop with her key, she'd without hesitation helped him break into the boss's file cabinet, using a couple of paper clips as a pick. She made copies of Sabrina's employment application for him, then turned off all the lights.

They'd done all sorts of kinky things on the floor and on the counter, and everywhere they could think of in the store. She wanted to come to his hotel, but he wasn't lying when he said he had to get up and leave early in the morning.

When he pulled to a stop next to her car, which was parked on a side street two blocks away from The Pit, he held the umbrella over her head as she put her key into the lock of her battered Toyota.

Before she could get inside, he kissed her long and hard, and let his hand roam down to her breast and gave it a little squeeze. When the kiss was over he handed her the umbrella. "Hold it for me," he said.

As she waited and held the umbrella over his head, he reached into his pocket and pulled out his money clip.

"What's that for?" she asked, her eyes wide at the sight of the crisp fifty-dollar bill.

"Just a reminder to keep what you told me between ourselves..."

Cerise tucked the money down her shirt, gave back his umbrella, plopped into her seat without the slightest bit of grace, "No worries, Paul. See you again, soon?"

Jack smiled indulgently, nodding in the affirmative, but it was a lie. He had no plans to see her again soon.

Smiling broadly, Cerise slammed her door shut, started her car, then after running her tongue over her lips in a lascivious manner and blowing him a wet kiss, she drove off into the night and Jack had to cover his mouth to keep from inhaling the cloud of exhaust fumes in her wake.

After her car disappeared around a corner, he stood there deciding what to do next. He wanted to return to his hotel room and shower and scrub away all traces of her skanky filth, but he knew that his benefactor would want an update soon.

He thought about that, not sure he was ready to make that call.

Cerise, the horny barista, was an excellent lay, but she'd also managed to extract a lot of money from him, the way a prostitute extracted money from a john. Jack Bressler didn't need to pay for sex. Women begged him for time in the sack. He'd given her money for information and to buy her silence, but it still felt like he'd engaged in a business transaction in exchange for sex.

He wrinkled his nose, as if there was something sour-smelling in the air. Her whole story about Sabrina going to Vancouver for some job smelled like something made up. Sabrina and a billionaire? It didn't make a lot of sense.

He had the address to this so-called father, so, why not check it out. After Sabrina took off – he'd used a portion of his benefactor's allowance to pay for a Private Investigator to track her down. He'd looked for her Volvo, but couldn't find it. He was cheap, so he only authorized a United States search, because it had never occurred to him that she would go north or try to leave the country.

He'd ended up tracking her down himself -- no thanks to the expensive PI. A simple Google Alert popped up in his email along with a link to the article in the Piedmont Gazette.

He had no doubt she'd just driven all the way. If he spotted her yellow Volvo in the driveway of the home in Skenet City, then he'd not have to worry about tracking her down on Vancouver Island, in which case, he'd have different news to report when he called in.

He punched the address into Google Maps and headed his car towards what Cerise had derisively referred to as Vancouver's hood. He drove fast, wanting to get his recognizance over with. He'd make his report, then hurry back to the hotel and stay under the shower until all the soap and the hot water was gone, until he scrubbed himself raw, and there were no more traces of Cerise on his body.

SABRINA

After my potential boss made his way upstairs, I sat on the bench, hugging myself as best I could. I was trying to get a grip, sucking in air, shuddering as I came to terms with all the shit that had gone down since leaving Vancouver. First, I found out that Jack not only knew that I was in Canada, but he'd also managed somehow to get my private cell phone. Then I thought about my destroyed car and how close I'd come to joining my mother. And then I thought about Harcourt Raymondson, and how he made my heart race.

After several minutes, I started to worry that he wasn't coming back.

Even with the two candles flickering, I couldn't stop staring up the stairs to the door as I willed my host to return.

After several more minutes, I noticed through a small window located at the top of the wall near the ceiling of the basement that the storm was still going strong, and yet, in the basement, I could hardly hear it.

Harcourt was right. It was the safest place in the house.

But he wasn't in the basement; he was moving around up there. I hoped he wouldn't get struck by lightning or fall through an open floorboard in the dark. I wrapped both arms around my shivering body and tried not to think such thoughts. He'd be fine. He'd be back in a moment.

As the weight of my arms pushed against my stomach I had a sudden urge to go to the bathroom. I hadn't gone since getting gas in Port Hardy. That was how long ago? I didn't want to think about it, or about the fact that I'd wasted those last dollars on gas I'd never get to use.

I got up and grabbed the candle off the file cabinet and went over to the door under the stairs, praying it was a bathroom and not a storage cabinet. To my relief I saw a toilet and a sink in the very tiny space. Since I knew I'd hear him coming in time to close the doors if I had to, I left the door open and the candle on the floor in front of the door and took care of business fast.

When I was done, I washed my hands in the sink and wiped them off on my wet clothes.

Then I almost fell back into the toilet when I caught a look at my face. My natural hair—which I'd tried so hard to tame back at Ellis's house only that morning—was sticking out in a million directions like my head had been struck by lightning. My face was dirty, and there were minor cuts and abrasions along my scalp and a trail of dried blood trickling down my forehead. I ran my fingers through my hair, pulling out errant pine needles and pieces of splintered twigs and leaves.

I turned the water back on, and using a wad of toilet paper, attempted to clean my face.

When I'd fixed myself up as best as I could, I returned to my bench and waited.

More time passed and my worries that something bad might have happened to Harcourt rose in me like a bad idea. My leg bounced. My hands rubbed up and down my jeans. And I was shivering again. My teeth started rattling so hard I had to suck in my tongue to keep from biting it off. Once again, I imagined Harcourt Raymondson injured up there somewhere, crying for me to help him as the blood drained from his body...

I was about of gather up enough courage to go up there with the candlestick and save his life like he'd saved mine when I had an even more terrible thought. What if he hadn't had a simple accident?

What if he wasn't coming because Jack had gotten to him first with a baseball bat?

What if Jack was at this very instant hunting for me, ready to give me the same treatment?

My muscles tensed. Then I heard a noise and I almost jumped out of my skin. Footsteps. Definitely footsteps. Someone was coming. I stood up, my eyes darting around wildly, looking for somewhere to hide. The door at the top of the stairs creaked open, and I froze in my tracks, unable to move. My eyes flew to the top of the stairs where the figure of the man stood silhouetted in the candlelight. My knees hit the back of the bench and buckled as I toppled backward over the bench and hit the concrete hard floor hard, my shoulders taking the brunt of the impact.

The figure ran down the stairs. "Ahhhh," I moaned, holding out my arms in front of me, as if that would protect me. "Please, don't hurt me," I begged.

10 HARCOURT

Before Harcourt could find suitable dry clothing for them both, his flashlight battery up and died. Forced to search with only ambient light, he'd taken much longer than he'd intended to. He moved slowly and carefully through his house, not wanting to fall or be injured. He'd rather show up downstairs a little late in one piece, than hurry and maybe not get back there at all.

He was relieved when he finally made it back to the basement. He opened the door and tried to balance the tall stack of clothing and towels in one arm as he made out the location of the steps, using the candlelight still flickering near Sabrina. When his eyes found her, still and motionless, standing and facing him, he sucked in a breath at the sight of her incredible body. She was like a fucking vision.

He was on his way down, unable to speak, thinking all sorts of unspeakable, sensual thoughts, when she vanished. Then he heard something fall and heard her cry out.

He rushed over to her.

She lay on her back with her legs still on the bench as if she'd fallen off. She had her face turned away, and both arms out in front of her, as if she were trying to block Harcourt from hitting her. "Don't hurt me," she pleaded. He saw that her eyes were squeezed shut.

"Sabrina, it's just me, Harcourt."

Her eyes popped open. "Oh, thank God."

She jumped to her feet and threw her arms around him. He felt her body quivering in his arms.

"Here, have a seat. Who the hell did you think I was?"

She gulped and pulled out of his arms. "I..." she said, her voice quivering, "I thought you might be..."

"Might be whom? Sabrina. Whom did you think I might be?" he asked and he put his hands on her shoulders to steady her.

She hesitated. "No one... I'm sorry, I'm fine." She twisted her body and Harcourt released her.

They stood there for a moment, neither saying anything.

"Here," Harcourt said at last. He reached down to where he'd placed the clothing and towels and went through the pile, handing her a stack. "Why don't you go change in there. It's a bathroom," he added.

She took the clothing, but didn't move.

Harcourt gave her a little shove. "Come on, Sabrina, you go first and then I'll go after you."

"Okay, thanks," she said and headed for the door under the stairs.

As she walked away from him, Harcourt caught his first glimpse of her figure from behind. While not as waterlogged as they had been when he first brought her into the basement, her clothing still clung to her body like shrink wrap, leaving little to the imagination. Blood rushed to his cock as he pictured her naked body beneath the soggy clothes.

"It's too dark in here," Sabrina called out from the bathroom.

"Right, let me bring you a candle," Harcourt said.

A moment later he stood before her holding the flickering candle, and looked down at her large trusting eyes. She didn't take her eyes off him and he couldn't take his eyes off her. The candle wax dripped on his finger.

"Right," he said, looking for a place to put the candle. The bathroom was too small, and there was no place to put it inside. So he left it on the floor in front of the open door.

"You can leave the door open. I'll go sit on the bench. I promise I won't look," he added with a grin.

"Okay," she said.

But she must not have trusted him fully, because after he'd taken the bench seat, he noticed that she'd closed the door more than he'd left it.

He found himself whistling, then stopped as he heard her starting to grunt and groan, as she clearly struggled to get out of her wet clothes.

"Need any help in there?" he asked, hopefully.

"No, I've got it," she said, but he detected a small chuckle. His face warmed at the idea that she might be flirting with him. And the thought warmed his body deep. He needed to get out of his wet clothes. He pulled off his shirt and saw the deep indentations on his forearms where she'd dug her nails into the skin. Seeing evidence of her body touching his, his pulse quickened. As he ran his fingertips along the groove, he closed his eyes and allowed his imagination to run wild. Sabrina's fingernails digging into his back as her beautiful face lit up in ecstasy and he entered her for the first time...

"Christ," he said as he realized that he was getting the boner to end all boners. His cock was tenting his wet jeans.

"Shit." He tried to think of what he could do to shut his cock the fuck down. It had been too long. He heard the water running in the sink, and afraid she might come out any second, he stuck the meat of his hand between his teeth and bit down hard, hoping the pain would divert some blood away from his cock.

"Fuck. Fuck. Fuck. Fuck," he grunted under his breath, when the biting only hurt but did nothing for his unwanted boner. When he heard the door squeak and saw the candlelight move, he grabbed his clothes and positioned them over his crotch, and dropped his shirt. He started to pick it up, but then she stepped out into the room and into the light.

It took all his strength not to walk over to her and scoop her up into his arms, and then march her up to the nearest dry bedroom. He'd never seen anything more beautiful in his life. She stood there, looking almost shy, her head down as she shifted from foot to foot. The sweatpants he'd brought for her must have been too long, because she'd rolled them up, exposing her shapely ankles and bare feet. The T-shirt he'd found for her was too tight and pressed against her ample chest. She must have taken off her bra, because Harcourt's cock did another somersault at the sight of her dark areolas surrounding her thick nipples. They poked against the thin fabric, and even as he gaped at her perfect breasts, they seemed to pebble and grow harder before his eyes.

"I'm sorry, they don't really fit. You're so tall," she said as if she had anything to be sorry about.

"What?" he said, realizing that he was talking to her. He dragged his eyes away from her chest and saw that she was looking away, shuffling from one foot to another as she held her hands behind her back.

"Thanks for the clothes," she said. Harcourt saw that she was looking down his body. Shit. He'd been so mesmerized by her body in his clothes he'd completely forgotten to keep his stack of dry clothes over his renegade cock. He slammed them back into place.

"My turn," he said, his voice almost squeaking with nerves and embarrassment as his neck heated up like it was on fucking fire. He felt like he was in junior high again.

"What?" she said. He wasn't sure—perhaps he was imaging it—but he thought he might have seen a look in her eyes, something along the lines of a knowing smile. Damn it. He pushed past her, keeping the clothes over his junk and turning his body so she didn't get any physical proof of what he feared she might already suspect.

If she said anything, he'd deny, deny, deny. When he made it into the bathroom, he went inside and shut the door without thinking, leaving the candle outside. He stood there in the pitch dark, trying to catch his breath.

"You want the candle?" she asked. Damn it, she was right outside the door.

"No, I'm fine," he squeaked. What was with the fucking squeaking? Get it together, man!

"All right," Sabrina said. He heard her walk away, and he proceeded to feel around. He found the sink, turned on the water and splashed his face until he could feel his dick retreat.

He sat on the edge of the toilet and pulled off his shoes, socks, and pants in the dark. He forced himself not to make any unnecessary noises, as challenging as it was to remove the damn wet clothes.

He sat naked and felt around for his dry clothes, trying to determine which way was front and back. He decided to take a chance and opened the door a crack, letting in some light. He picked up the dry pair of jeans and tried to step into them. But he missed the leg hole and started to hop on one foot and almost fell against the door, exposing his ass to Sabrina.

Catching himself in time, he tried again. With his jeans on but his shirt still off, he opened the door another crack, just to make sure he wouldn't put his T-shirt on backwards.

With the improved light in the room, and his shirt on as it should be, he moved back to the sink and checked his hair and face. He smoothed his hair down, then glanced down in the sink. And what he saw there, lying in the bottom of the basin, made his cock jerk back to life. Damn.

He wasn't imagining things when he'd speculated that Sabrina wasn't wearing a bra, because there it was in its glory. He picked it up. Roomy cups. He put it to his nose and inhaled. Then he felt like a pervert and put it back, and spotted another strip of black lace fabric. When he held up the bikini underwear his cock became erect so fast it almost poked out of his jeans. He let out a groan of masculine pain.

"Are you all right in there?" He felt the air move as the door opened. "Harcourt?"

Shit. She was standing right outside the door, poking her head in. He turned his body around. He pulled the door closed. "Hey, how 'bout a little privacy," he said.

"Sorry," she said. "But I heard you moaning in there."

"I wasn't moaning, I don't know what you're talking about. Go sit down, I'll come out when I'm ready," he said.

"Okay, but don't be long, it's boring out here without you."

His chest filled. She wanted his company. Damn. When Harcourt finally was ready to come out of the bathroom, he knew he had to get out of that basement. The worst of the storm seemed to have passed, so he said, "You hungry?"

"I could eat."

11 SABRINA

When he'd first come out of the bathroom, I hadn't been able to control myself. It was all I could do not to drop my jaw and gape at his six plus feet worth of sexual dream-come-true. Tall, and muscular and strong, he stood there, in his tight dry jeans and even tighter shirt, staring at me as if not sure what to do. Then he shifted from one foot to another and ran a hand through his tousled hair.

Beads of sweat broke out on the back of my neck and chest. I wasn't sure what to do. What to say. I bit my lip, then tugged on the too-tight shirt hoping to get some air on my flaming chest. But the friction, only made my nipples harden. They ached, making me want to lift my shirt and beg him to suck away the pain. I knew what I wanted to do...

I swallowed hard, and tore my eyes away from that hunk of sex-God standing in front of me. He didn't move, and I could tell he was watching me. It made me shiver, just thinking about what he might be thinking.

Stop it! Get a grip!

He was my prospective employer. Nothing more.

Besides, that wasn't the only reason I had no right to think such thoughts.

I glanced up at him, finally, as part of me hoped to catch in his eyes the same need that grew inside me. But, he didn't meet my eye. He looked away, and stared at the wall. Deflated, I tried to brush it off and going for cheerful said, "You said something about dinner?"

"Yes," he said.

He handed me a candle and led us upstairs, each of us holding the candle for light, like goths. As we carefully mounted the steps, it took all my strength to fight the temptation to feel up the muscles on his tight ass. As I joined him at the top of the stairs, I caught a whiff of his masculine scent. Please make the first move, I begged him telepathically. But he didn't seem to get my message, because he trudged ahead towards wherever dinner was waiting, and held back his hand to make sure I stayed close.

Forced to deal with walking over obstacles and debris strewn around the storm damaged house, I focused on where I was placing my bare feet and tried to let go of the disappointment that Harcourt Raymondson was a gentleman and not the kind of man who would take advantage of a damsel in distress. Bummer.

Whatever I'd seen in the basement, the signs that he had a physical attraction to me, wouldn't matter if he had the strength to hold himself against temptation and stick up for a higher standard. He was probably the kind of man with high moral fiber and strong ethics. The kind who would never act on his base desires. And if I tried to tempt him, what if he was repulsed. What if he rejected me? I had to let go of these crazy sex thoughts and remember why I had come in the first place. I needed to be hired by this man. I needed a fucking job, not to fuck the boss.

"Watch your step," he said.

Exactly what I was thinking.

I'd better watch my step.

Realizing that he wasn't talking metaphorically, I started to watch where I placed my bare feet. But, that wasn't as easy to do as it sounded. A single candle bouncing around near my face didn't exactly light up the floor. There was some ambient light coming in through the windows, despite the clouds and rain and almost set sun. But, as we moved deeper into the house, candlelight was all we had to guide our way and it was difficult to watch where I stepped.

When we came to top of the tree which was laying against the back wall of his house, Harcourt said. "Hand me your candle."

I gave it to him and he took both candles and leaped onto the top of the tree trunk, then jumped onto the other side and put both candles down. When he returned the shadow of his body bounced off the wall, making him appear as big as a bear. He reached down and pulled me up.

When I was situated on the top of the tree, he let himself down then held his arms out for me. I gave him my hand and he grabbed me around my waist, and as if I was light as some skinny model, he lifted he over and sat me onto the ground.

"Ahh, shit, owie, owie, ouch!" I hopped on my uninjured foot and grabbed onto his arm as I tried to stop the pain pulsing on my foot. As I lifted my leg to see what had happened, he grabbed a candle and shone it on my foot.

"Shit, I'm so sorry. Your foot is bleeding." His eyes were wild for a minute, but then his focus returned. "Hang on, I'm carrying you the rest of the way."

I tried to stop him, but he ignored my protest and lifted me like a sack of rice and carried me fast to the kitchen, muttering all the way. "I'm so sorry, I'm so sorry. I never should have let you out of that basement in bare feet. There's glass everywhere. I'm so sorry."

"No, it's not your fault," I said, but then my foot bumped into something and I let out a yelp of pain.

"Sorry," he said, as I wrapped my arms around his neck, and tried to draw my body into a smaller target for the next piece of furniture in our path. Closer to his body, I breathed in his masculine scent and almost forgot the pain in my foot.

My eyes darted up and he continued to move me down a hallway. I risked a glance at his face, and in the candle light, I could see that he was in deep concentration, his neck thrust forward, as he scrunched his brows together as he peered into the gloomy interior space. My heart skipped a beat. Is this what it feels like to have a man look out for you?

Well, I thought, as I recalled my near-death experience and how he'd pulled me from my car just in the nick of time. He certainly had been my hero so far, that evening. My body relaxed and my knees went back to a natural position. "We're almost there," he said as stepped through a doorway and entered a formal dining room which was almost completely dark. At the other end of the room, there was a dim glow.

"A few more feet, and we'll be there," he promised.

I was about to say something, nice and reassuring, and perhaps lift my finger to feel the line of his jaw, but stopped when my foot throbbed, reminding me that I still had a piece of glass sticking out of my flesh. I pressed my body closer into his, and closed my eyes, then begged the pain in my foot to stop ruining an otherwise perfect moment.

Harcourt was so relieved when he managed to get Sabrina into the kitchen where he could tend to her foot. He took her to the window where there was still a bit of fading high northern light, and sat her down on a chair. "Keep your foot up," he said.

"Okay, thanks, I'm sorry," she said.

"You've got nothing to be sorry about." He pulled over another chair and gently lifted her leg and pushed the chair under it so that it supported just her calf.

"Wait here," he said after he caught his breath. "Let me go back and get the candles." Without the burden of carrying a full-grown full-figured woman, Harcourt made the trip in short order.

"You still okay over there?" he called out as he rummaged around his kitchen trying to find the first-aid kit. He thought of the outdoor leadership camp he'd attended years ago, where he'd learned some basic rules of first aid. Rule one, when someone needed an injury tended to, the person administering needed to wash his hands, when possible. Germs and infection, they explained, were the enemy.

She moaned, and he decided to look for the kit later. First he needed to get that piece of glass out of her foot. After washing his hands at the kitchen sink, Harcourt grabbed the roll of paper towels from the counter and walked back to Sabrina and got to work. Gently lifting her leg, he sat on the chair, turning it perpendicular so he could rest her leg onto his thigh. She winced as he laid it down.

"Try to relax," he said.

It crossed his mind just how close a part of her body was to a part of his body, but the erection that had hampered him in the basement was no longer an issue. He was in his protective mode. He wanted to take care of her right now. She had an injury that was entirely his fault for not thinking about the fact that she was walking through his storm-damaged home in bare feet.

He lifted her foot up by the ankle and examined the wound from different angles. With the candle held close, he could see the glint of glass protruding from her foot. It was the shape and size of a tortilla chip, and almost as thin, but only a tiny portion of it had wedged into her foot. Still, there was quite a bit of blood pooled around it. He had to get it out.

"I'm going to take it out, Sabrina," he said as he readied a wad of paper towel to catch any blood once he removed the glass. "Are you ready?"

She nodded, looking at him with her brown and trusting eyes. Harcourt's chest squeezed. "This will probably hurt, but I need you not to move, and stay extremely still. Do you think you can do that, Sabrina?"

She nodded again.

He adjusted the candlestick on the floor close to her foot, then took a deep breath as he leaned into the task. Her breathing quickened as if in anticipation of the pain to come. He put his free hand on her ankle and held it firmly. She gripped the chair with both hands to steady herself. "Shh, good girl, you're doing great. It'll all be over soon."

Using the fingers of his right hand like tweezers, Harcourt carefully extracted the glass, taking care to pull it out in the same trajectory that it had gone in. When the glass popped out, Sabrina gasped, making a sound that was a cross between relief and pain.

"That's it, it's going to be all better now," he said, as he put the glass on the table and gently pressed the paper towel against the wound. The cut wasn't as bad as he feared and the bleeding stopped quickly. Relief flooded his body and he let out a breath which he'd not realized he'd been holding in.

"I think you're going to be all right."

"Are you sure?"

"I am," he said, but he was still concerned that there might be an errant sliver of glass still in her foot. Using a fresh wad of paper towel, he carefully pressed and prodded the areas around the wound, watching her stunning face for signs of pain. But there were none.

When the bleeding had been reduced to a trickle, he started to lift her foot off his thigh. But he changed his mind, and he bent his head down and kissed the top of her foot.

"I'm so sorry you got hurt, Sabrina," he said as his mouth hovered just over her skin.

He turned his face to consider her eyes, and the look that passed between them sent a shiver of longing through Harcourt's body. He kissed it again, more perfunctory this time, then set her leg back on the chair. The moment he stood up, she bent her knee and held onto her ankle so she could get a look at her wound. Harcourt ripped off some clean sheets of paper towel, and handing them to her said, "Keep applying pressure. I'm going to find that first-aid kit and something to kill the germs."

He found it on the top shelf of the pantry where he also found a bottle of vodka, and when he returned to her side, he held her hand in one of his as he poured the stinking but germ-killing liquid over her wound.

"Why are you being so nice to me?" she asked, after he wrapped the last bit of surgical tape around her dressing.

"Outback courtesy, Ms. Cane. I'm sure you'd do the same for me if things were reversed."

"I guess," she said.

He looked at his work, then got up and went to the kitchen, returning a moment later with a large plastic bag. "What's that for?"

"I'm going to wrap your foot to keep the germs out."

Once he had her foot cocooned inside two plastic shopping bags, and had secured it to her ankle with surgical tape so it wouldn't slip off, Harcourt admired his work.

"I think you'll live now."

"Thanks Dr. Billionaire," she said.

"The name's Harcourt, little lady," he said, dipping an imaginary cowboy hat. "But you can call me Hark."

"Why thank you kindly, kind sir," Sabrina said. She gazed up at him and for a moment Harcourt felt a tug toward her and wanted to reach down and take her face in his hands and kiss those sweet lips.

Outside a grumbling roll of thunder brought him back to his senses, and he realized that she'd been watching him. Damn.

Sabrina looked away when he tried to catch her eye. "Did you say something about having food in the house? I'm starving."

12 HARCOURT

Harcourt frequently glanced over his shoulder to check on his patient while he whipped up dinner. It was supposed to have taken place in the dining room, but with no electricity and no windows, the dining room was much darker than the breakfast nook by the window in the kitchen where Sabrina already sat.

"So, tell me about yourself," he asked as he dished buttered pasta on the plates, then ladled reheated spaghetti sauce.

"What do you want to know?"

"I saw that article about you. Let's start with that."

He thought she'd start right in on it, but Sabrina didn't respond.

He went to the refrigerator and pulled out the salad and the Mason jar. He shook Molly's ranch dressing, then drizzled it over the handfuls of salad he'd placed next to the steaming spaghetti.

"Sabrina? Everything all right? Don't want to talk about that?" he said as he opened the bottle of wine and poured them each a glass.

"Not particularly," Sabrina grumbled, then turned away from him as she stared out the window.

Harcourt put the wine glasses on the breakfast table, then brought over two forks and two spoons. "All righty then," he said, trying again to keep the conversation going as he ripped off and folded paper towels for napkins and placed them under each setting of flatware. "Let's not talk about your fascinating past. How about your present?"

"Okay," she murmured as she took a sip of the wine.

"How long have you lived in Vancouver?" he asked as he placed the dinner plates on the table and took his seat.

"Uh," Sabrina said, "Ah, I—" she stuttered. She gripped her fork and stared at him, as if waiting for him to ring a bell before she could eat.

"Dig in, Sabrina, go ahead."

And she did. Harcourt watched Sabrina eat with a focused intensity as if she thought it might be her last meal. She made appreciative noises with every bite. "Yum, this is so good," she said, her face lit up in a kind of food orgasm. "Did you make it?" she asked with a sense of wonder in her eyes.

Without thinking, he picked up his napkin and wiped away a bit of sauce which had dripped out of the corner of her mouth.

She ducked her head and grabbed at her own napkin and swiped at her face. "Sorry," she said as if she'd done something wrong.

"No worries," Harcourt said, as she went back to focusing on eating her food.

They ate the rest of the meal in silence. She couldn't keep her eyes off what her fork was doing, and he couldn't keep his eyes off what her mouth was doing. Harcourt ate a little, but his appetite was for something other than pasta and tossed salad.

After she'd cleaned her plate, he stood. "Can I take your plate?" he said, reaching out for it.

"No," she said, and she gripped the sides with both hands.

He stared at her, confused. Why would she want an empty plate?

Still holding it with a death grip in her two hands, she lifted it up and with her eyes going wide and needful as a puppy begging for table scraps she said, "More please."

A wave of need ran through him. A need to give her anything she wanted. To fill her plate and keep it full. He wanted to make her happy, he wanted to give her everything.

"Harcourt?" Sabrina said. "Can I have a little more, please? It's so good," she added, as if that explained her appetite.

Harcourt shook his head.

"Of course," he said and he went to the stove and dished out a slightly less full plate of everything than he'd given her before. He turned the water on loud in the sink as he muttered under his breath through gritted teeth as he worked, scolding himself for getting attached to the woman. "She's just pussy. Nothing more. Stop getting attached, you moron. She's just a means to an end. She's just pussy, pussy, pussy, pussy..."

"What did you say?"

"Nothing, I didn't say anything."

But when he returned with her second plate of food, he found that he couldn't look at her as his means to an end. She wasn't a fuck toy. She was too sweet, too vulnerable. He had to give up on that plan. As soon as she was done eating, he'd drive her into town and check her into her hotel.

In the morning, he'd take her out for breakfast at the Diversion Grill. Then he'd tell her that with the damage to his house and all, he'd decided to put the art project on hold. Then he'd write her a check to get her a new car, with maybe a little extra for her trouble in coming out, and then hire her a helicopter and send her back to Vancouver and try to forget about her.

He needed a different kind of woman for his first fuck out of the gate. A more experienced and worldly woman, a woman who he could get his rocks off on. Sabrina Cane wasn't one-night-stand material. Harcourt had a creeping feeling that if he ever got inside that woman, he might never want to come out again.

"I'm stuffed," Sabrina said and made a little sound and covered her mouth.

She'd picked up her plate, with food still on it. "Thanks again, that was so good."

He took the plate and placed it into the sink. Thunder rumbled in the distance. Harcourt checked his watch. Almost nine o'clock. He needed to get her in his car and get her to town. They couldn't stay in the house. When the sun went down, they'd be stuck in the dark. One of the candles had already burnt down to the nub; the other only had a few minutes to go. He wasn't sure he could keep his hands off her all night. It was time. Tell her you're going to take her to the motel now.

"It's sure getting dark," she said as the shifted in her chair. "What do you want to do now?"

Harcourt laughed, trying to cover the vivid thought that bolted into his dirty mind. Fuck. Tell her you're taking her to town. Tell her, you moron.

He didn't want to end this perfect night with that perfect woman too soon. His head popped up as he remembered his purchases, and he had a sudden brilliant idea. "You smoke?"

"God, yes. I mean, it's been a while, but after today—I think a smoke would really hit the spot."

In the fading light, Harcourt looked around the kitchen, trying to locate the paper bag from Hammond's. "What are you looking for?"

"The bag with my smokes," he said. Then he remembered that it also had extra candles and the condoms. Maybe they could stay all night.

"Is this it?" Sabrina said holding a paper bag in the air, as she started to unravel the top.

He was on her in an instant, pulling the bag out of her hand, his face heating up as he imagined her seeing the condoms. To cover himself and his rash act, he went to the kitchen counter and pulled out two of the candles and lit them. As he lit the second one, the candle on the table flickered out and he brought one of the jar candles and placed it in front of her. "See, didn't have a moment to lose," he laughed, pointing to the dead candle.

"I guess not," Sabrina said, as her mouth curved into a smile.

"I'll be right back," he said, and he took the bag which still had the box of condoms and moved through the swinging door into the formal dining room. It was dark as pitch in there, but he didn't care. He reached inside the bag, took out the box of condoms, ripped it open, then pulled out several packets to put in his pocket.

"Three or four," he asked himself. Six, responded his dirty mind.

He grabbed three more and stuffed them into the back pockets of his jeans, then taking out the last candle, stuffed the condoms back in the bag and hid them behind the Chinese planter.

With the pack of Marlboros rolled up into his sleeve, he returned to kitchen.

When she saw him, she looked up at him expectantly.

"Let's go outside and have that smoke," he said. After helping her to her feet, he helped walk her outside. He cleared away pine needles and water from the bench with several swipes of his hand, then held the swing so it wouldn't move as she sat.

"This is nice," she said.

Even though it was late, the sun setting low in the north, but it was getting considerably darker by the second. "Let me get a candle."

When he returned, he sat the candle onto the ground, grateful that it was in a jar and impervious to the steady wind. She eyed his shoulder. "Right," he said as he unraveled Marlboros from his sleeve. He struggled to get them out and felt like an idiot. He handed her the unopened pack, and watched as she expertly ripped away the plastic outer wrapping, planted it under her fine ass so it wouldn't become litter in the wind, the tapped the opened box of smokes against the back of her palm. She pulled the first cigarette out with two fingers, then placed it in her mouth, then handed him the pack.

He thought how James Dean would do it, and pulled the cigarette out between his teeth, almost biting it in half before he switched to holding it with his lips.

She watched him. He gulped. Her eyes seemed to sparkle with mischief. Something light and winged bounced against the inside of his stomach.

"It's pretty here," she said, as she held out her cigarette. "Got a light?"

He looked at her. "It sure is."

Harcourt just stood there, staring at her, watching the last of the day's light disappear into her eyes.

"Are you going to light my cigarette, or not?"

"Oh, yes, sorry," he said.

Sabrina smiled as he held up the match. Needing to be close to her, and not just to light her cigarette, he sat down on the porch swing beside her. The heat from her body moved right through his shirt. She turned toward him, the cigarette in her mouth, leaning toward the match. He struck the match, but then the wind quickly blew it out.

"Let me try again," he said.

This time he cupped his hand over the flame and she leaned in even closer, closing the gap between them, as her cigarette shivered between her lips. He envied the cigarette. He wanted to rip it out of her mouth and replace it with his lips, his mouth, his tongue, his fingertips. He breathed in her scent, apples and fresh grass, and tamarind? The end of her cigarette glowed and she pulled away. She sucked on it greedily, her eyes rolling back in pleasure. He pulled back to watch her, and saw the smoke come out, lost quickly in the wind. She was so young, so beautiful, so haunted.

"Aren't you going to have one?" Sabrina asked.

"Oh, yeah."

Harcourt hadn't had a cigarette since college, but he occasionally indulged in a good cigar. He lit his cigarette, using the same cupped hand method. Then he thought about his running and the importance of keeping his lungs clear, and he tried not to inhale. He let the smoke fill his mouth, turning his head away so she wouldn't see his cheeks puffing out like a chipmunk. Then, not wanting to seem like a wimp, he tried to control the exhalation through his lips so it would appear he smoked like anyone else.

He glanced over at Sabrina, then let out the rest of the smoke all at once and gulped in some air. She hadn't been watching to see if he knew how to smoke. She finished her cigarette and was looking around the side of the bench, as if hoping to find a coffee can or some other kind of ashtray.

".Just toss it out there. We'll pick up the butts in the morning."

"Can I have another one, please?"

He pulled out the pack of cigarettes from his shirt pocket and gave her the pack and the matches. He was already feeling a little lightheaded, even though he hadn't inhaled, and he'd only had one drag. He surely didn't want to smoke a second, not now, maybe not ever.

He discreetly dropped his cigarette onto the wet ground under the bench. It sizzled out immediately.

He handed her the pack. "You keep them. I'm not much of a smoker," he admitted. He liked being honest with this woman. It felt better. "Bought them on a whim."

"Okay."

They sat together, in silence. "That was some storm, huh?" Sabrina said after a while.

Even though it was nearly completely dark now, signs of the storm's wrath were everywhere. Tree branches, pine cones, and other debris were scattered all over the porch and the driveway. Harcourt knew that what they saw in the back of the house was nothing to what he'd see at the front of the house come daylight.

I sat on the bench next to Harcourt, wearing his clothes, my foot ensconced in a plastic bag. Yet all I felt was peace, safety, and comfort in his presence. Every time I looked at him, my eyes flew to his mouth, his lips. All I could think about was how it would feel if I kissed him.

But each time I got the urge I told myself no. I mean, it wasn't right. He was a potential client, not a potential lover, and besides, I was... well, unavailable for such things. Wasn't I?

It was getting darker and darker by the second, so I reached down and picked up the candle. I set it between us, so that one, I could see him better, and two, that it might keep me from trying to jump his bones.

But he didn't like that plan. He picked up the candle and moved it to his side out of our way, then he put his arms around my shoulders and pulled me close.

I gasped at the contact and the warmth, at how right it felt to be in his arms.

I wasn't sure if he was coming on to me or just trying to keep me warm against the growing chill. Was he being pro-tective, and caring, or was he making a move?

Damn it. I so hoped he would. Then I could succumb to my baser instinct and not feel as guilty, because who could resist a man like Harcourt Raymondson? Not me.

He didn't try anything though. He just ran his hand up and down my arm as we sat in a comfortable silence. After a few moments, I relaxed into it. It was nice. Right. Soothing.

I'd never been comfortable like that with a man before. I'd always been uptight, worried, second-guessing myself. Certainly, Jack and I had never sat in a comfortable silence. Jack always wanted something from me, always had a critical eye out, complaining about my weight, or my table manners or the way my hair never stayed put.

And when we were together he always wanted something from me: a fast blow job, or a quickie from behind, whether I was in the mood or not. And if he didn't want sex, he wanted me to listen to him talk for hours on end about how he'd been screwed out of his career as a television newscaster and how the movie was going to make him, once and for all. Or he'd lecture me on how I wasn't trying hard enough to bring back my psychic abilities and get on with the business of trying to locate all those missing kids.

That thought made me groan. That had been by far the cruelest thing he'd ever done.

He didn't even care if I had the psychic skills, he wanted me to fake it. To give those poor people false hopes—all to further his aims.

Well, if he hadn't hit me again, I'd still have left him. The idea that they expected me to read those heartbreaking letters on camera in the vain hope that one of them might trigger me to do what I'd done before, and go into a fugue state, just like when I was ten-years old. When I'd had a psychotic breakdown and managed to help the police save two children from certain death. It was never going to happen again. I don't know how I did it or why, but it was just a fluke. I was no more psychic than Harcourt Raymondson.

There'd been bags of those damn letters in my bedroom, when I'd run away from Jack. Even though I couldn't bear to look at them, I'd grabbed a few of the unopened letters, on my way out the door and stashed deep into the bowels of my handbag, telling myself that I might want to do what Jack suggested and at least try to see if I still had a gift. But, so far, they remained unopened. It hurt, just thinking about them.

I must have stiffened up, because Harcourt said, "You all right, sugar?"

I relaxed as his fingers moved from my back to my head. He stroked my hair, and Jack and the other creeps faded from my mind as I snuggled in closer to Harcourt.

"You know," he said, as he continued to cuddle with me on the porch swing, "I'm mighty glad you came up to my ranch, little lady," he said with a laugh.

I couldn't help it. I laughed hard.

"That's the worst cowboy accent I ever heard."

The swing rocked gently, and my uncovered foot started to feel chilled. I moved it to his leg and rubbed it against his calf for warmth. He just held me tighter, his arms back around my shoulder.

This was how a couple should feel together I thought. Not stressed, always on pins and needles, never afraid.

I decided then and there that when I finally got rid of the Jack problem, I'd look for a man like Harcourt. Of course, I knew that Harcourt Raymondson would never be relationship material for me, not for the long haul, certainly. I mean, he might be all right with a brief sexual relationship, but that would be all. Wouldn't it? I mean, he's a billionaire and I'm just a—what? An illegal immigrant, with no money and no job, avoiding my contractual obligations to the movie studio on that film I never wanted to be a part of, oh and I'm currently on the run from my abusive....

? Yeah, like that was the basis of a long-lasting relationship. Not.

Still, something seemed to be happening between us. I told myself that it was okay because it was only for a few days, only for a little while. Didn't I deserve to enjoy a few hours of passion?

Beside me, Harcourt's breathing became heavy and his arm relaxed, then drooped to the bench.

I laughed. Harcourt had fallen asleep.

How sweet.

After making sure his breathing was good and deep, I turned my body toward him and bent my leg over his and leaned against his chest. Drinking in his masculine perfection, I let myself dream for just a moment.

Harcourt

"That's so pretty," Sabrina said.

She seemed breathless, and was adjusting herself in the seat next to him, and Harcourt realized that he must have dozed off.

"I'm sorry, did I fall asleep?"

"Only for a second," Sabrina said, "but you have to see this. Isn't it beautiful?" She was pointing up to the sky, but he couldn't take his eyes off her.

"What's pretty, besides you?" Harcourt asked, as he gently moved a strand of hair out of her eyes.

She'd been looking out into the night, but at those words she turned back toward him. Their eyes locked. Harcourt saw her lips part and heard the intake of a breath. Her eyes scanned his face as if she were searching for something desperately important. Perhaps he imagined it, but it seemed as if she rose in her seat, bringing her face closer to his. Harcourt's heart thumped in his ears. She wanted him to kiss her. He tilted his head toward her and started to lean in, already tasting her luscious lips in his mind. She stiffened and she pulled away, turning her head back toward the sky.

Masking the flush of embarrassment at his near misstep, Harcourt sat back in his seat and started rocking the swing by pushing his weight against his feet. "What was it you wanted to show me?"

Sabrina breathed in and out quickly, as if she too was relieved to have gotten out of a sticky situation. She shifted her body and shimmied away from him, creating separation. She pointed to the sky. "Look at the moon."

This time Harcourt tore his eyes away from her, too embarrassed at what he might see. He'd gone too far. Damn it.

He followed her hand and saw what she was looking at: a half-moon peeking through a break in the storm. Behind the moon, the sky was a dark midnight blue, turned even darker as each new star flickered into sight. And as if their lack of contact could not be endured another second, he felt her fingers reach for his. A moment later, their hands entwined.

This time, he didn't stop himself, nor did she try to stop him. He turned his body toward hers and cupped her face in his hands. "Sabrina Cane, I'm going to kiss you now. Hold still."

He put his hand behind her neck and secured her in place, not willing to let another chance go by. And when their lips met, the sensation of the heat of her mouth, the soft need in the way her lips trembled besides his, made all the pain and all the bad memories and guilt fade away. Her lips parted and his tongue dipped inside, and for just a moment, he entered a state of grace, as if Sabrina's kiss could heal his aching soul. Something flickered at the edge of his closed eyes, just as his need grew strong again deep inside. When Sabrina pulled away from him this time, he felt something other than doubt. He felt fear. "What is it?"

"Someone's coming," she said, her eyes wide with panic.

13 Sabrina

I panicked. It was Jack, it had to be. He'd found me, but if he saw me with Harcourt with my lips swollen and my face flushed...

"Calm down, Sabrina," Harcourt said, trying to hold my face as he stared into my eyes.

I swatted his arms away as my eyes darted, expecting to see Jack appear out of some dark shadow with a baseball bat and take a lunge for us.

"We need to hide," I said.

"Sabrina, hide from whom, hide from what?"

I shook my head, not wanting to tell him, not wanting to admit that I'd just let him kiss a married woman. The vehicle had stopped approaching, and I realized that it was on the other side of the house. I grabbed my heart in relief. Maybe he could hide me in the pantry.

"Sabrina, honey, what's wrong? What are you so afraid of?"

A short burst of a siren filled the air, a loud wop, wop, and it made me jump. "See, I told you, nothing to worry about, Sabrina. Just the local volunteer fire department coming to make sure we're okay after that storm."

A moment later, red and blue lights danced in the trees overhead and I knew he had to be right. Relief flooded me and my knees buckled as we made it to the kitchen door. Harcourt caught me. "Here, sit at the table. I'll go get the candle and then I'll find out who has come to pay us a visit."

The private jet dipped its wings as it banked away from the Atlantic Coast and turned toward the west. The man in the expensive suit loosened his tie and sat back in his seat. His stewardess, a pretty blonde from Sweden, brought him a drink on a tray and sat in down at the table in front of him.

"Vill there be anything else?" she asked, as she un-snapped the buttons to her blouse.

Besides the stewardess and the pilot, the man had the jet to himself.

He pondered her offer, but he wasn't in the mood. He had thinking to do. He had plans to make.

"Not now, Hildy. Bring me the Black Label and a bottle of water and a glass, then make yourself scarce."

"Okay, whatever you say."

She yawned and he was glad to postpone. He preferred his pussy well-rested. Booking his flight at the last minute in the middle of the night had not garnered the freshest crew, but it made it easier to slip away and not be followed by the press. As long as the pilot was awake, he didn't care. He'd land in San Francisco at sunrise, then work his way up to his ultimate destination, in a way that would make anyone hoping to track him fail. His private jet would be parked in the Bay Area, and anyone searching for him would assume the same thing. He had a stand-in, ready to make an appearance at a public event at the appropriate times. All the wheels were in motion. There was only one loose thread, and fortunately, that thread was about to get cut.

After Hildy left his part of the cabin and closed the privacy door, he opened the bottle of water and took a sip. Then he poured himself half a glass of the Johnny Walker scotch whiskey. He pulled out his briefcase, unlocked it, then opened it. The jet banked again, and when he looked out the window, he could see Lake Superior down below. It looked like a sheet of black ice. His lips twitched in satisfaction. Then he pulled the tab and opened the FedEx envelope.

He slugged back a measure of the scotch, relishing the feel of the warm liquid as it slid into his belly. Pulling out the documents from the envelope, he read the article, copied from last week's Vancouver Sentinel.

Valuable Artwork from Mysterious Talent Sold for Peanuts at Vancouver Coffee House

An artist whose identity remained a closely held secret most of her life, after she'd become an anonymous child celebrity when she'd single-handedly helped police solve a major child kidnapping crime when she was just ten-years old, has turned up in Vancouver according to informed sources. Her identity no longer a secret after the press release from Merge Right Studios, a film company located in Los Angeles, California, she's become a highly sought-after artist. Her artworks have sold out fast at her art shows, sponsored by the studio. To learn that she's been selling her artwork at the Piedmont Coffee House in Vancouver for coffee house prices was a boon for the art critic who told the Sentinel of his discovery.

After that introduction, the article became a regurgitation of the promotional materials promoting the upcoming movie. His movie.

After skimming through the rest of the article, the man put it back in his briefcase and considered an alternate plan. Originally, when he'd heard that Jack thought he knew where she was hiding, he'd told him to get up to Vancouver and find her, then get her back to Hollywood at all costs. But now that he had a chance to reconsider the situation, and she'd so recently been in the Canadian press, he wondered if that was a mistake.

He'd originally wanted her back in LA so he could keep her in his sights, just in case her visions started coming back and she had any insights she shouldn't before he'd had a chance to make himself scarce. But the appeal of her story and the Canadian connection offered the perfect storm if he could bring her into the plan.

Yes. That's what he'd do. As soon as he landed, he'd notify Jack to find her, but not approach her. He didn't want to risk her running again. As soon as she was located, he'd get a more competent man to ensure Sabrina was where he wanted her.

The man smiled as he pictured just how it would all play out. It would be the perfect way to keep the story front and center, in both Canada and the US. And this time, they wouldn't dare to downplay his role. The third kidnapper would suddenly matter again. The third kidnapper who'd been all but ignored, forgotten, even though he'd gotten away with the two million dollars and one of the kids.

Finally, they'd revisit his all but forgotten first crime and they'd realize he'd struck again. And this time he wouldn't be ignored. He'd be famous again and he'd be the most wanted man in the world. And this time he wouldn't hide his identity. This time he wanted them to know. Once he'd finished his last spectacular kidnapping, and his plans to become a ghost were all set—he'd make sure they knew his real name.

Yes. He grinned and leaned back in his chair, then sat up and poured himself another drink. Very soon, everyone would know who Peter Talbert really was. A true, criminal mastermind.

The anticipation and excitement and the thrill of what would soon unfold burned like fire inside him. His cock came to life.

"Hildy!" he called toward the front of the plane.

She appeared a few moments later, looking fresh enough, but at that point, he'd fuck her dead.

"Did you vant something sir?" said Hildy, who'd just slid open the door to his side of the plane.

"Yes, I changed my mind. Get in here, pull up your skirt, bend over, and hang onto that seat."

"Yes, sir," Hildy said with a little squeal of delight. Then she did as she was told.

14 Harcourt

Harcourt used the illumination from the fire engines which were aimed inside the front of the house to pick his way through the debris and work his way toward the front door. Through the opening created by the tree, he could just see the firetruck with its lights flashing, forced to stop in his driveway as it was blocked by the tree. As he watched a fireman appeared at the top of the trunk, aiming the beam of a powerful flashlight over the scene. It fell on what was left of Sabrina's car. The fireman turned around and yelled to the men behind him. Harcourt noticed for the first time that Sabrina's crushed car still had its lights on. They were weak, but he had no doubt that the firemen were thinking that they had a victim still trapped into the car.

Harcourt climbed over a large branch, blocking his way to his front door, then pushed it open and stepped outside. He ran toward the men, waving his arms and shouting, "Hey!"

The fireman on the tree trunk had jumped to the ground and shone his powerful light at Harcourt's face.

Harcourt covered his eyes.

"Shine that somewhere else," he snapped.

"Are you all right?" yelled the fireman.

"I'm fine," Harcourt said.

Another fireman appeared on top of the fallen piece of tree trunk, this one hefting a bulky square medical bag. He jumped to the ground and ran over to the car, where the first fireman was busy shining his flashlight inside, trying to assess the condition of the victim.

"I can't see anyone," shouted the first fireman to the other. He set down his bag, lit up his own flashlight, and joined the scan of the car.

"There's no one inside. I got her out," Harcourt shouted.

The two firemen turned to Harcourt, appraising him, then they looked back at the crushed car. Harcourt could see as they shone their lights over the damage that the front seats of the car were caved in.

One of the firemen spoke. "So, you're saying there was someone in the car when that tree fell on her? And you got her out? Is she still alive?"

"Yes, I got her out. She's got some scrapes and bruises and a nasty cut on her foot, but I think she's going to live."

"You sure you're all right, sir?"

"I'm fine."

"Where's the girl?"

Harcourt showed them the way through his house. Sabrina was where he left her, and her face had a look of fear until he came into the room and nodded to her that these nice firemen were going to fix her up.

The paramedic took a look at her foot, pulling away Harcourt's attempts at first aid. He prodded and poked and then applied another bandage.

When they were done checking her over and also treating the abrasion on her forehead along her scalp, another car drove up, this time using the access road to the back of his house. Mark Pearson got out of his police cruiser, the bar lights on his car adding to the light show illuminating his backyard.

"Twice in the same day, Harcourt. It's got to be a record," he said as bounded up onto the porch and took Harcourt's hand, shaking it.

Then he excused himself and had a chat with the men. When he came back, Harcourt was afraid he'd want him to drive her to the next hospital, which was all the way in Port Hardy, a two-hour drive away. Sitting in an emergency room for hours was not how he'd hoped to spend his evening. Mark spoke with Sabrina briefly, in a low voice. Apparently satisfied that she was fine, he turned to Harcourt and said, "You know, Harcourt, I'm not going to let you stay here. I'm afraid I'm going to have to call this place unsafe until further notice."

"That's fine. I'll drive her into town. I'll get us a couple of rooms at the motel."

"Not likely," said the volunteer fireman who handled the medical bag.

"Why not?"

Mark stepped in to explain. "Because the storm took out the bridge, and your house isn't the first one we've seen like this. Okay, maybe it's the worst we've seen so far tonight, but the point it—a lot of people are looking for alternative shelter tonight, and the motel is fully booked. They've even got whole families staying in the rooms."

"They can go to the school," said a young fireman with red hair. "It's been set up as a temporary shelter."

Harcourt groaned. The idea of having to watch her sleep on some cot in some auditorium surrounded by a bunch of strangers had zero appeal, not when he wanted to hold her and watch her sleep in his arms. Then he remembered something.

"Did you see Molly's house when you drove by? Was it damaged?" He had a key to Molly's house.

"Didn't look damaged," said the firemen with the red hair. "Yeah, it was fine, as far as I could tell."

"Then we'll go there," Harcourt said.

A radio crackled in Mark Pearson's belt. He took it out and spoke into it.

"Captain, we've got a car accident at Highway 90 near Tamarac Wash."

"Injuries?"

"Nothing serious, but one of the vehicles went down an embankment."

"Is the tow truck underway?"

"Calling them next," said the voice on the radio.

"All right, I'll get one of the engines right over. ETA fifteen, twenty minutes. We're up in Dogwood Canyon."

"Roger."

After ending his radio call, Captain Pearson said to Harcourt, "I'm not leaving until you leave, Harcourt. I'm not kidding. This place isn't safe. So, come on, get that girl in your car and let's go."

Harcourt found his car keys and Molly's extra house key on the key rack by the back door.

"What about my shoes?" Sabrina said, pointing to her one bare foot and the newly fixed foot that didn't have a plastic bag over it this time.

"Where are they?"

"In the basement," Harcourt said.

"Forget your shoes. I'm not letting anyone that far into this house. Not until we can get a better look at the damage in daylight."

The constable was true to his word. The firemen and paramedics walked around the outside of the house to get to their vehicles, and soon left. Harcourt carried Sabrina to the Mercedes, while Mark watched, then he started his car and followed Harcourt off his property and all the way to Molly's house.

He walked around Molly's house, aiming his flashlight at the structure, looking for damage.

Then he waited for Harcourt to open the front door, and he stepped inside, waving his flashlight around to look for signs of structural damage.

He sniffed the air.

He seemed to be deciding.

"So, do we have your blessing?" Harcourt asked.

Mark put his hand on Harcourt's arm, patting it. "You have my blessing, Harcourt," he said. "Just don't expect too much, too soon."

Harcourt saw Mark glance over at Harcourt's Mercedes, where Sabrina had been told to wait, as he said those words. He suddenly understood the meaning.

He waited for Constable Pearson's tail lights to disappear around the bend in the road before going to the car.

She wanted to walk, but Harcourt insisted, and a moment later he carried Sabrina Cane over the threshold.

15   SABRINA

I lay in the comfort of Harcourt's powerful arms as he carried me over the threshold into his neighbor's house. The sound of the constable's car faded in the distance, and Harcourt closed the door behind him, leaving us both in the dark.

But I didn't need to see. All I needed to do was feel.

As soon as the door clicked shut, Harcourt's lips were on mine and my fingers were wrapped in his hair, pulling him closer. He stumbled into what had to be a living room and we kissed and pawed at each other, unable to speak. He put me on my feet and we desperately tore off our clothes.

I was on my back, panting with desire, with need, stripping his sweatpants off my ankles when I heard the tear of plastic. I knew he was putting on a condom. Neither of us spoke as we succumbed to the inevitable, his fingers swirling my juices to life before he plunged into me, and I met his thrust with my rising hips. He sunk inside me all the way to the hilt, and I moaned in ecstasy as he filled me completely, and I gasped at the size of him.

He purred, and spoke his first word in my ear, "Oh, Sabrina," and then his mouth did all the talking. I arched my chest toward him, dropping my head back and exposing my neck as he worshiped me with his mouth. He continued to move in and out of me, rocking me, fucking me deep and hard as the wind screamed in the trees outside.

My fingernails dug into his shoulders and his mouth covered mine, swallowing my gasps of pleasure as the intensity of our union filled my being. When his hand reached between our bodies and his fingertip found my clit and as he continued to fill me, I felt him take my lower lip in his mouth and he sucked on it hard as we both shuddered our release.

We stayed on the carpeted floor, becoming aware of furniture and other objects close to our bodies in that room. But neither of us seemed to care that there was a sofa leg between our feet, or a coffee table leg poking into our sides. All that mattered was that we were together, our naked and sweating bodies entwined like vines as he stayed inside me.

He came out and I heard the condom come off. He disappeared, cursing as he banged his toe on something. I lay there, feeling more at peace than I'd ever felt in my life. I watched the clouds move outside and smiled at the moon as she peeked behind the cloud and cast a silvery light on his perfect ass. He settled back on the floor beside me, then shoved the couch and the table away and covered us both in a clean-smelling sheet.

I sit up. I'm in a small room, sitting cross-legged on the floor, my hands covered with something. Sticky, drying, glue? I look up and there's a picture on the wall. A picture I made. There are three children in the picture, a little girl and two little boys. They are looking at me with big tearful eyes, hands reaching out to me. "Help us," they say in unison. Behind them, I see the two brothers, the men with the thick skulls, bug eyes, and matching broken noses. They're trying to cover their faces so I can't show who they are. But I'm not interested in them. My eyes travel to the other man on the wall. He's taller than the other two and he's coming toward me. He pops out of the wall and his hands are reaching for my throat. I want to scream, but my jaw won't move. I stare at his missing face, because I can't not look. I try to recoil but my body is frozen. His fingers are at my throat, pressing, squeezing. I try to lift my hands to pull his fingers off my throat, but I'm paralyzed. I try again to scream, but nothing but a piteous moan escapes my lips.

"Sabrina! Sabrina, wake up!"

It took a while for me to stop convulsing and come out of my dream, but as soon as I do I remember it all over again. I'm shaking as it all comes flooding back to me. I hadn't had that dream for months, and it had never been so vivid. Harcourt insisted on helping me out of the living room and into one of the bedrooms. Somehow, while I'd been sleeping, I guess he managed to locate a flashlight with a decent light. I was dripping in sweat, and he took me into the bathroom.

"You need to shower that off," he said as he turned on the water to get it warm.

I felt too weak to stand up in the shower, and was grateful when he took me in his arms and stepped into the shower with me. He was still naked, just like me, and he held me close as the warm water washed away the nightmare and the sweat.

He soaped me down and rinsed me off, then dried me with a towel. He carried me to a large bed and tucked me under the covers. He even brought me a glass of water and held up my shoulders and the back of my head as I drank.

He didn't speak or ask me about the dream, for which I was grateful, but he also didn't try to join me under the covers. I wasn't sure how I felt about that.

When I fell asleep for the second time that night, I had no more dreams that I could recall. And when I woke a few hours later, the faint early rays of dawn lit up the bedroom.

I heard loud banging noises coming from somewhere in the house.

I got up and decided to investigate.

Every night after he'd been fed and given his time in the washroom, the young boy who was almost a man waited for the sound of the key turning in the lock in his door. Then he moved his bedding to the floor, and curled up near the tiny crack at the base of the wall in the windowless room. Caleb always stayed awake as long as he could, listening hard for sounds of an approaching car.

When Sir or the other twin came to relieve her sister, he would hear the sounds of tires on the rough dirt track, long before he saw signs of headlights bouncing like long white dragonfly wings in the woods. If he heard anything, he would immediately throw himself on his stomach and shield his eyes so he could peer through the small sliver in the wall that looked out onto the dirt driveway in front of the cabin. Through his secret spy hole, which he'd discreetly made larger over the last five years, Caleb observed everything. He knew the license plate of the car the sisters shared, and one day, if he was very attentive, he hoped to see what Sir looked like. He hoped to see the face of the man behind the mask. And when he did, he would go to sleep and send the picture to his angel, so she could find him and take him away.

As usual, Harcourt woke at the crack of dawn. But, instead of dreading the day and dutifully reaching for his running shoes, Harcourt took a moment to savor the feeling of waking up with a smile on his face. And then he remembered why he was so happy. Sabrina Cane, what an incredible woman. And having sex with her had not been what he'd expected, and yet it had been everything he could have wanted or needed. He used the bathroom, then tiptoed to her room, opening the door with care so as not to disturb her. She lay sound asleep, her beautiful body outlined by the sheets only. She'd thrown off the covers.

His stomach growled and he decided to cook them both breakfast.

He walked into Molly's orderly kitchen and began his search for the coffee supplies. As he ground the beans and filled water for the coffee pot, then pressed the button to start brewing. But nothing happened.

He slapped his head. "No electricity, you idiot."

He checked the stove and was grateful for the gas burners. He found a metal strainer, a sauce pan, and a bowl and started boiling water for coffee.

As he continued to try to sort out breakfast, he realized to his surprise that he was humming. Fucking humming. He couldn't remember the last time he'd done that. He looked around. Maybe it was Molly's cheerful kitchen with her yellow painted walls and gleaming white appliances. Or maybe it was Sabrina. Something undeniable swelled in his chest. He breathed it in. Happiness.

Giving in to the feeling, Harcourt switched from humming to whistling as he inexpertly cracked a dozen eggs into a bowl. He extracted most of the broken shell bits afterward with a metal spoon. Then he added milk, after first smelling it to make sure it was still fresh, the way he'd seen his housekeeper do. Then he found a mill of pepper and ground a little into the mix. He pinched in some salt, then beat the mixture confidently with a fork.

That's how Molly made her scrambled eggs, and they were always perfect. A simple tune whistled its way onto

Harcourt's lips as he opened and closed the pantry doors, looking for something else to add to the breakfast. Harcourt realized that he was feeling something he hadn't felt in a long time. An eagerness to face his day.

Despite his good intentions and the good start, breakfast got out of hand. Harcourt could out-business the next businessman to the tune of the billions of dollars he made, but getting a breakfast on the table, the kind that Molly would prepare if she were in her own kitchen, proved more daunting than Harcourt would have expected. After he accidentally knocked a raw egg onto the floor, Harcourt forgot the eggs cooking in the frying pan as he searched for a way to clean up the sticky mess. When the smell of burning eggs hit his nostrils, he got up fast, too fast. Losing his balance as he attempted to turn off the burner and move the eggs off the grate at the same time, Harcourt reached out to stop his fall.

The box of recently opened Bisquick upended, and fell off the counter onto his head, just as his ass hit the floor.

"Need a hand?"

Sabrina stood there, hands on the doorjamb, laughing so hard as she shook her head that Harcourt could see the tears filling her eyes.

Harcourt wiped some of the flour off his face and stared back at the girl who had the nerve to point her finger at him as she continued to double over laughing.

"Oh, you think this is funny, do you?"

"I do," she said, nodding her head vigorously, her brown eyes sparkling with delight.

Harcourt was stealthy and scooped up as much of the flour as he could get. And then he rose, a mischievous smile tugging at this lips, eyes on his prey.

"What? No!"

He pounced and she yelped, squealing with laughter and delight as she tried to run away. The pink floral bathrobe she'd borrowed from Molly opened, revealing her incredible curves. She tried to avoid him, but he was too fast. In an instant, he reached her from behind and ground the handful of flour into her hair.

They laughed and wrestled and hurtled the pancake mix at each other like children in a snow fight, until they could no longer keep their hands off each other. They rolled on the floor, bodies tangled up like snakes as they kissed, and groped, and craved each other until they stopped to catch a breath.

They made love in the shower and then again on the bathroom floor.

Afterward, a quiet descended upon the house, and upon the occupants as if they were truly strangers to each other. They cooked the eggs and made pancakes, then set about the chore of putting Molly's kitchen back into its original pristine order.

Harcourt found his lips tasting her neck, and his fingers holding onto her hips. He couldn't not touch her as she stood in front of the sink, washing the last of the dishes.

She leaned back into him, sighing happily, but then her body stiffened and she pulled away. He felt a sudden rush of fear, as if she would soon be leaving him. He wanted to reach out and hold her, hold onto the moment. She stared at him with an earnest and searching look, her face needing to find something in him, to know some inner truth.

He lifted a brow, telling her to ask her question, telling her that he'd tell her anything, anything at all she wanted to know.

He saw her throat bob, and her eyes drop for a moment. She was desperate for the answer and yet afraid to ask the question.

"What is it, Sabrina?" he asked, lifting her chin with his finger.

"Does it ever go away?"

Harcourt knew what she meant by her question. If he'd been asked that question twenty-four hours ago, his answer would have been an emphatic no, it never goes away.

But that was before meeting Sabrina and letting her into his life, sharing her body. The pain had gone away when he was inside her, when she was rolling under him as they laughed on the floor. The pain had been freed from his body.

But it was coming back, and this time with a different kind of pain. Guilt.

He moved to the window, but didn't see anything beyond the glass. "It doesn't go away, not even for an instant." He felt the harshness in his tone and it made him cringe. He was taking his anger out on her for bringing them up when he should have been angry at himself for forgetting his wife and son so easily.

Sabrina took a tentative step toward him, her body language regretful, apologetic. "I'm sorry, I shouldn't—"

"No, you have nothing to be sorry for." Harcourt's jaw muscles worked as he tried to get his emotions in check. Again, the sharp tone in his voice. Why was he being such a dick to her? It wasn't her fault. He was the one.

"I'm going for a walk," he said.

"Good idea, I'll come with you."

"No, I'd rather go by myself."

I tried not to feel the loss that seemed to grow in my gut each moment that Harcourt stayed away. As soon as he walked out the door, I knew I'd made a terrible mistake. Not just the mistake of bringing up a clearly sensitive subject, reminding him about his loss, asking him the inane question if the pain ever went away... I'd also made the terrible mistake of jumping into the sack with this man to begin with. I don't know what had gotten into me.

I rationalized, telling myself that it was all those circumstances. God and nature conspired to bring us together, trying to make me forget my troubles—forget everything—as I zoned out in a sexual haze.

And yet it hadn't just been about the sex, or the release. A part of me couldn't deny some kind a deeper connection, a bond, a common thread.

Harcourt was a man in the midst of healing, and I was a woman who seemed to gash open my wounds and tear off the scabs, never allowing those things that had injured my heart and mind to ever have the chance to fully heal. Maybe

I felt closer to Harcourt than I'd ever felt to another man, because his pain was as raw as mine, maybe even rawer.

After cleaning up the mess in the kitchen so it looked almost as good as how we'd found it, I straightened the mess in the living room and tidied the guest bedroom where we'd spent the night. As a courtesy, and considering what we'd done under the covers, I stripped the sheets and put them on top of the laundry.

I took a shower using the cheap coconut shampoo to get the flour and egg out of my hair. When I stepped out and dried off, I couldn't bring myself to dress in Harcourt's flour-stained and too-long sweatpants.

So, with one towel wrapped around my hair and one wrapped around my body, I went down the hall and found the owner of the house's room to look for clothes I might borrow. Her underwear was far too big and extremely un-sexy, so I bypassed them. Her pants were too wide in the waist and too short in the legs, so they were out as well. I found a bright yellow cotton summer dress with white flower trim along the bodice that I prayed would fit. I slipped it over my head. It was a little too short for my long body and a little too snug around my breasts, but it was close enough. Best of all, it was clean.

I looked next for shoes, but her feet were too small. After digging around in the bottom of her closet, I got lucky when I found a pair of thin-soled summer sandals that looked like she'd gotten them at some beauty salon after a pedicure. They were the one-size-fits-all kind of shoe that fit no one.

They were clearly too big for her feet, and just a little too small for mine—but it was best option I had.

In her bathroom, I found some eye-makeup remover and got rid of the traces of mascara and smeared eyeliner under my eye.

"You had no business doing that," I said out loud, scolding myself in the mirror as I fluffed my hair in the towel. "He's a man in pain, and you're not exactly single."

My reflection didn't seem to care about my opinion.

Dressed, I went to the living room and sat down, determined to be cool if he ever returned. I'd insist that he take me back to the house so I could get my things out of my car, then I'd ask for a ride into town. I'd move into the shelter until there was a way to get back to Vancouver. I'd pack my things and go on the run again, to somewhere else, and forget about the billionaire with those sad, hazel eyes.

Then I thought about my car. It wouldn't be easy to bolt without a car.

I thought about what he'd said, how he'd promised and look after the claim for my car. I'd lie low in Vancouver until he filed the claim and I got the check. Then I could say goodbye to Ellis and Jeanette and the boys and head out into the sunset...

Jeanette!

I'd totally forgotten about Jeannette. She had to be worried sick about me. I needed to call her.

In the corner of Molly's living room on a polished, maple-stained side table, I saw a telephone. I ran over to it and lifted the receiver, listening. Dead. I depressed the switch repeatedly. Nothing. Dead as a doornail.

I thought about how mad Jeanette was going to be if I didn't get word to her soon.

I let out a sigh of frustration. It was already the next day, probably close to eight in the morning. She had to be freaked.

I'd promised to text her after arriving on Vancouver Island, but that was before I got that call from Jack and I dropped and broke my phone.

Shit. Jack.

Outside, I could hear footsteps approaching. I sat up straight and tightened my jaw, chin out, determined to be firm, determined not to succumb to his charms.

I needed to get my shit out of my car and get my butt into town, so I could find a way to get word to Jeanette and Ellis that Jack was in town.

Jack Bressler stood on the bow of the ship, smoking his one daily cigarette a little earlier than usual, as he waited for the ferry to dock at the east end of Vancouver Island. He'd arrived at the terminal on the mainland an hour before the scheduled departure. He wanted to get an early start, track her down, then have time to figure out how to get her to come back with him, and then back to Hollywood, per his benefactor's request. Having her back at the studio would do a lot to get the film back on track. It made sense.

Jack's eyes narrowed as he thought about how Sabrina's behavior was screwing things up for him. When she'd first taken off, he thought she'd return in a few days, but when it became apparent that she'd taken off for good, he'd had to scramble to cover up for her absences both at the art galleries and at the studio. He'd taken too long to inform his benefactor of the situation, and he'd paid the price for doing that. His benefactor scared the shit out of him, even on a good day, and he told him to find her or else.

Fortunately, he'd not followed through on his threat after the first month and even the second she was gone. Jack had no choice but to divert some of his clothing allowance to hire a private eye. He should have done that right away. It only took the dude a week once he was hired.

Jack had more reasons than pleasing this benefactor to want the movie to get back on track. He'd managed to finagle himself a role in the film. But without Sabrina, they wouldn't need his film. Sabrina was the key to everything, and even though he was getting close, she was still at large.

His eyes narrowed. There was no one too close. He started to speak to her, the way he did when he was angry with nothing to punch. "You're a little bitch, Sabrina. You've gone and fucked things up for me. You stupid skank. Papa's not at all happy about that," he said between gritted teeth, then he ground his cigarette out on the rail of the ship, picturing the rail as her face.

He tossed the cigarette into the sea and turned around, leaning his back against the rail. He sighed. He wouldn't burn her face with a cigarette. If he did, his benefactor would probably put a hit out on him. He wasn't that kind of man. Hell, he'd never hurt her all that much. She overreacted. They all did. Sabrina needed to get off her high horse and forgive him. Realize what a catch he was. She needed to come back to him. She needed to stand by her man. That was the real problem here. She needed to get straightened out. There was nothing wrong with him.

Once the ferry landed, Jack hit the road, stopping just once to fill his tank with gas. Everywhere he saw signs of storm damage, which occurred the night before. It had been a crazy storm, and had kept him up much of the night in Vancouver even in his steel hotel, but per the news reports he'd heard on the radio, Vancouver Island received the brunt of the storm. He spotted several road crews busy with chainsaws as they cut through fallen trees which had already been dragged off the road so people could drive. In several spots, lanes were closed due to flooding. Due to all the road work, traffic was heavy. His progress was slower than he'd planned.

But once he made it past Port Hardy and headed on the highway which would take him to the northernmost edge of Vancouver Island, traffic thinned considerably and Jack made up time by putting his foot down on the gas.

And he enjoyed almost no traffic on the road as he raced through over uninhabited wilderness, heading inland toward mountains. Everywhere he looked, there was nothing but forests. Jack Bressler didn't much appreciate beauty unless it was naked and standing in front of him or lying in his bed, but even he felt a rush of awe as he drove under a canopy of tall dark trees, and made his way up into the foothills. It was so dark under the trees that he put on his headlights. As he rounded a curve, driving faster than the posted speed, he slammed his brakes hard and had to swerve to avoid hitting a car.

When he caught his breath, and reversed back into his lane, he realized that there was a line of stopped cars ahead of him, all with their lights on in the dark tree-covered road. "Crap," he muttered. And out of habit he honked his horn.

It didn't do any good. The car far in front released its brake lights and inched forward. This went on, stop and go, for almost twenty minutes. Jack finally saw something up ahead. He assumed that there was some horrific accident and wondered if there was enough light to get a good shot if someone was dead at the scene. When he realized that it wasn't an accident, but a roadblock of some kind, he slammed the heel of his hand against his horn again.

"Knock it off, buddy," shouted the man in the car ahead.

And when Jack saw his finger shoot out of the window, he was tempted to put on the emergency brake and rip that fucker out of his car, then put him back inside in pieces. He jerked his head, getting out the kink in his neck, and worked his jaw until the urge went away. Eventually, he saw that all the cars ahead of him were being forced to turn around up by the lights. When he got close enough to read the flashing LED road sign, he wanted run over the rent-a-cop motioning for him to turn around.

Reluctantly, Jack made the turn, but not before carefully reading the sign again.

Road Closed. No Access to Diversion. Bridge Out.

Back in Port Hardy, he stopped and had a meal. After the meal, he started looking for a room. Since several people were stranded because of the bridge being out, there wasn't a vacant room in town. Cursing his luck, he bought another pack of smokes, deciding to up his daily allotment to four while he was on the island, and took the turnoff toward Victoria. He was sure he'd be able to find a room there, and since driving to Diversion wasn't a possibility, he'd look into renting a helicopter.

16 HARCOURT

As Harcourt walked through the woods behind Molly McCarthy's cottage, he marveled at how fast something could change. The weather for one. Less than a dozen hours before, the clouds had let loose a torrent of rain and wind so intense it was if God himself was leaning back, aiming a firehose at the island, and trying to wash it back into the sea. For another, his own mood had drastically changed. A hailstorm of guilt threatened to cloud his judgment and throw him back into the arms of despair.

But the walk had revived and refreshed him, helped him see things straight. He'd overreacted. Sabrina Cane was a beautiful woman, and having sex with her had been like a booster shot for hope again in his life. Yes, it had hurt to realize that for the time he'd been with her, he hadn't thought about his wife and son. He hadn't been gripped by the crippling pain. But what was so bad about that? Was he supposed to only know pain and grief for the rest of his life? Is that what Sharon would have wanted, or even little Cedric? If they loved him, wouldn't they want him to someday know joy again?

As he worked his way back toward the cottage, the wind picked up, dry and warm. In the trees above, the last memories of the night's storm—droplets of quickly evaporating water—formed at the ends of the needles and glinted like a million diamonds with each movement in the breeze.

Harcourt wanted to get back to her. To touch her, to kiss her, to learn more of who she was. He picked up his pace. As he found the trail leading back to Molly's cottage, his body tingled in anticipation. All he could think of was cupping her face in his hands and looking into her stunning brown eyes as he moved inside her.

But she might be upset that he'd walked out on her without an explanation. He'd have to smooth things over, bring her back on board. It wouldn't be difficult, he told himself. He'd just apologize for getting a little weird. She'd understand and they'd return to whatever it was they had going.

He'd been right when he told himself that he needed to think with his dick again. Sex would help him out of his pit. He needed to get his shit together and get back to New York, and take back what was rightfully his. Sabrina was a godsend, just what the doctor ordered. He'd do his best to keep her close for as long as he could. And when that ship sailed, he'd find another woman, and then another...

But he had a hard time even picturing another piece of ass. For some reason, the only body he wanted to touch, to fuck, to know in every way, was hers.

All right, he told himself. Then do what you can to keep her around.

As he took a detour up a trail that led to a rocky outcrop up a hill, he considered the myriad of possibilities. At the top of the trail, he could make out the rooftops of Diversion in the distance, and as he scanned the small town, he was reminded of the world he'd built, his corporation, his baby. He thought about the conference call and the work that he needed to do in New York. It was Saturday and the special board meeting would be held on Wednesday. He needed to get to work on that, get to New York, start gathering his team. Then another thought crystalized in his mind, the kind of insightful vision that made him the man he was. He could take Sabrina to New York with him.

Molly had turned him down, but he'd expected that she might. Sabrina Cane, on the other hand, might be more amenable to the idea. He'd certainly had some ideas for making it worth her while.

When Harcourt pushed open the door and stepped inside Molly's house, he felt a little nervous about what he intended to ask of her. He had no doubt that he could explain away his behavior, or that she'd forgive him, or that they couldn't get things back to where they had been.

But the house had a stillness, a silence that he hadn't expected. "Sabrina?"

There was no answer. Harcourt moved through the tiny living room, where Molly's tidy hand and good life was evident throughout. Clean and neat, the furniture was comfortable and welcoming. Doilies protected the gleaming polished wood of a coffee table. Tasteful groupings of photographs in intricately carved wooden frames showed a life filled with memories, friends and family, events with the garden club, and faded images of a former husband in his suit at their wedding, and in his military uniform.

"Sabrina, are you here?"

When he made it into the kitchen, he pulled up short. Sabrina sat at the small kitchen table, wearing a dress and shoes she must have found in Molly's closet. She sat stiffly in the bright, sunny kitchen, but the look on her face was anything but sunny.

"Sabrina, are you all right?"

"No, I'm not."

"What's wrong."

She lifted her hand, indicating the house. "This, all of this, us. I don't know what I'm doing here. I don't belong here. I want to go back."

"But my project. The commission. Aren't you interested?" Harcourt was grasping at straws.

"Look, just give me a ride to your house so I can get my things, then give me a ride to town. I'll get out of your hair."

"You're not in my hair. Sabrina, what's gotten into you?"

Harcourt moved toward her, hoping that if he could just touch her, hold her, kiss her, this mood would pass as fast as the storm. But she stiffened and pulled away from his touch, then stood up.

"Just give me a ride, please. Please, Harcourt."

Harcourt felt as if a log had been let loose to slam into his gut. His ego felt bruised as well. If she didn't want him, he wasn't the kind of man that begged for a woman's affections.

"Fine," he said and went to get his keys.

They rode in silence the one mile up the windy road to his house. But when they turned into his driveway they had to stop because a tree blocked the road. Harcourt stopped the Mercedes and the two of them got out and walked toward the fallen tree. Harcourt saw that the giant pine which he thought had been totally felled by the lightning had only been split down the middle, a half-trunk left to fall on his house and slap some of its thicker branches on Sabrina's car. Harcourt helped her onto the trunk and they both stood high enough where they could see the devastation that was once was her car.

"I'm still alive?" Sabrina asked, as she pinched herself.

"It shifted after I got you out," Harcourt said, his lips twitching into a tentative grin.

"Well, thanks," she said, smirking beautifully. Then her body turned toward his house. "Oh, Harcourt, I'm so sorry."

He tentatively put his arm around her and she gave him a little hug.

"It's nothing that time and money can't fix," he said, pulling her closer. He dropped his face to her hair. She smelled like rain and coconuts. After a moment, she pulled away. He let her go gently, then jumped down and helped her do the same. "Let's see if we can get any of your things out."

None of the doors were accessible, but since the windows were broken, Harcourt broke off one of the smaller branches from a stick he found on the ground, and used it to fish around until he caught the strap of her purse. She wanted to help, but he told her to stay back. "Too dangerous."

"Then you shouldn't be doing it, either." They both turned at the sound. A large man dressed in the uniform of the Canadian Mounties stood on top of the stump, looking down on them.

"And why not, Constable... I don't think I've had the pleasure?" said Harcourt, not changing his position.

"My name is Constable Hobday, I'm with the RCMP. I'm not going to ask you again. Please step away from the vehicle, sir."

"But I've almost got it," Harcourt said, trying to appeal to the man's common sense.

"I just need my purse, and the things from my trunk," Sabrina added, trying to sound sweet and pleading with the constable.

"Mr. Raymondson. You are Mr. Raymondson, I presume," the constable asked.

"I am," Harcourt said as his back stiffened both from annoyance and holding the uncomfortable position. He pulled back from the car, but held onto his stick. He stretched his back as he stood up straight then turned to face the unwanted officer of the law.

Hobday said, "I understand that your house had been condemned. I've come to make that official. Until we can get a state inspector in here from Victoria, no one, not even you, Mr. Raymondson, has the right to wander around this property or its grounds."

"Oh, come on," Harcourt said, never having heard of such a rule.

Constable Hobday pulled himself up to his full height, which made him look even bigger as he towered over them on the fallen tree-trunk. He didn't raise his voice, but instead lowered it, making the threat even more pronounced. "Mr. Raymondson, this is your last chance. Put down that stick and step away from the vehicle."

"Or what, you'll arrest me for trespassing at my own goddamn house?"

"No, I'll arrest you for being an idiot. Just get away from the car, Raymondson."

Sabrina was tense. She'd seen people get beat up bad for being only half as disrespectful to the cops as Harcourt was being. "Please, Harcourt, I'm okay," she said.

Harcourt seemed to realize that she was there, and the anger on his face turned to concern. He quickly put down the stick, then he stepped away from the car with his hands up in the air, to show he wasn't a threat,.

Then he headed over to the tree and climbed on top, and had a private word with the policeman. "Can you give me any idea how long it will take before this inspector can check out the house?"

Hobday kept his voice down. "With the bridge being out, the only way in or out is via helicopter or boat. With the storm coming back soon and the harbors all trashed, that would be dumb—so, yeah—probably going to take a while before we can get an inspector, couple of days for sure, maybe longer."

"You got here by helicopter?" Sabrina asked, who'd inched toward them to eavesdrop.

"Ma'am, please hold your position," Hobday said.

Sabrina stopped and felt her cheeks flame up. Stupid cop, treating me like some criminal.

"Yes, did you come by helicopter?" Harcourt asked, realizing that with the bridge being out that would be the way he could still get to New York.

Hobday had no trouble answering his question. "No, I drove in yesterday on an inspection. I'm trapped just like everyone else."

"Fair enough," Harcourt said, picking up on the best way to handle the man. He jumped onto the other side of the log, away from Sabrina. He motioned Hobday to join him.

"What?" Hobday asked.

"I've got a little problem. My work, my laptop, my cell phone, it's all in the house. And that's what I came here for. I know I can get to it safely, then get right out again. If you let me do that, I promise you, I'll stay away until you give me the green light."

Constable Hobday seemed to chew on that.

"All right, but only if I can go with you. If I think it's safe I'll let you grab your things. If not, you drive away and I don't want to see you here again until the inspector gives the all-clear. Deal?"

"Deal."

I was furious. They thought I couldn't hear, but I heard every word. The two men came over the trunk again and Harcourt told me to wait in the car. "But what about my purse?" I hissed, hoping Hobday wouldn't hear me. He did.

"Ma'am, please go back to the car," he scolded. What was with this guy? He had that look like he didn't think much of people who weren't white. I knew better than to get into an argument with a man like him, especially when he had a badge and a gun.

I bit back the retort edging to leave my lips, smiled sweetly at him, and almost curtsied. I headed for the trunk and with some effort managed to heave myself over. Just in case Hobday still had his eye on me, I went all the way to Harcourt's Mercedes and even opened the passenger door. But instead of getting inside, I just left the door open. It would look like I was inside, but keeping the air flowing.

I crept back toward the tree trunk, crouching low as I walked. When I got back on the trunk again, both men were out of sight. I scrambled over the tree and set let myself down as carefully as I could. Then I picked my way over the debris to my pulverized Volvo.

I tried the trunk, but it was jammed shut. I saw a gaping hole on the side of the trunk. The hole was small, but I managed to get my hand inside. I positioned myself next to the car and pushed my hand through, then groped around, feeling for anything small enough to pull out. I felt something soft, and then heard a tinkling sound. My shaman bag.

It took a little maneuvering to pull it out, and unfortunately I tore off a few of the beads, but I managed to get it. It sparkled in the sunlight, and I set it on top of the car. Then I went to get my purse, wincing when something sharp and hard poked through my useless sandals.

Relieved that it was just a sharp rock and not another piece of glass in my foot, I proceeded more carefully. I picked up the stick Harcourt had been using, and mimicked what he'd done before. Eyeing my purse inside the crushed Volvo, I leaned against the car for support. "Come on, you," I said, urging the tip of the stick into the strap of my purse. When it caught hold, I felt elated. I let my body weight fall against the car, and used both hands to lift the tip of the heavy stick like I was baiting a hook in slow motion. Soon, my purse was good and caught, so I started to move backward to pull it out of the car. I tripped on something, lost my balance, and the next thing I knew I was on my ass.

Fortunately, the stick and the purse also joined me on the ground. I heard something, and I thought they were approaching. I scrambled to my feet, and grabbed my purse and my grandmother's shaman bag. I scrambled over the tree, then stayed low to the ground as I hurried back to the car, my heart beating wildly. At the car, I had a view of the house, and realized that they weren't coming back yet. In fact, I saw motion at a second-story window.

I gasped in relief and took a minute to compose myself. My body vibrated with adrenaline. I felt like such a naughty girl, violating a direct order from a cop. Then I realized that my big white leather purse wouldn't exactly escape his notice if he were to look in the car. Harcourt would probably be cool about me going to get it, but I couldn't be sure about Constable Hobbledick or whatever his name was. He might take umbrage at my disobedience.

And then another realization hit me, turning my stomach into a whirl of knots. I wasn't exactly sure if I was living in Canada legally. At the border, I told them I was just coming up for the day. I didn't apply for a tourist visa, or anything like that. But, I'd been in the country now for almost three months. For all I knew I was here, illegally. If me breaking his direct orders pissed him off enough, and he wanted to look at my passport, I bet he'd just love to get me deported. I decided that I had better hurry up and hide my purse, and the shaman bag while I was at it. I stood on my tiptoes, looking for signs of them. I couldn't see them in the upstairs anymore, so I figured they'd be back soon. I hustled to the back of the Mercedes, and when I opened the back door, I groaned. Harcourt's SUV was clean, with nothing in the large trunk space except for a wool blanket folded neatly in the corner. I considered tucking my items under the blanket, but Harcourt was coming back with his own things. The possibility that he might move the blanket to put his things inside, and that the officer might spot my purse and put two and two together—my indolence and disrespect revealed—well, that made me reluctant to resort to that choice.

The voices were getting closer. Shit.

I lifted the floor mat, relieved to find some room in the spare tire well with a place to hide my purse. I stuffed my purse and the shaman bag inside. When I put the floor mat back down, there was a slight bump, but it wasn't very obvious. I didn't have time to worry about it, because the voices were getting closer. I closed the door as silently as I could and walked back to my seat.

Harcourt and the constable appeared a few moments later over the top of the fallen tree, with the Constable carrying Harcourt's suitcase. Harcourt had his arms full carrying a large briefcase with a laptop on top, wrapped in its heavy power adapter.

"Hey," he said, when he saw me.

"Hey," I replied.

After Harcourt put his suitcase in the back and his laptop on the back seat, exposing all my would-be hiding places as I feared, the officer of the law spoke to Harcourt.

"Stay out of here without my permission, are you clear?"

"Okay, boss, whatever you say," Harcourt said. Harcourt's lips were in a thin line, and he didn't speak to me as we drove away. I wasn't sure if he was still mad at me, or pissed at the cop. I wanted to reach for his hand and tell him how wonderful I felt in his arms, but it was obvious he was done with me.

I fell into a brooding silence of my own and stared out the window, hardly seeing all the damage from the storm as we made our way out of the mountainous section of Dogwood Canyon where Harcourt and Molly made their homes.

I had my purse, so I could go if there was a way out. I knew that's what I should do, but somehow, I couldn't bring myself to do it. And not just because I was dying to spend more time with Harcourt Raymondson. Not just because I wasn't ready to end our love affair. What dawned on me was that I had nowhere to go. If I got back to Vancouver, odds were good that Jack would be waiting for me, and now that that stupid article had been out almost a week, there was a chance that someone from the Canadian immigration department might be looking for me as well.

I stared out the window as we drove toward Diversion, trying to think of a way to stick around without coming off like a lovesick billionaire-chasing gold digger.

He should know that I didn't really want to go. I was sulking, making a point. If I meant anything at all to him, he should realize that I was expecting him to talk me out of my plan to bolt and to blow off the job. He should understand that I had no real desire to put a fast end to whatever kind of relationship we'd started. But Harcourt hadn't tried hard at all to talk me out of it. He'd been far too willing to go along with my plan.

As if he'd welcomed the easy departure, as if he was about to end things himself.

Maybe he was. He got what he wanted. Slam, bam, thank you, ma'am.

When Harcourt came back with Constable Hobday and the few things he'd been allowed to take out of his own house, he noticed that Sabrina was acting strange, cagey, quiet. She wasn't about to change her mind about going, apparently.

Fine, whatever.

Harcourt tightened his lips, and he matched her silence as he attempted to drive her toward town. Sunlight shone through scattered puffy clouds and the tall canopy of pines overhead, cleaving the graveled road like theater spotlights. Harcourt jerked the wheel sharply, tossing Sabrina and himself from side to side as he avoided the broken tree branches and other vegetative debris which littered the graveled road. Sabrina's jaw was tight, as she supported herself with one hand gripping the seat, the other hand white knuckled on the hand hold, but she didn't say anything. Obviously, she hadn't changed her mind. Obviously, she still wanted to just go.

Maybe it was just as well. He'd wanted to get laid, fuck a woman's brains out, get that out of his system, and he'd accomplished his objective.

Now that he had his phone and his laptop, he'd set her up somewhere, then get himself a place where he could get to work. It was good that she seemed to be done with him, because he needed to get her out of his hair. She was a distraction, a stunning, incredible distraction, but he didn't need that now. He had more important things to worry about.

If she was up for another round under the sheets before he found a way to get out of town, that would be great—if not, that was okay, too. Now that he'd pulled the beast out of hibernation, there'd be plenty of other women to fuck if he wanted, he told himself.

But as he drove, he couldn't help but look at her with a sideways glance. She was playing with her hair and looked pensive, uncertain.

Maybe she didn't want it to end, either?

No. He had to stop. This was just lust and nothing more. He'd had his fun and now it was time to move on. He couldn't care for her, not this quickly, not this soon. Hadn't he sworn to himself and to God during his darkest days that he'd never care for anyone again, to love anyone the way he'd cared for and loved Sharon and his son? Hadn't he made a promise not to set himself up for that same kind of heart-ripping pain?

It would be easier this way. She was a threat to that promise. She was far too tempting and likely to work her way into his heart. Get her to town and drop her off and wish her well, he told himself. Then move on with your fucking life.

Yeah. That's what he'd do.

17   SABRINA

As we drove onto the main road which would take us to town, I could tell Harcourt was angry with me. He'd just given me a wild ride in his SUV coming out of Dogwood Canyon, along with the silent treatment. I wanted to break the ice, to say something. I wanted to let him know I'd changed my mind.

When we got to the intersection at the bottom of the hill, I noticed a sign with hand-written lettering flapping on the other side of the T-section of the road. "Look," I said, unable to resist the urge to read the sign out loud, like a little kid. "Bridge Out, No Access to Port Hardy."

Harcourt just grunted and didn't say another word. I fell back against my seat again. What was the use? He drove fast, clearly in a hurry to get rid of me. The main road to town was lined with asphalt and already cleared of obstacles and debris.

But then I perked up. This bridge thing was a good deal. Even if he was tired of me, he couldn't exactly send me back home. Maybe I could still salvage the job, given the little extra time.

Maybe he'd want me back in his arms again. I shook my head.

I kept remembering a little detail that I wanted to forget. Even if he wanted me back, I shouldn't be doing this, and not just because he was a potential employer.

The fact was, I had no business chasing a romance.

I could hear his jaw muscles working, as if he was holding back something he wanted to say.

I ignored it. I had to be practical. God knew I needed the money. Especially, after that damn article and with Jack on my trail.

I wasn't likely to get another under-the-table job, even if I could find another place to live. I couldn't stay in Vancouver much longer. He'd figure out where I lived, where Jeannette and Ellis lived. I wished I could find a working phone and warn Jeannette about Jack.

But first I needed to convince Harcourt to let me stick around, to give me the job.

I'd keep my skirts down, and we'd let that part of our relationship remain in the past.

I'd do a bang-up job for him, and he'd pay me enough to help me hire an attorney so I could deal with the Jack problem.

"Harcourt," I said, deciding that I'd better put my idea out there before he dropped me off in front of some shelter and pushed me out of the car, never wanting to speak to me again.

"Yes, Sabrina?" There was an edge to his voice when he spoke, his mouth tight, lips thin as my chances of salvaging this gig. "I really need that job if you're still looking for an artist. I hope our little mishap doesn't ruin my chance to bid on the work."

"Mishap? Is that what you call it?" He glanced at me, squinting his eyes. I couldn't tell if he was amused or angry.

"Look, I'm sorry, I didn't mean for that to happen. All the things that happened, the tree on my car, and ... I got a little needy, that's all it was."

He flexed his lips, working his mouth without showing teeth or smiling, as if he was trying to make sense of my words. "Look, Sabrina, I'm not sure what happened either, but right now I can't even go to my own property—and since that jackass constable, whatshisname—"

"Constable Hobbledick?" Sabrina said.

Harcourt laughed, and Sabrina snorted, then covered her mouth.

"Since Constable Jackass wouldn't let me get your purse and you don't have a passport, I understand that you're going to need to stay here for a while. Since your car was damaged on my property, I'll make sure you don't have to sleep in the woods. I'll make sure you're taken care of... but..."

"But what?" I said, unable to hide the hurt in my voice.

"As for the project, I'm not even sure right now that I'm up for having it done. Tell you what. If after we get your purse and the greenlight to explore the property again—if I'm still in town, I'll consider letting you bid on the job."

"Fine," I said, then I fell into a silence. His words seemed so analytical, cold, unfeeling. Son of a bitch. On the plusside, at least he agreed with me that the Royal Canadian Mountie Constable Hobbledick was a jackass. It made me wonder what he'd said to make Harcourt dislike the man.

Then it occurred to me that Hobbledick probably made a racist remark. I couldn't help but feel a little bit heartened by the possibility, because if that was what happened, it was comforting to know that Harcourt would find such behavior repulsive. Good for Harcourt.

As we drove into Diversion, I was struck with how pretty the town looked. All the buildings were painted in bright colors, red, orange, blue, white and green. My stomach twisted, telling me to feed myself and I blurted out without thinking, "I'm hungry."

Harcourt turned to me, and my heart leapt at the hint of a smile in his eyes.

His hand reached out and his knuckle jabbed gently against my chin. His hazel eyes were soft. "Hello, hungry." I wanted to lean over and kiss him and throw my arms around his neck. Instead I ducked my head shyly, causing my wild, untamed hair to fall over my face. I hoped that it hid the unstoppable grin that spread across my face.

Harcourt's troubled mood had thawed as he drove into town. Sabrina had changed her mind about leaving. She wanted to stay. He tried not to admit to himself, how good it felt to know.

He'd meant what he said about taking care of her.

In the center of town, he pulled into the dirt lot next to Diversion Grill which was owned by Mark Pearson and his wife Maggie. Even though the sign said, Diversion Grill all the locals called it, Mark and Maggie's Grill. He found a spot, and backed in to park the car. He'd been thinking about Sabrina's foot, and how if he was going to do the honorable thing and take care of her after letting her get injured in his home, he should make sure she had a professional look at it again. The bandages the paramedic had put on her foot washed off after their lovemaking, the food fight, and the multiple showers. He couldn't find more than a package of Band-Aids in Molly's house, and Sabrina was walking around in those flimsy flip-flops.

She wanted to stay. She wanted the job. Even if he decided to forgo the project, or at least, forgo the way he'd been obsessing about it up until he'd met Sabrina. Even if he would be going to New York soon and leaving her to do the job without his supervision, it was the least he could do for her after getting her into the mess that destroyed her car and probably would give her foot pain for the rest of her life.

When he turned off the engine, she started to open her door.

"No, wait," he said. He jumped out of the car and ran around the front to her side, opening the door for her.

"This is very gentlemanly of you," she said as she took his offered arm and stepped down gently onto the dirt road. She was still wearing Molly's floral cotton dress, which was a little too small for her, and pressed against her full breasts and ample hips. It was obvious from the way her nipples pressed against the fabric that she hadn't found a bra in Molly's drawers. Then he remembered that her bra and panties were still in his basement sink, in the condemned house. He imagined her naked and panty-free under that dress.

He sucked in a sharp breath.

He felt a strong urge to lift her up, put her back inside the car, then drive her to the nearest isolated spot. He'd push up that skirt and find out how pretty she was in the light of day, and taste her sweetness for the first time.

He patted his pack pocket and felt the last of the condoms. He'd gone through five. Five times he'd fucked her and hadn't once gone down on her, or her down on him. Well, that was just wrong. He couldn't end things with her yet. Not without tasting her heavenly juices on his tongue.

"Hark?" said Sabrina.

Hark's head shot up, and heat spotted his cheeks as it dawned on him that he'd been staring intently at her crotch while his mind was lost in his sexual musings. "Sorry, thinking about something else."

"Clearly," Sabrina said, as a knowing smile lit up her eyes. "You gonna help me out or not?"

He offered her his arm and she grabbed onto it gratefully, but as she stepped onto the ground, her foot slipped. He caught her and kept her from falling. "After we eat, we're going to get you some better shoes, and some clothes."

"You don't have to do that," Sabrina said.

As they walked toward the front door of the Diversion Grill, Sabrina stopped and tugged Harcourt's arm. She dropped back, closed her eyes, and sniffed the air. "What's that smell?"

Harcourt sniffed the air as well until he caught the scent. It was just smoke, probably a wood fire coming out of a chimney, or maybe someone burning trash. But then it dawned on him he'd smelled something similar when they were driving into town, too far to be smelling a fire in someone's fireplace. Now that she'd pointed it out, it was much stronger out in the open than it had been the Mercedes ventilation system.

"Look at that," he said. He swiped his fingers over the top of the newspaper stand, and it came away with a layer of ash. He smelled it.

"What is it?"

"Ash."

"Look, it's on the car," Sabrina said. "And look, it's coming out of the sky."

Sure enough, there were tiny flakes of ash falling from the sky.

Harcourt moved out into the street to get a better look around. Then he saw it. A dark plume of smoke rising over the trees, back where they'd just come from.

"It's a forest fire," he announced as he checked for traffic, then helped her walk to the street where she could see the smoke.

"Oh no, Harcourt, it's so big."

A bell clanged, startling them back to the sidewalk, and the door to the Diversion Volunteer Fire clanked open. Harcourt and Sabrina watched as men scurried about, preparing their trucks to roll off to the fire.

One of the men, fully dressed in his heavy fireman's pants, coat, and helmet, walked to the center of the road and halted traffic in both directions. An old vintage fire-engine backed into the road, then turned around and re-versed back into the fire department's driveway.

"Why aren't they leaving to put out the fire?" Sabrina asked.

"Because not everyone is there yet. They're volunteers. It might take a while to get a full crew," Harcourt explained.

"Oh," she said.

"Let's eat," Harcourt said. "We can watch from inside." But as he headed toward the front door, a memory flashed into his mind.

He was home for once, relaxing in the main house, read-ing reports on his laptop, while Cedric played quietly nearby. Suddenly Cedric started jumping up and down, and Harcourt heard the sound of a siren approaching. "The fire-man. The fireman!" Cedric screamed excitedly. Cedric dragged Harcourt out of his chair and made him go outside so he could watch as the fire engine went by. A knife twisted in Harcourt's gut.

When Harcourt was five years old, he never dreamed of being a fireman, like Cedric did. All he'd ever wanted to do was impress his father, to show him that he was worthy. All he ever wanted to do was be the best, to turn money into more money, power into more power. He'd spent his whole life being the hot shot, chasing money and power, and what had it gotten him? Nothing.

The only thing he'd ever done right in his life was Sharon and Cedric. Then he'd fucked that up too. He didn't appreciate them when he'd had the chance, and when push came to shove, he'd let them down.

Sharon didn't want what he continued to seek. Sharon didn't want to live in New York, or have Cedric experience a household filled with all the trappings of wealth and none of the warmth of family. She'd wanted to go back to Canada, to live on Vancouver Island. She'd wanted someplace where no one would treat her or her son like a billionaire's kid. She'd wanted desperately for Harcourt to quit his job, to enjoy the massive fortune he'd already accumulated, to stay with her in paradise at least till their son was of age. If he'd only listened. If he'd only heard her, they'd still be alive.

"Harcourt, are you all right?" Sabrina asked. "I said, you don't think the fire is close to your house, do you?"

Harcourt let out a breath. He hadn't realized she been talking to him. "Sorry, Sabrina," he said. Then he considered her question as he tried to shut the memories of Sharon and Cedric out of his mind, because it hadn't occurred to him that his house might be at risk.

He looked more carefully in the direction of the smoke. Maybe it was closer to his house then he'd thought. The fire engine's siren sounded, startling them both, and a huge puff of black diesel fumes plumed out of the back of the engine as the first of the two Diversion Volunteer Fire Department Engine's rolled down the street.

"I guess we should eat while there's still a town," Harcourt quipped.

"Yeah, I guess so."

As they approached the front door of the grill, Harcourt glanced through the windows, and he could see that the inside of the grill was packed with people. There were a few seats at the counter, though, which would be good enough. The door flung open, and Mark Pearson rushed out. Harcourt had to pull Sabrina quickly out of the way so the two wouldn't collide. Mark continued past as if he hadn't seen them, and raced across the street toward the fire station. A stout woman wearing an apron shot out of the diner, and ran after Mark. "Wait, Mark, take this."

Mark turned around, and came running back. He took the large paper sack out of the woman's hands then kissed her long and hard. The woman jabbed her finger into his chest, and said something, then hurried back inside the diner. Mark, who'd come back to the sidewalk so he wouldn't stand in the street, took a moment to look in the bag. Harcourt was close enough to get a whiff. It smelled like ham and cheese sandwiches on whole wheat. Harcourt's stomach growled again. He stepped over to his good acquaintance.

"Hey Mark, what's going on?"

"Harcourt?" Mark seemed surprised to see him. Then his eyes fell on Sabrina as she approached.

Mark lowered his voice and motioned for Harcourt to walk with him, out of earshot of his guest.

"What is it? What's wrong?" Harcourt asked, picking up on Mark's somber mood.

"We've got a massive forest fire to deal with, and with the bridge washed out, we're going to be on our own for a while. Trouble is, we're short-handed. Ever worked on a fire line before? We could sure use the extra hands."

"What, me? You want me to volunteer?" Harcourt's pulse quickened and adrenaline pumped through his veins.

"Yes, it's not rocket science."

"Yeah, of course. Tell me what I need to do."

"Come with me now to the station. I'll suit you up."

"Now?"

"Yeah, the fire isn't going to wait for you to get your fucking manicure first, rich boy."

Harcourt could see from the expression in his eyes that he was just kidding. "Sure, I better tell Sabrina."

"I'll tell her," Mark said.

Mark followed Harcourt over to Sabrina, who'd decided to wait under the awning in front of the grill. "Hey Sabrina," Mark said.

"I'm sorry, I don't remember your name," Sabrina admitted.

"Mark Pearson, we met last night?"

"Of course, I remember you. I just forgot your name, I'm sorry."

"Hey, nothing to be sorry about. Listen, Sabrina, I'm going to have to borrow Harcourt for a while."

Harcourt spoke. "Look Mark, I'm not sure. I need to get Sabrina situated, since my house is off-limits. I want to help, but... I don't want to leave her stranded."

Sabrina's face showed alarm. "What are you talking about, Harcourt? Where are you going?"

"They need volunteers to fight the fire," Harcourt explained.

"I'm sorry, what?"

"Maggie," Mark Pearson shouted as stuck his head through the front door. "Can you please come out here, sugar?"

Maggie came out a moment later, wiping her hands on her apron. "I thought you were leaving?"

Across the street, someone shouted for Mark to hurry up. "Sabrina, this is my wife Maggie. She'll get you situated while Harcourt and I save the day. Come on, Hark. We've got to go."

Harcourt pulled his keys out of his pocket, took a wad of money out of his wallet, and stuffed them both into her hand. "Here, you take the car, get clothes, food, and for God's sake, get a pair of decent shoes. Get whatever you need. I'll track you down later when I get back."

Harcourt could see the fear and alarm in Sabrina's eyes, and it made him uncertain about what he needed to do.

"Hark, we've got to go," Mark said as the driver on the fire engine honked the horn.

"I'm sorry, I've got to go," Harcourt said, looking from Sabrina to the waiting firemen.

"Come on, Sabrina," Maggie said to her. "Let me get you something to eat, then I'll help you, okay?"

Harcourt gave Sabrina one last look, started to reach for her, then changed his mind. He turned and jogged to the fire station.

As Harcourt waited for a fellow fireman to find a pair of boots in his size, he looked back to the diner and saw the back of Sabrina's head with her wild black hair as she sat at the counter. His stomach lurched as he had the sudden thought that he might never see her again. He wanted to run back and kiss her for good luck.

"Here, try these," said one of the firemen, holding out a pair of boots.

Harcourt turned away from the diner, and put on the boots. They fit.

I sat at the counter, too stunned to drink the coffee that had materialized the moment I sat down. What the hell just happened? How was it possible that Harcourt was going off to fight a fire?

"Sabrina?" said the woman I believed they called Maggie.

"Yes, Maggie is it?" I asked.

"That's right, sugar. I'm Maggie, and that was my husband, Mark."

"Right," I said, without much enthusiasm. I felt numb. Lost. Harcourt was going off to fight a fire? How was that even possible?

"Can I get you something to eat?"

"Uh, sure," I said. But I wasn't hungry anymore. "I'll be right back."

I spun off the stool, and hurried out of the diner. The fire truck was still there, but the engine was running and it was fully out of the firehouse. I searched the men, suited and already in the truck, looking for Harcourt. Then I saw him, walking in his heavy equipment toward the back of the truck.

"Harcourt, wait," I shouted, waving my arms as I tried to get his attention, but the noise of the truck engine was too loud and he didn't seem to hear me. I ran across the street, startled when brakes squealed and a horn blasted as a car narrowly missed slamming into me. My heart raced from the near collision, but I didn't care.

The big engine was on the move, and I waved my arms, stepping in front of it. The driver of the firetruck slammed on his brakes. I ran to the back where I'd last seen Harcourt, and saw that he'd mounted a platform on the back. "Sabrina, what are you doing here?"

I ran up to him and wrapped my arms around his legs, his knees lining up with my face. "Oh, Harcourt, please be safe," I said, meaning it desperately. He reached down pulled me up, and held me in his arms. Then he kissed me, like it might be for the last time.

The horn blared. "Cool it, Romeo." Mark shouted from the front.

Reluctantly he put me back on the ground. I didn't want to let him go. I ran after him, my fingers grasping to touch him one last time. I felt tears on my cheeks, then realized that I was behaving like some sentimental lovesick idiot. I stopped chasing and stood there with a stoic look on my face.

Harcourt yelled out as the truck drove away, over the din of the siren, "Don't worry, Sabrina. I'll be back, I promise."

Harcourt wrapped his gloved fingers tight around a metal hand rail after almost falling off after that disorienting kiss. As the fire engine flew over the giant potholes made deeper by the recent storm, Harcourt had to dig his boots into the diamond plated metal platform and hang on for dear life just to keep from flying off the back. Surges of adrenaline rushed through him as the fire engine picked up speed, heading toward the black smoke rising in the distant sky.

He was excited, despite the logical part of this brain telling him to jump off before it was too late. The little voice was telling him that he was a businessman, a CEO, a fucking billionaire, not some kind of hero.

But another part of him couldn't get that last kiss out of his mind. The way she'd looked at him, as if her life would end if he didn't return. The way she looked at him as if her heart would break with pride for what he was about to go do. He closed his eyes and relived that last kiss and the warmth from her touch that seemed to spread through his body, out of control, like the forest fire apparently raging in the woods beyond his house.

18 JEANNETTE

"Tyler, leave Jerrod alone!" Jeannette said, as her oldest child chased his little brother through Ellis's small kitchen. Jeannette was about to lose her last nerve.

"Let the boys be boys, child," Ellis said.

The boys ran off into the living room, screeching with delight, as they continued their game. Jeanette let out a breath, then brought the two steaming hot mugs of tea to the table, putting one in front of her father. It was mint tea and the aroma filled the kitchen.

She wrapped her hands around the mug, warming them, though it was not a cold day. Her shoulders slumped, and she sniffed back tears. "Oh, Daddy, I'm really worried about Sabrina. She should have called by now."

"Why don't you call the person who hired her. A billionaire, you say?"

"I can't find the number. His assistant called when I was working at the coffee shop. Sabrina called her back from there. I wrote it down, but Sabrina took the number. I don't know how to get in touch."

"Can you look it up?"

"Nobody lists their telephone number anymore, Daddy."

"You say he owns a company?"

"Yeah," Jeanette said, starting to see where he was going with this. "Good idea, Daddy."

She jumped up and kissed him gently on the side of his face, then reached for her hot tea and carried it into the living room, carefully sidestepping Jerrod and Tyler who were wrestling over that stupid turtle again.

When she got to the spare bedroom where she and the boys had slept the previous night, she closed the door behind her, relishing the instant reduction in noise. She found a pen and the back of a Lands End catalog with a bit of room to write some numbers if she got lucky. She turned on her laptop, plugged it in, and did some deep breathing exercises while she waited for the old computer to power up. Using Pearl's password, the sweet lady who lived next door and was happy to share her WiFi with anyone close, Jeannette accessed the internet and got to work.

As she expected, there was no listing for a Harcourt Raymondson, or any Raymondson in Diversion, Vancouver Island, B.C. But she did get a number for Raymondson Industries in New York City.

"Raymondson Industries. How, may I direct your call?"

"Harcourt Raymondson, please."

"One moment."

"Office of the President. How may I help you?"

"I'd like to speak with Harcourt Raymondson, please. It's urgent."

"I'm sorry, but Mr. Raymondson is not available. What is this in regard to?"

"My sister. She's missing. And she was supposed to be working at his house on Vancouver Island. I just need his telephone number so I can make sure she's safe."

"I'm sorry, I can't give out that information."

"Can you leave a message for Mr. Raymondson and ask him to call me as soon as possible?"

"I'll be happy to do that, miss. May I have your name and telephone number please?"

Two hours later Jeannette sat in the kitchen, which reeked of the peanut butter and jelly sandwiches she'd just made, ready for the boys as soon as they woke up from their naps.

She stared at her cell phone, willing it to ring. "Come on," she said to her phone. No matter how hard she tried not to worry, she couldn't stop imaging the worst. Sabrina knew she was supposed to call her. Why hadn't she called? Why hadn't the frickin' billionaire called?

She poured herself a glass of Coke and turned on the small television Ellis kept in the kitchen.

She wanted to get her mind off Sabrina.

Using the remote, she flipped through channels. There was a soap opera she hadn't watched in years, and Judge Judy which she'd never cared for, and a movie made for television that would probably last four hours and have more commercial breaks than actual movie scenes. She was about to turn it off when she saw the words BREAKING NEWS on the screen.

Unable to resist, she turned up the volume and sat back in her chair.

"Breaking News. Channel Four Action News has just learned that a forest fire is raging out of control in the desolate northern end of Vancouver Island."

Jeanette put down her glass of Coke hard on the table, causing the soda to slosh over the lip of the glass and onto her hands. She grabbed a tissue from the box Ellis kept on the table next to his stack of magazines and newspapers, and cleaned up the mess.

On the screen, the image moved to a press conference, where an official in a fire chief's uniform stood behind a podium and spoke into a mic.

"We are very concerned about the Diversion fire, which at this point has burned over a thousand acres due west of town. Diversion has a population of four hundred people and the nearby First Nations reservation has two hundred more people. We believe the fire was started by last night's record-breaking storm system, which not only started the fire due to lightning but also damaged the Talhkahaw'ka river Bridge, which has been closed.

"Since the main road goes over that bridge and is the only way in or out of the area, we are unable to send additional fire engines and crews to support the two-engine local volunteer fire department. It also means that those residents and visitors on the wrong side of the inaccessible bridge are stuck as well. We are concerned that if the fire reaches the populated areas, evacuation may become problematic. We are currently working to get air firefighting assets to the area and ground crews flown in as early as tomorrow, we hope. We will keep you posted as more information becomes available to us. Thank you."

On screen, cameras flashed and reporters shouted questions, but the fire chief walked off the podium, refusing to say any more. The shot changed to two reporters sitting in the Channel Four studios. The male broadcaster said, "As you've just heard, hundreds of residents are trapped in the path of a deadly fire burning out of control near Diversion. Stay tuned to Channel Four Action News for the latest updates on the breaking story."

Jeannette stood up and spun around in the kitchen, wringing her hands and shouting, "Shit, shit, shit, shit, please Sabrina, please be okay."

Caleb couldn't remember much of his life before he was brought to the cabin, just a vague sense that he was once happy. But he was barely walking when they took him away from what he couldn't remember anymore. He remembered the night when he forgot his name. He remembered how he begged his caretaker, Babette or Olga, he couldn't be sure, to tell him what his name was. He remembered how she'd just laughed in his face.

She told him that Sir was coming and he'd have a new name soon enough.

Caleb cried himself to sleep each night after he forgot his name, lamenting the loss of something so precious, something as personal as one's own name. On the third night after he forgot who he was, he had the dream that would give him hope for the rest of his days.

And after that night, and after that dream, Caleb stopped crying.

He didn't cry when the cruelest of the twins beat him with a stick until his body was bruised and bleeding and covered with welts. He didn't cry when she held his head under water in the bath repeatedly, all because he'd stolen her whiskey, and poured it into the loamy soil outside the cabin.

Nor did he cry on the worst night of all, when Sir came with the other little boy...

Caleb didn't need to cry because he had an angel on his side, a dark and beautiful angel, or so said his dreams.

19 SABRINA

REPLACEMENT After punching in the right set of After Harcourt disappeared on the back of the fire engine, I
got myself together and walked back to the Diversion Grill.
I sat in my seat and stared into my coffee. Before I could
take a sip of the coffee that had probably gone cold, Maggie's hand appeared and she yanked my coffee cup away.

"Here, let me get you a fresh one, honey," she said.

"Thanks," I said, as I sipped the steaming-hot coffee and
inhaled the fragrant aroma. My mind was spinning. I didn't
know what to think, what to feel.

"You okay, sweetie?"

My head popped up as I remembered that I still needed
to contact Jeannette. She was probably jumping out of her

skin with worry by now. "Do you have a phone that works? I really need to get ahold of my sister in Vancouver."

"I'm sorry, dear. As far as I've heard, there isn't a landline or a cell phone in town that's worked since last night's storm. But you could try the satellite phone over at the police station. That's assuming Mark didn't take it with him."

"That's great," I said, starting to get up. "Where's the police station?"

"It's just up the road, on the next corner, between the tackle store and Jimmy's Mail Stop, but I doubt anyone will be there. I mean, with Mark fighting the fire, it's probably closed."

"Oh," I said, my disappointment showing as I slumped my shoulders. Anxiety flooded my countenance as I remembered that Jack was out there, and that I needed to warn Jeannette to stay clear of him.

"Listen, Sabrina... may I call you Sabrina?"

"Sure."

"When my daughter gets here in a half an hour or so, I'll have her mind the store, and I'll walk you over there. I've got a key. How's that sound?"

"I appreciate your help," I said.

"In the meantime, you should eat something. Keep up your strength. It's probably going to be a long day."

"You don't need to get me breakfast," I said, even though my stomach was beginning to growl.

"Nonsense," Maggie said.

While I waited for my breakfast, the bell over the front door to the diner pinged, and I saw a worn-out-looking young woman enter the Grill, dragging two rumpled children behind her. Maggie bustled over to the them, with a huge smile on her face. "Why hello Elaine, Petey, Suzie."

"Come for breakfast?"

"Hi Mags," Elaine said with a deep yawn.

Maggie did a quick scan of the small Grill. A booth had recently been vacated, but it still had empty dishes on it. "Give me a second." I watched her quickly ready the table, bussing the dishes to a plastic tray set up at the end of the counter, then she wiped off the table with several fast swipes of a damp rag. "Here, you guys. Please, have a seat," she said, motioning to the table. Take a load off. Elaine, don't take offense, but you look terrible. Like you didn't sleep a wink last night."

"We barely did," admitted Elaine. She directed her children to the booth and helped the littlest one, Suzie, by lifting her into her seat. Maggie returned with a plastic booster seat, and Elaine helped her daughter into it.

Elaine went on. "We had to spend the night at the shelter, but they weren't expecting so many people and they ran out of cots. Petey and Suzie, lucky little grunions, were small enough that they got to share a cot. But a couple of the other parents and I had to make due on the floor in sleeping bags. Not what you'd call five-star accommodations. I didn't sleep much."

"Your house was damaged in the storm? Elaine, I'm so sorry, I hadn't heard." Maggie's pleasant face had lost its cheery expression, and showed sincere concern.

"Yup. Wind came in like a tornado. Tore a hunk of our roof clean off. Right above the bedrooms. Then the trees attacked the house. Well, that's what it seemed like."

"Like in Harry Potter," Little Petey added.

"Absolutely, just like right out of Harry Potter. It was scareee, Mags, scareee!"

"That's terrible, Elaine, I'm so sorry that happened. Where's Charlie?"

"Oh, he's catching some Z's at the shelter. He was out all night with some of the other men from our neighborhood, going from house to house, making sure no one was injured or trapped."

"And no one was?"

"Nope. Our house definitely got the worst of it in our neck of the woods."

"You know, if you don't mind sharing a room with the kids, we've got a spare guest room downstairs at our house. I'd hate for you to have to spend another night in the shelter," Maggie said.

"Oh, that's mighty kind of you Maggie, but I've got it covered. We're going up to my sister's farmhouse in Crab Apple Ravine—it's where I keep my horse. She's out of town and we've been going up there every day to feed the goats and the pig, so tonight, we'll just move in and stay there until they open the bridge and my sister can come back and kick us out."

"She wouldn't kick you out," Maggie said. I could tell Maggie was about to go attend other customers when the mother spoke up, her tone conspiratorial, excited. "Did you hear about Hark?"

I'd been casually eavesdropping up to that point. The woman lowered her voice and I couldn't make out what she was saying. I pretended to have an itch at the top of my foot and could cock my ear and stay with the conversation.

"—had a woman up at his place last night. I hear they spent the night together, alone, in Molly's house, since his was trashed by the storm. Can you bu-leeeve it? Ooh, ooh, boy howdy, Hark Raymondson back in the game. I can't wait for the phones to get back online."

"Why is that?" Maggie asked, and I could sense the discomfort in her voice.

By then I'd stopped scratching my foot and I was doing my best not to turn around to say something, I'd regret.

"Because I have to call Becky, you know, my sister. She's had her eye on that man forever, and not just because he's richer than God. Becky thinks he's gooooor-geous!"

I thought about setting her straight, explaining that I was no one's "lady friend," that I was no one's "main squeeze." But then I remembered that I'd probably been spotted by at least a few people in that talkative town as I ran blindly across the street to give him a desperate, parting kiss at the back of the damn firetruck. I felt a blush climbing up my neck, but I kept my nose high in the air. When Maggie came over a few minutes later to reheat my coffee, she didn't say anything, but her eyebrows were lifted into a knowing "you can't fool me" way.

If push came to shove, I'd deny everything. Deny, deny, deny.

Maggie cleared her throat loudly.

"Can I get some more coffee please?" I said, unable to mask the trace of resentment in my voice. I caught Elaine's eye and the bob of Maggie's head in my direction, silently informing Elaine who exactly she'd just been talking about. Elaine's eyes widened, then she had the good grace to look away and duck her head, and help her little girl by passing her a crayon and a coloring sheet.

What had happened was a fluke—past tense—a mistake. I had to remember that I had no business doing what I did. I certainly couldn't justify continuing the behavior. I'd just made a mistake, and it wouldn't do to compound it by keeping it up. No more funny business, I decided. If I was fortunate to get the opportunity to work for Mr. Harcourt Raymondson, it would be strictly business from that moment on.

Nothing else.

Harcourt's body was already sore by the time the truck drove past his house. Lester Faraday, a stout and bearded tattoo artist who'd been sharing the ride at the back of the truck, reached over and punched Harcourt's arm to get his attention and shouted over the engine noise.

"Holy, shit, look at that!" He was pointing to the sight of a Sabrina's crunched car, and behind it the massive hunk of tree harpooned into his house.

"I know, that's my place. I was there," Harcourt yelled.

Lester's face broke into a grin. "You're the dude? The billionaire? I didn't put two and two together."

"What?"

"Nothing man. Sorry about your house."

"Thanks," Harcourt said.

As the engine slowed down before preparing to climb a steep grade, Lester spoke again. "Someone said there was a person in that car when the tree fell. Is that true?"

"Yeah, there was." The engine noise got louder again as the truck began its climb.

"How the hell did she get out alive?"

"What?" Harcourt shouted.

"I said, it's a fucking miracle she got out alive."

Harcourt could only nod in agreement. As the truck rounded the curve on the road above his property he took a long hard look at the smashed yellow car.

A chill went down the back of his spine, and for the first time since Sabrina's arrival into his life, he had the sensation that there was more to her presence in his life than just a boost to his idle libido. It was as if the unseen hand of God had held onto the tree trunk, just long enough so he could save her from the car. It was like Sabrina's survival was mandatory to God's greater plan, and that He'd sent Harcourt to save her just in time, so she'd be there to serve some higher purpose yet to be revealed.

He stared back at the yellow car under the tree, and squinted as he thought he saw something. A flash of sunlight on the metal, a shadow cast from the trees, whatever it was, there seemed for a moment to be some form rising from behind it. The truck hit a bump, causing Harcourt to look away. When he glanced back, whatever he'd seen was gone.

"Hang on," Faraday shouted sometime later, after they'd been driving on old logging roads, which hadn't been used in years.

They'd gotten deeper and deeper into the forest and closer to the fire with each mile. Harcourt saw a turn up ahead, a fire road that ran straight up the side of the hill like a gash. Mark, who was driving the truck, honked his horn to make sure his crew knew to hang on. Then he made a sharp turn and down-shifted. Slowly, engine groaning from the strain, they began the almost vertical ascent to the top of the hill.

Harcourt and Faraday stopped talking as they concentrated on holding tight, the air around them swirling with heat. Harcourt imagined his body melting away, his fingers sliding off, and his body falling off the back of the firetruck, the way meat falls off barbecue ribs.

By the time they made it to the top of the ridge, Harcourt's fingers felt numb from gripping the handles tight, and for the first time, he could see the fire. The acrid smoke filled his lungs as it settled around them like fog.

"We should have put on our respirators," Lester said, coughing as the truck made it the bottom of the ravine and came to a stop.

Faraday yelled, "Over there," after he'd helped Harcourt into the self-contained breathing apparatus and explained how it worked.

The larger truck had arrived some time before, and the crews blasting water onto the flames gratefully accepted their relief as Harcourt and the other men took over the hoses.

Harcourt's body pumped with adrenaline, but he followed the directions of the captain and the other more experienced firefighters, aiming the water to stop the fire exactly where they told him to aim it. He couldn't help but think of how proud Cedric would be if he could see his father now. He'd done many things in his life which most men could only dream of accomplishing, but right now, he had one goal and one goal only: to do what he could to support these brave men and save his town from this fire.

I didn't think I'd have any appetite, but when my food arrived, I changed my mind.

A plate big enough to serve a small turkey was set before me and I gaped at the breakfast, salivating at the delicious smell. Not only was there a steaming, succulent omelet as big as a football dripping with melted cheese, there were sides of pan-fried rosemary potatoes, and two discs of Canadian bacon the size of hockey pucks.

MIA CALDWELL

I was about to make a crack about having enough food to feed an army when Maggie came back with a basket filled with steaming-hot rolls.

I shrugged and picked up my fork. In addition to the melted cheese, the omelet was topped off with a dollop of crème fresh and a sprinkle of chopped chives. When I cut it open with my fork, I could see a filling of chopped ripe tomatoes, grilled sweet onions, and more melted cheese. I took a bite, and moaned with appreciation.

"Mmmm, this is good," I mouthed to Maggie, who was standing, eyes twinkling as she awaited my verdict. I grabbed my napkin and wiped off the bit of burning tomato and cheese off my lip.

"Glad you like it," Maggie said before returning to her other customers.

As I dug into my breakfast, alternating bites of food with sips of the fresh-squeezed orange juice Maggie added to my feast, I marveled at how it was possible to get such gourmet fare in the middle of nowhere. I wondered why I was so ravenous, and then I thought about all those times Harcourt had been inside me. Three, four times, in less than twelve hours, each time the fast, animal-intense kind of sex that left you panting for more. We'd been insatiable with each other.

Thinking about Harcourt made the muscles between my legs contract. I closed my eyes, remembering how it felt to have him inside me. I wanted more.

My eyes popped open. Was it possible? How was it possible? We'd had all that delicious, mind-blowing sex, but not once had I feasted on his cock. And more importantly, not once had he sucked on my clit. And yet I'd orgasmed every time?

I'd never had a vaginal orgasm with Jack or any other man. How had he done it? I thought back and remembered how he'd always moved his fingers between my legs, how he'd always thrummed at my clit with his fingers. Good man, I thought. And if he could do that with his cock and his fingers, what kind of orgasm would I have at the end of his lips and tongue? I gasped, remembering that first time he'd come inside me, when he'd tried to suck in my lower lip.

"Jeezus," I moaned as my body hummed with the memory.

"You all right, sugar?"

I opened my eyes. Maggie was at the other end of the counter staring at me.

"Yes, I'm fine," I said, taking another bite of the omelet. "Ahhhhhh, it's just so good."

"I'm glad you like it," she said and got back to work.

I put down my fork. I couldn't eat any more. I thought about Harcourt and where we were at.

First off, a night of amazing sex, and then we came to this kind of unspoken agreement to call it a day. But then I freaked out at the idea that he went running off to fight a fire, and chased after him like a lovesick puppy, kissing him right out in public?

All right. Fine. That was all me. But then again, he had kissed me back. Hadn't he?

Maybe he wasn't ready to call it a day yet, either.

Then I thought about something else. With the bridge being out, I'd be stuck in Diversion for a least a few more days. Shouldn't I plan to make the most of my time, stranded in paradise?

Wouldn't he want that as well?

Shouldn't we at least have sex one more time, just so we could experience each other orally?

I groaned. Just the thought of holding his cock in my hand and finding its edges and curves with my mouth made me suck in air. I tugged at the tight bodice of Molly's dress, flapping air on my heated bosom. I closed my eyes again and felt my tongue trace across my lips. To wrap my lips around his large … Damn, I was horny.

Noticing a bathroom at the far end of the diner, I got off my seat and went inside.

Five minutes later, I felt a whole lot better, having relieved an itch in a very wet part of my body.

When I came out of the bathroom, Maggie was holding up a plastic bag which appeared to contain my uneaten breakfast to-go.

"There you are. Good."

There were two young women in their late teens standing next to her, behind the counter.

"Sabrina, this is my daughter Lynette and her friend Tahkina. They're going to man the store for a bit while you and I do some investigating."

I wasn't sure what she meant by that, but I went over to meet the two young women. If Maggie hadn't introduced us, I could have easily guessed that Lynette was her daughter, because take away a hundred pounds and thirty years and they were the same person. Same round face and body, same pale freckled skin, same rosy cheeks and same strawberry-blonde hair.

Tahkina, on the other hand, was clearly not related. She was thin, with a muscular, athletic build and long glossy black hair she wore in a ponytail over one shoulder. She had the distinct look of the First Nations people.

"Girls, this is Sabrina Cane. She's an artist working for Mr. Raymondson."

Lynette reached over the counter and gave me her hand. "Nice to meet you," she said. I was both impressed and charmed by her fearlessness in greeting a stranger. It had taken me years just to look strangers in the eye. I still sometimes struggled with anxiety when meeting new people.

Tahkina was less forthcoming, giving me only a slight nod in acknowledgment after our introductions. She had a wary look about her. I could relate to Tahkina a lot more than Maggie's cheerful, trusting daughter.

"Mom says you're staying with Mr. Raymondson?" Lynette's eyes sparkled with curiosity as if she'd heard the same rumors that Elaine had. I glanced behind me, and realized that Elaine and her two kids had left sometime before. One less bit of news for her sister Betty, I thought.

"No, I'm not staying with Mr. Raymondson, but I am stuck here for a while, like everyone else."

"Stuck here?" Maggie said. "You say that like it's a bad thing."

"Mom," Lynette said, exasperated that her mother could be so dense. "She's talking about the bridge—you know—the one that is out? Isn't that insane? I heard that some people think that it was more than the storm, that someone deliberately blew it up. You know, like way back when?"

"Now, now, Lynette," Maggie said, waggling a finger at her daughter. "Don't you go spreading any rumors. I'm sure that's not true. Probably got struck by lightning in just the right spot, that's all."

"Whatever you say, Mom," Lynette said with a huff. Then her voice became more subdued. "Mom? Do you think Daddy's okay? I'm worried about the fire."

"Your father is just fine. Listen, girls, I need you to put on aprons and mind the shop. I'm going to take Sabrina over to the station to use the satellite phone. Can you handle that?"

"I'm hungry," Lynette whined.

"Have Carlos whip something up. You can eat between customers."

"All right," Lynette said and her eyes lit up.

"Thanks Mrs. P.," Tahkina said.

I figured Carlos's culinary skills were appreciated far and wide in this town.

Yeah, Mrs. P.," Tahkina added, "maybe later you can take me home? I was going to have one of my cousins pick me up, but none of the phones are working."

"Of course, Tahkina, after the rush, I'd be happy to drive you back. Now, you two, don't burn this place down before I get back."

"We won't," Lynette said.

"Yeah, let's make this quick," Maggie told me as we headed out the door. People walking past us on the street greeted Maggie, but she just nodded and kept moving. She was a woman on a mission, with no time to stop and chat.

After we'd walked past the first block in the three-block town, I asked, "Where can I buy some clothes?"

She pointed to an across the street, toward an old building that took up half of the next block. "Hammond's. Hammond's General Store."

That rang a bell, since I'd spent some time before heading out for the interview with the billionaire doing a little research on the place I was coming to. I'd found a cool blog when I'd Googled Diversion. I read one of the articles, which were excerpts from a local history book the site was trying to sell. I remembered reading about one fascinating story.

At one point, there was a conflict between the logging company and the local indigenous peoples. With the completion of a bridge, trucks could get into the area and logging was suddenly profitable. But the logging rights that came with the town were inadequate for the logging companies' needs. So they started cutting in sacred groves, areas where they had no rights to log. The First Nations people as well as tree-hugging non-indigenous people from both Canada and the States protested by making a human shield on the bridge. When four local First Nations men were discovered the next morning murdered under the bridge at the bottom of the ravine, the indigenous people fought back, destroying the bridge.

I slowed my walk for a moment, twitching my mouth from side to side. Was the current damage to the bridge man-made? No, I decided. Not likely. There would be no reason. Based on the story, the tragedy had become such a big blot on the government who'd looked the other way while the logging company did its worst, that laws were passed soon after and the entire region surrounding Diversion and the reservation were turned into a logging-free national park for one hundred years.

Apparently, the original Hammond's General Store owner was an advocate for the First Nations people and helped to bring justice to their cause. I hoped that I'd get to meet a Hammond family member when I went shopping after calling my sis. Maybe, if they had it for sale, I could grab a copy of the history book. Diversion was growing on me.

On the next block, we passed several storefronts which I noticed were all closed. Fred's Bait and Tackle, for one, but also a used bookstore. Considering that it was the middle of the day on a Saturday, I thought that was a bad sign.

I stopped to stare into the display of one shop, which had no signage other than a sticky note taped to the door which said, Closed Due to Fire. It was by far the strangest shop I'd ever seen, with a bizarre combination of stuffed dead animals and buckets of fresh flowers. I laughed out loud.

"Are you coming?" Maggie hollered. She'd already crossed the next street.

I sprinted to catch up, but stopped when my pedicure flip-flops tried to slide off my feet. Man, I couldn't wait to get new shoes. Catching up, I peered through the window, covered with partially opened blinds, noticing that the Diversion RCMP police substation looked closed.

"I've never been to a police station that wasn't open twenty-four hours."

"It's just a satellite station," Maggie said as she hunted for the right key. "Mark's the only stationed law officer in town. He keeps regular part-time business hours, but other than that, he only uses it to detain someone while he waits for the Port Hardy RCMP to take custody."

"Mark's the only Mountie in town? What about Hobbledick?"

"I'm sorry, what? Who?"

"My bad. His name was Constable Hobdart, or Hobday, something like that."

"Honey, I still don't know who you're talking about, since Mark's the only RCMP in town. Like I said, others come in to haul away lawbreakers or if anything major happens, and sometime they come by for inspections. I've never heard of any Constable Hobday, or even a Hobbledick."

"That's strange," I mused. "Because I absolutely ran into him at Harcourt's house this morning. And I hope you'll pardon my language, but he was a real asshole. Do you know he wouldn't let me get my purse out of my car, but he let Harcourt go into his damaged house to get his things?"

Maggie's glance fell to my shoulder at that comment. And I figured it was the first time she'd noticed that I didn't have a purse on me. She shrugged, then went back to looking for the right key. "It's strange that I've never heard of him before, but I suppose he could be new to the force. Mark probably knew all about it, and just hadn't gotten around to telling me."

Maggie smiled as she seemed to find the right key, and as she placed it into the keyhole, I started thinking about what to tell Jeannette to explain what had taken me so long to check in.

"That's strange."

"What? Key doesn't work?"

"No, that's not it."

She pushed open the door. "It wasn't locked."

We stepped inside and Maggie switched on the lights. The Diversion Police Station was a small rectangular storefront approximately twenty by thirty feet. There was a reception area in front, desks and office equipment in the middle, some walled-in rooms down the back side, and what looked like a combination interrogation and holding cell at the back left. I leaned over the rail, scanning for the satellite phone.

"Where is it?" I asked.

"Not here," she said. "I'm sorry, Sabrina. Looks like Mark took it with him."

I sniffed back a sudden urge to start crying, looking away before Maggie could see. I hated making Jeannette worry. I hated that I couldn't get word to her that I was just fine. I hated that I was letting this shit get to me. I needed to buck up and deal.

"Come on, I've got to get back. Let's go," Maggie said after she locked up the station. I followed back toward the Grill, slowing to take another look at the taxidermy florist shop, laughing out loud when I spotted a stuffed rat next to a bucket of sunflowers.

"Sabrina, you should go to Hammond's now before they run out of whatever you need. Looks like it's already getting crowded. Word's getting out about the bridge and the fire, looks like."

The store did look crowded. "Okay, I'll come back to the Grill when I'm done. Thanks for trying to help me," I added.

"Sabrina, don't lose heart. I'll ask around; surely someone else has a satellite phone."

"Thanks," I said, and I meant it.

I'd planned to go back to the Grill to get my purse, but with more people heading over there every second, I decided to make do with the wad of cash that Harcourt had handed me. I ran across the street toward the store.

Behind the store, I noticed with a shock a huge cloud of black smoke in the distance billowing off toward where Harcourt lived. My stomach lurched at the thought that he was out there, close to the fire. I bit back my fears and stopped as a car drove by. I followed it as it got into a line, which I realized was to a gas station.

Of course, no gas trucks could drive in, so people wanted to fill up while they still could.

I counted six cars at Eddy's Gas and Garage, and made a mental note to drive Harcourt's SUV over there and fill it up for him while we had the chance.

Hammond's was packed with more people than I'd originally expected, and their voices bounced loudly off the solid wood walls. I could see in an instant that some of the shelves were looking a little bare. I made a beeline for the clothing section, and made fast decisions, not bothering to try anything on. I found a pair of jeans in my size, a few long-sleeved T-shirts, a jacket, and even a pair of cross-trainers in my size. I got socks and not the sexiest underwear I'd ever seen, but it wasn't white and the pack was bikini, so I figured they'd do.

I almost cried out with glee when I found a sports bra that was big enough not to smash me to smithereens. Then I took all my purchases to the checkout line. There was a book on Diversion history which I was sure was the one they'd promoted on the blog I'd read, so I added it to my pile.

"Are you a Hammond?" I asked the middle-aged woman who was running the register, after slumping my purchases onto the counter, relieved to free my arms.

She shook her head in a distracted way. The line behind me had grown to over seven folks while I'd waited, and obviously the clerk wasn't up for chitchat. Still, I'd asked her a question, she could at least answer. So, I asked it again. "Are you a Hammond?"

"No, I'm not. I just work for Mr. Hammond."

"Is he here?" I asked.

"No, he's off today because he's fighting the fire," she said as she gave me my change and handed me my purchases stuffed in a large plastic-handled bag. "Next, please."

My feet hurt from walking around in those useless shoes, so before leaving the store, I went back to the dressing room and changed into some of my new clothes.

"Nice clothes. Get them at Hammond's?" asked Lynette as soon as I walked into the Grill.

I nodded, then looked around for Maggie and didn't see her, then remembered she promised to take Lynette's friend home.

"Were you able to make your call?" Lynette asked.

"Nope, didn't your mom tell you? Looks like your dad took the satellite phone."

"Oh," Lynette said.

"Where's your mom? Did she leave to take Tahkina home?"

"Not, yet," said a voice behind me. It was Tahkina, at the counter, apron off, no longer part of the staff.

I asked Lynette, "Where is she?"

"Office, trying to get Dad on the radio." She nodded toward the back.

"Your mom said she'd ask about satellite phones. Do you know if she found anyone that had one?

"We've got one," said Tahkina.

"You have?"

"Yup."

Maggie came out of her office, a strained expression on her face. She spotted me and forced a smile. "Hey Sabrina, glad you found some new clothes." Her smile faltered. "Tahkina, you ready?"

Tahkina hopped off her stool.

"Wait a minute," I said. "Can I come along?"

Maggie cocked her head, so I explained. "Tahkina says she's got a satellite phone. I really need to get ahold of my sister."

"You've got a sat phone?"

"Yeah, on the rez, at Bella Bella's house."

A loud crackling sound came and filled the room. Maggie held up a finger, shushing us, then ran toward her office. "Mark to Maggie, Mark to Maggie, over."

Lynette hollered after her mother, "Ma, what about Tah-kina?"

Maggie's head shot out of the back door. "Sabrina, you take her. Kill two birds…" Then she shut the door.

I hesitated. Part of me wanted to go stand by the door and make sure Harcourt was okay, but the other part of me didn't want to miss my chance to get to call Jeanette.

I pulled Harcourt's Mercedes key out of my pocket and said. "I'm all yours, Tahkina. Show me the way."

On the night when Caleb's diligence was finally rewarded, he heard the crunch of tires on the dirt road. He flattened himself on the floor as he'd practiced, and moved his eye right to the hole.

He did not fear being seen or observed, because he knew from previous reconnoitering that unless a light was on in his room at night, no one from the ground could possibly see him. Even still, his heart pounded and his pulse raced.

A large sedan approached, windows so dark no one appeared to be driving. It stopped in the circular clearing in front of the two-story cabin. The engine turned off, but the headlights stayed on. The light bounced off the side of the house and into the tall trees which surrounded his prison, causing a greenish glow on the scene.

Olga got out first, and not from the driver's side. He hadn't seen Olga for over a month. She opened the rear door of the car and after a moment came out with another child in her arms. Caleb stared, expecting to see the usual drugged-out child. But this one was wide awake and crying. For a split second, Caleb imagined that they'd decided to bring him a friend. But then he chased the foolish hope away. Caleb wasn't naïve.

Caleb turned his attentions back to the long black car. He saw Babette come out of the cabin. She went to the back of the car and lifted suitcases out, and started to roll one inside. When Sir stepped out from the driver's side of the car, Caleb let out an involuntary gasp and pulled away from the wall. When he got back, he held his breath. Had he imagined it? Was Sir not wearing his mask?

As he focused once again toward the scene, he flinched, realizing that Sir's head seemed to be scanning the area, as if he'd heard Caleb's unfortunate noise. His first instinct was to move away and not be seen, but then he remembered. No one could see anything from the ground.

Caleb remained at this post, refusing to blink or close his eyes, willing Sir to turn his face in his direction.

Caleb strained his eyes, trying to make out wisps of perception, trying to memorize whatever hint of a feature that he could, but it was too dark. And then a miracle happened. His dark angel was watching and she spread her wings, disturbing the thick clouds overhead. The moon appeared for just a moment, illuminating the enemy with a silvery light. Though Caleb knew he hadn't made another sound revealing his presence, Sir turned around and looked right at him. At last, Caleb saw the man's face, the face of the man who thought he could destroy his life. Caleb could not stop the shudder than ran to the end of his fingers and down to his toes.

The man walked away, and out of Caleb's line of sight.

Later, when he tried to recall what he'd seen, he could not remember if the man's face was fat or thin, dark or pale, angular or rounded. He could not recall if he had a large nose, or a high or low forehead, or whether he was bald or had long, thick hair. He couldn't recall the man's mouth, or if there was a beard or a mustache, or a dimple.

All he could remember was his eyes.

Cold, cruel eyes.

20 SABRINA

"Turn right," Tahkina said after we'd driven in almost total silence for the last fifteen minutes out of Diversion and toward her village, that everyone called the "rez." I turned Harcourt's Mercedes onto the unpaved road, and slowed way down as it bounced over deep ruts.

"Just over the top of the rise," she said, pointing ahead.

I said, "Do you mind if I ask you a question?"

"You can ask."

"What makes you think that the bridge wasn't struck by lightning? Is it because of what happened before?"

For the first time since getting in the car, she eyed me with something other than disinterest. "You know about that?"

"A little," I said. "I know that someone dynamited the bridge, way back in the Sixties, to stop the lumber company from cutting down trees."

Her eyes danced. "You got that right. But that wasn't the only reason. Four of my people were murdered on that bridge."

"Yes, I read that too. A horrible thing."

She nodded.

"But there's no more lumber activity out here anymore and no protests from what I can tell, so answer me this... why would anyone want to disable the bridge?"

"I don't know why, but Grandma Bella Bella saw a dark spirit in her vision a few days ago, a dark spirit she said that would test us all."

I felt the air rise on my arms. "Your grandma has visions?"

"Yes, she's not my real grandma. Everyone calls her Grandma. She's a shaman, a medicine woman."

Sabrina felt the hairs rise on the back of her neck.

"And she's the one with the satellite phone?"

"That's right."

"Over there," she said, pointing up a street. "The red house, way over there, do you see it?"

"Yeah, I see it." I started to turn.

"No, can you take me to my house first?"

"Sure."

After dropping her off in front of her house, I headed back toward the red house, stopping outside. I was excited to meet a shaman. I went to the back of Harcourt's car and pulled my purse out of the back. Maybe, if she was cool and I liked her, I'd show her my shaman bag.

After I closed the door to the SUV, I was startled to see an old woman in black jeans and a long red jacket with multicolored embroidery standing in the doorway smiling at me.

She had gray hair that hung to her head like a cloud, curious black eyes, and white but broken teeth inside a broad smile.

"I've been waiting for you," she said as she came closer.

I felt a chill on the back of my legs.

"I'm Sabrina Cane," I said.

"Sabrina," said the old woman, as she took my hands in both of hers. Her hands were gnarled, the color and texture of tanned buffalo hide, but they were warm. She was short, just over five feet, but there was a power in her grip and the way she held my eye.

"Ms. Bella Bella?" I said.

She laughed. A beautiful sound, which reminded me of the chimes on my shaman bag. I gripped my bag tighter. "Just call me just Grandma or just Bella Bella, take your pick."

I stiffened as I realized she hadn't let go of my hand, but instead had flipped it over and was studying my palm. She nodded her head as if confirming something in her mind.

"Uh, I was hoping I could use your satellite phone," I said.

She let go of my hand. "Come in, child, come in."

MIA CALDWELL

The interior of the small house was cluttered, but clean.
A pair of striped cats stretched on top of a table. I followed
her to a small room, off the foyer. Inside, there was a desk,
a copier, and to my great relief a satellite phone.

"Let me get it going for you, dear," she said. She walked
over to it, and flipped a switch, and a few minutes later, I
heard a dial tone. Relieved, I picked up the phone and then
I put it back down.

"What is it?"

"I don't know any numbers by heart."

"Ah," she said. "That makes calling difficult. Call information?"

"They just have cell phones, and no one lists their cell
phone these days." I felt deflated, and close to tears.

"Let me make you something to drink. Sit there. Think
on it. Maybe it will come to you."

I nodded, and sat on the chair by the satellite phone,
feeling like a total idiot. Why hadn't I thought of that before? Then it occurred to me that Ellis might still have a
landline. Maybe he was old school and it was still listed. I
picked up the phone and dialed information. "May I have
the listing for Ellis Hawkins, Vancouver," I asked.

"I'm sorry, there's no listing."

"Uh, darn," I said, about to hang up. Then I thought of
something else. "Wait. How about the Piedmont Coffee
House, in Vancouver?"

"I'll put you through."

The phone rang and rang, and for a moment I thought
that maybe the business was closed, and then I remembered

that it was Saturday in the middle of the day and there was no way it wasn't open and probably packed. I figured they were short staffed, since I'd stopped showing up for work, or that Cerise was out having a cigarette and Mike was left to man the store alone.

I hoped that when the phone was answered that it would be Mike. I'd never liked Cerise much, and it seemed the feeling was mutual. Even if I got ahold of her and asked to relay the message that I was fine to Jeanette, I couldn't be sure she'd comply.

"Piedmont Coffee," came a sullen female voice.

Shit. Cerise.

"Hi Cerise, it's Sabrina," I said, trying to sound cheerful, like we were old buds.

"Who?"

I wanted to reach through the cell phone and slap her.

"Sabrina Cane, Jeannette's sister?"

"Oh, yeah, hey, I'm kind of busy right now."

"Wait," I said, sensing that she was going to hang up on me. "I need you to do me a favor."

"We've got a bad connection. I can barely understand you."

"It's a satellite phone," I said. "Please, this will only take a second."

"What do you want?" She'd said it like I was asking her to make some extreme sacrifice.

"Can you get a message to Jeannette, please? Tell her that I made it to Diversion, and that I'm fine?"

"Whatever," she said. "I've got customers."

The line went dead.

"You got through?" said Bella Bella from the doorway. She didn't have any tea in her hand and I wondered for a moment if she might not be a little senile.

"Yeah, I found someone," I said, sighing. I got up, thinking I should take my leave and head back to town. I needed to figure out where I was going to stay until the bridge was fixed. Plus, I was worried about Harcourt. I wanted to get back to the Grill and find out what news Maggie had gotten from Mark.

"Thanks for letting me use the phone, Bella Bella," I said.

She nodded and reached for my arm. "There's something I'd like to show you."

I thought she was going to lead me to a sitting room and serve that tea, but instead, she led me into a bedroom.

"Sit."

There were no chairs in the room, but she pointed to the bed, so I sat on it. On one side of the room a curtain ran the length of the wall, blocking whatever was behind it. She pulled the curtain aside, revealing a wall covered with floor-to-ceiling shelves. On each shelf were a myriad of items, books and bottles, jars and bowls, tin boxes and wooden boxes, and stacks of twigs and piles of rocks. One shelf had dried flowers and plants hanging from hooks. One shelf had cups with feathers sticking out of them. In still another, there were baskets filled with little dolls. And when I saw them, I had a sudden and powerful recollection of the last place I'd been when I'd seen my mother smile.

The woman my mother had visited, I now realized, was a shaman just like my mother, just like the old lady before me, just like Bella Bella.

"You like?" she said, pointing to the wall, the smile on her face twinkling in her eyes. "Go ahead, take a look."

I gulped. Despite the memory, despite my reluctance to follow in my mother's footsteps, despite the denial I clung to about my so-called gift, I couldn't help but be drawn to the wall. I left the bed and walked over. Bella Bella busied herself as I examined the treasures, retrieving an electric tea pot from one of the shelves. She disappeared behind a door and I heard water running. She brought back the tea kettle, plugged it in, then found an old cast iron tea pot and placed it on the middle of the table.

She hummed to herself, darting in front of me to take down first one jar and then another. Each time she took out a portion and placed it inside the tea pot. I didn't recognize the names on the labels, as they all seemed to be in another language, but I recognized some of the herbs by sight and smell. In addition to chamomile, I recognized yarrow, clove, and burdock root amongst the half-dozen ingredients in the tea.

She stopped and rubbed her chin, then grabbed a small stepstool from the corner and struggled to open it up.

"Can I get something down for you?" I asked.

"Yes, my dear. Up top, in the green jar."

The shelf was high and as tall as I was. I had to stretch to reach it. I held it out for her. Bella Bella shook her head. "No. Put it on the table. Then go back and sit on the bed."

I did as I was told.

She continued her set up for our "tea," and I began to feel more and more comfortable with each passing moment. It was as if she were my own family, a kindred spirit. I felt safe and quiet and at ease. Once she'd gotten what she needed for the tea, including two tea cups, she brought down an intricately carved wooden box and added it to the other items on the table. Then she went to the basket filled with little dolls.

One by one, she picked up the items on the table, holding them up into the air over her head. Each time she chanted words which meant nothing to me, but I understood what she was doing. I'd seen my mother do something similar before she died. Bella Bella, just like my mother, was a shaman preparing to do magic, or a ritual, or whatever you call it. Before she began, she was blessing her tools.

The last item she blessed was the carved wooden box.

Having blessed each item, she brought over the tea kettle and poured hot water into the pot, filling the room with the aroma of clove, and chamomile and several scents I didn't recognize. While the tea steeped, she opened the blessed green glass jar and removed three root-like objects that resembled flattened sticks.

From inside her jacket pockets, she found a spool of multicolored braided threads, and slowly wrapped the three sticks together, twisting the thread around the sticks several times until she created a tight bundle.

She poured tea into the two cups, her old hand strong and not shaking in the least. "Come," she said, beckoning me to join her. After I sat cross-legged in front of my cup, she spoke. "We shamans must stick together, no?"

I was stunned. How could she possibly know that I came from a family of shamans?

"I saw a vision and you were in it," she said, as if that explained everything.

"I was?"

"Drink," she said, pointing to my tea.

She held hers in both hands and slowly sipped the hot tea. I couldn't disrespect her after all her hospitality, after letting me use her satellite phone, so I sipped my tea. It was scalding hot and it burned my tongue. I blew on it gently and had another sip. It tasted of the forest, of the desert, of the sea.

"How long has it been?" she asked. I didn't know what she meant, and I must have shown that in my face. "Since your last vision?"

I nodded and closed my eyes, trying to recall. How long had it been? Ever since the day I'd lost my mother, I'd suffered from horrible nightmares, many of them too vivid. Later, I found myself having dreams during the day, sometimes after I became upset, and sometimes they seemed like visions more than nightmares. And sometimes, people would tell me that I'd been in a trance and I couldn't remember what had happened to me. It felt like I'd slipped into someone else's body and mind, only to forget what had happened the moment the trance was over. How long had it been since I had last seen a world through another person's eyes?

"A long time," I answered and took another sip of the tea. There was a bitter taste that time, and my throat burned a little. Bella Bella's face showed sadness, as if that were a bad thing. Didn't she get it? I didn't want to have visions. They locked me up when I had visions. Visions were not my friend.

I stood up. Had she given me something, something that would bring them back on?

"Don't worry, child," she said. "If you want to see again, that is what the bark is for."

She put down her tea and stood, wincing imperceptibly as her old knees cracked. She bent down and handed me the bundle of jerky-like twigs. "Only a few chews of the bark, then sit quietly. Picture yourself traveling to the underworld. When you get there, call to your spirit guides to show you the way to wherever it is you want to go. And remember—don't chew and drive."

I remembered my shaman bag in my purse. I should open it now, and maybe Bella Bella could explain what the things inside it were for.

"Bella Bella," I asked as she sat there in deep contemplation.

"Yes, my child."

"Have you ever seen one of these," I asked, as I grabbed my purse and pulled out my shaman bag.

Her eyes lit up, and she squealed like a happy child and clapped her hands together, and then whistled.

I tried to hand it to her.

"Oh, no, a shaman never touches another shaman's bag," she said. "What do you have in there? I'm dying to know."

"I've never opened it," I admitted.

"Child, fix that right now. Go ahead."

I worked at the ties, and unlike before when I couldn't budge the knot, it opened right up. I laid the bag on the table and dumped out the contents.

She stood over me, hands clasped behind her back as she dropped her head to peer closely at each item. She was muttering in a language that made no sense to me.

She clapped her hand, then made a face. "No, no, no, not good."

"What?"

"Those black knobby balls. Throw them out. They're widow balls and they're far too old." She went to the corner and picked up a metal trashcan and brought it over to me.

"What are widow balls for?" I asked, reluctant to let go of anything that came from my Mamago, via my mother.

She gave me a look, like she thought I might be stupid, but said, "Another time. Please, put them in the trashcan."

I picked them up, between two fingers, and started to sniff one. "No," she shouted, leaping into the air. "Don't even think about that," she said slapping it out of my hand. Then she grabbed the trashcan and shoved it in front of me. "Please. Throw them away, then go wash your hands."

Accepting that these widow balls were bad news, I felt a little hurt that my own mother would leave something dangerous for me, but I shrugged it off. I didn't like that I was getting rid of something my mother had wanted me to have, so when Bella Bella wasn't looking, I reached under the table and picked up one of the widow balls that had rolled out of sight and stashed it into my front pocket.

After washing my hands thoroughly in the bathroom, I returned to my seat, where Bella Bella poured the tea.

I sipped mine. Then I looked at the other items that had fallen out of my bag. There were several small and polished animal bones, a doll with no eyes, like ones on her shelf, some minerals and crystals, and a pendant on a chain. I turned it over and gasped. It was beautiful. Inlaid in a setting of burnished metal was a hunk of amber the size of a halved egg. Carved into the surface of the amber was a picture of an owl, with big owl eyes.

"Oh my goodness. You need to wear that, child. You're so lucky, you know. To have an owl as your spirit guide means you've got the gift of sight."

"It does?"

"Oh, most certainly. Put it on, put it on." She ducked her head and looked around, then whispered. "There's a bad spirit around, I've felt it. Don't wait. Put it on, child, put it on, and don't take it off."

Not wanting to be rude, I put the chain over my head and felt a rush of electricity on my chest as the amber and metal pendant rested on my bosom.

I placed my fingers around it and felt a kind of heat.

"It's warm," I said.

"Yes, yes, that means it's working." She stood up and clapped her hands again and then spun around, and almost tipped over.

She laughed and spread out her skirts, then sat down again, pouring more tea into my cup.

"The owl is mighty and powerful and deadly and wise," she rattled on. I left the pendant on my chest, hoping it wouldn't burn a hole in me. "And the owl sees things others cannot see, especially at night."

I thought about my visions, and I wondered if maybe there was something to my "gift" after all. Then I knew I should go. "Thank you," I said as I started to pack up the items back into my bag.

"Wait," she said when I started to get up. "Don't forget your vision sticks."

I took the vision sticks and the shaman bag and my purse and thanked Bella Bella for her kindness.

Bella Bella didn't walk me outside, so I sat in Harcourt's car for a moment and sorted out the bundle of sticks. I wanted them inside my shaman bag, since they were a shaman tool, but there were too many of them. I unraveled the string and removed a few sticks and put them in my jeans pocket. I put the rest back in my bag, and worried that I might get pulled over by Constable Hobbledick and he'd be pissed if he saw my purse. I took it to the back and stashed it next to the spare tire, under the mat.

21 CALEB

On the night after he'd seen his enemy's eyes through his secret peephole, Caleb barely slept.

He stayed up most of the night listening to the little boy cry. They'd put him in the room next to his, a room with a window, a room Caleb hoped he'd someday get to have as his own. But after that night he no longer wanted that room.

That night, after he was certain that Sir and the twins had gone to sleep, Caleb had wanted multiple times to call through the wall, to comfort the child, to call out to him, to rescue him.

But he didn't dare. Eventually, the child fell asleep and despite his intentions to stay awake, so did Caleb.

In the morning when Babette opened his door, she dragged Caleb into the room down the hall, the room where the boy had cried most of the night. Caleb could hear no crying then. No sounds but the creaking of the door as Babette prodded him inside.

Sir, was there, as he'd expected. Sitting in a chair, his back erect, his gloved hands calm on his lap. His masked face stared at the window, toward the trees, as if he hadn't noticed Caleb coming in the room. But Caleb knew better. Sir always knew.

Caleb's eyes traveled toward the bed, which was shrouded in a shadow cast by the window pane, cleaving the bed like a triangle. In the shadowed portion of the bed, Caleb could see the outline of a small boy underneath blankets, his head raised upon a pillow as if asleep. Caleb knew better. He knew of breath and the motion that comes from inhalation. He knew of the sounds of sleep. There was no motion, no sounds.

Caleb knew not to speak unless spoken to, so he stood there waiting.

"Caleb, you have asked me to tell you what your purpose will be someday, is that not true?"

Caleb nodded, his throat dry as he tried to swallow.

The man with the mask over his face spoke again. "Come close, Caleb. See for yourself."

Obediently, Caleb stepped toward the boy, covering his eyes from the glare of the morning sun. When he could see, it surprised him how peaceful the boy looked, despite the berry-red hole in his forehead and the child's open, yet non-seeing eyes.

Caleb turned toward Sir, refusing to let the tears fall, refusing to tremble, refusing to throw up.

"I see that you do understand the purpose you will some-day serve."

It wasn't a question, so Caleb did not respond.

Sir's masked face seemed to pinch slightly, as if per-turbed how unperturbed Caleb had been by the demonstra-tion. Caleb didn't tremble, or flinch. He remained as still as a rock on a windless day.

"Do you understand your purpose, Caleb?" The anger in the man's voice was palpable.

Caleb forced himself not to smile as he sensed anger blos-soming behind the mask. It felt good to have power over the monster, to manipulate his emotions, his temper. Caleb did understand and he nodded, and said what he knew the man wanted him to say. "Yes, sir."

"Babette, take him back to his room," yelled Sir.

Caleb didn't think about his future, or the fate that was supposed to befall him as she led him back to his room, because he only felt a sense of triumph, a sense of joy. Sir might think he had power over him, but Sir didn't know his heart, didn't know his resolve. Sir had no idea that Caleb was aware of his true purpose in life—his purpose was to vanquish the monster... even if it meant destroying himself.

"Let's go find out what's happening," Maggie said the moment I walked into the Grill. There were no customers and one of the kitchen workers was mopping the floor.

"Are you closing already?" I asked.

"Yep. I don't want to worry about feeding other people when my husband and those other firemen are going to be starved when they come off that mountain. I'm going to find out the news on the TV, then I'm going to start getting supper ready for the men. Come with?"

"Okay," I said, not sure where we were going, but glad to have something to do for the rest of the day other than sit at a counter staring at a coffee cup.

"You want me to drive?" I asked when we got outside.

"No, it's a short walk."

We headed in the same direction we'd gone before when we'd visited the police station, but turned right at the end of block. We walked down a narrow alley till we came to a set of stone steps going down. Through an open door, I could hear loud voices, and the sound of clinking glasses. "Are we going to a bar?"

Molly didn't answer. Above the door, a sign answered my question as we entered the The Shipwreck Pub.

That made me think about that blog again, and a particularly interesting fact. Diversion had not always been called by that name. Originally, it went by the name Upper Shipwreck, since it was up-river from the natural, but deceptive harbor known as Shipwreck Cove.

Years after the sorry incident at the bridge, and a real estate crash, the city fathers wanted to spruce up the town's image and felt that the name Upper Shipwreck had contributed to the town's bad luck. Some called the name cursed. So they held a town-naming contest and the winning name fit the town's new primary source of revenue, namely tourist dollars for those who appreciated serious river rafting, fishing, and incredible hiking.

Diversion won out, and the town's luck had been better ever since.

Inside the bar was dark and smelled of draft beer and stale cigarettes, but my eyes were drawn immediately to the large television mounted on the wall. The volume was turned off, but that didn't stop the crowd of patrons from keeping their eyes glued on the screen. The television repeatedly showed the same clips. Fires burning. People standing around. Officials talking to reporters. Air tankers dropping water and chemicals onto the fire.

Maggie pushed her way to the bar, and I did my best to stay right behind her. "What's the word, Mitch?"

Mitch, the bartender, was in his mid-sixties with a beer belly and a large mole under his right eye. He wiped a glass with a bar rag as he pulled his gaze from the television. His face lit up in surprise. "Hey ya, Maggie. Don't usually see you here this time of day. What's the word on the fire? You tell me. Any word from Mark? Can I get you something?"

"No, thanks. I just came to find out what's on the news. Mark says it's bigger than he thought and they're planning of staying up all day to do what they can."

"That's not good," the bartender said, shaking his head.

"I know, I'm worried sick, Mitch."

"Quiet," someone shouted. The patrons stopped talking as Mitch turned up the volume. It was the top of the hour.

"Time for a recap and the latest news. It was the biggest wildfire breakout in British Columbia in over forty years. Seven different fires burned across the province. The largest and the fire using the most resources was in the national forests fifty miles northeast of Vancouver."

"What about us?" shouted a man, then he guzzled a huge sip of his beer.

"Another troubling development is the Diversion fire. While there is no immediate threat to populated areas, we are concerned because we have extremely limited assets on the ground and no way to bring in new fire engines, since the bridge to town was closed after receiving extensive damage from last night's storm. We are, however, making arrangements to drop in relief firefighters by helicopter and hope to have air tankers routed to the area by sometime tomorrow..."

"Tomorrow," several people shouted in disbelief.

Maggie grabbed my arm. "Let's go, I've heard enough."

As disheartening as the Shipwreck Pub was, it managed to fire Maggie up. "It's worse than I thought," she complained as we walked back. "No wonder Mark thinks he has to stay up there all day. Well, I'll be damned if I'm going to let them drive all the way back to town before they can get fed."

I was grateful for my new cross-trainers, because I had to jog to keep up with Maggie, and I had the longer legs. "I wish I could think of a place to set up a basecamp," she said as we approached the Grill. "Do you think Harcourt would mind if we used his house? His is pretty darn close to where they were going."

"That's not an option. It's condemned. Tree in the middle of his house, remember?"

"Oh, yes, that's right. What about Molly's? Didn't you spend the night in that house? There's no major damage there, is there? Do you think Molly would mind?"

I wondered why she was asking me. I'd never met the woman. But then again, if she was like most people I'd met in the town, she probably wouldn't mind.

"I've got the keys to her house, I think, in Harcourt's car."

For the rest of the day, time flew by. Anyone Maggie could get near the Grill was recruited to get out the word to the wives, girlfriends, and family members of all the firefighters. They came in droves, bringing supplies and working in the kitchen. By five o'clock, the cars were packed with tables, plates, chairs, and everything else we needed to set up a base camp. They'd loaded all the hot food in Harcourt's car, and I was just getting in line with the caravan heading out when I saw Harcourt's gas gauge was only a quarter full. I managed to shout out my dilemma to Tweety, one of the wives, and she said she'd let everyone know that I'd be a little late.

It took almost twenty minutes before I made it to the front of the line at Eddy's Gas and Garage. Eddy jogged over to inform me that he was rationing gas, and that I could have only ten gallons, and no double dipping. But after I explained what was in the back, and who it was for, he wanted to see. I opened the rear and after I gave him a piece of Maggie's fried chicken, and he saw all the other catering supplies, he was convinced. Eddie insisted that I fill up the car and refused to let me pay for it.

I drove as fast as I could back without disturbing the food, and was beyond overjoyed when I managed to find my way back to Dogwood Canyon and Molly's house without GPS or a co-pilot. But then my joy dropped a notch. I'd expected to see both firetrucks already there, along with all the firemen milling about, anxiously awaiting the main courses in the back of Harcourt's car. All I saw were the volunteers.

As soon as I turned off the engine, they descended on me en masse and made quick work of removing the food and taking it to the tables set up in Molly's side yard. When everything had been removed, I drove the SUV up the street and parked in front of several other cars. Then I walked back to join the others and find out what I could do to help.

As I got close, I looked up at the sound of a loud rumbling noise overhead.

"About time," shouted one of the volunteers. Then she pointed up in the sky toward three water tankers flying our way. Everyone present burst into spontaneous and grateful cheers and applause.

"How long will they fly the planes?" I asked the volunteer closest to me.

"Hi, you must be Sabrina, I'm Carol Faraday." Carol Faraday was dainty and blonde. She offered me her hand and I shook it. "As to your question, I know for a fact that they won't fly after dark. Probably they'll stop around eight, maybe sooner."

I nodded. Carol said, "Lester's been a volunteer for two years. I was surprised to hear that Harcourt volunteered. How long have you two been together?"

I gulped and felt heat rise in my cheeks. "Uh, we're not a couple."

"Sure," Carol said, as she gave a sly grin.

Ignoring her look, I focused on watching the planes as they got closer to the bank of smoke in the distance. "I wish they could have gotten here a little sooner," I said.

"You and me both," said Carol.

From behind us, someone shouted, "Look!"

We all looked at the planes, just in time to see them each drop purple fire retardant onto their target. When the purple stuff hit the fire, even though we couldn't see any flames from our position, a massive white cloud of steam billowed up. Everyone cheered.

"Yes!" Carol shouted, then she gave my hand a victory slap.

The air tankers, done with their first drops, banked and made a slow turn, heading back to where they came from.

"Where are they going?" I asked.

"Port Hardy," someone said.

We all looked back where the planes had dropped their firefighting chemicals, and there was a dip in the celebratory mood. As quickly as the white clouds of steam had risen from the ground, new thicker, taller, angrier black clouds had taken their place, as if the fire was responding to the threat of being extinguished by consuming nearby fuel faster in a gluttonous act of rage.

We got back to work. While we worked, no one spoke their fears. The air tankers only made three more drops, each seemingly as useless as the one before. At eight o'clock sharp they made the last drop, then banked not toward Port Hardy, but toward the mainland.

"I wish they'd get back here," Maggie confessed to me around 8:30 p.m. when someone had made coffee for the volunteers and brought out the fudge to munch on. A few hours earlier a member of the Kiwanis club had dropped by with a generator, some outdoor lights, and a coffee pot.

When 9:00 p.m. rolled around and darkness pressed in, so did the doom and gloom in the camp.

I had a sudden thought that I should go find a quiet place to chew on a vision stick, to see if I could "see" what had happened to the men, when I heard someone shouting. "They're coming, they're coming!"

Something broke inside me.

I burst into grateful tears and joined the other women racing to the road. We stood in the middle of the road, cheering and applauding as the first fire engine came to a halt twenty yards off the road. As their men jumped off, each of the volunteers who had a man on the largest of the two engines started running up the hill to meet up with her man.

But there were two engines that were supposed to be coming down the hill, and so far, only one had appeared. Those who didn't see their firemen on the truck stayed behind with me as we watched on the road, anxiously awaiting a sighting of the second truck.

As the new arrivals walked back toward the camp, I saw Mark Pearson embracing Maggie and walked over to him. I was about to ask him about the other engine when Carol Faraday beat me to it. "Where's the other truck?"

Mark stepped away from Maggie and I noticed the other fireman had moved close to the constable. Mark took off his fireman's hat, and rested it at his side. His face looked tired and miserable.

"I'm so sorry," he said, not able to look at me or Carol.

Then he dropped his head.

"No!!!" Carol wailed. "No!!" She collapsed into grief, and I grabbed onto her and she almost took me down to the ground with her. I tried to comfort her even as my own heart was crushing under the news, and tears ran down my face.

22 JEANNETTE

After a long day of worrying about her sister, Jeannette's nerves were on edge. And it wasn't helping that the boys were trying to drive her nuts. They wouldn't let up. They wanted her to play that stupid Teenage Ninja Mutant Turtles movie in their grandfather's VCR. She'd wanted to stretch out on the long couch in the living room and watch the news, her eyes glued to any information that might give her updates about the worrisome forest fires burning near Sabrina on Vancouver Island.

Deciding that she couldn't stand to see the same shots, interviews, and soundbites repeatedly with nothing new having been reported for the last hour, Jeannette gave in and helped the boys start the movie.

Ellis had been taking a nap, so she went into the kitchen and started opening cabinets looking for where he hid his rum.

"Looking for this, daughter?" he said from behind her. She'd climbed up onto the counter and almost fell off. With her hand on her heart, she smiled. And let herself back onto the floor.

He'd come into the kitchen without her noticing, not even his ragged breath. In his hand he held his bottle of Momento Amber.

"Come sit with me, daughter," he said, "but get us a couple of glasses first."

Jeannette found two glasses and brought them to the table, and Ellis was already pouring before she sat down. "I'm really worried, Daddy," Jeannette said after she finished her first glass.

"Worrying won't help her, but praying might," he said.

Jeannette looked at her father. He was never the kind of man to go to church.

For the first time, she noticed that he was holding something else in his hand.

Jeannette breathed in the rum, inhaling the discreet anise and orange peel scents. "What is that?" she asked as she took her first sip. It was warm and soothed her, calming her almost instantly as it went down.

"It's a Sangoma doll," Ellis said, holding it up to eye level. Jeanette took it and turned it around so she could see it from all sides. It was very unremarkable: stuffed burlap in simple a shape, two pudgy legs and arms, and a head and a torso. Jeannette noticed the doll had no eyes or facial features. It reminded her a lot of the voodoo dolls that people stuck pins into. "It used to belong to Ziviki," Ellis said as he took it back.

"Ziviki? Sabrina's mother? I don't understand."

"Neither do I, to tell you the truth. Ziviki was a shaman from our tribe, and I remember seeing the old medicine men and woman rubbing these dolls when they were hoping for some outcome. I thought I'd try it later, you know, if I start to really worry about her."

"You're not too worried now?" Jeannette asked.

"Well, I'm a little worried, but not so much that I need to pretend to do magic," he said with a laugh.

Jeannette turned down the second drink. She didn't want to be incapacitated in case Sabrina needed to get picked up or something. She got up to wash out her glass. Then she made two cups of tea. Sleepytime for Ellis, and regular Lipton for herself. She didn't want to go to sleep before she was sure Sabrina was okay.

She'd just set Ellis's tea in front of him when Jerrod and Tyler ran into the room, excitement all over their faces. "Movie over, boys?" she asked, forcing a smile. The boys hadn't asked about their missing aunt, nor had they asked about the fires that were all over the news and stressing out Western Canada. They were blissfully clueless about what was going on. She envied them.

"Mommy, Mommy," Jerrod said, "Why are there so many people outside?"

"What are you talking about?"

Following her sons back into the living room, she went to the window where Tyler had pulled back the curtains. They motioned her over and the boys proudly showed her their discovery. Jeannette's eyes went wide and her jaw dropped at the sight.

In front of her father's small house, two television vans had been parked with their satellite dishes jacked up to the sky. Plus, there were several vehicles parked around them, most of them double parked in the street. She recognized the names of the major broadcasters, Channel 8 and Channel 4. In addition to the vehicles, a dozen of more people, men and woman, all of them white, were gathering and speaking to men holding cameras and lights. And then as if one entity, the crowd turned and started moving toward her father's front door. What the hell? She dropped the curtains and flattened her back against the window.

Then the doorbell rang.

Jerrod stood with his thumb in his mouth, and his other hand holding on tight to his turtle. Next to him, Tyler looked up at her, his usual big brother bravery replaced with concern.

"You two, go stay with your granddaddy," she said sharply, her tone clearly not willing to take any guff. The boys ran into the kitchen and her younger son burst into tears, sensing his mother's fear.

"Jeannette, who is it?" called Ellis from the kitchen, as the doorbell ringing was replaced by a series of loud knocks on the door. "Just some people at the door. You keep the boys in the kitchen, okay, Daddy?"

As soon as Jeannette opened the door, she was hit with lights as cameras flashed and videos hummed as the men and women of the press jostled for the chance to be the first reporter to stuff a microphone in her face. She almost closed the door at the barrage of shouted questions.

"Are you Sabrina Cane?"

"Are you the child psychic?"

"Do you know where Baby Adalyn is?"

"Is Baby Adalyn still alive?"

"Can you tell us who the kidnapper is?"

Jeannette, who'd been unable to absorb what was happening, stepped out onto the porch and squinted her eyes against the glare of the camera. "What are you people talking about?"

"Are you Sabrina Cane?" the man with the perfect hair asked.

"No, she's my sister," Jeannette replied.

"Can we talk to her? Is she here?" shouted two other people from behind him.

"No, she's not here. I'm going inside now." More questions were shouted at her as Jeannette slid back into the house and closed the door, and even with the door closed, she could make out what they were saying. She staggered backward, holding her hand against the living room couch, staring at the shouting shadows that looked like zombies as they crowded her father's front windows.

"Is she here?" someone asked.

"Is she going to help?" another person shouted.

"Does she know who kidnapped Baby Adalyn?"

"Where's Sabrina?"

Baby Adalyn has been kidnapped? Holy Jesus, Jeanette thought, that was terrible news. But why did they think Sabrina could help? Then she remembered the article. The writer had gone to a lot of trouble to explain Sabrina's alleged past. It explained how she'd helped police identify the kidnappers and her help had saved two of the three children.

Had someone shown the parents the article? Were they so desperate that they were pulling out any stops? Could she blame them?

"Mommy, what's going on?" Jerrod said.

That damn Ninja Turtle soundtrack was stuck on a loop on the VCR, so she unplugged it and told the boys to get to their rooms.

They didn't argue, and she collapsed on a stuffed chair and tried to think. She could tell the news zombies were still outside. She could see their shadows reflecting against the curtains as they walked on her father's lawn. What the heck did Sabrina have to do with a poor kidnapped baby? For the first time since hearing about the fires, Jeannette was grateful that Sabrina was off on Vancouver Island. At least she didn't have to deal with this.

Jeannette felt sweat trickling down her forehead as she had another thought. Even though Sabrina was the wrong person and had nothing to do with this kidnapping, now that the media was in her face, wouldn't the Canadian government take note and recognize that she'd outstayed her tourist visa? She felt an urge to pack up the boys and her father and slip out the back, and run away somewhere... anywhere...

But instead, she walked back into the kitchen and took the rum bottle and took a swig, not bothering to get a glass.

"Child, what is it?" Ellis said, his eyes wide. Jeannette walked over to the small television set they kept in kitchen and turned it on, moving the dial until she came to the news. She needed more information before she could come up with a plan.

As she watched the news, everything fell into place. Chance and Sky were like Canadian royalty, and their Baby Adalyn was like a princess to the nation. Somehow the couple must have heard about Sabrina's one-time fluke of a gift—when she for some strange reason had helped save some other kidnapped children by creating a mural of the kidnappers when she was only ten years old. While she waited for the commercials to end and the news to come back on, she presumed that Chance and Sky, desperate for any hope that could bring their daughter to them, had announced to the media that they wanted Sabrina Cane's help.

Jeannette couldn't blame them. It was the most horrible and the worst nightmare any parent could go through. To experience the loss of a child, especially by some sicko kidnappers, was too horrible to think about.

But Sabrina couldn't help. Sabrina was no more psychic than she was. Or at least that's what Sabrina claimed. Why else had she been so eager to leave Jack and the stupid movie. Okay, maybe because he'd beat her up, but it was also because they'd wanted her to start trying to solve other missing children cases. Hell, they'd put out a press release asking for letters.

Sabrina hated that they wanted her to do that. She hated that they were getting the hopes up of these poor parents. She hated that they were trying to promote their stupid movie at the expense of others.

Sabrina was certain that her one-time deal was just a strange occurrence, a mystery, an oddity. She was convinced that she had no psychic abilities. Jeannette wanted to talk to Sabrina, to get her opinion on what to do. But she had no idea if Sabrina was dead or alive because that jackass billionaire on Vancouver Island refused to return her calls and put her mind at ease.

Jeanette looked up as a light bulb turned on inside her head. "Daddy, stay here."

Jeanette went straight to the front door and opened it. The people who'd been crowding around her front door minutes ago had retreated to the sidewalk. They were standing in front of their camera operators, spread out from each other slightly, each reporter having Ellis's house as a backdrop as they gave or prepared to give their evening report.

They were going to tell their television viewing audience that they were standing in front of the home where Sabrina Cane lived, the woman the whole world seemed to be looking for. "Hey, hey, hey!" Jeannette shouted, her hands cuffed into a megaphone. "I have something I want to tell you."

Like a stampede, the television journalists and their camera crews rushed forward to get the shot. They started shouting their questions again, and Jeannette shoved her arm out in front of her and showed them her palm, urging them to shut the hell up. When she turned, she looked at each of them sternly, daring them to interrupt her. Everyone fell silent as they waited for her to speak.

Her voice shook, but she was clear and loud. "Please set up for a shot. I have an announcement to make. I'll be back in ten minutes." As soon as she turned around to go back inside, they starting shouting questions again. She slammed the door and almost tripped over Tyler and Jerrod.

"I thought I told you boys to go to bed."

"Ah, Ma," they complained.

The small child pretended to be asleep, tried to be brave and not make a sound when the mean lady who wore the strange clothes opened the door to the man. The child craned hard to hear what was being said.

"Out?" asked the man.

"No, just asleep."

"I need the child out and blindfolded and you need to pack."

"Me? I'm coming with you. How much should I pack?"

"Whatever you want. You're not coming back."

"I'll need time. An hour perhaps."

"You have twenty minutes."

"May I ask where we're going?"

"To visit your sister."

"Very good, sir."

The child, who was soon to receive his nickname, Fox, tried to control his quivering lips to maintain his fake slumber.

"Oh, Babette..."

"Yes, sir?"

"Wear something else. You look like a gypsy horror show."

"Very good, sir. My apologies. I wasn't expecting you."

"Hurry up, and make sure the child can't see anything. Give him a double dose. Get me out of my office when you're ready."

"Very good, sir."

After purchasing a copy of the Seattle Sun, the man with the long hair and beard, jaywalked across the street and got onto the bus bound for Puget Sound. He set the large, custom-made duffle bag on the seat beside him and mused at how easy it had been for him to get from point A to point B, unobserved. He'd flown on the corporate jet to San Francisco as himself, where he'd checked into his hotel, and hired a limousine as himself. He'd even picked up his registration materials at the two-day conference on global trade, and had been seen by many a colleague who could confirm his whereabouts.

But as soon as everyone slipped inside the two-hour key-note breakfast, he'd disappeared. Changing into a hotel uniform and putting on a mustache, he walked through the kitchen and into the back.

An Uber driver was waiting for him, one he'd called with a fake ID, credit card, and phone he'd set up for the purpose. The Uber driver took him to a place downtown, where he met up with his helicopter pilot, who flew him under the radar all the way to Seattle.

One more hour on a bus and he'd arrive at the padlocked garage, where everything he needed to accomplish for his next big crime was waiting for him.

He had barely slept, and the bus ride would take an hour, but even though his eyes were closed and it looked like he was taking a nap, he couldn't sleep.

He sat there the entire time, eyeballs racing under his eyelids as he thought through his plan in his head, going back through every nuance and detail until he was convinced he'd forgotten nothing, and that it could not fail.

The buzz of anticipation was building inside him. He couldn't wait.

23 SABRINA

The other firemen detached themselves from their women and came over to Mark, all of them with their hats in their hands, heads down with sorrow. Mark spoke. "They went off to do something on their own, and then we lost contact. We stayed up as long as we could. We went as far as we could in the last direction we'd seen them go. But then the fire blocked our access. There was no way we could get there. I couldn't risk my other men. I'm so sorry."

He looked away, as if unable to face the truth, or the women whose loved ones had been left behind.

At that point the word had spread almost as fast as the fire burning beyond the ridge. The news of the horrible turn of events hit like showers of boulders falling from the sky. Crushing everyone into bundles of grief and sorrow.

But I wasn't ready to cry, or to wail, or to join those needing the comfort of anyone's embrace. I couldn't believe it. I couldn't accept it. I wouldn't accept it until I saw for myself.

I wanted to see the truth. Maybe Mark had made a mistake. Harcourt Raymondson was on that engine, and he was a billionaire. Billionaires were smart, weren't they? I couldn't accept that a billionaire could let himself perish in a fire. I wouldn't believe it. Not until I saw it with my own eyes.

Taking a piece of vision stick from my pocket, I moved away from the others and sat behind a tree. I took a tentative chew as a flash of something hit the corner of my eye. I looked out through the trees into dark trees, east of Dogwood Canyon road, and saw it again. A pair of headlights. Big wide headlights.

"Look!" I shouted, my voice raspy, as if afraid to hope.

"Oh, my God, it's them!" someone shouted.

The group of mourning women cried even louder, but this time tears of joy and relief.

As the fire engine turned onto Dogwood Canyon Road and rumbled toward us, there was a burst of applause and hugs. The men whistled and slapped each other on the back.

Maggie shouted, "Ladies, let's get this show on the road. Dinner's up, boys."

Those women and volunteers who'd already gotten their loved ones back safe got to work getting the dinner ready. But Carol and myself and two other women ran up the road, eager to get to the firetruck first.

As if not wanting to wait another second, the smaller engine screeched to a halt fifty yards up the road, and the men inside peeled off it and started walking down the hill.

"Lester, oh, Lester," Carol Faraday cried as she ran past me toward her husband. He, and the other two firemen that walked beside him, looked like they'd been through hell.

I hurried forward, turning my head, trying to spot Harcourt, but I didn't see him. Another catering volunteer, a delightful older woman named Tweety, didn't run up the hill, but embraced her husband when he made it to where she'd waited for him.

I felt a rock settle in my stomach.

There didn't appear to be anyone left on the truck.

Where was Harcourt? Had they forgotten about him? Was he still up in the forest, all alone?

I noticed a fireman who must have been single, because there was no tearful reunion for him. He smiled broadly as he walked past me, but with a weariness impossible to mistake.

"Wait," I said as I ran toward him. "Where's Harcourt?"

"Ma'am," he said, and I wondered if he could hear me. He had headphones over his ears. I pointed to them.

His eyes widened, then he nodded and pulled them off his head. "Sorry, what did you say?" he shouted.

"Where's Harcourt?" I asked, too fearful of his answer.

The single fireman scrunched up his face for a moment, clearly puzzled by my concern. He shrugged. "Hark? Oh, he's back there somewhere," he said.

"Thank you," I said, bursting into tears again like a blithering idiot. I stopped, composed myself, wiped away my tears, and with my heart on the verge of exploding from relief, I sprinted up the hill as fast as I could and threw myself around the back of the fire engine and smashed right into him.

"Oh, Harcourt, thank God. I thought you ... I thought you had died," I said, as my eyes filled with fresh tears again.

"Sabrina?" Harcourt said, as if he'd never expected me to pop out from the side of the truck.

I just hugged him, even though he was too big with his massive, smoky coat to wrap my arms very far, but I didn't care. I was just so happy he was alive. He gently pulled my arms away and lifted my chin. "Sabrina, what are you doing up here?"

"I brought you fried chicken," I said, as I tried desperately to retain some composure, to fight back the tears of joy which threatened to soak my grateful face and reveal just how much he meant to me.

"You brought me fried chicken, did you?"

He was teasing me.

"Oh, you," I said, hitting his arm. I was just so damn happy to be with him again. I'd been so devastated when I'd thought I'd lost him forever.

Even though we were going downhill to Molly's house, Harcourt walked slow and with some pain.

"You're walking funny," I said.

"You'd be walking funny too if you just had a long day at work in hell."

That shut me up, but I couldn't stop myself from sighing with a deep and profound sense of relief as I clung onto his arm and leaned against him as we made our way back to basecamp. "Let me get back to work," I said.

Some of the food stations weren't manned, as several of the women were busy helping the men take off their gear and wash up at the washing station. Since I'd provided Ellis's secret recipe, I took point behind the fried chicken platter and eagerly served the men as they got in line.

24 JACK BRESSLER

After leaving a message with his benefactor that getting to Sabrina by car was not an option due to the road closures out of Port Hardy, Jack Bressler watched the television behind the bar with vague interest and wished the bartender would turn around so he could get another beer.

He knew the man never cared about expenses, so he figured he was authorized to take a helicopter to go fetch Sabrina and he'd considered that option. Trouble was, there were none available, all of them fully booked. People apparently were trying to get there to evacuate loved ones, or to deliver additional firefighting personnel. His only hope of getting to Diversion was if one of the helicopter companies had a cancellation, or one of the existing bookings agreed to let him tag along, since he was willing to pay for any available spot.

But so far, no go. And with night coming, he knew the helicopters would be discontinuing flights. He'd booked a room in a pit of a place just up the road, and he wasn't looking forward to going to it. The bar was crowded with people, others probably trying the same as he was for a way to get a flight. He scanned the room for any potential lays, and his eyes fell on an older woman who seemed to be alone and not terribly unattractive. But she wasn't pretty, either.

He needed another beer. He was toying with the last French fry on his plate, dipping it in the strange curry-flavored ketchup the Canadians seemed to enjoy, when he noticed people in the bar raising their voices, shouting to each other and pointing to the television screen. Someone shouted to the bartender, "Eh, turn it up!"

Jack and the rest of the bar patrons all turned their attention to the screen and shushed anyone that dared utter a sound as they strained to hear the report.

Across the screen ran a flashing red and black sign. Stay Tuned for Breaking News.

A male broadcaster with a handsome face and perfect hair stared into the camera lens. His face was serious and sad, as if something terrible had happened. For a moment, Jack thought that perhaps everyone in Diversion had perished in the fire, and his first thought wasn't how he'd miss his wife, but what that could mean to his future, to his hopes to getting his career back as a television broadcaster himself.

The man on the screen who Jack believed was far less attractive than he was, seemed to be waiting for someone to give him the cue to continue. Waiting no doubt for the teleprompter to roll.

"Vancouver Channel 8 News has learned just now that Baby Adalyn, the daughter of Canadian television stars Sky Rochelle and Chance Sanders, has been kidnapped. Furthermore, her nanny was shot and killed during the abduction. The Seattle Police Department will be holding a press conference shortly to discuss this tragic news."

Jack, not being particularly familiar with Canadian television stars, or terribly fond of children for that matter, found it difficult to relate to the outrage and shock that suddenly permeated the bar.

Instead, he decided to take another stab at getting the barkeep's attention.

"Fucking wrong, that is," the bartender said to Jack after he waved him to come over.

"One more," Jack said as he pushed his glass forward. The bartender took it and started pulling the draft.

"It's starting," someone shouted. "Turn it up."

The bartender set aside Jack's beer, which wasn't quite full, turned and reached for the remote, and pointed it at the screen while he turned it up.

Jack felt a little put out, but turned his attention to the screen.

Reporters had their cameras at a podium, and a man in uniform climbed onto the stage to a stand with several microphones. Behind him stood several men, all in uniforms or suits, standing grim-faced. The man tapped the mic, and at the upper edge of the screen titles appeared in the center of the podium.

M. Farnsworth, Seattle Chief of Police.

He cleared his throat and appeared to read from a statement.

"Sometime between eleven o'clock and noon today, Gracile Ramirez, a fifty-seven-year-old employee of the Sanders family, was shot to death as she took Baby Adalyn for a walk in her stroller on the grounds of the family's vacation home in Puget Sound. Her body was discovered by the cook, after the nanny and baby failed to return. Police found the nanny, but no sign of the baby. The stroller was left behind. The US and Canada are coordinating the efforts to find the child—"

Jack sighed loudly, already bored with the news story, his attention back on his drink, "Uh, can I have that beer, please?"

"Shut it," the bartender snapped.

Bored, but with nothing better to do, Jack focused his attention back on the police chief's statement. "We don't normally release pertinent details and evidence; however, we've decided to share the ransom note. Anyone who has information regarding the meaning of this note is to call the 800 number on the screen or their local police."

A female police officer stepped in front of the podium, holding a framed note. Everyone in the bar quieted, and everyone but Jack leaned toward the television as if hoping to see the note soonest. But not Jack. Jack saw his chance and leaned over the counter and grabbed his beer.

He picked up the beer and took a sip, smiling at his cleverness and watched over the rim of his glass as the Channel 8 camera focused on the note. For a second, he didn't grasp what he was seeing, but then the penny dropped and so did his glass.

"Fuck," Jack shouted as beer flew out of the glass and all over his clothes. The glass broke when it hit the ground, but Jack couldn't take his eyes off the screen.

On the note, plain as day, were two words. Each letter was cut out of a magazine or another printed document. Two words that sent a shiver up his spine.

Ask Sabrina.

Jack's mind reeled as the bartender cursed. Jack threw money on the counter and bolted out of the bar, and ran out into the street.

He stopped and put his hands on his knees as he tried to slow his pounding heart.

He'd always known that his benefactor was an asshole, but he hadn't pegged him for a kidnapper. For the first time since agreeing to work for the man, Jack experienced a feeling of dread. As he paced up and down the street, having the fifth cigarette of the day, he pondered what to do. Should he take off? Bolt? Go into hiding?

No. That would be difficult. And besides, his benefactor needed him to make the movie. Yeah, kidnapping a baby was an extreme way to get some publicity, but the more he thought about it, the more fucking genius it was.

And it would do him good as well. The movie's success was his success, and it would help him retain his former celebrity. If the movie went national, no international attention thanks to the high-profile kidnapping, then maybe he could get back behind the camera again, and not in some dipwad town like Albuquerque.

"Oh, shit!" he shouted into the night as he thought about something else—that frickin' article.

If the authorities got to Sabrina first, it wouldn't be hard. Cerise was probably already on the phone trying for that reward money, giving them all the same info she'd given him.

If the press or the cops got to her first, it would be just what his benefactor wanted. Jack wouldn't be needed anymore. He'd be expendable. Dead.

No, he had to get to Sabrina first and figure out a way to keep her under his control. Use access to her as leverage, until he could figure a way out of the mess. He had to make it so that he would become an indispensable part of his benefactor's plans, and do it without letting his benefactor know that he was on to him.

He needed Sabrina. He needed to get to Diversion. The only way in was by helicopter, and he'd already come up short. Now with the news it was going to become more impossible.

"Damn," he said as he pulled off his shirt to fight the sweat in the stuffy room.

How to get a helicopter ride?

He'd already beat his head against the wall trying to book passage. What else could he do? He watched as a helicopter lifted into the night at the end of the block. Maybe he could break into the office, find the names of a passenger on upcoming flights, go to their home and roofie them so they'd miss their flight. Then he'd just happen to be there, seriously bribe the staff to let him know the moment there was a spare seat... Make sure they knew he was ready to pay extra to fly standby...

"That's it!" Jack said as his head snapped up at the brilliant idea.

Convinced that his new plan would work, he went on to consider how to get Sabrina to cooperate. He went over to his suitcase and felt around an inside pocket and pulled out the baggie of drugs he'd purchased while checking out the house Sabrina had allegedly been living in. He'd stopped on the corner where two men had stood in the rain under a street lamp with tennis shoes tied together, and had purchased the Horny Boy Special.

Four Mexican Valiums, four Adderalls, and four doses of Ecstasy. That should do the trick.

Jack smiled, and grabbed his cell phone. He knew exactly what to do to get a fast ride to Diversion.

Harcourt joined the rest of the firemen, who were were seated at the feast set up for them in Molly's driveway. All the men were digging in with as much gusto as totally exhausted, yet hungry firemen could muster, but Harcourt found that he didn't have much appetite. Something was causing a prickle of anxiety. He turned and looked back over the ridge of the hill. The smoke seemed thicker, darker, closer.

The radio next to the plate of food in front of Mark let out a loud squack, followed by the shrill sound of static.

Mark put down the piece of fried chicken, and quickly grabbed his radio.

"Base to Pearson, come in Pearson," said the voice on the other line.

"Pearson here. Over."

"This is base. Just got CB radio call from Elaine Reese. She's staying at her sister's house at the top of Crab Apple Ravine. Says they can see the fire coming at them over the southeast ridge. She's got two kids, a horse, and a bunch of animals and her sister's out of town. She needs help. Urgent. Are you close?"

"10-4."

"Dinner's over, men," Mark said as he wiped his mouth with a napkin. "Everyone suit up, the night is young." There were groans of protest, but that didn't stop the men from scurrying into their clothes.

"I need someone with a small vehicle to help evacuate a mother and two kids. Elaine Reese, last house at the top of the street. Any volunteers?"

"I'll do it," Harcourt said, surprising himself.

"Fine," Mark said. "You can get there before we can, just put that family in your car and get them out of there. We'll be up, but we're going to need to get water first, out tanks are dry."

Faraday said, "Where's the water source, Captain?"

"Bottom of Crab Apple Ravine."

While the men hurried to get dressed and reclaim their firetrucks, Harcourt limped over to Sabrina. "Give me the keys," he said, holding out his hand.

Sabrina gave him a wide-eyed look, then surprised him. "No way," she said, dropped her tongs into the tray of fried chicken in front of her. Before he could stop her, she ran around the table and bolted with surprising speed out of the driveway, then sprinted to his car.

He watched her move, then shaking his head, even as a small smile formed on his face, he hurried to catch up with her, before she drove off without him.

"Sabrina!" Harcourt shouted as he chased after me. I didn't have a limp and I got to the car first, and let myself into the passenger seat and had my safety belt on and the engine started before Harcourt could get to my door.

I hit the lock before he could open it and pull me out.

"Sabrina!"

"You're not going to talk me out of it. Get in the passenger seat. You're wasting time."

Harcourt shrugged and reluctantly got into the car. I put the car in gear and gunned the engine. "Which way?" I asked.

He grunted, then pointed down the hill. I drove as fast as I could, and followed his directions, turning right at the bottom of the hill, then turning right again onto a road which wound up a steep hill, thick with younger-looking pines. We rounded the corner, and saw the first home. "Should we knock on that door?" I asked, as I slowed down at the first driveway.

Harcourt looked outside for signs of the fire. I could see an orange glow lighting up the clouds far ahead of us. "Just honk the horn real loud and let's keep going. Let's get to Elaine and get those kids out of there, and then we can work our way down."

I kept my fist firm against the horn as I drove fast up the hill. It was full dark by this point and as we approached the last house on the street, the one occupied by the family requesting assistance, I got the first close-up sign of the fire that had been taunting the entire community all day.

"Holy mother of—" I said as I stared at the bright strip of yellow and red flame racing down the hill behind the old farm house.

"Help us," shouted a woman standing in front of an SUV with its lights on.

"Stay in the car, Sabrina," Harcourt ordered, then he got out and hurried over to the woman. I recognized her from the Grill, and peered into the car and saw the two kids. Suzy and Peety? Then I remembered also that she had a sister, Betsy? Becky—a woman with designs on Harcourt. I put that thought out of my head, and tried not to think about how close the wall of flames was looming behind the house.

After another minute of following Harcourt's pointless orders, I got tired of feeling useless. I stepped on the emergency brake, but left the engine running and made sure all the doors were unlocked.

When I stepped out of the well-protected car, I almost got back inside. It felt like I was stepping into an oven being heated inside another oven. And the air was so thick with smoke I could hardly breathe.

I moved closer to Harcourt and Elaine, who was gesticulating wildly and saying words I couldn't hear over the roar of the approaching fire.

"Is everyone out?" Harcourt yelled. Elaine nodded. "Then what are you waiting for?"

"I can't. My horse is still in the barn. And we've got goats and a baby pig."

I scanned the yard until I saw a pen with animals in it. "I'll get the goats and the pig, you get the horse," I said, and before he could stop me I was back inside the SUV, releasing the emergency brake and turning my head around so I could back up to the pen.

Elaine and the kids drove away and I saw Harcourt go into the truck which had a horse trailer attached and start the engine, then backed it up close to the barn. Harcourt ran around the back, flung open the trailer's door, then went into the barn. As soon as the door was opened, I heard the scream of the horse and almost dropped the two-by-four I'd picked up to give the goats a ramp.

Horses were dangerous, especially frightened horses. I held onto my pendant for a moment, sending a silent prayer to my shaman ancestors that Harcourt didn't get kicked in the head by the noble beast. I saw out of the corner of my eye that Harcourt was getting the horse into the trailer, and I got to work opening the gate.

As soon as the gate was partially opened, all three goats ran immediately up my makeshift ramp, and trampled and fell against each other inside the back of the SUV. "Good job, goaties," I said as I peered in the gloom for the pig. Fortunately, Mr. Piggy was a small pet-type of pig, but he was also son of a bitch. He wouldn't let me pick him up, and kept slipping out of my grasp and running through my legs every time I got close. Sensing that the fire was getting closer, and becoming more than a little lightheaded from all the smoke, I managed to corner the little pig, then pounced. I slipped and slid in the mud, but when I got to my feet I lifted the pig in triumph.

"Got you," I said as I ran over to the SUV, and not wanting to risk having the goats get out, threw the pig into the rear seat.

I was catching my breath when an explosion made me duck and cover my head.

"Sabrina, are you all right?" Harcourt shouted from behind the horse trailer.

"I'm fine, what the hell was that?"

"Propane tank," he yelled over the screams of the horse. "Sabrina, I'm not kidding. You need to go, now. That's an order."

"Are you sure you're okay?" I said. The horse was in the trailer, so I nodded and got in the car and drove down the hill. I then turned left to go to basecamp, just as one of the fire engines pulled up at a fire hydrant and the men popped out to pump water into what I assumed was an empty tank, before heading up the hill. I stopped the car.

"Harcourt's still up there, and that house is almost on fire," I yelled.

Mark was standing there with his white fire chief's hat and he gave me a thumbs up. I saw the smaller truck start to move as several men jumped on board, and felt a great relief knowing Harcourt was going to be all right.

Harcourt was grateful to have the horse inside the trailer, and he'd just finished making sure the door was secure when he saw the back of the barn catch fire. "In the nick of time, old gal," he said to the horse. Then he heard a sound that made him stop in his tracks. A barking sound.

He turned toward the house and saw that a dog was scratching at the window inside Elaine's house. He made a beeline for the door, just as the roof caught fire, sending smoke and ash and sparks all around him. Covering his mouth and nose with his shirt, and wishing to God that he'd brought his SCBA, he stayed as low as he could until he made it to the front door.

Fearing a back draft if he opened the front door too fast, he used his shirt to cushion the burning heat of the metal doorknob, and feeling it singe his skin, he grit his teeth and turned the knob. He pulled the door open just a little, then waited.

The dog wasn't interested in waiting and it pushed its body nose-first through the gap in the door, throwing Harcourt backward just as a blast of superheated air and fire shot out the door.

Harcourt went out for a second, but was awakened by barking and something cold and rough licking his face.

Then strong arms lifted him away from the fire and dragged him away from the falling, burning debris field. He was put on a stretcher and carried even farther away, and then someone covered his mouth with a breathing device.

He coughed out the smoke, and eventually came around.

"You gave us a scare buddy," Mark said, as one of the other firemen checked his vitals.

"Did Sabrina get back all right?" Harcourt asked.

Something pressed at Harcourt's elbow. Mark shouted, "I thought I told you people to secure that dog." Then he turned to Harcourt. "You've made a new friend."

Harcourt felt weak, but he lifted his hand and pet the grateful dog.

When Harcourt and the rest of the firemen came back to basecamp with Elaine's sister's dog, I thought the townspeople were going to throw him a damn parade. My chest burst with pride at his apparent heroics. But soon attentions were changed to the fire which had moved away from Crab Apple Ravine and was headed toward Dogwood Canyon.

"Everyone out," Mark ordered and we all started to pack like crazy. The firetrucks went back to the main highway to fill up the empty tanks, and Harcourt was told to hang out at basecamp and get a ride back with Sabrina.

But as soon as the firemen who weren't suffering from smoke inhalation and could still work had gone, Harcourt came over to me and asked me for his keys.

I thought he was just going to go sit in the car, so I didn't think anything of it, but when I looked back to see if he was resting, the car was gone.

At first I panicked, thinking he'd left me, but then I saw the rear taillights going up the road. "Of course," I said to myself. "His house is at risk; he's just going to get a few things out while he still has time."

I thought about saying something, but decided it wasn't my place. I chewed on my nails and got back to work, helping everyone load the catering tables and chairs into the last vehicles still around.

Maggie came over. "You've got Molly's key?" she asked.

"I do."

"Why don't you go in there and wash off whatever that is all over your face, clothes, and hair?"

Grateful not to be covered in pig shit, I took her advice, taking the flashlight she lent me to find the bathroom and illuminate the room as I showered with my clothes still on. When I got out, I dried my hair in a towel and squeezed out my clothes as best I could. I felt the vision stick in back pocket and took them out and rinsed them in the sink. Then I felt something knobby in my front pocket and took that out. "Oh, yeah," I said, holding up the weird pod-like object—what had Bella Bella called it? I dropped it into the sink. "Widow Maker," I said, using two fingers to run it under the water. I was still intrigued, so I wrapped it into several sheets of tissue paper, then washed my hands until I was sure I'd gotten rid of all traces.

"Sabrina, get out here," Maggie yelled. Since I was already dressed, albeit soaking wet, I grabbed the flashlight and sloshed my way outside.

As soon as Mark and the rest of the firemen left, Harcourt got the key to his SUV from Sabrina by acting like he wanted to just go sit in it for a bit. But the moment Sabrina turned her back, he picked up the fire mask and gloves and hurried to the car.

He checked the rear view mirror as he drove away with his lights off, sure no one had noticed. But even if they had, he hadn't planned on being stopped. His house was in the line of fire and there was something up there he couldn't, wouldn't let burn.

As he took off onto the back road behind his mansion, the one that led straight up to Sharon's cottage, he cursed when he saw how close the fire was coming, threatening his property with two fingers of flame oozing like lava down the hill. He accelerated. Inside the car the goats and the pigs made a ruckus and a stink like he'd never smelled in his life, but he didn't care.

He brought the SUV to a screeching halt in front of the cottage, then put on his gloves and mask as he hurried up the stone steps to the front door. He didn't have the key and was about to kick in the door when an explosion ripped into the air, throwing him to the ground. He covered his head as a huge ball of fire billowed into the sky, and he knew that his hotel-sized propane tank at the back of the mansion had just blown.

He was about to kick in the door when he realized that it wasn't locked, and that it lay cockeyed off one hinge as if someone had already kicked the door in. With no time to worry about why that might be, Harcourt hurried toward the padded window seat just as the roof overhead caught fire, and the room glowed bright orange, the heat burning the hair off his neck.

He only had seconds before he, the photos, and the whole house were engulfed in the flames.

Outside, the goats and the pigs were screaming, probably feeling the heat. He lifted the lid to the window seat and screamed, and reeled back in horror, tripping over a stack of Italian floor tiles. "Fuck, Jesus, Fuck. What the hell?" he shouted, and saw the walls beginning to go up in flames.

He decided. He went back to the box, scooped up the evil thing in one of the blankets, and secured it to the floor with his feet. Then he got what he'd came for, the box of photos. With the box secured under his arm, he wrapped the horrid thing in one of the blankets, and carrying it like a bag of Santa's toys, hurtled to the door and got out of the house just as it went up in flames.

Afraid the car was going to catch on fire, he opened the front door, threw all the items onto the seat, and put the car into gear and floored it away from danger. The rear fish-tailed and before he could get control, the car skidded right into a wall of flames. The animals were hysterical and he thought they'd break out of the car, but he somehow managed to get the car back under control and sped for Dogwood Canyon Road.

When he'd gotten far enough away from the fire that he could open a window, he rolled them down, then stopped at the side of the road. He felt sick, and not just from the heat and the smoke, but from that horrible thing sitting in the car, that horrible thing in the blanket.

By the time he made his way back down the hill, the Number 2 Engine was just coming up to find him.

They waved him past and turned around, clearly not interested in trying to save the houses already fully engulfed on the hill.

Sabrina came running up to him as soon as he parked the car.

He didn't want to talk to her.

He couldn't face her right now.

"Mark," he said, and coughed more than was necessary. "Can you have Maggie take Sabrina back to your place? I need to talk to you about something."

25 JACK BRESSLER

Jack sat on the bed in his shitty motel room after searching for more news about the Baby Adalyn story. After reading everything he could get his hands on to get a firm grasp of the story, he found the telephone number for the Vancouver Channel 8 news desk and made the call.

It took a while before he got through to someone who would listen to his pitch, but Jack knew how the news media worked, and he soon had them eating out of his hand.

Jack had been a broadcast journalist for years, one of the best in Albuquerque, before—well, before an unfortunate incident involving his temper and a woman working at the station got him suspended and apparently blackballed from working as a television news broadcaster again in that town. He'd moved to Los Angeles, hoping to parlay his good looks and experience into career as an actor. But that had not gone well. He was hungry and considering adult films the day he'd run into his benefactor. That's when he made the deal with the devil to use his charms and other talents to seduce one Sabrina Cane.

He hadn't expected later to be informed that he was to marry her, because Jack had never wanted to marry anyone, or be tied down in any way. Of course, his benefactor made the proposition hard to refuse, giving him a house in his name in a great part of town and increasing his monthly salary. The benefactor was right about the importance of marrying Sabrina, because when Jack eventually pitched the movie script written by the benefactor—but to anyone that asked, written entirely by Jack—the fact that Jack was married to the mysterious Sabrina helped. The studio knew that as her husband, Jack could give the studio access to the woman, that she would agree to "out" herself, and thus help promote the film.

The studio bought the movie rights to the script. And when Jack offered to help fund the venture by coming in as an investor in the production, to the tune of one million dollars channeled secretly to Jack via his benefactor, the studio executives gave the film the green light.

And for a while, everything was going great. Sabrina co-operated. She signed the contract he put gave her and re-luctantly got in front of the camera, dutifully sharing her recollections for the documentary side of the film. She worked in the studio the benefactor's money had built for her in the back of their great house, cranking out one piece after the other.

Her art was dark and mysterious, haunting, ghostly.

She didn't fight with him when the studio wanted to put her art out for sale. She dressed for the gallery openings and private auctions and posed for photos in the designer dresses the studio sent around, but remained quiet, uncomfortable on camera, and reluctant to speak. Her shyness and vulnerability only made the mystery about her grow. Soon her artwork became the hot ticket in town, selling like hotcakes, and the money came rolling in—and Jack made sure he handled her money as her business manager.

Everything was going fantastic. The film studio was thrilled by her popularity and the success of her art sales, and Hollywood's best actors were lining up to get cast in the film. Fractured Fourth of July, the current working title, was going to be the best movie ever. Drama, fiction, based on a true story, maybe Oscar-worthy. Jack was to be in the film, interviewed as the husband of the troubled young woman, all part of the documentary piece.

Once the film hit distribution, and Jack's face had been seen by the masses, he knew that his troubles would be over. The benefactor would pull the salary once his movie was made, but so what? He could walk away from married life unless Sabrina's art kept selling, because there would be a million job offers back in his chosen profession.

But that was before Sabrina had to go and ruin everything.

After he made the announcement that Sabrina was looking for crimes to solve, for missing children to find, Sabrina flipped out.

When the letters starting coming in to the studio, and boy did they come in, she refused to read them.

She started behaving strange, having nightmares which kept Jack up all night. She started acting crazy, and out of it, like she didn't seem to know who she was. She was terrified to go in her studio, and refused to make any more art. She became afraid to leave the house, specifically the spare bedroom she moved into because she didn't want to sleep in the same bed as Jack anymore. The studio was flipping out because she missed scheduled shoots for her interviews.

She became irrational, and wild, screaming like a banshee if he even tried to have sex with her.

Jack only did what any man would do; he went out and found his comfort somewhere else.

And when she calmed down enough to go to a gallery showing that was already scheduled, he figured he could bring the woman he was fucking to his home.

It was unfortunate that she found him with the woman, but what did she expect? She wasn't letting him get any, so how the hell could she have the nerve to be jealous?

So, yeah, he lost it.

She was going to mess up everything, piss off his benefactor, shut down the film.

He was mad. Who wouldn't be?

After the woman he'd been fucking in their marital bedroom was long gone, Jack gave in to his urges. He let his frustrations out. He knocked his useless wife around a little, but she deserved it. She deserved much worse than he gave her. What he did to her was nothing. Nothing broken, just some bruises that would heal right up.

But did she forgive him when he begged her to?

Nope.

She had to be a total bitch about it. She had to overreact.

She locked herself in her bedroom, and the next day she ran off, fucking up everything he'd worked for. Just when his life was about to get back on track.

But all's well that ends well, Jack thought as he lay back in his bed and closed his eyes and stripped off his boxers. He'd managed to speak with the right person at Channel 8 news, and his future was bright again. Everything was going to fall back into place now. The whole clusterfuck about to get back under control.

Jack looked forward to what the next day would bring, as he jacked himself off in that dingy motel room. Not only was he going to get a first-class ride into Diversion on the Channel 8 news helicopter first thing in the morning, he was going to get his meal ticket back.

Best of all, he'd negotiated the deal with Channel 8. If they shot film of him tracking down his wife and rescuing her from the burning town, he'd give Channel 8 exclusive access to the most sought-after person in Canada now. The one person who could help save Baby Adalyn. His wife and the person the kidnapper said to talk to. He'd be the one on camera to ask Sabrina.

And when he was done, Jack's picture would be broadcast all over the United States, all over Canada. Jack was about to get famous.

And there was no way in hell he would let that spoiled, fucked-up woman screw things up for him again. This time, he'd make sure she stayed in line.

It took fifteen minutes before Jeanette was ready to make her television debut.

The boys refused to go to sleep, but they did agree to stay quiet by the window while she did her thing. She'd put on a little makeup and fixed her hair a bit, and changed into a blouse that wasn't stained with peanut butter and jelly. And just before heading back outside, she got her laptop powered up and took a moment to Google the story. Afraid that they might get called to a bigger story if she didn't get out there soon, she went to the door and reminded her excited boys to keep quiet by putting her finger over her mouth.

When she stepped outside, bright lights illuminated her father's porch. She closed the door.

The reporters were hushed as they waited for her to speak. She pulled her shoulders back, and smoothed her hair. She stared into the closest camera. "First, my family and I are very saddened to hear of the kidnapping of Baby Adalyn. We are all praying for her safe recovery. As for my sister, Sabrina Cane, I can confirm that she was the child psychic artist involved in steering police to rescue two of three children during the infamous Seattle Fourth of July kidnappings ten years ago."

She paused, and all she could hear was the hum of the television cameras. She looked out and noticed that all the neighbors on Ellis's street were standing in the background, watching the scene with unmasked curiosity.

"Some of you asked if Sabrina was currently consulting with the parents of the kidnapped child. I can't answer that question, because my sister Sabrina Cane is missing."

She let that sink in. A few questions were shouted, and Jeanette held up her open palm. The questions stopped.

"We need the media and the public's help in finding her. She was last known to have been traveling to Vancouver Island, to Diversion in the heart of the wildfire. She was to meet with Harcourt Raymondson of Raymondson Industries, and I've been unable to get ahold of either of them. I hope that you can track her down, and Sabrina or Mr. Raymondson, if you hear this, please let me know that Sabrina is safe. We are very worried about her."

The questions came fast and furious, but Jeannette was done. She went back into her house and closed the door, collapsing against it as her excited children ran into her arms.

26 HARCOURT

No one argued with Harcourt, probably because the man had just lost two houses.

Harcourt sensed that Sabrina was upset that he wasn't talking to her, but he couldn't face her. Not after what he'd found in Sharon's cottage.

Mark ended up driving the SUV and Harcourt pretended to sleep, waking up in time to help Mark drop off the goats and the pig at the emergency animal shelter set up at the Diversion Secondary School.

Before Mark had gotten into the car, he'd transferred the dreaded item to the back, then threw the pig in with the goats to protect the evidence.

Mark had already insisted that Harcourt stay at his house, and since there was nowhere else to go, he didn't argue. What he was afraid of though, as he contemplated how to explain what he had in the back seat, was whether Mark would decide to make him spend the night in a cell instead of in the guest room at his house.

"You all right?" Mark asked. "Was there something you wanted to show me?"

Harcourt took a deep breath. "Can you take me to the police station?"

"Why Hark, do you want me to arrest you?" Mark said with a laugh.

"Not really, but you might want to when you see what I've got to show you."

Mark pressed him to explain what he was talking about, but Harcourt refused to say anything about it. "I'll show you when we get there."

"Whatever, you say, buddy," Mark said as he stifled a yawn. "Whatever the fuck you say."

They drove in silence the rest of the way, and Harcourt kept thinking about the damning evidence in the back seat. God had sent one of his soldiers to plant that horrible thing in Sharon's cottage. A reminder to him that he had already abandoned his wife and son once before. God was punishing him for fucking around so soon, for enjoying his life again with Sabrina Cane. He was fooling himself. He'd never be happy again. He didn't deserve to be.

When Mark and Maggie and I watched Harcourt's house burn, it was like seeing the end of the world, and I couldn't stop kicking myself for not telling Mark earlier where he'd gone.

But just like before, just when I thought all was lost, Harcourt came driving out of the smoke with the live animals still in his car. I ran up to him, ready for the happy reunion moment, but he refused to talk to me. He wouldn't even look at me.

I tried to understand and not take it personally when he asked Mark to have Maggie drive me to her house for the night. My body stiffened and my nose went up in the air and I crossed my arms over my chest. Two can play at that game. In a sniffy tone, I said, "Maggie, are you sure you don't mind having me? I'd be happy to go to the shelter."

"Nonsense," Maggie said. "Of course we don't mind."

I was about to get into Maggie's minivan and not give Harcourt a second glance when I realized I was missing something. My purse.

"Wait," I shouted, racing back to the SUV. Harcourt was slumped in the passenger seat and turned his back to me, and Mark was already behind the wheel. "What?" Mark asked.

"I need to get my purse," I shouted. Harcourt's head shot up, and I saw the look of bewilderment in his face. "No way, you can't let her do that. It's not safe."

"What are you talking about?" I said, angrier than ever at Hark. He had a lot of nerve keeping a woman from her purse.

He turned and looked at me, his voice pleading. "Sabrina, you can't go up there, it's too late, and it's not safe. I won't let you."

And then it hit me. I'd never told him that I'd violated Hobbledick's orders and fetched the purse out of my crushed Volvo. For a split second, I felt shame and embarrassment for getting caught, but then I got over both emotions darn fast. What business was it of Harcourt's? I crossed my arms, and narrowed my eyes. I owed him no explanation. I spoke to Mark directly, avoiding Harcourt's eyes.

"My purse is in the rear of this vehicle. Please ask him to unlock it, so I may get my property."

I stomped toward the back of the car, and heard Harcourt open his door. "Wait," he said.

"Well, fuck you," I muttered under my breath. I flung open the door and something hit me square in the chest, knocking the wind out of me and slamming me to the ground. I did what any self-respecting female would do under the circumstances. I screamed.

"Get!"

"You!"

"Here!"

The men yelled and finally one of the them managed to grab the one billy goat that got away by the scruff. I scrambled to my feet and heard Maggie laughing uncontrollably. "Oh, Sabrina," she said. "You're going to need another shower."

I looked to see if Harcourt found the whole thing funny, but he'd gone back inside the car and closed the door behind him.

I explained to Mark where I kept my purse, and after more cursing and blocking of goats, he extracted it and handed it to me.

"Is Harcourt all right?" I heard Maggie ask Mark in a hushed voice.

"The man just lost his home, two homes. Give him a break."

Harcourt was quiet as Mark drove him down the mountain to town. They went to the shelter, and put the goats and the pig in the pen. Then they headed to the fire station. As they drove, Harcourt stared at the sky above the western mountains. A half-moon had risen behind strip of a smoky clouds and it hovered like a long magic carpet above the ridge of the westward mountains. Through the clouds, the moon cast an eerie red glow over the entire town of Diversion.

"So, what's in the blanket?"

Harcourt suddenly felt very tired. "Did you say there was a police station in town?"

"Yeah," Mark said, "I was going to go there after the fire station. But if you want to turn yourself in or something we can go there first."

Mark had a smile on his face, but it faltered.

"Seriously, buddy, what's going on?"

"Can we go to the police station first? This is something I need you to see."

Inside the police station, Mark turned on the lights and opened the door to the interrogation room in the back.

"I found this in Sharon's cottage," Harcourt said.

He unwrapped the blanket. "Holy shit," Mark said. "Christ. Is that what I think it is?"

"Yes. I'm afraid so."

"Is it real?"

"I think it might be."

"You know that's the skull of a child, Harcourt."

"I know."

"Holy fuck. And you have no idea who the child is, or how it got there?"

"I think I might have an idea or two."

Mark stood up and put his hand on his firearm. His face was tense with disappointment. "Do I need to read you your rights, Harcourt? Are you confessing to murdering your own child?"

"No, no. Of course, not."

"Then how the hell did this get in your possession?"

"Listen, will you fucking listen already?"

Harcourt slumped back in his chair and Mark took his hand away from his gun.

"All right, I'll listen."

For the next thirty minutes, Harcourt told Mark everything. How he'd always felt guilty about his wife and son's death because of his insistence that they fly to Seattle to meet him, and how it had made it hard for him to stop mourning, hard for him to go back to work. But after that video conference call where he realized Peter Talbert's game, he started thinking about things, about little signs that someone had maybe caused the accident, and had set it up so that Harcourt would feel responsible.

"So you think this Peter Talbert guy might have deliberately caused their deaths?"

"I don't have another explanation."

"I thought the bodies were never discovered?"

"Well, that's what I was told. But remember when they came with some of the clothing, Cedric's fireman hat, the other pieces of the plane?"

"Yeah."

"What if Peter Talbert sent someone out there after the cops gave up, after I'd identified the clothing after they had a shut case? What if he sent divers down and recovered the bodies? I mean, there's signs that the skull was in water. Aren't those barnacle markings? It had to be pulled up from the sea. It's the only explanation."

"That's a little far-fetched, don't you think?" Mark said. "I mean, why go to all that trouble and then a year later put it in your wife's cottage?"

"He's trying to make me mad, make me get declared insane, unfit to run my company. He's been conniving all along, telling me that things were fine and dandy, telling me to take the time I need. But I think he could tell on that conference call that I wasn't going to take his shit lying down. Maybe by planting the skull of my son on my property he could get me arrested, or make me kill myself. Whatever, the board would probably balk at letting me be president again, not if I was being investigated for the murder of my wife and son."

Mark used the bathroom. Harcourt did as well, then they left the eerie skull sitting on the desk and Mark made a pot of coffee.

"So, what's with the note?" he asked.

"I'm not sure."

"Didn't he think that if you found this shit in your cabin that you would be smart enough not to run and tell the police?" Mark snickered. "Oh, wait, that's exactly what you did."

"Look, I'm crushed to have my son's skull in that room. If I hadn't already spent a year coming to terms with the fact that he was dead, I'd probably want to put a bullet in my brain. But it's just a skull now. I say we run it up the flagpole. Have forensics look at the note, try and find fingerprints, DNA, anything that might tie it to Peter. I am an innocent man. I did not tamper with that plane. I did not kill my wife and son. I'll hire the best lawyer in the world, if I have to—later. But for right now, you are my only friend."

"So, what do you want me to do?"

"Just lock it up somewhere and keep it safe until I can find a way to prove that Peter is trying to frame me."

"I could get into trouble," Mark said. "I don't know."

"Look, I'm not asking you not to take this up the chain of command. I'm just telling you to sit on it for a day or two. I mean, you've got a fire burning, limited support personnel, a bridge that no one can cross, and there's just you and Hobbledick to police the whole town. It's understandable that something like this might not get handled for a—"

"Who?"

"What?"

"You said there's just me and Hobbledick? What the fuck does that mean?"

"Constable Hobday, I mean, sorry—he was at my house yesterday morning when Sabrina and I went up there to get some things out of my house and out of her car. Total asshole. He let me get my laptop and cell phone and some clothes, but refused to let me go to Sharon's cottage…"

"Hark?"

"Mark, are you telling me that you've never heard of an RCMP constable named Hobday? You never told that man to go to my property and officially condemn it?"

"No, and no. Absolutely not."

Both men were silent, and then Harcourt hit his fist into his hand, "That's why."

"That's why what?" Mark asked.

"It all makes sense."

Mark raised his voice. "No the fuck it doesn't. What are you talking about?"

"Sorry," Harcourt said as he took in a deep breath. "I thought he was just being a major dick, because after he let me get my laptop and cell phone out of the part of the house that was damaged, he wouldn't budge when I told him I needed to get something out of Sharon's cottage. He got all asshole cop on me, no offense. It was because he'd already planted the damn skull and he didn't want me to find it. That fucking bastard."

"Now, now, Harcourt, calm down. Don't jump to conclusions. That doesn't prove anything. Let me get on the radio and make some inquiries about the dude. For all I know he's legitimate and he heard me on the radio mentioning that it was off-limits because of the damage."

Harcourt poured a coffee for himself, and asked Mark with his cup if he wanted one too. Mark nodded and he poured Mark's coffee as both men sat there and pondered what they knew.

Then Mark went over to his radio and started to move dials around. "Son of a bitch!" he said as he slammed his foot against the desk.

Harcourt sprayed coffee onto the floor. "Shit, Mark, what the fuck?"

"Radio's not working. All right, I'm buying your theory now, that son of a bitch."

"See, I told you."

"Just shut up and help me get the car loaded."

They worked without much chatter, each man's face a study in irritation and growing outrage, but also concentration as they put on gloves and worked to transfer the evidence into large plastic evidence bags. Following procedure, Mark filled out an evidence log, and made stickers for each bag. Harcourt wrote out a statement on the typewriter and signed it. He explained in detail how and where and when he found the items, what had taken place with Constable Hobday prior to the discovery of the skull, and how, where, and when he'd voluntarily handed over the evidence to the police. Mark looked at it, and they both signed it, then he made a copy for the office files and taped the original to the bag with the most damning evidence, a human child's skull.

"Now what?" Harcourt asked as they looked at the transparent bags against the far wall, which looked like eerie donations waiting for pickup to a charity store. "We leave those here?"

"Not with Hobday having a key to this place," Mark said. Then he stood up. "Fucking A."

"What?" Harcourt asked.

"The armory. Fuck."

Before Harcourt could get out of his seat at the table where he'd typed up his statement, Mark had moved to the back of the police station and was going through his keys. He found the one he wanted and opened the door.

"Well, that's some good news," he said as he expelled a breath. Light flooded the inside of the armory. Harcourt came around his side and peeked in. The room was small, but the walls had weapons covering about every surface, plus there was a tall metal supply shelf stuffed with boxes of ammo. "Everything still here?" Harcourt asked.

"Looks like it."

"So, we store it in there, then?" Harcourt asked.

Mark whirled around and glared at Harcourt. "Look, buddy, why don't you stop telling me how to do my job?"

"What?" Harcourt said, putting his hands up and taking a step back.

"You've been too up in my face on this matter, and you have nothing to do with it. It's police business."

Harcourt's face heated. "What the fuck are you talking about? I wasn't trying to tell you what to do."

Mark's voice got louder. "You know, you shouldn't even be in here. Poking your nose around where it doesn't belong. Why don't you wait outside and let me finish my job?"

"Fine," Harcourt said. He went to the table to grab his keys. He'd just sit in the car in the back and wait.

"No, you don't." Mark said, pulling the keys out of Harcourt's hands. Then he pointed to the front door. "Wait out there, and I'm still driving until I say otherwise."

Harcourt rubbed his face, trying to stop the biting retort waiting on his lips. "Fine," he said, then stormed out.

Mark poked his head out the door. "Don't leave that spot or I'll have you arrested."

Harcourt heard the door lock behind him, followed by the sound of the blinds being adjusted, so Harcourt couldn't see what was happening inside. He banged his fist against the window. "Fuck, you, Mark," he barked through the double-pane glass.

Then he paced back and forth on the sidewalk, trying to understand Mark's sudden change in mood. He looked around. The streets of Diversion were empty. The air was thick with the smell of fire. And even though it was the middle of the night, there was an ominous red glow bouncing off the black sky. Harcourt was bone tired. He never should have told Mark about the skull. Or at least waited until morning after getting some sleep. Maybe that's all that was wrong with Mark. Long day for him too. He was just tired.

He slumped down, sitting with his back against the wall, when his Mercedes beeped open.

He got up and realized that there was a narrow foot path next to the police station which led to the alley in the back. He couldn't resist the urge. Running fast, but on the balls of his feet so he wouldn't be heard, he made his way to the end of the path and peeked around toward his car.

"What the fuck?" he whispered to himself as Mark proceeded to load a large black plastic bag into the back of his truck. It looked like he was going to put the evidence in the car and not leave it in the station.

That bit of intel was a comfort. It meant that he didn't trust Hobday.

Mark went back inside, came back with another bag, also in black plastic, about the size and weight of the second evidence bag. When Mark went back inside again, Harcourt could hear sounds inside the building, as if he was throwing metal things around. A few minutes later, the back door opened and something heavy and metallic clanged onto the ground. Then the back door of the police station was locked and Harcourt saw Mark heave a heavy-looking duffel bag into the back.

He knew it had to have weapons in it.

Mark slammed the door shut and Harcourt pulled his face back behind the corner, breathing hard. When he heard the front door open and the car fire up, he sprinted back to the front of the police station. He was leaning casually against the window of the police station, trying to calm his breathing when Mark pulled up.

"Get in," Mark said.

As he entered, he saw that Mark was moving a large envelope off the seat. Harcourt could read the words printed in the upper corner.

Dogwood Canyon Case

Neither man spoke as they drove, and Harcourt was too exhausted to care about anything except getting some sleep.

27 SABRINA

When Maggie and I arrived at her house, she sent me straight to the guest room, where I was ordered to take a shower. She wanted to take my dirty clothes and wash them for me, but I was thinking about my shaman herbs and didn't want her messing with them.

"Let me bring them down to you after my shower," I said.

She came back a few moments later with a nightgown and a robe, and let me be.

After my shower and after removing all my vision sticks and the last of the money I'd received from Harcourt, I took my clothes down the hall. As I'd promised I put them in the laundry room. Maggie wasn't around, but I could hear water running upstairs. Assuming she was taking her own shower,

I started the load of clothes myself, putting them on a speed wash. After having a glass of milk, I headed back to my room.

We'd been back at the house almost an hour since leaving Dogwood Canyon and it troubled me that Mark and Harcourt still hadn't returned. I wanted to knock on Maggie's door and ask her about it, but the house was so quiet, I'd suspected she'd already gone to bed.

Hungry, I went back to the kitchen and helped myself to some crackers and another glass of milk.

I was too wired to sleep, so I ambled into the living room and turned on a lamp. The living room had a comfortable, lived-in feeling with overstuffed chairs and couches arranged around a coffee table. I sat on the plush couch and ran my fingers over the stack of coffee-table books, noticing the titles. Trees of Western Canada, and The Organic Farmer, and Mushroom Hunting in Canada.

I didn't feel much like reading, so I got up when I noticed the wall of photos down the hall. I turned on the light so I could see what I'd missed when I'd walked past before and started at one end, staring at each photo as if visiting art in a museum.

A wave of sadness washed over me, like it always did when I looked at another family's wall of photos. Over the years, as I'd gone from foster home to foster home, I'd stare at these walls of belonging, hoping that one day there'd be my picture on the wall.

Of course, the foster parents probably did put my picture up after I left, not that I'd ever returned to find out, but it wasn't the same as being in a real family.

My chest tightened as I thought about Jeannette and Ellis. Had Cerise passed along the word that I was okay, or was Jeannette going out of her mind with worry? I put my hand on the wall to steady myself as I thought of something else. The darn fire was all over the news, and if Jeannette hadn't gotten word from Cerise, hell, even if Cerise told her I made it Diversion, the news of the fire had to be stressing her out.

I was about to leave the hallway and go see if I could find a landline and make another attempt at a call, when a picture on the wall caught my eye, and I stopped dead in my tracks.

Most of the pictures I'd been admiring so far were the one's you'd expect. Mark and Maggie and their daughter at various stages of their lives. There were also pictures of other friends and relatives scattered throughout, but this one had none of the Pearson family in the picture.

This one was of a different family.

Raymondson Family Moves in After Completing Dogwood Mansion Renovations read the headline of a framed article. I stepped closer for a better look at Harcourt and his family.

His petite wife with her willowy body was at home in a smart pantsuit and hair straight out of Mayberry. On his other side, he holds onto a scrawny boy whose head barely comes up to Harcourt's thigh. Three or four years old, I estimate. I notice the same thatch of unruly brown hair as his father and my breath catches. Hark is relaxed, acknowledging the camera, a serene glow on his face. His wife and son don't seem to know the camera is there. They only have beaming, loving eyes glued on the man in the middle.

My chest squeezed hard and I had to look away. Just like his home, those people were gone for good.

I understood how that felt. Oh, did I understand...

I was five years old when my mother and I went to visit an old friend of hers that was living in the south of Seattle, but who had once lived in the same village that my mother had come from in Africa.

We'd visited her a few times before, and as usual, they wanted me to keep busy in the living room while they got to play in a back room in the house. But that night I was bored watching television, so I'd crept back into the room and peeked through the door.

"Hey, you, little one," said my mother's friend when she spotted me spying on them.

Momma started to scold me, but her friend said, "Watch what we do, little one—someday you'll be a shaman just like us. It's in your blood."

I didn't know what a shaman was, but I was happy not to be excluded from their game. The room had a wall of colorful objects and they played their game standing in front of it. They wouldn't let me near it, but they gave me a doll to play with, a strange little doll with no eyes.

I sat quietly and watched as they continued their game. They lit candles, moved around the room, and burned smoking twigs that filled the room with a strong smoke that made me sneeze. They spoke in the language of my mother's tribe, and then they started to sing and chant.

At one point they shared the same decorated bottle, and even from the back of the room, the strong smell made me wipe my nose. I thought they'd swallowed the foul drink, but a second later they both started spraying it out of their mouths all over their toy wall.

Candles hissed, and I squealed with delight.

Their singing and dancing and chanting got more crazy, so I jumped out of my chair and started to mimic them, waving my arms, and trying to copy their sounds.

When they'd finished, I remember my mother's friend picking me up in the air and kissing me on my forehead, then saying to my mother, "Oh, your little Sabrina, she's a natural. Did you feel the power she brought?"

Then she turned to me. "Sabrina, you'll make a fine shaman someday. It's in your blood, and it's right here."

She tapped so hard on my chest in the spot where my heart was that it almost hurt. And yet I felt so proud. I was going to be a great shaman...

As we drove back home, I kept trying to get my mother to explain what a shaman was, and how soon I'd be one. She said that a shaman was a person who could make things happen, and heal people and bring harmony to the world.

She told me to let her concentrate on her driving, because a bad storm had come up. Each mile, her good mood changed. It was raining like crazy and the windshield wipers were going full blast. My mother leaned forward in her seat as she tried to see through the sheets of rain.

"Momma?" I said, worried because she seemed so worried.

And that's when she turned to and looked at me, then reached over and grazed her knuckles across my cheek.

"I love you, Sabby," she said, her voice the saddest I ever heard.

I remember smiling at her, and I was about to tell her that I loved her too, but then that's when the accident happened, and the words never had a chance to leave my lips.

I remember coming awake, crying because of the pain on my forehead, and then I saw my momma, sitting right next to me, her eyes open still looking out the window. No matter how loud I screamed, or how much I begged, she wouldn't look at me, she wouldn't turn her head, she wouldn't move. I tried to reach out to her, to touch her, but my hands couldn't reach her. My legs were stuck and I was pinned in my seat. The rain wouldn't stop, and some of it ran over my mother's still face and body through the crack in the windshield.

I remembered what they'd told me, that someday I'd be a great shaman. Helpless and alone, I cried all night long, trying to be the great shaman right then and there, trying to make the magic that would that would bring my momma back to life.

But I couldn't do it.

I failed.

I wasn't a shaman, like they'd said...

I wiped my nose with the back of my arm, and forced away that horrible memory from my mind.

I looked at the picture of Harcourt and his happy family one more time, and found my eyes focusing on the little boy. Hairs rose on the back of my arm, and I felt a powerful connection to that child.

I shook my head. That made no sense at all. Clearly, I was in desperate need of sleep.

I turned off the light in the hallway and went back to my room. But I didn't crawl into bed, nor turn off the lights in my room. I was still too wired to sleep.

Something was nagging at the back of my mind. I thought about the image of Harcourt's little boy again. What was his name? Oh, yes. They'd mentioned it in the article. Sharon and Cedric.

That made me think of the stack of letters I'd brought along to read. That's why the picture of little Cedric was getting to me. It reminded me of the pictures of the missing boys and girls sent by those hopeful parents, courtesy of Merge Right Studio's bullshit publicity stunt.

I thought about my mother's friend from way back then. She'd said I would be a great shaman someday, and Bella Bella, who'd never met me or even heard of me before, said the same thing.

Maybe there was something to it.

Pulling my purse onto my lap as I sat on the edge of the still-made bed, I pulled out the small stack of letters. It was just a sampling of the ones that had arrived in giant mail bags after the studio made their announcement.

I'd decided to take some with me as evidence of cruel and unusual punishment before I split, to show to an attorney if I could ever afford one. But after having ignored them for a few months, I was working up the courage to open a few more. I guess that's why I'd brought them on the trip with me.

But at that moment, I was glad that I had.

Something had happened when I was ten. Call it magic, or a psychic phenomenon, or signs of severe mental illness, or whatever you want—there was no doubt that I'd seen through the eyes of those two kids I'd saved. How else could you explain me going into what the shrinks called a fugue state, then proceeding to draw detailed pictures of children I'd never seen before? That included the clothing they were actually wearing, and then also detailed pictures of their two kidnappers. There was no other explanation. Like Bella Bella had said, I had the gift.

For the first time since I was five years old, I was excited about trying to be a shaman.

I spread out the letters beside me on the bed and opened the first one.

It took all I could do not to start bawling as I read the account of the family who'd last seen their child in front of an ice cream store while vacationing in northwest Oregon. All the letters included at least one photo, often more of the missing child. This little boy whose name was Alex was a goofy, big-eared six-year-old boy with freckles and a missing front tooth.

I closed my eyes, and held up his picture to my forehead with one hand, and found that my other hand was holding onto the amber owl at my throat.

I rubbed the owl, and tried to picture the child in my mind's eye.

"Alex, are you still alive?" I asked.

Nothing.

I sighed and put away the letters. I thought about chewing some vision stick, but then I found myself yawning violently and my eyes were heavy as stones. I went to the bathroom one last time for the night, noticing the guest toothbrush and toothpaste Maggie had left for me. After brushing my teeth, I turned off the lights and crawled into bed.

My last thought before falling asleep was that I should get up and check to make sure Harcourt and Mark had made it back safe. But I was too tired, and the thought quickly faded as exhaustion took over.

.

28 HARCOURT

At 2 a.m. when they got back to Mark's house, Harcourt was dead on his feet. Mark locked Hark's car in the garage. As they walked through the mudroom, where a washer and dryer sat with a stack of folded clean clothes on one side, Harcourt held out his hand to his friend. "Can I have my keys?"

Mark opened the door into the house and they stepped into the kitchen. He opened the refrigerator and pulled out a shrink-wrapped plate of cut sandwiches and grabbed them each a beer.

"My keys?" Harcourt said, ignoring the food and the beer.

"Look. I think it's best that your car and everything in it remains in police custody for now," Mark said before taking a slug of his beer and then a bite of his sandwich.

Harcourt shrugged, popped off the cap to his beer, gulped some down, then started eating as well. When he'd finished eating, his head didn't hurt as much and his thoughts had cleared a bit.

"Can you at least bring in my briefcase? It's just in the back seat," he added.

Mark groaned as he stood up and tried to roll away a kink in his neck. "Can it wait until morning?"

"No, not really. I've got some work I need to do. Please, Mark."

"Whatever."

A few moments later, Mark called for Harcourt to come to the mudroom.

Harcourt saw that his friend was lifting the briefcase with two fingers and placing it into the utility sink. "You clean this off before you take it into Maggie's house, or you and I will both regret it."

"I understand." Harcourt said.

As if her ears were burning, Maggie appeared in the doorway of the mudroom, holding a bundle of folded clothes and towels in her arms. "Glad you guys finally made it home. What took you so long?"

"This and that, Maggie. Firemen stuff."

"Oh, yeah?" she said, her eyes narrowing. But then the suspicious expression vanished as she yawned.

Harcourt lifted his eyebrow at her outfit, and the corners of his mouth gave an upward tug. In her fluffy pink bathrobe and fluffy pink slippers, Maggie was almost comically cute.

"These are for you," she said to Harcourt, indicating the items in her arms.

"Thank you," Harcourt said as he reached for them.

Maggie spun away, "Not so fast. Harcourt, I want you to use our room. It's the first door on your right at the top of the stairs. Please take a shower, then put these clothes on. Leave your dirty clothes on the bathroom floor and I'll see that they're washed."

Maggie had a hand on her hip as she gave Harcourt a stern look, as if daring him to fight her. Harcourt lifted his eyebrow, glanced at Mark who was giving him the "you better not try and argue with her" look. He shrugged, then taking care not to touch anything with his soot-stained clothes, headed up the stairs with Maggie right behind him.

After he'd finished his shower, and dressed in Mark's pajamas, Harcourt went into the kitchen to let them know he was done. Maggie got up sleepily from her seat at the kitchen table and showed him where she'd made up a bed for him on the couch in the living room.

"Thank you for doing this," Harcourt said.

After Mark and Maggie left to go to their room, Harcourt switched off the light and settled onto the couch. His thoughts went back to Sabrina. They hadn't said a word about her, and he wondered if she was even there. Of course she was he told himself, then crawled under the covers.

In the dark, he stared at the unfamiliar ceiling, and thought about Sabrina.

He'd been a real dick to her, after coming off the hill.

The way he refused to talk to her, refused to even look at her.

It wasn't her fault that two of his homes had burned down.

It wasn't her fault that he'd found Cedric's skull in his wife's cottage.

It wasn't her fault that someone was trying to frame him for murder.

He was closing his eyes when he heard footsteps on the stairs. The pink slippers appeared around the corner, and Harcourt sat up and saw Maggie moving toward the mud-room, holding his and Mark's clothes at arm's length.

"Hey Maggie," Harcourt said, trying not to scare her. "I take it Sabrina's here somewhere?"

"Yes, she is," Maggie said, then seemed to wait for more on that subject.

"Thanks for having me," Harcourt said instead.

"Of course."

She paused.

"I'm really, really sorry about your house, Harcourt."

"Thanks," Harcourt replied. The loss of two homes wasn't what was on his mind, but he didn't want to explain that to Maggie. "Maggie, you look beat. My mind is still spinning. If you want, I'd be happy to transfer those clothes to the dryer when they're done."

"Would you mind?"

"Not at all."

Not wanting to sit in the dark while he waited for the clothes to finish washing, Harcourt went into the kitchen and had another beer.

To start the dryer, he had to pull out a load of clothes. When he started folding them, and realized that they were the jeans and T-shirt that Sabrina had been wearing, his heart raced.

Once he'd had the dryer going, he went back into the living room. He tugged off his pajama top, relishing the cool air against his skin. He never slept in pajamas, even on the coldest night. Acknowledging an urge to take a leak, he got up and walked down the hallway, then opened the door to what he thought was the bathroom. As soon as he realized his mistake, he pulled the door shut, then changed his mind and inched the door back open.

Sabrina lay on a bed at the other end of the room. Silvery moonlight came through the uncurtained window, illuminating her curves. Harcourt had to grab onto the frame of the door to stop himself from moving into the room and crawling under the covers and just holding that vision in his arms all night.

Shaking his head, he closed the door. He leaned his back against the wall and rubbed at his forehead.

He didn't have time for this.

Stumbling down the hall, he found the correct door and splashed cold water on his face, all the while the image of amazing body throbbed behind his eyelids.

He splashed more water on his face, and after drying it with a towel, he stared into the mirror. Placing his hands on the side of the sink, he dropped his head.

Sabrina. What the hell have you done to me, woman?

"Fuck it," he said, and was about ready to go back through that door and at least sit by her bed and breathe in her scent for a moment, when a wiser voice prevailed and stopped him.

Instead, he relieved himself, washed his hands, and reminded himself that there were times when thinking with his dick was absolutely the wrong move. And this would be one of those times. There were too many issues to deal with; too many serious problems that required his full concentration.

A shit storm was coming with his name on it.

This was not the time to get distracted by that woman.

Hadn't she already distracted him enough?

Convinced that he'd talked himself out of making a big mistake, Harcourt headed back down the hallway and didn't allow himself to even look at her door. Tomorrow he'd think clearer, he told himself. But first he needed to get some sleep. In the morning, he'd unvolunteer himself, and hope that Mark would be too busy with the fire to do anything drastic, like lock him up.

On his way back to the living room, Harcourt remembered his briefcase in the mudroom.

Deciding that he'd clean it in the morning, he opened it and got out his checkbook and a pad and a pen.

He wrote out a check which he hoped would cover her car and a few day's expenses, then wrote a note, saying, "I wish you well."

He stared at the note, then ripped it up.

He could at least have the balls to say thank you and goodbye.

He'd give her the check in the morning, and be quick about his explanation. Before she could do something or say something that might make him regret his decision, he'd go for a walk toward downtown and do his best to stay clear of Sabrina Cane.

It was almost three in the morning when Harcourt finally felt sleep approach, but his last thoughts before his body finally succumbed to slumber was the image of Sabrina, her face flushed with excitement as she rose from the muck, a squealing Mr. Piggy safely in her arms.

I woke up with a start. I was in a strange room, and it took me a moment to place where I was.

Mark and Maggie's house. Right.

I sat up as other memories came to the forefront. A massive mansion. Harcourt's home a blazing inferno on the hill.

Then I remembered his face after he'd come back. The deadness, the sadness, the distance.

I shut my eyes tight against the pain as the memory of how he seemed to want nothing to do with me slammed against the inside of my head.

"Sheesh, give the dude a break!" I said as I slammed my fist against the pillow. "Not everything is about you."

Eventually, I had to get up and just make sure they'd made it back. I tiptoed into the living room and my heart leapt at the sight of Harcourt lying on the couch. I'd left the Tiffany lamp on in my bedroom and it cast just enough light that I could make out his features.

"God, you're beautiful," I whispered as I saw his bare chest rise and fall.

Satisfied that the men were back, I returned to my room, but something was nagging me and keeping me from falling asleep. Thinking I'd figure out what was troubling me in the morning, I crawled back under the covers and lay there, waiting for sleep.

And then it hit me.

I rose out of bed, breathing hard.

Throwing back my shoulder, I opened the door and stalked into the living room.

For once in my life, I wasn't going to wait for other people to hand me crumbs.

I wanted to make love to Harcourt Raymondson one last time, and this time I was going to make sure I got to feel what he tasted like in my mouth.

Harcourt is lying naked on his back in a field of rose petals. His eyes are closed, and he can't see what's happening, but he recognizes the sensation. Between his legs something wet and smooth and warm and soft is feeling around, seeking, pleasuring. He moans into the scent of rose petals, when an eager tongue joins the lips in prodding, tasting, sucking, gently tugging him to life. The rush of blood seems to flow from his brain through his body, past his heart to his cock. It's the kind of dream you don't want to disturb. He doesn't want to wake up…. Not yet.

Despite his attempts to stay asleep, a rush of pleasure quakes through his loins, opening Harcourt's eyes, evaporating the bed of rose petals. He sits up slightly, afraid to move too quick, afraid to disturb the deliciousness, the heat. Shock at the scene playing out before him is replaced quickly by joy and delight and a powerful urge to thrust. But he doesn't move, fearing that any movement would break the spell and wake him up.

He must be dreaming… it's too amazing to be real.

Harcourt was lying on his back on the couch watching Sabrina's head slowing rising, then falling over his alert shaft. After a moment of shock and alarm, he gave in to the dream-come-true and caressed the smooth skin at the base of her neck. She groaned, back arching at his touch and swallowed him in deeper. He shut his eyes and savored the feel of her lips, his mind barely registering that they were in Mark and Maggie's living room, with Mark and Maggie just up the stairs. What if they came down?

Her fingers tickled his abs as her mouth continued bringing him fully awake.

"Sabrina," he murmured. She lifted her eyes, his blood pumping at the sight of the fire in them. She kept her luscious lips moving around him, pressing like a gentle vise.

He was engorged, harder than he'd ever been, and when she finally released her lips from his shaft, there was a popping sound followed by a smacking noise as his freshly sprung cock flew free and bounced against her face.

Sabrina's eyes widened, and laughter danced in her eyes.

Harcourt groaned deeply, and threw back his head as she gripped him and began to tease the rim with her tongue.

"Fuck," he said.

His chest heaved up and down and his hips rocked with her movements. His hands couldn't stop reaching for her skin, touching, caressing. He realized that while he'd still been asleep, Sabrina had pulled his pajamas down, and he felt them binding his feet at the ankles.

Wanting his legs free for what would come next, he carefully removed the pants using his feet and toes. Sabrina had managed to suck him deep into her throat.

"Oh, God, Sabrina."

His balls were filling up. He felt heat building at the base of his spine. He wasn't ready to come yet. Not until...

Gently, but firmly, he put his hands on her head and shoulders and guided his cock out of her mouth.

She beamed at him, her burnished skin glistening with moonlight and pre-cum. Her chest heaved from her exertions and she seemed unwilling to let him go, her tongue flicking back toward her need. He'd never seen anything sexier in his life.

She didn't want to stop.

She wanted to make him come.

She wanted to bring him pleasure.

God, what a woman.

"Sabrina, please," he said as he gently moved her away from his cock. She didn't fight him. She wanted to please him. He reached for the fabric of her nightgown and lifted it off her body, and sucked in air at the sight of her breasts bouncing in the moonlight.

"Come here," he said as he got off the couch and guided her onto her back.

He climbed up onto the couch and positioned one knee between the couch and the woman beneath him, then placed his other foot securely on the floor. Sabrina's fingers guided his cock back into her mouth, and he leaned over her body and rested his cheek against her stomach, taking a moment to fill his lungs with her scent.

And then he lifted her up, one hand cupping her buttock, while he spread her knees with his face. "Sabrina, do you taste as good as you feel?" he asked, teasing the inside of her thighs with a flick of his tongue. She raised her hips toward him, but continued sucking his cock.

His first taste of her hot pussy sent him over the edge.

Something inside let loose, like a dandelion blowing in the wind. He slurped and sucked and brought in his fingers, not holding back, until she convulsed around him, and his body let go.

Time seemed to stop as the pleasure blocked all thoughts, all troubles, all worries, all sadness, all pain.

After their breathing had become less ragged, he realized they'd fallen onto the carpet.

He helped her up onto the couch and held her close, kissing her lips, savoring the moment.

A loud crackling noise made them both jump.

Sabrina hurried to find her night gown, and Harcourt helped her into it. They started to giggle as he searched for his pants, and stumbled as he hopped on one foot trying to put them on.

"Hurry," she laughed.

The sound came again, and Harcourt recognized the crackle of a radio.

"Hammond to Pearson, Hammond to Pearson. Come in."

Harcourt saw that there was a radio next to the TV. Harcourt went over to the radio as he heard movement upstairs.

"Go," Harcourt said to Sabrina.

He smiled as she rushed, giggling, back to her room.

He turned on a nearby light, so he could figure out the radio, then answered.

"Harcourt Raymondson, here. Mark's sleeping. Over."

"Wake him up. It's urgent," said Hammond.

29 SABRINA

My heart raced and I couldn't stop smiling as I threw myself into my room and tried to stifle my giggles with a pillow. I'd never done anything so bold in my life, and it had paid off big. Damn.

Quivering energy bolted through my sated body and my mind swooned.

Hearing voices in the living room, I got under the covers in case Maggie thought to check on me. The men spoke in urgent, yet hushed voices in the other room as they prepared to deal with a fire crisis of some kind. I couldn't resist the urge to keep dip my hand under the cotton sheets and touch myself, where so recently Harcourt had ravished me with his lips.

Each press of my fingers against my aching, soaking sex reminded me that we weren't finished. I needed him back inside me, and my fingers coaxed and circled until my back arched and my breathing quickened.

The slam of the front door, followed by the turn of a car's engine, startled me back to the present. Mark and Harcourt were heading out. Putting on the robe which lay on the overstuffed chair, I stumbled into the bathroom and stared at my swollen lips. I put my hands to my face and breathed in his scent, and felt the tears begin to fall.

I knew it was over. I had to cut things off.

If I didn't, I might never be able to pry myself away from that man.

I couldn't risk staying with him, because the longer I did, the more likely he'd discover my secret. And if he knew that...

I closed my eyes, not wanting to face that scenario.

With a heavy heart, I made my decision. In the morning, I'd ask Maggie to take me to the shelter while the men caught up on their sleep. And despite my commitment to ending the affair, I didn't want to let go of him, not yet. I ran my nose along my arm, sensing for traces of Harcourt, memorizing his musk.

Knowing that he'd have to face these hard times without a friend only added to the guilt. But what kind of friend, what kind of lover, kept such a secret as I'd done? No, he was better off without me. On top of everything else he was going through, I couldn't let Jack's anger and jealousy add to his pile of troubles. No. If I ended it now, before things got more serious, there was hope that both of us would come out whole.

I lay there, not believing a word of what I'd decided to do, and wrapped my arms up to my face, trying to memorize the scent of his body which still lingered on my skin. I kept hanging on to the last moments we'd been together until I eventually dropped my arms and cried myself to sleep.

I'm in a forest. I'm running through the trees. Something is chasing me, and I try to turn my head to look behind me, but I can't see anything. My heart is pounding and the forest thins. I'm in a clearing now and I stop. I spin around, but my feet aren't moving. It's as if I'm on a Lazy Susan, a carousel, a music box.

I'm back in that room again and I'm cross-legged on the floor. My hands are holding a giant pair of scissors. I'm cutting paper, faster, faster, and with each cut the floor fills. The sea of snipped paper grows around me, and I stand up, but I can't stop cutting. My hands are sticky and my mind thinks "glue," but when I look my hands, I don't see glue, only blood. The blood is pouring out of my fingertips, and adding to the paper sea. "No," I try to say as the sea of paper and blood fills the room.

I try to walk to the door, to move my arms to swim to safety, but I can't move. The bloody paper sea rises to my neck. I'm going to drown. I want to scream for help, but my jaw is frozen shut. And then I hear it. The voices. The voices of all the missing children. "Help us," they say in a chorus. "Help find us."

"I can't," I say, "I don't know how."

A young boy crawls out of a dark tunnel, reaching out to me. "Yes, you can, you have to."

My eyes open and the boy and the sea are gone. I lift my hands in the air and stare at my fingers. It's not blood, but there is something sticky. Then I remember the wall. I turn toward it, and rip out another piece of paper from the big book. I see the color I need for the little boy's eyes and start to tear, tear, tear.

"Sabrina, what are you doing?" There's a woman standing before me in a pink fluffy robe. She's throwing a blanket over my naked body that I keep pushing away. I'm too hot for a blanket. "Sabrina, Sabrina, wake up," she shouts.

"I need scissors and glue," I tell her, then go back to the table and flip the pages in the large book. A page with colorful mushrooms appears and I see what I'm looking for. I grab the edge and begin to tear.

"Mom, what the hell is going on?"

Another person is in the room, but she isn't wearing fluffy slippers. Maybe she can help me. "Scissors, glue?" Neither person makes a move to help me out, but I can't worry about that now. I've got an image to create. I move back to my spot on the plush carpeted floor and gather up my already torn sheets of paper. I move away from the fluffy pink woman and the girl in the red sweatpants and sit myself back down, crossing my legs as I concentrate on my pile.

The image I want to create comes into my mind in wisps of colors and shapes and I know what I must do. I start sorting. Dark colors on the right. Light colors on the left.

Oranges with yellows, blues with greens, violets and purples with reds, and all the skin-toned pieces sorted by race.

"Mom, what's going on? Why is she naked?"

"Just help me, Lynette," I hear the fluffy woman say.

"Where are we going?" I ask, protesting, as they pull me off the floor. "No," I moan, trying to catch the memory, the vision, the image before it's all gone.

"You're sleepwalking, Sabrina. Please let us take you back to bed..."

They are so nice I don't fight them. But maybe they can help. "Can I have scissors and glue?"

The girl in the red sweatpants doesn't like that plan. She whispers into the fluffy lady's ear, loud enough for me to hear. "Mom, don't you dare give her scissors." Which makes me sad.

Fluffy shushes the negative Nelly in the red sweats and promises me that I can have all the scissors and glue I want after I take a short nap. As a wave of exhaustions threatens to buckle my limbs, I don't argue and let them guide me to an unfamiliar room and place me onto an unfamiliar bed...

30 CONSTABLE HOBDAY

If not for the clouds of black smoke lingering over the town like a toxic London fog, Constable Hobday would have been facing the dawn with a cloudless sky. Sweat beaded from his forehead as he hoisted himself up the steel joists of the cell phone tower, and secured his finger around the metal box. He grunted, giving the box a yank, and the magnetic hold released. He dropped the box to the ground, wishing he'd climbed down as his head throbbed at the impact.

He took a moment to shake away the discomfort as he regretted those extra beers at the local bar. But then again, he needed information, and in a small town there was no place like the local drinking hole for that.

He'd meant to get up to the tower before dawn, so no one would see him in his police car, but the drinking had screwed up that plan. It still hadn't been daylight for long and it was unlikely that anyone would notice or care about the Mountie near the cell tower.

He got to work, turning his back so the glaring sunlight wouldn't blind him. He unscrewed the cover then removed the batteries. He tore open a new pack of 9-volts and slotted them inside. He screwed on the metal cover and was about to climb up and hide the device under a joist when he decided to test the device first. If he was caught in possession of a signal disrupter like the one he had, he could get into a lot of trouble, as such devices were illegal in both the US and Canada. But he'd managed to obtain one, since they were available for sale in Russia and China, used by the governments to prevent free speech and prop up lies. He checked his phone, expecting to see no signal, but instead he had three bars of coverage.

"Damn it, I don't need this right now," he said the silence around him.

He unscrewed the cover, and checked the battery placement. They were properly set within the device. He pulled out the batteries, and using his tongue to test for a charge, he discovered that one of the brand new 9-volts was a fucking dud. Since he had no other choice, he took one of the drained, but not totally dead batteries and replaced the dud. When he checked his phone again, the cell coverage was no longer available.

He put the cover back, and put the box up closer than before. He'd just have to get better batteries and get back as soon as possible. Given that one of the batteries was close to the end of its life, Hobday didn't know if the cell disrupter would work for the rest of the day, or die in the next ten minutes. He hoped that if the coverage did come back, Harcourt wouldn't notice, or wouldn't be able to arrange his way out of Diversion. After cursing himself for buying off-brand batteries, Hobday let himself slide as much as walk back down the steep, craggy hill to his car. Once he was inside, after wiping the grit and dirt off his uniform pants, he gunned the engine and headed back to town.

He was due to call in again in just three hours for another report, and he wasn't looking forward to it.

Needing name-brand 9-volts to put in the cell phone disrupter, Hobday went to Eddy's Gas and Garage, since it was only 7 a.m. and the general store wouldn't open till nine. Inside the market, he found what he was looking for, and decided to buy a coffee and Danish to go. The bell chimed and two of the locals walked in. Hobday grabbed a magazine to cover his purchase, then read it and sipped some coffee, opting to check out once the two newcomers had gone.

"Did you see the TV folks out there?"

"Yup, they were taking pictures of the town, last I saw."

Hobday looked out the window, not pleased that television crews were in town. He wondered how they'd arrived and for a moment he feared that his work on the bridge had been inadequate and the they'd fixed it already.

"Excuse me, boys," he said walking over to the two men.

They stiffened, not an uncommon response to his presence, especially when he was in uniform. "Who's in town? Television people?"

"Yes, Constable, Channel 8 and Channel 4."

"How did they get in here? Is the bridge fixed?"

"Helicopter..."

"Is there an airfield in town?"

"Yup, they used to do tours up there until the company shut down, but the port is still good, so that's where they're going. Heard they got the radio tower up and running too."

"Interesting. Mind telling me where it is?"

After the boys gave him directions, which oddly enough were only a mile past his cell phone tower, Hobday bought the magazine and started back to his car. He'd filled up, so he didn't need more gas. He'd just opened his door when he overheard more of the young men's conversation.

"I bet those media idiots will end up at Dogwood Canyon today. You hear about the mansion burning down? Crying shame. You heading up there?"

"Nope, I'm going to the reservation. I need to call my aunt."

"What, they've got reception up there?"

"No, but that old witch doctor lady has a satellite phone. I hear she's letting anyone who needs to use it and have a few minutes of time. I need to call my mom in Montreal. She's probably been worried sick about me."

Hobday went back inside and asked Eddy, "Can you tell me how to get to the reservation?"

"The rez?"

"Yes."

Armed with two bits of disturbing news, the existence of a way in and out—namely a helicopter port and the existence of a second satellite phone—made Hobday reconsider his call into the boss. Especially since he'd lost track of his target, and with his house no longer in play, he wasn't sure he'd be able to track him down again.

He tried to decide what to do first. After much consideration, he decided. First, he'd secure the second satellite phone to prevent Harcourt from having a way to call out. Then he'd replace the batteries in the disrupter and then he'd check out the helicopter port and see what he could find out. If Harcourt had somehow managed to make a reservation, he could use his badge to keep him from taking the flight. If the helicopter option proved unlikely, then he could drive up to the property and hopefully catch Harcourt returning to go through the rubble.

It would be nice to see his face when he found the surprise.

And if Harcourt didn't come, he could be a visible threat and keep the curious reporters and neighbors from finding the surprise before Harcourt did.

Worried that curiosity seekers could be already up on the hill, Hobday pressed down the gas and hurried toward the reservation.

MIA CALDWELL

The emergency which had forced Harcourt and Mark to leave the house early was somewhat of a letdown. Simon Duvet, a man in his late sixties who'd lived in Diversion all his life, was a notorious alcoholic who managed to get himself into trouble about once every quarter. That morning, a neighbor walking his dog spotted Simon stuck on his roof. By the time Harcourt and Mark arrived, Lester Faraday, who was a neighbor, had already roused Fred Hammond who also didn't live far away. They'd managed to extract the man from the roof without letting him fall.

"What's his condition, Lester?" Mark asked when they arrived.

"Drunk," Lester said. "You want him to sleep it off in your jail, or should we put him inside in his bed?"

"His house is fine," Mark said. "I don't have time to deal with him today."

"10-4 boss."

Lester and Fred scooped up the man under both arms and Harcourt and Mark lifted his feet. Together they carried him inside and plopped him onto his bed.

"If you see any alcohol in the house, hide it somewhere in the garage. Oh, and don't forget, we're still having roll-call at eight sharp."

"I was hoping to get the day off," Fred said.

"Me too," Lester said.

"Me three," Mark quipped, "But then again, I also want to have a town to live in, so I'm planning on showing up to work. I expect you to as well."

"Just keep paying us the big bucks."

"Your check is in the mail."

Harcourt and Mark watched the other volunteers drive back to their homes, and Harcourt asked Mark what he planned to do next. After Sabrina's surprise visit in the night, he no longer felt a need to end the relationship.

Mark looked at his watch. "It's a little early, but let's go to the station. I'd like to get on the radio and let some people know about what we found on your property before the others come in. I'd also like to touch base with BC Fire."

Cecil Moore, who'd been with the Diversion Volunteer Fire Department for over ten years and who'd stayed behind when the others went up to the hill the day before, had already opened up the station, and had both engines parked in the driveway. He was hosing down the smaller of the two engines. The water running down the driveway and into the gutters was black with soot. He saluted Mark and nodded to Harcourt.

Mark went inside to get on the radio, after indicating to Harcourt that he'd prefer to work in private. Harcourt went out front to speak with Cecil, who was putting the finishing touches on his truck wash.

Harcourt said, "I need to make some important telephone calls. Any idea how I can do that?"

"Have you tried your cell phone?"

"What? I thought the cell reception was out."

"Well, I just made a call, so I guess they fixed it."

Even though they'd left in a hurry that morning, Harcourt took the time to grab his briefcase and his cell phone.

At the moment, they were both inside Mark's police car. The door was unlocked, so he got his cell phone, but left his briefcase in the car. "I need a charger," he said to Cecil.

"What kind? Android or iPhone?"

"iPhone," Harcourt said.

"Good. There's usually one set up in the break room next to the coffee pot."

Harcourt found the charger next to the coffee pot as Cecil predicted. His phone was completely dead, and he knew it would take a while before he could even power it up. Since there was no coffee brewing and he certainly could use a cup, Harcourt decided to make some. By the time the coffee pot was half-full, his phone beeped to life. As Cecil had said, there were a few bars of coverage. Harcourt saw that there were multiple voicemails waiting to be heard, but he decided that those could wait.

He scrolled through his contacts, then dialed Molly McCarthy.

"Molly, it's me, Harcourt."

"Oh, thank God, Harcourt. I saw on the news about your house. I'm so sorry. Are you all right?"

"I'm fine. Listen, Molly, I need you to do something for me. It's very important. Do you have a pen and paper?"

After he gave her instructions for what he needed her to do, he paused.

"Harcourt?"

"Molly, I don't know yet, but the fire might have taken your home as well. I'm sorry, if that's the case."

There was silence on the other line.

"Molly?"

"If it's gone, it's gone, and there's nothing much I can do about that, is there?"

"Well, maybe it was spared. Call back later and try and reach Mark Pearson. I'm sure he'll have word a little later today when his men go back up the mountain to fight the fire."

"What about you?" she asked.

"I'll stay in town, so I can get to the helicopter port as soon as I get the good word from you regarding my ride out of here."

"Mr. Raymondson, can I ask you a question?"

"Of course."

"Have you been watching the news?"

"No, not really. Is there something I should know?"

"Actually, there is something…" Molly hesitated. "It's about that artist you hired, Sabrina Cane? Did she ever show up? Do you know where she is?"

"Yes, why? I mean, she's been here the whole time. What's this all about?"

"Well, she's kind of a top story. There's kind a lot of people looking for her. You should turn her—"

There was dead air. "Molly? Molly?" Harcourt checked the phone, expecting that it ran out of power, that he'd pulled his head away from the short cord without thinking and had disconnected the charge. But the screen was lit up, and while there wasn't a lot of power, there was enough. What was missing was the bars indicating cell phone reception. There were no more bars.

"Shit," Harcourt said.

"Problem?" Harcourt's heart raced. Mark was reaching for the coffee pot. Had he heard him on the phone? He hated not being totally honest with Mark, not admitting that he was trying to get out of Diversion. He needed to get back to the states and get a lawyer who would protect him from whomever was plotting against him, and away from Canada's confusing legal system.

"Just the damn cell coverage. Cecil said it was live again. I tried to call Molly, but I couldn't get through. Does your cell phone work?"

"You had coverage? That's strange," Mark pulled his cell phone out of his pocket and shook his head. "Nothing on mine."

"Oh, well, maybe Cecil was mistaken, or maybe it was some kind of sun-spot fluke."

Harcourt plugged his phone back into the charger, then came over to Mark so he could speak and not be overheard. "Did you make the call to the you-know-who people?"

Mark was stiff.

"I haven't had a chance to do that yet. I've been talking to BC Fire so far. Just needed some coffee."

"What's going on with the fire?"

"Listen, Harcourt, why don't you help Cecil with the equipment? I'll brief everyone at roll call."

Harcourt nodded, but his stomach twisted. Mark was behaving strangely, as if he'd decided that Harcourt was guilty. Maybe the reason he wanted to make his radio calls privately was because he was arranging for his arrest. The idea that Mark could think for one second that he was capable of committing such a heinous crime hurt Harcourt to the core, but also reminded him that he was on his own and that he had to do what he could to look out for himself.

At eight fifteen, when the rest of the Diversion volunteers had arrived for the morning briefing, Mark finally came out of the captain's office. He didn't look Harcourt in the eye. Mark spoke to his gathered troops, his expression serious. "I hope that you all got plenty of rest, because today might be another long one. I've been on the radio with BC Fire most of the morning. We've got good news and bad news."

"I want the good news first," Lester shouted.

"The good news is that we had four air tankers flying since first light, and they've reported that the Dogwood Canyon fire is now 90 percent contained. More good news is that there appear to have only been five structures burned, including the two on your property, Harcourt."

That was the first time he acknowledged Harcourt's presence, or looked at him. Harcourt nodded.

"So, counting your houses and the rental up the hill, only two homes burned down on Crab Apple Ravine. One of them was vacant. From a property standpoint, it could have been much worse."

"You're saying that Molly's house is still standing?" Fred Hammond asked. Everyone knew that Fred Hammond, who'd been a widower now going on four years, was sweet on Molly McCarthy.

"Apparently so, Fred," Mark said.

"What's the bad news?" asked Cecil Moore.

"There's a couple bits of bad news, Cecil. For starters, as I said earlier, the Dogwood Canyon fire was reported to be 90 percent contained, but the 10 percent that wasn't contained is due to a finger of fire which ran up the shoreline overnight. Unfortunately, it's burned its way up to Shipwreck Harbor."

"Shipwreck Harbor," Lester repeated, clearly alarmed by the news.

"That's right Lester, Shipwreck Harbor, and I need not remind most of you that Diversion was once known as Upper Shipwreck. For obvious reasons this means this is a very alarming development."

Several of the men stood up, as if to get to their gear sooner, to head out and stop the fire before it made it to their town and the homes and the people they cared about.

"The other bad news is that after calling in the containment numbers, BC Fire rerouted three of the four water tankers before it noticed where the last bit of the fire was going, and left us with just one for clean-up."

"Shouldn't one be enough?" inquired Cecil Moore.

"I don't know about being enough, but one would be helpful. Trouble is, the water tanker they left for us was grounded. Engine trouble. Which means for the foreseeable future, we've got zero air support."

"Shit. Isn't the reservation the first stop up the river canyon?" asked Fred Hammond.

"Yeah, and Diversion comes next," Faraday pointed out.

There was a long silence in the room as the danger of the situation sunk in.

Cecil Moore spoke first. "What are your orders, Captain?"

Mark's brows narrowed and he pressed his mouth together as he came up with a plan.

"Okay, here's what we're going to do. Lester, Cecil, you're in charge of protecting the reservation. Get both engines up there and place them between the fire and the reservation. Make sure both trucks are filled with water. Make sure you have full crews on the fire line."

Lester and Cecil nodded, and Cecil spoke up. "Both tanks are full and ready to go."

"Good, Cecil."

Fred started to get up.

"Fred, you need to stay in town. You're in charge of the getting the word out. First, you need to find people willing to help evacuate the rez—I'm talking anyone with a pickup truck and van, and SUV, provided they've got enough gas. Get them up there right away. Harcourt and I will go up there in my cruiser and I'll make sure they understand that the evacuation order is mandatory, not voluntary. Then I'll leave Harcourt in charge of making sure people leave, and then I'll come up and join Lester and Cecil at the fire."

Fred said, "Do you want me to come up and help?"

"No, after you get the evacuation volunteers headed to the rez, I need you to get the word out in town that people should start preparing to evacuate. Make sure everyone knows what's going on. Make sure no one is left stuck without a way to move, should the fire get through the rez, then come down the hill."

"Will do, Captain," Fred said.

Once his orders were given, Mark motioned for Harcourt to join him in his car. Harcourt grabbed his cell phone first and didn't bother to check for bars. He put it in his pocket. They drove quietly, until Harcourt noticed that Mark wasn't going toward the reservation, but rather back into the heart of town. "Where are we going?"

"I need to talk to Maggie. Someone has to ready the gymnasium for all those evacuees."

Harcourt stayed in the car while Mark went inside, because he was hoping that he had cell coverage back and wanted to know if Molly had any luck getting him a flight out of Diversion. But there were still no bars. He dropped the phone into his lap when a horn honked behind him. Harcourt checked the rear view mirror. It was Maggie in her minivan. She jumped out of the car and raced toward Mark, who'd stepped back onto the porch. Harcourt immediately sensed trouble when he saw the look on her face.

Harcourt opened the car door, and planted his feet on the ground, and listened to Maggie.

"Oh Mark, thank God you're here. I was just on my way to the station to find you—"

"What's going on Maggie? What's wrong? Is Lynette okay?"

"She's fine, it's Sabrina."

Harcourt's chest squeezed, and he stood up and hurried over. "What's wrong, what's happened to Sabrina?" He pushed past them and climbed up the stairs to the front door.

"She's not in the house," Maggie said.

"Where is she?" Harcourt asked.

"That's just the trouble, I don't know where she is." Maggie's voice was a bit hysterical.

Mark spoke in a calm, firm voice and held out his hand toward Harcourt, requesting that he calm down as well. "Maggie, please tell us exactly what's going on."

Maggie took a deep breath, then spoke. "After you left, we all went back to sleep, but then I heard something, and when I got up, Sabrina was... well, she was acting very strange. Lynette and I found her, uh, naked in the living room, tearing up paper and trying to stick it to the wall. She was totally out of it, babbling incoherently. Lynette and I decided that she was sleepwalking, and we got her to go back to bed."

She took a breath.

"So she was sleepwalking, and then she went back to bed. What happened?"

"Yeah, she did, I even checked on her and she was asleep. She was sleeping hard when I took Lynette over to her friend's house for the day. I thought Sabrina would be there when I got back, and I'd planned to drag her to the Grill so I could keep an eye on her. But she wasn't in her room when I got home."

"Did she maybe go for a walk?" Harcourt said, running his hand through his hair. "Maybe she's just taking a walk."

"No, Harcourt. She's not on some walk." Maggie's voice was firm. "She took your car, Harcourt. She drove away without saying anything, not a word."

"She took the Mercedes? How did she do that?" Mark said. "I had the keys in our bedroom."

"I don't know, Mark, I guess she found them." Maggie sounded upset and annoyed. "Which reminds me, why in God's green earth were Harcourt's car keys in our bedroom?"

As if Mark couldn't accept the truth that Sabrina had taken the car, he stormed into the house, through the living room and kitchen and mudroom, then opened the door to the garage. Harcourt was right behind him. Maggie wasn't making this shit up. Harcourt's Mercedes and the compromising items inside it were gone.

Back inside the kitchen, Harcourt spoke. "I don't understand what could have happened to her. Explain it again. You said she was sleepwalking and ripping up magazines? None of this makes any sense. Where would she even go with the car?"

"Maybe she was sleep driving. I've heard people do that, especially when on certain medications."

"Was Sabrina on any medications?" Harcourt asked.

Mark was calm. "Maggie, try hard. Is there anything, anything at all that you can tell us that might help us find out where she went?"

"Only that she mentioned the shaman a couple of times, something about how the shaman was right? But I don't get how that can help."

"As in the shaman at the rez?" Mark asked.

"Who knows?"

Mark said, "Listen, Maggie. Forget about opening the Grill today. You're going to be too busy for that."

"What's going on?"

"I came home to tell you that I'm going to order a mandatory evacuation of the reservation. Don't panic, but the fire has made its way to Shipwreck Harbor. Harcourt and I will worry about Sabrina. In the meantime, I need you to gather volunteers and get the evacuation center ready. Can you do that?"

"Of course, Mark."

"One more thing. Take your cell phone and charger with you. There's been some indications of a signal. It might come in handy."

"Okay."

"One more thing. Get Lynette and keep her with you. She can help at the center. I don't want you separated. If we can't stop the fire at the rez..."

"I understand; we'll all be next."

Mark drove his cruiser fast, with sirens and lights on, heading to the reservation. On the road, they passed some of the volunteers already recruited to help with the evacuation, and a tourist company Jeep transporting two men, one a very fat man with a massive video camera in his lap.

"Reporters," Mark said, more to himself than to Harcourt. "Just stay out of my way."

In the center of the reservation, Mark pulled over. "Go over there to the Tribal Community Center and make sure that the word is getting out that the evacuation is mandatory. Make sure they know that people are coming up to help with transportation. Don't take no for an answer."

"Will do."

Harcourt grabbed his briefcase and got out of the car, and Mark gave him a funny look.

"This isn't a business meeting."

"I realize that." Harcourt didn't feel the need to explain further, and Mark sped away, headed toward the clouds of smoke looming with menace at the far end of the reservation.

Harcourt found several leaders of the reservation already telling the populace to prepare to evacuate. He explained that townspeople would be arriving soon, and sure enough, the first of several volunteers arrived. The tribal leaders seemed to have the situation under control. Harcourt decided to turn his attentions to finding Sabrina.

"Is there a shaman in the village?"

"Yes. Grandma Bella Bella. Go east two streets to a big red house. Can't miss it."

The first thing Harcourt saw when he spotted the red house was his car. Relief flooded him. He ran over to it and looked inside, but Sabrina wasn't in it. He tried the doors, which were open, and checked the back. The items in the bags were still there and the keys were in the ignition. He took them out and locked the car.

At least this way, Sabrina couldn't leave when he wasn't looking. She had to be close. He began walking up the steps when he noticed the RCMP cruiser parked a few cars away from his Mercedes. He was about to knock on the door to ask for the shaman when he caught a glimpse of Officer Hobbledick inside the house, carrying something in his arms. Not wanting to have a confrontation with the man at that moment, Harcourt moved around to the side of the house and waited.

A few moments later, the door opened and Harcourt saw Hobbledick hurry to his vehicle with something in his arms. Hobbledick glanced around, as if making sure he wasn't being observed, then he popped open the trunk and stashed whatever he'd been carrying inside. The RCMP officer got into the cruiser and started the engine and was reversing out of his space when the car stopped. Harcourt understood why when he spotted the dozen men and women all dressed in full ceremonial garb coming toward the red house. They turned and disappeared around the other side of the house. Hobbledick turned off his engine, and followed after them.

Harcourt cursed, and tasted fresh ash from the fire in his nostrils, and had to cover his mouth to hide the sound of a cough. The fire was coming closer. He needed to find Sabrina.

Jack Bressler was so proud of himself. He'd managed to convince the BCTV Channel 8 news to put him on the helicopter instead of Marcus Burrard, the usual hot-shot reporter, and had given him a cameraman for the job. He wasn't sure how long it would take to find Sabrina, especially since he'd already heard that the mansion had burned down. He decided, after taking advantage of transport offered by an enterprising young driver who had a business giving tourists a view of the wilds from his Jeep, that he'd just act like a real reporter and he'd find Sabrina soon enough.

He was standing in town doing some reports about the town of Diversion when he heard that people were being sent to the reservation to help with an emergency evacuation because the fire now threatened it.

That was news, and he would provide his viewers a first-hand report. Maybe if he was lucky, he'd get shots of the village burning to the ground. He sighed deeply with satisfaction. He was back in front of the lens. Back where he belonged.

Sabrina was important, but once he found her, he'd have to leave straight away. He hoped he'd have a little time to report the news first.

But then he spotted the Channel 4 helicopter banking toward the helicopter port, and he worried that if they were here looking for Sabrina—thanks to the announcement from her sister that Sabrina was here—that he might not get her in time.

Reluctantly, he gave up his plans to go to the reservation, and started making inquiries.

"Hey, have you seen a pretty black woman up in these parts?"

"You mean Harcourt's new gal?"

Jack had to bite his tongue. "Possibly."

"Isn't that her in that car?"

Jack followed the woman's finger which pointed toward a black Mercedes SUV that looked like it hadn't been washed in a year. Inside it, he saw Sabrina coming toward them, driving erratically.

Jack and the talkative town woman jumped onto the sidewalk. "Well," huffed the woman, clearly not pleased with Sabrina's driving skills. The SUV headed down a side road that seemed to lead out of town.

"Where do you think she's going?"

"I suspect she's joining the other volunteers that are evacuating the rez."

Jack didn't thank the woman. He shouted for his overweight cameraman to get his fat ass to the Jeep. Then he jumped into the passenger seat and hollered to the driver as he pointed toward the SUV. "Follow that car."

"Jesus, don't stop," Jack barked when the Jeep driver stopped, allowing a young mother pushing a stroller and holding the hand of a walking toddler to cross the street.

"I have to," the driver said, nodding with a good-natured smile at the pedestrians.

Jack leaned over in his seat and took hold of the wheel, yanking on it. "Go around them. Come on, you're losing her."

The driver reluctantly did as he was told, his good-natured attitude vanishing. Instead he tried to calm the customer. "Look, you don't need to worry, we'll catch up."

But they didn't, and while Jack caught sight of Sabrina's car as it drove up the windy mountain, the Jeep slowed as it found itself behind a caravan of a slower-moving vehicles.

"Drive around them, you moron!" Jack shouted.

The driver had enough. He jerked the wheel, and pulled off into a turnaround, coming to a screeching halt in the dirt.

"What the hell are you doing?" Jack asked.

"Get the fuck out of my jeep," the driver said.

Jack climbed out, and his cameraman started to get up. "Stay put," Jack said.

He walked around to the driver's side of the car and opened the door, then reached in and grabbed the smaller driver by the scruff of the neck. He yanked him out of the car and pulled him away from the car, maintaining a tight grip of the man's collar.

"What the hell are you—"

Jack didn't let him finish his sentence. He pulled his arm back and punched the man in the nose.

The man fell back onto the ground, groaning as he grabbed onto his face. Blood trickled down through the fingers grasping at his broken nose.

Jack got in the driver's seat and put the car into gear and drove away, leaving the driver in the dust.

Jack glanced in the rear view and noticed that the cameraman they'd sent from Channel 8 news looked a little stunned by what he'd just done, but he was either too frightened or too smart to say anything, which suited Jack just fine. As they got closer to the top of the hill, the cameraman found his voice. "Hey, that fire looks pretty close. Mind if I start shooting?"

"Yes, get lots of establishing shots," Jack said.

Jack rubbed his hand over his sore knuckles, and breathed in deeply, expanding his chest. He was in his element now, a reporter again and this close to reclaiming his wife. As the Jeep sped past the stand of poplar trees that lined the main road toward to the entrance of the Talhka-haw'ka reservation, Jack slammed the brakes when a runaway goat appeared out of nowhere right in front of him.

He was forced to drive slowly to avoid hitting anything in the bedlam around him. People were everywhere, running around, loading up cars and trucks, dragging screaming children and barking dogs in their wake. In the distance, smoke rose up in large black plumes, making visibility bad, and breathing even worse. Behind him, Jack heard the whir of the camera. His cameraman was standing up in the back, the heavy camera mounted on his shoulder.

There were small side streets with homes, and he looked down them as he drove by, scanning for signs of Sabrina, or signs of the black Mercedes SUV she'd been driving. He turned when he spotted it, parked haphazardly outside a large red house.

As he approached, he noticed several people dressed in what appeared to be ceremonial clothing at the front of the red house. As he watched, they started toward the back of the house. They weren't in a hurry, and they certainly didn't look like they were trying to evacuate. His reporter radar went off, and he wondered if there might be a good story back there. He also wondered if Sabrina was there.

"Where are you going?" the cameraman asked as Jack put the Jeep in park, removed the key, and jumped out.

"Just keep that camera rolling and follow me," Jack said.

Jack, who had parked the Jeep a few houses away from the red house and Sabrina's car, walked by it and looked inside. She was not in the car. He moved to the side of the house and walked the same path he'd seen the others walk, and the cameraman followed behind him.

"Holy crap," said the cameraman, when they rounded the corner of the house and saw what was happening.

"Turn it off for a minute and set up for my report. Over there."

Jack had spotted Sabrina immediately, but there was no way he was going to interrupt her or the others at that moment by alerting her to his presence. He stayed well away from the activities with his back to it. He knew a golden opportunity when he saw it, a true money-in-the-bank kind of scene. He felt a surge of excitement in his body. It was better than anything he might have thought to arrange, or stage, for dramatic effect. Behind him, there was a ritual happening, and the woman who would help launch his fame and fortune was right in the middle of it. Perfect.

"Get the rain dance in the background," Jack said as he pointed to a spot where he wanted his cameraman to stand. While the cameraman readied the shot, Jack took a powder compact he always kept in his pocket and checked his teeth for food. He smoothed his hair, then powdered away the bit of shine that always reflected off his nose. He straightened his shoulders and took a deep breath, and nodded to the cameraman to start recording.

When the red light came on, he put on a serious face, then spoke with his eyes looking directly into the camera lens.

"This is Jack Bressler, guest correspondent for Channel 8 News Vancouver. The Diversion fire has taken a new turn for the worse, and is now threatening to rip through the main part of the reservation. The town is being evacuated as we speak, but behind me, you are seeing several people who aren't willing to leave yet. What are they doing? I believe they are attempting to fight the fire with magic. They are attempting to summon the powers of nature to bring down rain. At this time, the only clouds in the sky are the clouds of smoke."

Jack fake-coughed a moment, designed to show how he was in the middle of a dangerous situation. Then he motioned for his cameraman to get a picture of the area around the house and the growing wall of smoke in the sky as the fire continued to move toward them. When the camera was back on his upper third, he continued reporting.

"There is more going on than just a front-row seat to a rain dance, folks. I want you to focus on the tall woman in the center of the group, the one with the black hair. Channel 8 Vancouver has found the most sought-after person in Canada and Washington today. Ladies and gentlemen, may I present to you my missing wife, Sabrina Cane. The Sabrina that everyone is looking for."

He paused, letting that bombshell announcement sink in as the camera closed in on Sabrina. He watched her. She held a doll in the air, and she was singing something he couldn't hear or understand as she swayed in her spot in the circle. Jack faced the camera.

"After the rain dance is over, I will take my wife away from Diversion and back to the Channel 8 Studios. Stay tuned for the exclusive report—when I will personally, and on camera, ask Sabrina how to find Baby Adalyn."

Just then there was a rumble in the air, and shouts from the people watching the dance as a pine tree exploded into flames. The cameraman lifted the camera to catch the burning tree, lighting up the sky in the distance. Sabrina broke from the edges of the circle and moved into the center. Her hands held a doll and she lifted it high into the sky. Her eyes appeared to be rolled back into her head and her singing became loud and shrill, her words from a different language, unintelligible.

Above the dancers, great dark blue clouds formed, seemingly out of nowhere, rising rapidly in the sky.

The dancing in the circle became more frantic, and the singing, louder, faster.

The blue-white cloud grew and grew, until it filled and darkened the sky overhead. The singing rose to a fevered pitch. Energy sparked around the circle, causing the hair on the back of Jack's neck to stand on end. Suddenly, there was a force of energy that ripped through the circle of dancers, causing each of them to fly backward.

And with their collapse, lighting ripped through the clouds, followed by a roar of thunder that made Jack's heart squeeze in fear. He gathered himself as the rain came down in torrents, yelling toward his cameraman. "Did you see that? Did you see this miracle? It happened because they had the help of Sabrina Cane. My wife, the woman who saved those children ten years ago. Sabrina Cane, the miracle worker who will save Baby Adalyn."

The rain was coming down in buckets by the time Jack made it to Sabrina's side. The other dancers who'd collapsed at the end of their little magic trick had risen, and along with the other spectators had gone to seek shelter while they celebrated their success.

"Turn that off and help me get her out of here," Jack ordered his cameraman. But his cameraman had run to the shelter of the house and was dripping wet, shaking his head. Now that Jack had finished his newscast, he needed to get Sabrina back to the helicopter, and back to Vancouver. Their little broadcast wouldn't be seen by anyone until his crew performed an upload at the helicopter. But there had been spectators that probably heard Jack's announcement of who the woman was.

Police and authorities from two countries were currently searching for the mysterious Sabrina, and he'd already spotted other members of the media in town. He needed to get out of Diversion before the other reporters showed up, and for sure before some RCMP cop or some other asshole with a badge and a gun tried to take Sabrina away from him. They would hand her over to the Canadian Secret Intelligence Service, and ruin his plans to make television broadcast history. He'd get her back to the Jeep, give her a sip of the water he'd already doctored with a good dose of Mexican Valium, so she wouldn't give him any trouble by raising a fuss, then they'd get back to the helicopter and go straight to Channel 8 headquarters in Vancouver. Time was of the essence.

My mouth was dry, so dry, and my head felt like it was filled with fuzz. It was raining all around me, but not on me. I wanted to drink and I opened my mouth and put my head back, but no rain fell into my mouth.

I didn't know where I was. And then I recognized the shaman's backyard. I couldn't remember getting there. There were people milling about. Maybe one of them knew.

There was something in my hand. One of my mother's dolls. I put it in my pocket, and felt something inside. I pulled it out. Pieces of a stick. I smelled it, and had a sudden memory. It was the vision stick, and I'd decided to test it. I was back at Mark and Maggie's house, after another dream.

I wanted to read some letters and see if I could help, see if I had it in me, face my duty in life. I remember eating the vision stick, and walking through the house, and seeing a picture... a picture that sent me over to the other side. What was in that picture?

I scrunched my eyes tightly closed, trying to remember. It was a framed picture on the wall in the hallway. There was a picture of a man, a woman, and a tiny child standing in front of a big house. Billionaire Raymondson to Renovate Abandoned Mansion for Family.

I opened my eyes as a chill went through my body, and I suddenly understood what my vision meant. I needed to tell Harcourt, and I needed to find my purse, my shaman bag. I put the pieces of the vision stick back into my pocket and started to get up.

My vision was still blurred but there was someone standing over me, hands pulling me to my feet. I stared into the face as it came into focus...

The face spoke and I recognized the voice. "Sabrina, here, let me help you."

"Jack?"

Harcourt watched in wonder, mesmerized by the miracle, too stunned to move as the rain came down. But then he saw that Sabrina had collapsed and he started toward her to help her. He'd taken two steps when a massive person slammed into him, knocking him onto the ground. By the time he came around, he saw that some man was helping Sabrina to her feet. Harcourt got up and went to Sabrina's side and tugged at the man's arm. "She's with me."

"No she isn't," said the man and he gave Harcourt a push, knocking him off balance. Harcourt staggered backward, and felt his hands fall into fists. He was about to knock the man clear to Los Angeles when Sabrina opened her eyes and she stared at the man with recognition. "Jack?" she said.

"Sabrina are you all right?" Harcourt said, when he noticed her eyes widening with alarm. He grabbed the man's arm and yanked him away from Sabrina. "I said, let go of her. She's with me."

"And I said that was a crock of bull."

Harcourt shoved the man aside and tried to reach for Sabrina's arm to finish pulling her to her feet, but he didn't see the sucker punch. His jaw exploded with pain and he was knocked off his feet. He grabbed his jaw, then lunged toward the man. "Why you son of a bitch."

"What's going on here?"

A strong hand held Harcourt's arm, impeding his advance. He readied his fist to punch out whoever was trying to stop him, but stopped when he saw the uniform, and recognized Constable Hobbledick.

Harcourt forced himself to calm down. He straightened himself up, and although his breath was heaving, he spoke in as reasonable a tone as he could.

"Officer, I'm glad you're here. That man won't stop harassing my friend." Harcourt was alarmed to see that the man he was about to hit had used the interruption by the constable to lead Sabrina away.

"Hey, come back here!" Harcourt started to go, but was stopped as the constable tightened his grip. The last thing he wanted to do was get into this man's bad graces—or into his custody—with a skull in the back of the car.

"Stay here," Hobbledick ordered. Then he shouted at Sabrina and the reporter. "You sir, come here and leave the girl." The man who was trying to take Sabrina away stopped and turned around and glared at the man in the uniform without hiding his disdain. For a moment, Harcourt thought the man was considering disobeying the order. But he thought better of it. He left Sabrina standing next to a tree and walked back.

"What is going on?" Hobbledick asked.

Harcourt and the other man started talking at once. Hobbledick glared at Harcourt. "I already heard your side of this story. Kindly shut up while I hear his."

"This woman is my wife. I'm taking her home. That man tried to stop me," said the man.

Harcourt was outraged. "She's not your wife, you son of a bitch!

"Can you prove it?" Hobbledick asked the reporter.

"Why don't you just ask her?" Harcourt said, pointing to Sabrina.

Hobbledick didn't bother, so Harcourt yelled, "Sabrina. Sabrina. Tell this fine constable here that that asshole standing there is just that—some asshole and not your husband."

Sabrina didn't follow his suggestion. Her mouth opened, but no words came out. When she gave him a look of such utter sadness, such shame, a shell of hope that had been forming inside Harcourt's body since meeting Sabrina shattered into a million pieces.

"How about some wedding pictures, is that good enough for you?" said the asshole, as he puffed out his chest. The whole group had moved into the shelter of the back porch, except for Sabrina, who stood in the rain, and yet appeared to be untouched by it. The reporter pulled out his phone, and started thumbing through screens. "I'm Jack Bressler, and Sabrina Cane and I were married six months ago, in the United Sates."

His face lit up in triumph, and he turned his screen so Harcourt and the constable could see the photos. Lots and lots of photos. All pictures of a Las Vegas wedding, all of them clearly showing the wedding of the man standing there and Sabrina Cane. Sabrina was smiling and kissing him, her veil thrown back over her hair, her eyes glassy like she hadn't a care in the world. Harcourt's stomach lurched.

"Fine," he said.

Then he walked away, in the opposite direction from where Sabrina was standing. He thought he heard her voice, desperate and full of anguish, calling his name. But he never wanted to speak to her again or see her again. He had nothing to say to her. Nothing at all.

31   Caleb

Caleb never in a million years expected to have another child brought to the house and then left, both alive and in his care. But that was exactly what happened. One minute it was just Olga and him, the next minute, Babette had arrived and hauled in the skinniest little boy Caleb had ever seen.

Babette, who was clearly upset about something, told Caleb to "take care of the little brat, until we get back."

Then Olga and Babette drove off into the night.

The boy was drugged, but shivering, so Caleb carried him upstairs and put him into his bed. He wiped away dried snot and used a warm washcloth to clean the boy's hands. While the boy slept, Caleb turned over the house, going through every room that wasn't locked up, searching for anything he could use.

Caleb didn't believe for a second that they'd bought him a little playmate. The fact that the twins left him alone and seemed to be in a panic made him wonder if Sir was getting ready for Caleb to serve his purpose. Maybe that poor little boy had the same purpose to serve.

Caleb slept a few hours, then got up and cooked oatmeal. Since there was no milk, he boiled water and stirred in sugar until it dissolved. While the sugar water cooled, he took out the best of the apples—the ones that hadn't fully rotted in the bowl—and cut away the bad parts, and sliced the good pieces into the gruel. He found raisins and soaked them in the sugar water, then rested while he waited for the child to wake up.

The sound of whimpering and frightened shouts brought Caleb upstairs. The boy lay in the bed, covered up to this chin, and backed against the headboard when Caleb walked in.

He looked frightened, wary, then said in a high-pitched voice, "Where's Babette?"

"Not here," Caleb answered. "Are you hungry?"

The boy nodded.

"Can you walk?"

The boy nodded again.

Apparently, no longer afraid of Caleb, the boy stood up. The child wore ragged shorts with urine stains and a red-and-white shirt that needed also needed to be cleaned. Now that the child was standing, Caleb realized that he was taller then he'd thought. And maybe four or five or even six, and not the three or four he'd previously thought. Despite the boy's height, he was rail thin. His eyes were large and hazel, and seemed to dominate his small face.

"What's your name?" Caleb asked after the boy had finished his first bowl of oatmeal without saying a word.

"I don't remember."

32 SABRINA

I couldn't believe what was happening. I recognized where I was, but I had no idea how I'd gotten there. I felt drained, exhausted, and stimulated all at the same time. But mostly I felt crushed—crushed that Harcourt had found out the truth about me in the worst possible way.

I wanted to run after him, to explain things. But he gave me one long look, a look of utter shock, disappointment, and sadness.

How could I blame him? Jack had told him the truth about me... what I'd been unwilling, unable to admit to him myself. And when I didn't deny it, I basically confessed, and Harcourt came to understand that he'd been screwing around with a married woman, as Jack shoved those damn wedding photos in his face. Pictures from a wedding I couldn't remember.

I'd called after Harcourt when he turned and walked away from me, but he didn't slow down, he didn't stop, he didn't look at me again. I had no doubt at that moment that he hated me for lying to him, and for making him an unwitting participant in my immorality, my sin. My knees felt weak and I felt my body slumping back to the wet ground. Harcourt was done with me. Done.

Jack yanked on my arm, pulling me back to my feet. "Come on Sabrina, let's go!"

I didn't know what else to do. I let Jack pull me out of the backyard of the shaman's house, and to the front. The men who'd been with him before were climbing into a Jeep. Jack pushed me to the car.

I dug in my heels as it dawned on me what he was trying to do. He was trying to take me away. I might have ruined my chances with Harcourt Raymondson, and I might have decided that I needed to go back to LA to finish my contractual obligations with the film. And perhaps, learn about my shaman gifts and try and help some of those parents who were sending the heart-wrenching letters. I was ready to leave Canada and face the music back in LA, but I had no desire to subject myself to Jack's brutality again.

"Let me go," I said, and jerked my arm out of his grasp. Jack grabbed me back, and dug his fingers into my arm so tight I felt my skin break and I cried out in pain. Jack jerked my body to him, and held me in his iron grasp. My breath heaved, and I could feel panic setting in. I looked around wildly for help, but there was no one around.

"I need you to calm down and do exactly as I say, or I swear to God, Sabrina, I'll give you a beating so bad your last beating will seem like a love pat." He shook me hard to make his point, and I bit my tongue. "Are we clear?"

I could feel the tears falling down my face, but I resisted my body's desire to cry out in pain. I nodded vigorously, hoping he'd believe me. I told him that I'd cooperate, and not to hurt me anymore. I didn't struggle, and let him drag me to the front of the house.

Harcourt was devastated as he made his way back to the car. He sat in the driver's seat, and power-locked all the doors, then indulged himself in his sorrow. He breathed loudly through his nose as his anger grew. Sabrina had played him, played him like a fucking hammered dulcimer. He tried to understand why she'd done it. Not so he could forgive her, but so he could learn. She'd given him absolutely zero indications that she was involved with another man, let alone married to someone else.

Why did you do it?

She was a gold-digger. That was it. Clearly. Her husband, that Jack guy, was a celebrity, a reporter. Well, she obviously wanted to upgrade her social status. She wanted to land a billionaire. Maybe she imagined that she could charm him, make him fall in love with her. So much that he would gladly forgive her for cheating on her current husband.

Well, that wasn't going to happen.

Harcourt was about to take the Mercedes and drive up to the helicopter port and offer to give a million bucks to the first pilot that would fly him away when there was a knock on the window.

He saw that there was a short Talhkahaw'ka woman in full ceremonial garb standing there, motioning for him to open the door. He did.

"What?"

"He's a bad spirit. You must save her," she said.

Harcourt realized that the woman was putting her nose where it didn't belong. He was about to close the door and fire up the car when the woman shoved a large purse into his lap. "Would a good man drag a woman away kicking and screaming, and make her leave her purse behind?"

He was angry, and the idea that he'd witnessed any man dragging Sabrina away kicking and screaming sent his blood boiling. "What are you talking about?"

"She doesn't want to be with him. He is a bad man. Very bad."

The old woman reached in and pulled Harcourt out of the car. "Come this way. Hurry."

33 SABRINA

Jack made me get inside a large red Jeep and buckled me into the passenger seat. He reached under my legs and pulled up a water bottle and unscrewed the cap. He smiled at me. "Sorry I was angry, Sabrina. You look thirsty."

I was so very thirsty, my throat felt like sand and gravel inside a hole in a rock. He handed me a bottle of water, and I drank from it eagerly.

The cameraman was filming more shots of the town, and the storm putting out the fire in the distance.

"You need to be on camera for this," he yelled to Jack.

Jack said, "Stay in the car. Don't move or you'll regret it."

I nodded, too afraid to make him angry.

He walked over to where the cameraman wanted him to stand and began to make a report.

I realized that I could run. I could unbuckle myself and take off, find Harcourt, explain things, beg him to protect me from Jack. But Harcourt was already gone, and I couldn't bear what Jack would do to me if I made him angry. Out of fear and cowardice I sat there in the Jeep. I was telling myself to be patient, bide my time, and wait for a better opportunity to escape.

When Jack returned, I'd be meek and cooperative and not do anything to upset him. I would be no trouble for him, no trouble at all. I'd trick him into thinking that I was glad to be with him again, grateful that he'd come for me. I'd wait for the right moment to flee, and then I'd do it right this time. I'd go straight to one of those women's shelters, and get word back to Jeanette and Ellis. Trying to run now made no sense.

To be stuck in Diversion, in a town without a bridge, no car, and no friends, there was no telling how I'd end up. I'd have a hard time finding a place to hide from Jack. Short of begging Harcourt or Maggie and Mark to give me shelter and protection—something I couldn't do under the current circumstances—I'd just be a homeless rat, hiding in bushes and abandoned barns, starving until Jack found me and punished me for running again.

I suddenly realized that I didn't have my purse. I must have left it in the backyard. My chest tightened as Jack and the cameraman stopped their report and headed back to the car. I'd tell him about it, let him go get it for me. Yeah. Surely, he wouldn't begrudge me my identification and passport.

But when Jack and the cameraman finished their report and headed back to the car, I felt a surge of anger at the self-satisfied smirk on his face at the sight of seeing me malleable and pliant, waiting like a scared chicken in his car.

As they approached, a car screeched to a halt and several people came out of the car, one of them with a video camera, the other with a regular camera, and the third person dressed to be on camera.

"Hey Jack, look at those clowns from Channel 4," said his cameraman. "Hey, you slackers missed it."

A pretty female reporter ran straight toward me. "Sabrina, Sabrina Cane," she shouted, as her two associates trained their lenses on my face. "Is it true that you know where Baby Adalyn is? Can you tell us if she's still alive?"

"Shit," Jack said. Then he ran toward the Jeep and jumped into the driver's seat and started the engine. "Get the hell out of my way," he said.

"Sabrina Cane, where is Baby Adalyn?" shouted the reporter.

I wanted to tell her that I was being taken against my will, that Jack was an abusive husband and I needed police protection. I wanted to tell her that I didn't know anything about Baby Adalyn. I wanted to cry out for help, but I felt dizzy and my mouth couldn't form words.

Beyond the reporter and her cameramen, I saw Harcourt coming toward me. Behind him, Grandma Bella Bella. She was carrying something familiar. My purse. I tried hard to speak and finally my words came out, "Harcourt, help me."

The reporter turned her attention to Harcourt, who was running toward the Jeep. "Harcourt Raymondson? Are you Harcourt Raymondson, the man who's been hiding Sabrina?"

Harcourt stopped, apparently stunned by the reporter's attentions. I tried desperately to unclasp my safety belt, but the muscles in my fingers wouldn't obey me.

"I told you to behave!" Jack's open hand slammed against the back of my head, throwing my face into the dashboard. I cried out in pain, and I tried to scream for help, but I couldn't form the words.

"You son of a bitch," I heard Harcourt yell.

Jack kept my face against the dashboard a few seconds longer, then before the cameramen could swing their lenses around and get proof of Jack's brutality, Jack backed up the Jeep and roared away. Before we left the reservation, I lost the ability to think, to remember, to move...

When the little boy said he didn't remember his name, Caleb had to grab his chest because his heart wanted to fly out.

The same thing had happened to him, and his hate for Sir and his captors bubbled inside him.

"You've been with them a long time?" Caleb asked the boy.

"Yes."

"Would you like a bath?"

"Yes."

After Caleb stayed near the bath as he helped the boy with the soap and with washing his hair, Caleb dried him off and gave one of his clean T-shirts to wear while he washed the filthy closes.

The boy sat on the toilet, staring at Caleb while his clothes were washed in the bathtub.

After rinsing them clean, Caleb wrung out the boy's clothes as best he could, then wrapped them in a towel. "Let's hang these outside so they'll dry faster," Caleb said.

The boy followed Caleb outside, watching him intently with his big eyes. While the clothes dried under an overcast sky, Caleb sat on the stoop and read the boy a book.

The boy didn't seem interested in the story, so Caleb set the book down, and asked the boy, "How long have you been with them?"

"A long time."

"Do you remember anything before?"

The little boy's huge eyes brimmed. "I remember my mommy, my cottage, and my daddy," he said, then wiped his nose, dirtying Caleb's T-shirt.

"Do you remember their names?" Caleb asked, wishing he had memories that precise.

The little boy looked confused at the question.

"No, just Mommy and Daddy."

Caleb nodded. That made sense. Those were the names he'd used when talking to his parents. Those were the names they answered to when the little boy called for them. He'd probably never paid attention when they called each other by their real names.

"Tell me about the cottage."

The boy's face lit up. "I had a fairy garden, and it was magical."

"It was? That's nice."

After a while, the little boy fell asleep, and Caleb carried him inside and laid him onto the couch.

It was close to midday. Caleb worried.

Had they just left them there to starve? Were they planning on coming back? Caleb had a terrible feeling it would be for the last time. Every instinct inside him was screaming that he couldn't just wait for the bad thing to happen. Every instinct told him that he had to do something to protect the boy.

He considered hiding the boy in the woods. But then they'd be both killed by wolves.

Caleb's eyes went wide as he remembered the key.

Once, almost a year before, when Babette had gotten too drunk to lock her door, Caleb had gone into her room and taken her car keys. He'd meant to steal the car to drive away, but he'd never driven a car before and he couldn't figure out how to start it. Hearing noises in the house, he quickly took out the key and lay still, hoping Babette wouldn't come down. He heard a toilet flush, then found an owner's manual in the glove compartment. He took the book and his keys back upstairs, and noticed that there were two keys on the chain. He took one off and put it in his room, along with the car book. Then he waited until Babette was snoring and snuck back into her room, replacing the keys. He went back downstairs and put the key and the book in his secret hiding place under the stairs.

The next day Babette was too hungover to notice, and he never heard a word about the missing key or missing book.

Unfortunately, Babette decided to not drink during the rest of her stay, so he didn't get another chance to try the key. But in the months that had passed, he'd almost memorized the book and he was almost certain he'd figure out how to drive it if he ever got another chance.

When the boy's clothes were dry enough, Caleb woke him up and got him dressed, then opened a packet of salt crackers. While the boy ate, Caleb went to his secret hiding place and dug out the key. He tucked it deep into his pocket, then got his jacket from his room, and as an afterthought, grabbed his smallest blanket. It was summer, but the summers never got very warm in the mountains, and the boy was too skinny to stay warm.

If Babette or Olga came back in the car they always used, then he'd make a run for it and take the boy with him. It was their only chance.

While the boy watched, Caleb gathered up food and water and extra clothes. He used the blanket to make a pack. Then he hid it under the stairs.

As night fell, Caleb had a feeling that Babette and Olga would be coming soon. He'd stayed downstairs, not talking, not letting the little boy hum or make noises. He needed to hear the first signs of an approaching car. Not wanting the boy to get cold under the stairs, he'd decided to hide him at the very last second. He hoped Babette or Olga or whoever showed up would go upstairs to look for them, and then he'd make his move.

Caleb had intended to stay up all night, but sleep overcame him. He was having a sweet dream, being flown over the forest in the arms of his dark angel, when he was startled awake by the moans of the little boy. Fox was having a nightmare.

"It's okay," Caleb said, and jostled Fox awake.

"Caleb?" said Fox.

"Hush," Caleb said as he saw the shadows move across the room. "Don't make a sound!"

He lifted Fox into his arms, and hurtled down the steps and ducked under the stairs, lying on his back with Fox on top of him as he scooted toward the back of the secret hiding place.

They remained there, out of sight, still and quiet as stones. First one, and then a second car drove up. They didn't make a move or a sound when Olga screamed at Babette or when the two of them bounded down the steps and headed into the woods, each in a different direction, their flashlights bouncing angrily as they hunted for the missing boys.

As soon as Caleb felt they we far enough away, he said the word. "Go," and Fox scrambled out into the fresh air first, with Caleb right behind him. He looked at the two identical cars and hoped that he'd pick the correct one on his first try. He saw that one car was not so identical. It had more dings and dents than the other.

His mind flashed to Babette's legs, which had more marks, bruises, and scratches, evidence of all the times she'd stumbled into corners or had fallen down the stairs during one of her benders.

"That one," Caleb whispered and the two boys sprinted to the closest car.

34 HARCOURT

Harcourt shoved the reporter and her cameraman out of his way and hurried to the SUV. He couldn't believe what he'd seen. That brute had hit Sabrina upside the head, slamming her face into the dashboard, then grinding it in for good measure. He might be done with Sabrina as a lover, but no woman deserved that kind of treatment at the hands of a man. He'd be damned if he'd let that asshole get away with what he'd just seen him to do her.

He was inside the SUV and reaching to turn the key when the door to his car was flung open.

"Harcourt, where the fuck do you think you're going?"

Mark was standing there, looking furious.

"Stay out of this. I found Sabrina. I've got to go after her."

"Harcourt, step out of the car."

Harcourt saw that Mark had removed his weapon and was pointing it at him.

"Mark, what are you doing?"

"I told you to step out of the car. Do it, now. I'm not going to ask you again."

Harcourt put his hands in the air. He couldn't understand what had gotten into his friend. He stepped out of the car.

"Turn around," he ordered.

Harcourt complied.

"Put your hands behind your back."

"Wait just a moment."

"Do it!"

Harcourt moved his hands behind his back.

"Head against the car, legs spread."

"Jesus, Mark, what's gotten into you?"

Harcourt felt the cold steel clasp around his wrist, and the jerk on his shoulders as Mark handcuffed him. The two cameras from Channel 4 news were trained on his arrest.

Mark shoved him forward, then around the front of the car. "What the fuck, Mark?" Harcourt whispered.

Mark opened the passenger door and shoved Harcourt inside. He slammed the door shut, then ran around to the driver's seat. He holstered his weapon, then climbed inside.

Outside, the female reporter was shouting. "Why are you arresting Harcourt Raymondson? Did he kidnap Sabrina Cane? Did he kidnap Baby Adalyn?"

Mark ignored their questions and started the engine, then backed out and sped away.

Harcourt saw that the reporter and her crew were hurrying to get to their car to pursue them. "Mark, what in the name of hell is going on?"

"I'll tell you in a minute," he said.

Harcourt tried not to blow a gasket in frustration as Mark hurried out of the reservation. His mind was a jumble of confused emotions. First Sabrina goes missing, then she turns up, married to some abusive bastard, then Mark treats him like a criminal.

He saw Mark glance into the rear view mirror. He continued to speed up the windy road that led away from the reservation on the first flat land above Shipwreck Harbor.

"What's going on?" Harcourt asked.

"I'm getting you out of here so we can go after Sabrina," Mark said.

"What do you mean, you're getting me out of here?"

"You're my prisoner. I need to get you to Vancouver. Important police business. Do you understand?"

Harcourt did understand. "Why are you doing this?"

"Because, first of all, I'm after that reporter bastard. I want to get to him before someone tells me I have no case. Second of all, because I saw what he did to Sabrina. Who the hell does he think he is?"

"It's her husband," Harcourt said, and saying the words made his chest ache.

Mark's eyebrow lifted in surprise. "Well, hopefully not for long. She didn't look all that happy to be back with him, and if you think about it, sounds to me like she's been trying to stay away from the brute. I'd say she's not planning on staying married to the man, so I hope you aren't holding it against her."

Harcourt didn't respond. He did hold it against her. He'd help her get away from the man, and punch out his lights next chance he got, but he wasn't considering ever being with Sabrina again. Not after she didn't trust him enough to confide her little secret.

"So, you're going to get to this reporter bastard, and what? Arrest him for assaulting Sabrina? What if she's one of those battered wives that won't press charges? Then what will you do?"

"You don't understand, Harcourt. I'm not going to arrest him for hitting his wife, if that's what she is to him. I'm going to arrest him for assaulting a member of my community and for grand theft auto."

He yanked the wheel, stopping at the side of the road, where an ambulance and several people milled about. "Stay in the car," Mark said.

Mark headed over to the group and spoke to a young man sitting on the back of the ambulance. The victim, in his mid-twenties, sported a hipster beard and tattoos and looked vaguely familiar. A massive bandage covered his nose and a swelling black-and-yellow bruise shut his right eye. Mark wrote something on his notepad and the young man signed it. When Mark got back into the car and headed back on the road, he mentioned it before Harcourt pressed his purpose for stopping.

"I just needed to see for myself what that man did to him. That sweet kid owns the Jeep your buddy stole. Said he was doing the newsman a favor, and wasn't even going to charge him in the interest of helping the press. Well, I'm happy to say that's he's eager to press charges. Let's go get the bastard, shall we?"

"Where do you think he's taking her?" Harcourt asked.

"Flying her out on the news helicopter, no doubt, since that's how he got here."

"I see. And you don't think they're going to wait around for us to show up? Can you drive a little faster, since you had to take that detour?"

"I know where he's headed."

"You do?"

"Yeah, he's a reporter—and she's news. They'll go to the TV station, where else?"

"Great, then we'll just flap our wings and fly over to the mainland?"

"Harcourt, shut up, or I'll have to tighten those cuffs, and maybe I'll gag you as well."

"You wouldn't dare," Harcourt said.

Both men laughed.

As they climbed the road leading to the helicopter port which was gouged like a slice of cheese off the top of the ridge, they caught a few good views of the town below. The freak blue-green storm clouds hovered above the reservation and down toward Shipwreck Harbor. The rest of the skies over Diversion were clear. Harcourt considered what he'd read about Sabrina's childhood experience, about her psychic abilities, and wondered if he'd witnessed actual magic. And if she could summon rain, then maybe she'd seen those villains, way back when through the eyes of the child victims.

He had a fleeting and disturbing thought. What if her powers went beyond seeing visions through the troubled eyes of a child? What if she could communicate with the dead? Would he want her to try and speak to Sharon or Cedric?

Harcourt banished those thoughts from his mind. He only wanted to make sure she was safe, and not with that brute of a husband against her will. Then he'd get on with saving his job and after that deal with the fact that the mansion had burned down. Levelheaded leaders didn't waste time trying to talk to the dead.

"Fuck," Mark said as they rounded a bend. "We missed them."

Harcourt and Mark watched the Channel 8 news copter lifting into the sky. Mark pulled off the road and climbed out and opened Harcourt's door so he could see. Harcourt leaned out and watched the news copter fly away. From their angle, Harcourt could just make out Sabrina, strapped into a back seat, her head lolling against her chest as if asleep. A pain of regret ripped through his chest, and he felt a strong urge to call out her name, but resisted it. Mark came around to his door, but stopped. The helicopter changed its path and flew back toward them.

"What the fuck?" Mark said.

As they got over them, the helicopter leaned slightly giving both men a great view of Jack Bressler. He stared down at them both, a sick grin splitting his face, as he gave them the finger. The helicopter turned and this time continued on its way to Vancouver.

Mark kicked the ground. "What a fucking ass hat."

They drove in silence the rest of the way. Harcourt noticed the BCTV Channel 4 news helicopter waiting for its news crew to return, and noticed a man sitting at a pair of picnic benches, inside a sheltered structure. He was smoking a cigarette, and had his hand on a portable radio.

"You going to make him fly us back?" Harcourt asked, as Mark idled the SUV in the parking lot.

"Not him. We've got our own ride," he said. As if on cue a rumbling like a monster truck rally filled the air, and a moment later a slick, black helicopter appeared from behind the ridge and hovered in front, creating a tremendous circle of dust. It landed. Mark put the SUV in gear, driving though the access gate and bumped over the compressed dirt landing strip, stopping close to the helicopter.

"Who is that?" Harcourt asked.

"It doesn't matter. What matters is that we get off this island. You need to play the part. This guy thinks you're under arrest and if he hears otherwise, he won't give us a ride."

Harcourt nodded, ready to do what he had to do to rescue Sabrina, but groaned when he noticed the man at the picnic table watching them with unmasked curiosity. "Great," he muttered to himself. "I can see it now. My face on the nightly news, and the big headline: 'CEO Arrested for Child Murder.' Great. That should play well at the board meeting when I ask them to let me come back to my own fucking company."

Harcourt beat his bound fists against his seat in frustration, then settled down to observe through slit lids as Mark and the pilot met up and shook hands. The pilot, a man in his mid-forties, appeared to be the only man in the copter, and he didn't dress like a pilot, but more like a cop. Not because of his clothing. He wore khaki pants, a white dress shirt, and dark blue tie, but he also was packing. He had the posture and the bearing of law enforcement or military.

Mark and the pilot went to the back of the SUV, and proceeded to load the helicopter. Harcourt could tell by the way he carried it that Mark had chosen to transfer the skull, while the other man got stuck with the heavier bag with the weapons and ammo taken from the Diversion armory. After the luggage was stowed both men returned to the SUV, and stood outside Harcourt's door. The stranger glared at Harcourt behind his mirrored sunglasses, and stood in a ready stance, hand on the butt of his gun. It was obvious from the man's body language that he believed Harcourt to be guilty. Harcourt imagined the man thinking, "Do something punk. Make my day."

Harcourt's chest tightened, not out of fear, or because this man believed that he was the worst kind of scum, but because Sabrina might see the news report before he'd have a chance to explain.

"Get out," Mark said.

Harcourt did as he was told. Mark steered him toward the helicopter. Mark removed his cuffs just long enough for Harcourt to climb aboard, and when he put them back on, he cuffed one wrist to a metal hook on the side of his seat. Harcourt used his free hand to rub circulation back into his wrists and stretched his arm out, relieving the kink in his shoulders.

The pilot climbed inside and started his pre-flight check. Harcourt remained quiet, waiting for Mark to park the SUV and walk back. The moment Mark took his seat, the pilot lifted off and they flew fast toward the mainland. No one spoke, as each man was absorbed in his own thoughts. Harcourt's face turned toward the window, but he paid no attention to scenery below. When he closed his eyes, the same image appeared on his retinas. Sabrina's beautiful face being marred by that bastard's brutal hand. The closer they got to Vancouver, the tighter Harcourt's resolve became. He'd make that bastard pay for what he did to Sabrina.

Constable Hobday decided to skip switching cars, after letting the girlfriend go home with the man claiming to be her husband, and headed to the cell tower instead to change the battery. The freak storm had made the ground wet. He slipped many times before making it to the tower. After getting the disrupter back on track, he returned to his cruiser, muddy and cursing. He wiped his hands dry, and after having a cigarette to calm his nerves, made his call.

Before the latest events, he'd been hoping that his boss would answer, but now he was grateful that he got voicemail again. He made his report short and to the point, confirmed that Harcourt Raymondson was still in Diversion, and that cell phone service was out, and that he'd secured both of the towns' two satellite phones. He'd intended before to mention the girl staying with Harcourt, and to tell the boss that he'd learned her name, but decided against it, since she'd gone off with that reporter. A few more days babysitting the billionaire and keeping him stuck in Diversion, and this shitty assignment would be over he hoped.

He was driving back toward the cabin to shower and change into a clean uniform, and then try and track down Harcourt again when he saw Harcourt's SUV drive past. His target wasn't driving the car, he noticed, but appeared to be a passenger. Hobday didn't care, but he didn't want to be made, so he stayed well back as he followed the vehicle. When he saw them turn onto Helicopter Road, he cursed and gunned his engine, no longer caring if they made him or not. He be in deep shit with the boss if his target got away.

When the deer jumped in front of his cruiser, Hobday slammed on his brakes and jerked the wheel to avoid it. Too late. When he came to, his head pounded. He touched it and felt the swell of a bump where he'd smashed his head on the steering wheel. Someone pounded the window.

"You all right in there, officer?" asked a man. Hobday turned his head with care and eyed the man. A passerby had come to help.

"I hit a deer," Hobday said, feeling dazed.

"No shit, do you want it?" asked the man.

"What?"

"If you don't want it, I'll be happy to take it off your hands."

Hobday peered at the man. In his mid-sixties with leathery skin, he seemed far too interested in the damn deer. Anger rose inside Hobday, but dissipated as he heard the rumble of copter blades. The sound reminded him of something. He rubbed his face, trying to remember, but nothing was coming through.

Hobday pushed himself out of his cruiser and was hit fast by the stench of blood from the felled deer. Unlike the deer, his cruiser showed no signs of damage. And if it didn't have its nose sticking in the ditch, he would have backed up the car and continued to the helicopter port. It all came back to him: Harcourt and the other man, his target, his future, already gone, or if he was lucky, still up there waiting for a bird. He had to get to the helicopter port fast.

Hobday felt a tap on his shoulder. He reeled around fast, face twisted, hand on his weapon. "Whoa, sorry, didn't mean to scare you buddy—you want that buck, or not?"

Hobday rallied his composure as a thought occurred to him. He even put a smile on his face as he spoke to the irritant in overalls. "I tell you what, you help me pull my car out, and you can have the deer."

By the time Hobday's cruiser was pulled out of the ditch and he managed to drive the rest of the way to the helicopter port, there was no sign of Harcourt or the other man.

He parked his cruiser next to Harcourt's SUV and looked inside.

On the dirt landing field, the copter from Channel 4 news waited for their team to return, but the man waiting at one of the picnic benches appeared to be the pilot. Hobday made sure there was no one else around, then opened the trunk of his cruiser. He loaded his duffel bag with the things he would need. He zipped up the bag, setting it down on the ground, then after making sure he wasn't being observed, dug around until he found his ankle holster. He strapped it on, then found his snub nose. Two guns and a rifle should be sufficient. He locked his car, and carrying the heavy bag, with his rifle slung over one shoulder he approached the picnic table where the pilot sat watching him.

"Hey, Constable," said the pilot in a jovial tone that didn't match the nervous moves and the sweat beading on the pilot's forehead. "What's the word on those fires down there?"

He moved his hand near to the SIG Sauer at his waist, then after nodding towards the sole helicopter on the tarmac, said, "That's yours? You the pilot?"

"I am."

"I'm commandeering your helicopter under Canadian rule of law 15S3022."

"What? I've never heard of that law."

Hobday took a step forward and deepened his voice. "Sir, if you don't comply, you will be arrested. This is an order, not a request."

The man put his hands in the air. "All right, all right, whatever you say, buddy, whatever you say."

35 SABRINA

I woke up in a strange place. My face hurt and my head felt like it was stuffed with insulation. My ears are humming, or maybe that's my blood pumping, I'm not sure. I try to sit, then regret the fast motion, closing my eyes as I feel around. I'm in a bed, a small bed, perhaps twin size. I get up slower this time, breathing short shallow breaths as I regain my equilibrium.

The bed is pushed against the wall, next to a window with curtains. I reach for them, moving them aside to look where I am. Sun slants in, sharp and low, like it's late afternoon. I'm staring at the west, and I see what looks like a fire glinting beyond the cops of pines. I know it's just the sun, lying low and orange in the distance. I tug on the curtains, pulling them together, blocking the worst of the glaring light. Then I get up. Slowly. My head feels thick, like it's full of cotton, and my legs want to buckle beneath me, but soon I find enough strength, enough balance. I'm in a bedroom, but I've never been in it before. It's furnished with a bed, a metal folding chair. The chair faces a wall, painted white.

On the floor in front of the wall, there are boxes and bags, lots of them. I walk toward them, my hands out to my side for balance. I feel like I'm walking a tightrope. The boxes and bags are filled with art supplies, most of them items needed for making mosaics, but also items for drawing and painting. My head swims. I look down at my body, lifting my arms. I'm wearing a slouchy sweater, and underneath it I'm wearing a dress.

A flood of memories race into my head, making me dizzy. I barely get to the chair in time. I remember a man. Harcourt Raymondson. I remember every second I shared his body, every time we made love. Then I remember that look on his face—the disappointment, the sadness, the way he seemed to despise me when Jack informed him that I was a married woman, and showed him pictorial proof.

"No!" I said, groaning.

Outside my bedroom, I hear sounds, voices, drawers opening and closing. I go to the door and open it, then step into a dim hallway that opens into a large space with a living room on one side and a dining area and kitchen on the other. My chest tightens as I see my husband. His back is to me and he's scooping coffee out of a tin can.

My eye wanders to what looks like the front door to the house, and I start to walk toward it. Jack is whistling as he pours water into the coffee pot. "Ah, the princess is up. Very good. Sabrina, where are you going?"

I turn around. "Oh, hi, just getting the lay of the land."

He's all smiles and sweetness. It makes my head hurt. "Come sit at the table. I've got some food for you. You'll need to eat something before your big debut."

"Debut?"

He took a sandwich from a deli bag he got from the refrigerator and placed it in front of me. He poured a glass of orange juice and got me a paper towel for a napkin.

"What's going on, Jack?"

"Just eat, I'll talk to you in a minute."

Wheels crunch on gravel, and I see through the slats that a large van was pulling up. A moment later, the door opened and a fleshy man with balding hair began dragging in video equipment.

"Can I set up now?" he asked.

"Yes, hurry up."

The man took several trips to transfer his gear to the room. When he completed the task, Jack joined him in the room and shut the door. I heard their voices, but I couldn't make out what they were saying. I stared at the front door and considered running, but my legs wouldn't move. When Jack came out a few moments later, my heart pounded.

"Listen to me good, Sabrina."

"Yes," I said, still reeling from his prior abuse.

"I need you to go back in that room when I say to and do what you did when you were ten years old."

"What? I don't understand."

"It's not hard, Sabrina. Just like you helped find those two kids way back when, you need to help find Baby Adalyn. The whole world will be watching as you create your work of art."

I stared at him with horror as I comprehended his plan. "But, Jack, I can't. I don't know where she is. I don't know how I did it before. I can't," I said, pleading with him.

"You can and you will," he said. He leaned close and I could smell that sour odor that always came out of his breath. He pulled out his cell phone and scrolled along the screen until he found what he was looking for. Then he showed me and I almost fell off the chair. He had a picture, which looked like it had been taken of a newscast on a television screen—blurry and pixelated—but I had no doubt who the picture was of. It was a picture of my sister, Jeannette, standing on the stoop of my daddy's house, talking to the press. Talking about me.

"I see that you're starting to understand me," Jack said, his voice rich with triumph. I wanted to kick him in the balls the bash a chair over his head. But I didn't want to risk my sister. "I saw that she has a few kids and there's the old man as well. Several reasons for you to be fully cooperative, wouldn't you agree?"

I couldn't mask the tremor in my voice. "What are you saying, Jack?"

"I'm telling you that I have plans, and I don't want you fucking them up." He jabbed his index finger at the phone. "If you care about these people, then you do exactly as I ask, all right? No complaining. no running away. Am I making myself clear, Sabrina?"

At that moment the cameraman came out of the bedroom. Before, the room had been dim, cast in the fading afternoon light, but now a bright white light flooded out of the room.

"It's all set," said the cameraman, who for some reason wouldn't look me in the eye.

"And the van? Is it out of sight yet?"

"Not yet, but I'll find a spot in the back of the house. No one will see it."

"They better not," Jack said.

The cameraman didn't seem to like that tone. He also didn't make a move for the door.

"What?" Jack snapped.

"Just wondering something. When's she gonna be in that state again? What did you call it?"

"A fugue state," Jack said.

"Yeah, how soon before she starts?"

"I don't know. It's up to her. I think she needs some time to prep. Right, Sabrina?"

"Yes," I nodded. "I need to bless my tools."

Jack's face creased into a smug smile. He had me under his thumb again, doing his bidding again, gratified to see my eagerness to play along. It made me want to get one of those beer bottles and smash it against the floor and lash at his throat. But I just sat there. Powerless.

As soon as the man had started the van up, Jack grabbed me by the arm and hurried me back into the bedroom. He took me to the bathroom and shoved a plastic bag filled with lightweight items into the hands. "Fix your face," he said.

I cringed when I saw my face, then looked through the items in the bag. I pulled out the bottle of Cover Girl, and even though the color was a few shades too light for my skin, I got to work. After a moment, the ugly bruise which had formed on my split lip was less apparent.

I wetted a tissue to wipe away the dried blood, and used the lipstick and the mascara from the back to further improve my appearance. Jack stayed in the bathroom with me, standing far too close. "Let me explain what I need you to do," he said, watching me through the mirror. I nodded, but dropped my gaze.

His arm slid along my side and he handed me a snapshot. It was a press photo, from the one-year-old Baby Adalyn birthday celebration that had taken place less than a month before.

"This is Baby Adalyn," he said. "She needs your help. You need to do your thing, go into a trance, and then use that wall and all those art supplies over there to create an image of both the baby and whomever kidnapped her. Then we can send the police to save her."

"But, Jack. I can't. I told you before, I don't know how I did it when I was a kid. I can't just make it happen on demand. I don't know who the kidnappers are."

"Sabrina, Sabrina," he said, his tone implying my cluelessness. "I'm not trying to save the baby. I couldn't care less about the baby, so I don't care what you put up on that wall. So long as Baby Adalyn is in the image, you can make up a face for all I care. You can use this picture as a reference, but do me a favor—I mean, do your sister and her kids a favor—don't let anyone see that picture. Keep it off camera."

I nodded.

"So, you don't care who I put as the kidnapper?"

"Nope, I don't care. Just make up a person, or use a mask like you did last time."

I thought about that little child and her parents, desperate for her return. I thought about the false hope I'd be giving them, live and on TV. I felt a terrible sense of guilt, and shook my head. "Jack, we shouldn't be doing this. It's wrong."

Jack pushed his face next to mine, so for a moment it looked like I was a two-headed person. "It's not wrong, Sabrina. It's brilliant."

He stepped back as the front door opened and the cameraman came into the house.

He left me in the bathroom. In the bedroom, the two men spoke as I brushed on another layer of mascara. "Can we start now? Will it be live?" Jack asked.

"Yep, all set up. It'll be live just as soon as I press record."

After conning his way onto a helicopter, then stealing the pilot's car, Hobday normally would have immediately stolen another car, something non-descript. But the opportunity had fallen into his lap. Some moron with gold chains around his neck thought he could leave the keys in the ignition, leave the engine running, and no one would touch his wheels while he ran into a store to pay for gas. Idiot...

Now it was Hobday's vehicle. He knew he should find that third car to steal, something boring and ubiquitous, but he couldn't bring himself to trade in the car. It was the perfect tactical vehicle for his needs, other than the fact that it was brand new, and flashy, and easily spotted. But he could fix that, he told himself. And he needed a reliable car with power and four-wheel drive. The Cadillac Suburban cost more than two years of his regular RCMP salary. It was the kind of car he could only dream of. Just driving it made him hard. Who was it that said that the car was the man's true mistress?

Shit. There was no way he was going to ditch this car for some piece of shit Ford Focus, or Toyota. He'd hang onto this puppy, even if he had to bang it up, maybe rough up the exterior, so it didn't look so brand new. He breathed in the new leather smell, and ran his hands along the dash. There wasn't a speck of dirt or dust in it. And it was fully loaded, decked out to the max. It had all the authorized doodads, and a bunch of after-market bells and whistles, plus every electronic gadget a man could want in a car. It had a radar detector, GPS, rear view camera. It was the perfect car for the big trip, which he planned to take very soon.

He hadn't intended to kill the pilot. I just happened, like an epiphany. He was done working for the boss, done being a Mountie, done living in Canada. Killing the pilot made it impossible for him to change his mind, to go back being under the thumb of a man who'd never revealed his identity.

Now he had to run... far, far, away.

But first he intended to complete his assignment, and collect the money. He'd need it, now more than ever. All he had to do was find Harcourt Raymondson and make sure he couldn't get to New York on Wednesday. He'd take him out, hide his body somewhere, and send lies to his boss about his whereabouts, and his boss wouldn't be the wiser. When he didn't come to New York, his boss would send out his funds in the usual fashion, and he'd be inactive again until the next job came along. Only by then, when his boss tried to reach him, Hobday would be long gone.

All the more reason to dump the car, to begin removing all connections to his past—but he couldn't bring himself to do it. The car was making him hard. There were other ways, he knew. He made another decision, this time turning into a promising-looking underground parking structure. The old ticket booth was empty and there were no barriers going in or out. He drove inside and parking in a corner, got out and swapped license plates. He'd keep doing it several times until anyone looking for him would lose the trail. The best cars to swap plates with were the cars that didn't appear to get a lot of use—where the owners were unlikely to report that someone had fucked with it. After the plate was swapped, he had to brace himself for the next task.

"Time to get ugly, beautiful," he said to the car as he headed toward the concrete support beam. He winced and cringed at the sounds of scraping metal, but destroying the perfect finish and denting up the car would make it easier to hide it. He'd bang it up as much as he had to, and when he got out in the country he'd look for a field and fling dirt clods and mud at the car until it lost its shine. Yeah.

He drove away, then into a residential neighborhood, parking in front of an old motorhome. He lit up and tried to think how he would find Harcourt Raymondson. An alarm notification on his phone reminded him that he was due to provide another report in less than an hour. Maybe he'd just skip the call. That sometimes happened. With that decision made, he took a moment to admire his new wheels, and saw that there was a television tuner built into the dash. He turned it on, and after fiddling with the tools for a moment, he found the news, and his target.

Constable Hobday let out a whoop of excitement at the sight of Harcourt Raymondson's face plastered on the screen. The banner over Harcourt's image was icing on the fricking cake. It read, Breaking News: Child Murder Suspect Detained.

"This is fucking awesome, baby," he said stroking his new car's soft leather seat. The video showed Harcourt Raymondson being led into the Canadian Secret Intelligence Service building in handcuffs.

He couldn't have asked for a better outcome. With Harcourt behind bars, he could do whatever he needed to in order to lie low until Wednesday, and keep his new vehicle. This was perfect. The cops would be doing his job for him until Wednesday, then his bonus would be sent to his account, then he'd cash out and split and drive his new car all the way to Panama.

Then he had a more sobering thought and his usual angry countenance returned. What if Harcourt was arrested because his boss had planned it? Maybe the skull was intended for that purpose and not just to freak him out. Hobday wondered if his boss was thinking about doing something like that to him. Maybe he was going to rat him out. Maybe if the pilot murder was in the news and he'd been implicated in the crime, perhaps the boss man might decide to bail on giving him the bonus, claim he didn't deserve it, since the Harcourt was in custody. Or maybe he'd just say that he was too hot, too volatile, too much of a liability.

Maybe, once the boss found out, he'd rat him out.

Regret for taking the action he did evaporated Hobday's good mood. And when his cell phone buzzed, Hobday was startled, and he grabbed his chest. He recovered fast and scrambled out of the car, racing around to the passenger side and throwing open the door, so he could unzip his bag and get to the cell phone before his boss hung up.

"Boss," he said, catching it probably on the last ring.

"Have you seen the news?"

"Mr. Raymondson is in custody. Saw that. Guess the skull worked?"

"What? No. I don't care about him right now. Pay attention, Hobday. I'm talking about different news."

Hobday felt his jaw tighten. He hated it when his Boss spoke in that condescending tone.

"All right," Hobday said, forcing himself not to sound pissed.

"I told him to take the girl to one of my properties until I could make arrangements to get her over the border, but the idiot decided to put her on camera, and now he's not answering my calls or stopping this spectacle, even though I made myself quite clear."

"Okay, so you want me to make him stop?"

"Yes. Hobday, where are you currently?"

"Vancouver, sir. I followed Harcourt over after they arrested him."

"Good. Very good. I'm texting you an address where he should have her. I need you to go there and stop this stupid live cam. Then I want you to bring Sabrina to me tonight. Can you do that?"

Hobday's chest tingled. Did he just say bring her to him? Am I finally going to get a chance to meet the mysterious boss?

"What about the reporter?" Hobday asked, wondering if there might be a chance to make some bonus money.

There was a pause. "Yes. I would like you to fix that situation."

"Permanently?"

"Let's just say I'd like not to have to worry about him ever again."

"Will do, boss, and I assume I'll get the usual fee for that service? Any chance you'll have the cash when I deliver the girl?"

"Yes, Hobday, yes, I'll have the cash—stop annoying me with your stupid questions. Just confirm that you'll do this."

Hobday paused before answering. "Yes, I will, but..."

"But what?"

Hobday's voice had a slight catch in it. "I see no issues with taking care of the reporter or getting the girl, but I don't know where I'm supposed to take her, so I can't guarantee I can be there tonight."

There was a pause, and Hobday wondered if the man could read his intentions. "I'm not far, just over the border. I'll text you the coordinates after you confirm that you've got the girl. Send me her picture, preferably with a gag on."

Hobday felt a pang of disappointment. If the boss had been willing to give him his location, he could have skipped the assignment and started casing his target, and ended up with the bonus money without having to go to the trouble of killing and kidnapping first. "All right, boss, text me the address. I'll get right on it."

36 HARCOURT

When the helicopter arrived at Vancouver RCMP head-quarters, Harcourt was taken to an interrogation room, and told to wait. Mark had not been invited to join him. Harcourt sat in the holding cell with no contact from anyone.

When a deputy walked by, Harcourt yelled, "Hey, when can I speak to a lawyer?"

He didn't reply. A few minutes later, two men and a woman—one in an RCMP uniform and the other in plain clothes, but armed—appeared outside the glass doors to his cubicle. Mark was nowhere to be seen.

Harcourt's stomach twisted. Fuck. He'd handed over the skull, which was probably of his child. He'd admitted to Mark that it was on his property. He'd practically convicted himself.

"Mr. Raymondson?" The man in the gray suit and red tie stepped into the room first. The others crowded in behind him. The last person in, a compact woman with dark hair and hawk-like eyes, closed the door behind her. They all stared at Harcourt as if he were a curiosity. Harcourt would have tugged at his shirt collar to get some air, but his hands were still cuffed behind his back. He opted instead to ignore the closeness in the room, and sat up straight looking none of them in the eye, waiting for one of them to speak first.

"Mr. Raymondson. I'm special agent Calvin Vasquez, CSIS," said the olive-skinned man with the shaved head and body builder's heavy neck, "and this is Brenda Riggs, from the US FBI, and this is Sam Burton, homicide detective with Vancouver RCMP. We'd like to ask you a few questions, if that's all right?"

Harcourt felt sweat bead on his forehead, and hoped it wouldn't trickle into his face.

"Am I under arrest?"

"No, not yet," said Vasquez.

"Then un-cuff me, please."

Burton started to protest, but Vasquez put out his hand, stopping the man's comment. He opened the door and called for a deputy. He spoke to the deputy in a quiet whisper. "We'll have those off you soon enough," he said smoothly. "But while we wait for the key, how about you answer a few questions."

"How about we wait until I'm no longer being held against my will."

"Fine."

Five minutes later everyone in the room had begun to fidget and the FBI agent Riggs had propped open the door to get some air by the time a deputy returned with the cuff keys.

The door was closed as Harcourt rubbed circulation back into his wrists.

"Can we get started now?" asked Riggs of Vasquez once the door was closed again, and Harcourt appeared to be ready.

"Tell us how you came into possession of the skull."

"Where's Mark Pearson?" Harcourt said.

"We'd like to have you answer questions without him present, if that's all right?"

"Why?"

"Look Mr. Raymondson, can you just answer the question, please? How did you come into possession of the skull?"

Harcourt decided that he had nothing to lose by telling the truth regarding the skull. If it turned out to be Cedric's he knew he hadn't put it there, so whoever did would be of more interest to the police than he was.

"My house was about to burn down a few nights ago during the wildfires in Diversion, and since I was in the area working as a volunteer fireman, I thought I'd go to the cottage and try to save the only pictures I had of my wife and son. I went inside, opened the lid to the window seat where I kept the pictures, and that's the first time I saw the skull. Scared the crap out of me, I'm not ashamed to admit."

"So, you're saying you didn't put it there?" Riggs interjected.

"I didn't even know that it existed. My wife and son's bodies were never recovered after the accident, so it was a double shock for me to see my son's skull in that house."

"You admit that the skull is your son's?" Riggs pressed.

"I just assumed, but I don't know for sure. But who else could it belong to?"

"Why don't you tell us," Riggs said.

Vasquez put out his hand again to make Riggs back off and she stood against the wall, her hands crossed over her chest. Vasquez had a reasonable, conversational tone. "Mr. Raymondson, you said yourself that the bodies of your wife and son were lost at sea, so you can probably understand how puzzled we are that a skull from the bottom of the ocean could suddenly end up in your cottage. Any idea how that could have happened?"

Harcourt leaned forward. "Look, about six months ago, they found debris that appeared to be from the crash site. I identified possible fabric to the upholstery in the Cessna and I absolutely identified a fireman's helmet that belonged to my child. Maybe someone did a deep-sea dive and pulled up the body, and..."

"Why would someone go to all that trouble?" Vasquez asked.

"To frame me, or make me kill myself—take your pick."

"All right," Vasquez said in a reasonable tone. "Walk me through who might have done this and why?"

Harcourt proceeded to tell the assembled law enforcement officers his suspicions about Peter Talbert and how he believed the RCMP Constable Hobday might have planted the skull.

They all went outside and conferred in low voices, the female agent speaking sharply until they all became quiet. When the door was opened, the woman came back inside.

"Here's what we'll do," she said.

"I'm listening."

"We agree to listen to your side of the story and if we think you aren't blowing smoke up our assess, we will allow you to leave our custody—but not entirely."

"What?"

"Bear with me. You said you wanted to leave so you could find Sabrina Cane. Well, that's what we want to do as well. If we don't think you are full of shit after you tell us everything, then you will be free to go, but we will keep some of our people with you, and you will not be free to try and shake them."

Harcourt considered this. On the one hand, he'd be talking and waiving his rights to counsel. If they decided they didn't believe him, or if they had some evidence they weren't sharing with him, he could get himself into a deep load of shit. On the other hand, if they thought his story had some validity, and it matched what they'd heard already from Mark, maybe they'd give him the benefit of the doubt. Maybe they knew there was ticking clock for the kidnapped child and it was in their best interest to let things play out and not involve attorneys, subpoenas, and all the delays that came with it.

"Mr. Raymondson?"

"Where's Mark Pearson?"

"He's not a part of this," said the CSIS man.

"Let me revise my terms," Harcourt said.

"You can't—"

"Let him speak," said the woman.

"If you let Mark sit in on this and send that jerk out of here, I'll agree to speak to you now and tell you everything I know without an attorney, provided Mark and whomever else you want to send will be available to help me go find Sabrina, just as soon as we're done."

"He can't do that," protested the CSIS man.

They went back outside and the voices were louder this time, and the CSIS man left in a huff.

They waited outside and Harcourt's hopes grew as he saw an angry-looking Mark Pearson come into the room. The woman spoke to him and few minutes later, they shook hands.

She, Mark, and the FBI agent came into the room.

She spoke.

"We've agreed to your terms."

Harcourt told them everything, leaving nothing out except some of the more personal aspects of his relationship with Sabrina.

"I can't be certain if he's involved in any way, but I think you should look into a business associate of mine," Harcourt added after he'd finished explaining what had happened since the bridge collapsed.

"And who is that?"

"His name is Peter Talbert. He had an interest in keeping me away from New York. It's possible he hired this Constable Hobday to keep me in Diversion."

"Are you saying that the Constable is responsible for the bridge issues?"

"No, that was lightning, wasn't it?"

"We've been informed that there are signs that the damage was man-made. Explosives."

"Really?" Harcourt said.

"Then it would make sense," Harcourt said. "I was informed of the upcoming board meeting during the video conference, the morning before a storm was scheduled to blow across the island. With the bridge being out, and cell coverage down, it would be hard for me to get out of town and to the meeting to save my company from being taken over. That would be incentive for Talbert, don't you see?"

"That all seems a little far-fetched," said the FBI agent. "You say this constable blew up a bridge and then planted a child's skull in your house?"

"In the cottage."

"Why would he do that?"

"I don't know, to make me go mad? I didn't tell you that I'd been in mourning for close to a year, and that I was due to return to the company, business as usual, in just a few weeks. It was his last chance to make sure I didn't come back."

The FBI agent said, "All right, we'll look into him, but none of this helps us to find Sabrina Cane, or Baby Adalyn.

Is there anything in your mind that connects this Peter Talbert to either of them?"

Harcourt shook his head. "I think it's just a coincidence."

"I don't believe in coincidences."

Harcourt tugged at his handcuffs. "Can you guys release me and let me hit a bathroom, and then can we start figuring out how to find Sabrina?"

The FBI agent nodded, and Harcourt's cuffs were removed.

When he came out of the men's room, a deputy was waiting for him. "This way, sir."

Walking without restraints, Harcourt followed her to a stairwell, then up a flight of stairs. At the top, she led him down a hall until he arrived at the outside of a large conference room. It looked like a war room with twenty people staring at documents and television screens and writing things on chalkboards and hanging up pictures.

The FBI agent came forward. "We've confirmed a few things that make us inclined to trust you. Having said that, when you come inside that room over there, you are expected to keep what you hear and see to yourself. If we find out that you've contacted the media, or have done anything else to compromise what we're doing here, I will personally see that we come after you until you can't remember what freedom feels like. Are we clear?"

"Yes, of course."

Some of the people looked up. "Attention everyone. This is Harcourt Raymondson. He's acquainted with Sabrina Cane and is as interested in finding her as we are. He will be acting as a civilian consultant in this matter due to his recent contact with the woman. Please answer any of his questions and don't hesitate to keep him in the loop."

The FBI agent went to the television screen, then spoke to a deputy running the computer. "Can you replay for Mr. Raymondson the video coverage from earlier today? The rain dance?"

An hour later, Harcourt was part of the group, and even the CSIS agent who'd been reluctant to treat Harcourt like anything other than a criminal had come around. Seeing Sabrina's rain dance miracle seemed to give them direction. Harcourt insisted Sabrina couldn't be involved in the kidnapping, since she'd been as stuck in Diversion as he had been when the kidnapping occurred. Seeing the evidence of her magical powers, and reviewing the old footage of her escapades when she was ten years old, made them want to get to Sabrina. She might be legitimate, and she might lead them to the kidnappers or to Baby Adalyn herself.

"Turn that up!" barked a Vancouver detective as he pointed to a television screen.

Harcourt glanced at the screen and saw the words, Baby Adalyn Kidnapping—Exclusive Channel 8 Live Report flashing across the screen, then saw the still photo of what looked like two people in a bedroom. In the foreground, Jack Bressler was standing and holding a microphone. Behind him, a woman sat cross-legged on a bed. Sabrina. "There she is!"

"Quiet."

All other televisions were switched to Channel 8 and the room became silent as Jack Bressler gave his report.

"This is Jack Bressler with an exclusive live report for Channel 8 News Vancouver. As you know, from the rain dance miracle footage shown earlier today, my wife, the shaman Sabrina Cane, has been found. She is the woman referenced by the kidnappers in the 'Ask Sabrina' note, we believe. Ten years ago she famously helped police find two of three kidnapped children during the infamous Fourth of July kidnappings which took place in Seattle, Washington.

"My wife was not interested in having her gifts questioned by the authorities, so she requested that I take her to a safe place and let the world see her at work. I've arranged to have her gifts observed live on camera.

"As you can see, she is now going into her trance, or fugue state. Before she agreed to access her shaman gifts, I showed her a picture of Baby Adalyn and asked her to reach out to the child, to help determine her whereabouts, or even if she's still alive.

"Assuming she is able to connect with Baby Adalyn in the spiritual plane, she should then move to the art wall."

Jack stopped speaking as an unseen cameraman turned the camera away from the standing reporter and the woman on the bed, and focused on the other end of the room, pulling back to take in the large white wall.

"As you can see, we have a blank canvas here, and on the floor we have all the art supplies Sabrina will need. In the past, she's had her visions and created her art in private, so in a moment, I will leave the room. However, the camera will remain on, broadcasting a live feed.

"The images, if any, that Sabrina Cane creates will be seen by you the viewer at the same time any law enforcement agency gets a chance to view the image. This psychic shamanic gift comes from deep within her and can't be rushed, or accessed through police questioning. This is part of the reason we are keeping her away from authorities.

"At this time, Channel 8 News doesn't know where I am. I have borrowed a news van to do the live satellite feed, but otherwise, no Channel 8 executive can reveal our location. Sabrina, I know you can't hear me, but we are all hoping that you will be able to hear Baby Adalyn and that you will help us find her and bring her home to her parents."

With that, the camera remained pointed at the empty wall, and there was nothing else to see, since Jack had left and the door had closed. A few moments later, a new set of words came across the screen. Ask Sabrina Live Cam.

Riggs spoke to the captain of the RCMP. "I'd like to go to Channel 8."

"Fine, go ahead."

"We should come with you," Mark said.

The captain ignored Mark.

Another officer spoke to Riggs. "They'll just claim power of the press. They're not going to reveal their source."

"This isn't about revealing a source, it's about arresting Jack Bressler," Mark said. "Which is why Harcourt and I need to go."

"On what charge?" asked the captain.

"Assault and grand theft auto, just for starters," Mark said. He pulled the statement from the Jeep driver, which showed that he wanted to press charges. He handed it to the captain, whose face lit into a smile.

"Oh, this is damn good. But based on what we've got here, fuck grand theft auto and assault. I think we can easily shoot for felony carjacking on this one, and if Channel 8 gives us trouble we'll arrest all of them for harboring a dangerous criminal."

"Raymondson, Pearson, and Riggs, you get on up there first," the captain said and Harcourt and Mark were the first to their feet. "I need that arrest warrant yesterday, people," he yelled into the room. Then he went into his office and closed the door.

A deputy almost knocked them over as he ran into the room. He shouted, "There's a dead pilot."

"What?" Riggs said, and she stopped the man before he could run off.

"Call just came in on dispatch. They just found the body of one of Channel 4's helicopter pilots, shot up at Vancouver municipal, out in the parking lot."

The trip to Channel 8 news was delayed, and Harcourt was forced to stay in the car while Mark and Riggs office walked onto the scene with blessings from the Captain. Harcourt watched them. As CSI took photographs and surrounded the body with crime tape, Harcourt thought he recognized the man. It was the same man he'd seen sitting in the shaded area at the Diversion helicopter port, waiting for his reporters to return from filming the day's news about

Diversion's fire. He thought about Hobday, and he felt sick to his stomach. Had he done that? Is that the kind of sick fuck he was working with?

When Riggs and Mark returned to the car, they were grim-faced and didn't talk until they'd almost reached the Channel 8 news station.

"So what happened back there?" Harcourt asked as Riggs parked the undercover sedan.

"Looks like that was the pilot who'd flown a three-man crew to Diversion. Bastard was shot in the stomach. Probably bled out for hours before he was found," Mark said.

"Yeah, some shit hole you've got there, whoever the fucker is," Riggs said.

"So, you believe me? You think it's Hobbledick, don't you?" Harcourt said to Riggs.

"Please call him Hobday," Riggs snapped.

"Fine, whatever, do you think it was him, or not?"

Riggs gave up on looking for a parking spot and parked in a loading zone. She turned toward Hark. "If he's the rogue cop you think he is, hijacking a helicopter would be the fastest way to get off the island. So, yeah, I'm beginning to believe that he might be our man."

"What now?" Harcourt asked.

"I'm waiting for word that they've issued an arrest warrant, and then we wait for backup and then we go inside," Riggs said as she settled back for the stakeout.

"What if Jack walks out of the building before we get the warrant?"

"That's why we're here early," Mark explained, trying to calm Harcourt down.

Harcourt tapped on the Mark's headrest. "Hey, did anyone check on that news team in Diversion? Maybe they saw something."

Riggs nodded. She stepped out of the car and made a call, pacing pack and forth on the rain-dampened road.

"Well?" Harcourt asked when she got back in the car.

"They were already on it. They're also sending a team to check out the damage on the bridge."

A RCMP cruiser stopped at their side, and handed Riggs the arrest warrant.

"Stay in the car," she said to Harcourt.

And then everyone went in through the front doors.

They came out forty minutes later, cursing and grumbling.

Mark and Riggs laid it out for Harcourt.

Channel 8's legal counsel made it clear that they had no knowledge of the whereabouts of the reporter, or their news van. Jack was acting as a freelancer. He was neither an informant nor an employee. And since they didn't know where he was, and had no way to communicate with him, they could not be compelled to do so...

"Lawyers," Riggs and Mark both grunted at the same time.

"Now what?" Mark asked Riggs.

Harcourt saw a news van driving through an electronic gate just beyond where they were parked. It seemed to be the entrance to the station's vehicle pool and employee parking lot. "Quick, I need to bum a cigarette and a light," he said, jabbing smoker Riggs on the shoulder.

"What?"

"Just do it, and let me out. I have an idea."

Mark motioned to Riggs to give Harcourt what he wanted. Seconds later, Harcourt flew out the door and raced to the gate, slipping inside just before it clanged shut.

Once inside, he assessed the situation. Mark and Riggs screamed police. But in his jeans and long-sleeved flannel, and over a week's worth of scruffy beard, Harcourt knew that he looked like a man who belonged on the back lot. The sounds of someone running a hose filled his ears. He lit the cigarette and walked toward a man who was hosing down the news truck that had just come in.

"Hey ya," he said, in greeting to the car washer.

"Hey back at you," said the man.

"Leonard Merced," Harcourt said, giving the man his hand.

"I'm Buck. Buck LeFont."

"Listen, I'm new here. I'm supposed to find out if there's a spare news van I can get for later. Maybe this one. When will it be ready?"

"This one just came in. I'm supposed to wash it and gas it up, and check the fluids and stuff, and then the night crew has first dibs. Are you part of the night crew?"

"I guess I'll find out," Harcourt said, laughing a little.

"I'm not familiar with these. I mean, I just stand in front of the mic, normally. Anything cool I need to know about them?"

"Cool? In what way?"

"I don't know. I mean, say we have an accident or something, fall down a mountain, is there any way for you guys to find us?"

"Well, if we think to look for you, we could always use the GPS."

"No kidding, it's got GPS?"

"Yeah."

"How does that work? I mean, wow—that's pretty cool. I suppose you wouldn't be the one to do that. Probably some security drones upstairs, am I right?"

The man puffed out his chest. "Hell, no. I've got a system right over there. I can tell you where every one of our trucks are."

"You're shitting me," Harcourt said. "I don't believe you."

"I'll prove it to you."

The man put down his hose, then turned it off. Harcourt felt his heart race. He followed the man to a little shack. Inside, there was a console with a monitor. "We've got six news trucks. Right now, I've got one in the garage getting new brakes, three in the field, and one on loan, and the one you just saw."

"And they all have GPS?"

"Yup. See, look here." He flipped a switch on the console and the screen came on. It was a large map of Vancouver, as seen from far away.

"I don't see anything," Harcourt said.

"There, and there," Buck said, pointing to two tiny blinking lights on the screen. "Here, let me get a close-up." He turned a knob and the map view became closer. The blinking lights now showed numbers, T3 and T6, practically blinking on top of each other.

"So, those are Trucks 3 and 6? The one I just saw and the one in the garage."

"Exactly."

"What about the others? I mean these were close, but can you really find the ones far away?"

"Absolutely. I'll show you."

Buck moved the cursor, changing the view of the map, making it more macro, until he spotted another blinking light. "This is T1, the one on loan from earlier today."

Harcourt's pulse raced. "Oh, yeah, where's that on the map?"

"Uh, I'm not sure. Let me get in a little closer," Buck said. "Uh, looks like maybe a residential area, up near Seymour Lake, in North Vancouver? Let's find the other two."

The screen changed. "No, I want to see the one in North Vancouver again," Harcourt said.

"Hey, what is this?" Buck flicked off the screen. "Are you even with Channel 8? What did you say your name was?"

"Of course I'm with Channel 8. Hey, I didn't mean to upset you. I was just curious. I mean, why is a news van all the way up there, right?"

Buck's eyebrows knitted together. "Yeah, I see what you mean. But shit happens even in nice neighborhoods, so who knows?" He focused back on the location of T1. Harcourt memorized the coordinates and the name of the nearest street.

Harcourt heard a honking sound, and then the wop wop as if someone had let go a burst of a siren.

"Buck, I'll see you later when I come back with my crew."

"Okay, nice meeting you, Mr. Merced."

Repeating the numbers again and again in his head until he was sure he had them down, Harcourt hurried back to the car, he waved away their questions. "Hush. I need to write down a number. Pen, paper, fast," he ordered. Riggs handed him her notepad and pen. Harcourt held his breath as he wrote down the coordinates, praying he still had them right.

"What the hell?" Riggs asked when Harcourt gasped in air and sat back into his seat.

"I know where she is. I know where the news van is. These are the GPS coordinates."

Riggs made a call and a few minutes later had a street address and directions. Then she started the car, and they headed off to find Jack Bressler and Sabrina Cane.

37 PETER TALBERT

In the fading light, the man loitered at the edge of the clearing, waiting for the two-man helicopter to pick him up. He rubbed at his heavy beard, checking the application, the edges, feeling for residue and bumps and anything else that might give him away. The Hassidic Rabbi outfit had been waiting at the garage and he wrinkled his nose at the musty smell on his shawl. He switched the heavy duffle bag to his other hand, knowing he couldn't lay it on cool, damp ground. Wind whistled through the canopies as the helicopter approached from the south. He opened the zipped bag to let in a last blast of air, then leaned down to look at his accomplishment.

Her eyes were closed and she was sleeping the sleep of the drugged. "You're going to make me famous," he crooned.

Then he zipped the bag up and backed away, taking the child with him, as the helicopter completed its landing.

The pilot jumped out and ran over, too short to bother with ducking his head. The man's lip curled at the pilot's odd body: his prominent forehead, too short legs, and too long arms. The mini-pilot stuck out his hairy hand and the man shook it fast.

Hairy hands stared at the bag. "I've got storage in the back, Mr. Reigrod." He reached his long, hairy arm towards the bag.

"I'll keep it with me," the man said, then he started towards the helicopter.

"You got the money?" asked Hairy hands.

"It's all in here," said the man as he patted the bag.

He handed the pilot his destination, and the helicopter took off, flying close to the trees.

"That was quick," said Hairy hands after only a short time, "we're already here."

He motioned out the window and dipped the helicopter slightly so the man could see.

Even though it was almost dark, the man recognized the property as the old training camp, which had been idle for almost a decade. As the cabin came into view, the man directed the pilot to land in the clearing in front of the house.

The hairy-handed pilot said, "All here, buddy, time to pay up."

The man in the Hassidic robe said, "Why don't you come inside, and have a drink?"

"Don't mind if I do," said the pilot.

As he climbed out of the helicopter, he stumbled, and his luggage dropped hard to the ground. The duffle bag let out a whimper, then quieted.

"What did you say?" asked Hairy hands, who was busy shutting the bird off.

"Nothing, follow me."

A muscle twitched in the man's cheek – where were Babette and Olga? They were supposed to have come out and offered the man tea and cake, booze if he'd take it, laced with something to make him sleep. Then, he'd intended to shoot the man and let them bury him in the woods. He didn't need a pilot to make his escape, he only needed a helicopter. And now he had one.

He strode into the house first, planning to scold the idiot twins for not following his orders. Hairy hands was right behind him. "Nice place, you got here."

"Yes," the man said.

There was no sign of Babette or Olga anywhere. The bag began to whimper, and then cry.

The man saw the pilot's face change; saw his eyes go wide and his pudgy legs backing up towards the door. Before the helicopter pilot could make a lunge for the door, the man had his weapon out. "Hey, I'm cool man, you don't need to do that—" the pilot said as he held his hairy hands up in the air.

"Outside."

Hairy hands reeked of fear, and the little runt took off, bolting for the trees. Sighing, because this wasn't how it was supposed to happen, the man lifted the revolver, and thumbed off the safety, took aim and squeezed the trigger. The pilot shrieked, stumbled, then got up and kept lunging forwards. Though he had many talents, thought the man, a good aim wasn't one of them, so it pleased him that he'd managed to hit target at all from that distance. But, soon the distance was made up, as the pilot had fallen and wasn't getting up. The quivering waste of space, was now just a few feet in front of him. He took aim, paying no heed to the man's desperate pleas for mercy, or his useless attempts to protect himself with his hairy hands, and fired.

As he made his way out of the woods he paused to assessed his new situation. He'd learned that no matter how carefully he planned an operation, unforeseen circumstances often arose. When that happened, he needed to adjust. Keeping his gun up, he eased his way back into the clearing. Babette's car was in the driveway, so, he knew they were around somewhere. When they'd first failed to come down with their cake and tea smiles as planned, he'd originally assumed that they'd just fallen asleep on the job, or something. He pictured them snoring on the couch upstairs, while Caleb and the other child were locked in his bedroom. But, it was unlikely that the two of them could have slept through the screaming little man and his gun shots. "Babette, Olga," he called out as he entered the house, and walked past the baby, who'd gone back to sleep. But all he could hear was the hum of the refrigerator, and the wind rustling the trees outside.

Keeping the gun in both hands and out in front of him, he cleared the downstairs then headed upstairs.

He thrust open the door to the Babette and Olga's room, but it was empty. He checked the bathroom, which was also empty, then went back into the hall, and leaned against the wall. Panting. Trying to think things through.

He'd not counted on this. The twins had his loyal thugs for a more than a decade. He'd counted on them to be too lazy and stupid to guess that he'd decided to terminate their employment soon. But, obviously, he'd underestimated them.

Maybe instead of going back to the cabin with the other child, they'd taken both cars instead of just one? Maybe, they'd delivered the kid as requested so they could pack up some of their things. Maybe there were already on their way back to Bulgaria?

Hoping that they'd not bother taking the kids with them, the man dug out his key and approached Caleb's room at the end of the hall. At the sight of the unlocked and opened door, he sucked in a breath.

"Caleb?" he shouted. "Are you here?"

He paused before going inside, reminding himself that if Caleb or the other child was in the room, they'd both see his face. He'd not intended to wear his mask anymore at this stage of the plan, but given the new changes which he was going to have to make, he wished he'd at least brought it along. But, then, he let that worry go. Whatever adjustments would be needed to his plan, letting any of the children live long enough for a leisurely session with a police sketch artist, wasn't part of it.

Caleb's room was empty of the two captives, and the man's eye twitched violently at the sight. Babette and Olga had taken his children. His hands molded into tight fists and he punched at the wall.

"Ouch," he said the shook out his hand.

Downstairs, a baby's loud cries pierced the air, jolting him back to the present. He checked his watch, as he remembered the other threat. Hobday was headed his way. He'd timed, giving him the location and instructions as to where to bring the girl, to just before he'd started waiting for the helicopter ride. He'd sweetened the job with a promise of cash money, available on delivery of the girl, if he could get there sooner, rather than later. He'd hoped that Hobday would take the bait, but he also knew that Hobday was no fool.

In all those years, he'd had Hobday by the balls, making him do his bidding, he'd heard the hate and the threat that lingered behind the man's willingness to follow orders. He knew that the second Hobday learned who he was, or knew where to find him, he would be in the man's murderous cross-hairs.

He was counting on that.

Before, leaving Caleb's room, he checked under the bed and in the closet, then headed back downstairs towards the crying baby. Once in the living room, he went to the front door and scanned the woods for signs of life. Behind him, the brat's constant bawling seemed to bounced off the wall, and it was making his teeth hurt. The drug supplies in the storage garage had been compromised by some rats, he suspected, and he'd only had one dose to give the kid and she needed another. His teeth hurt from the noise.

"Shut up!" he shouted at the bag.

That only made the baby cry louder.

"If you don't shut up, I may not wait and let you live for the grand finale."

The finale. Just the thought of his glorious return to the world's stage calmed him. So what if Caleb and the other brat were gone? It wouldn't be as spectacular without the other children in the mix, but he still had the most important child in the bag. Laughing at his own joke, he ignored the baby and went into the kitchen, and washed the gun powder residue off his hands.

As he scrubbed them clean, making sure to not miss his fingernails, and rolling back the sleeves of his rabbi robe, so he could get to his forearms, he allowed himself to daydream.

Oh, they would be talking about him for decades, perhaps hundreds, maybe thousands of years. They would write books about him and they'd have a special course dedicated to studying his crimes and methods taught to all profilers, training at Quantico.

After drying his hands, visions of the future faded as the baby's intolerable racket ruined his musings. He had sudden urge, to zip the bag up tight and toss her onto the floor in the basement, and leave her there to cry all she wanted while he got ready for Hobday's imminent arrival.

"Of course," he said, then smiling headed for the basement. He'd forgotten about the drugs cabinet down there. He'd just give the little noise box another dose.

He glanced over at the yowling bundle by the door, and considered taking her downstairs into the basement. Probably best not to leave her alone. He rubbed at the sore muscles in his arm, reluctant to start carrying her around again. They might still call her Baby Adalyn, but the kid was past a year old and she weighed a ton. What was the worry? Babette and Olga and the others were long gone. Hairy hands the pilot wasn't going to give him any trouble. And Hobday was probably still looking for a place to cross the border.

He keyed open the basement door, and switched on the lights. The fluorescents flickered on, casting a sickly yellow light over the cluttered room. Making his way down the steep and rickety stairs, he negotiated boxes and broken furniture until he got to the medicine cabinet.

"You idiots," he said under his breath as he put the key away, since once again they'd failed to lock up the drugs. Tension gripped his neck and he jerked his head to one shoulder, trying to ease it. It didn't help.

Babette and Olga were sloppy, he despised sloppy. He'd hunt them down and make them pay for their treachery. He found the right vial, took it out and stood under the light as he refilled his syringe.

He locked up the medicine cabinet then started back towards the stairs when a crunch above him jolted him alert.

Was that footsteps? Was there somebody up there moving around? It sure as hell wasn't Baby Adalyn.

He pocketed the syringe in his shirt pocket, then after making sure the glass vial didn't roll off the table, he pulled his Ruger back out of the deep pocket of his Rabbi's robe and moved behind the shelter of a metal file cabinet. He held his breath, gun up, ready to fire, and all he could hear was the swish of the fringe on his shawl.

But, the he the squeak of the door. Someone was coming down. He peered around the corner prepared to blast whoever it was, dumb enough to stand at the top of the stairs. But, instead of a person, he realized that the door had been closed. The lock clicked. "No, you don't," he shouted, then tore towards the steps, but before he could get to them, the lights went out, plunging him into total darkness.

His chin bashed into a chair, but he didn't stop. Groping his way through the blackness, he made his way to the wall, then to the stairs. With his left hand on the wall, he ascended the steps, and when his fingers found the door knob and his fears were confirmed, he yanked on it, then kicked out at the door. "You fucking Bulgarian bitches!" he screamed, then heaved himself at the door, hoping to break it open.

But the attack on the door with his body only caused pain to tear through his shoulders. He wasn't a large man, nor terribly strong as men went. He tried the door again, but it still wouldn't budge. Those bitches had locked him in! Uselessly, he banged his fists against the door, then giving up rested his forehead against it. His body shook. He took deep gulps of air to steady himself. He reminded himself that he was too brilliant, too clever, and too diabolical to have been foiled so easily. If anyone could think of a way out of this mess, it was him.

He needed to assess, to think things through.

After his heart stopped pounding and his breathing had returned to normal, he put his ear to the solid door and listened. The first thing he noticed was that the baby wasn't crying anymore. No. He could hear it. But, it sounded less loud. His stomach tightened as he realized what that mean. Someone had picked up that baby and was moving her away from the cabin.

Without thinking it through, he took another run at the door, hitting it even harder than before, and almost dislocating his shoulder. After getting over the first yelps of pain, he started chanting the same threat into the door. "Babette and Olga, I'm going to kill you!"

When the car engine roared to life, followed by the sounds of tires spinning on the dirt driveway, he collapsed onto the floor and buried his head in his hands, his gut twisted as he grasped the mistake he'd made. They were lazy and incompetent, but they weren't as stupid as he wanted to believe. They'd heard about the million-dollar reward and they saw their chance and took it.

Anger bubbled up inside him again. "I'm going to rip you apart piece by piece," he roared. They'd ruined everything. All his plans. All his glory. And after all he'd done for them.

He got back on his feet and tried the door again, then dissolved into a full-on tantrum, screaming and stomping his

feet and slapping his arms around him, lashing out at anything in his path. "You fucking Bulgarian bitches!" As one
of his arm flails, caused a finger to bump against something
on the wall, lights flicked on for a split second, and then
went off. He stopped, and retraced his fingers, then found a
light switch on the wall. He turned on the lights, and the
fluorescents hissed and hummed, as he indulged in another
round of maniacal laughter. Once, he got that out of his
system, he looked at the obstacle. It was just a door. Surely,
he could get through it?

Then another thought drifted into his mind and his leg
muscles tensed at the thought. He had to get out of there
and fast. What if Babette and Olga, finally figured out that
this was their best chance to eliminate their number one
threat. Him? At any moment, they'd turn that car around
and do something to make sure that he never got out, never
came after them. That's what he'd do if the shoe was on the
other foot.

He couldn't breathe. After pulling out his wallet and keys
and placing his gun on the floor, he tugged off the damn
shawl and then the robe and threw them to the bottom of
the steps. It would only slow him down.

He saw the gun on ground and picked it up, then looked
at the door. Why the hell, not?

Touching the wall with his left hand, he took two steps
down until he was eye level with his target, then aimed the
gun. He hesitated, not sure what part of the door to hit. He
tried to think where would be the best spot to aim, settling

on the sides of the door knob. Holding his breath and sighting the target he fired off the first round. The recoil almost knocked him off the steps, but he caught himself, then walked up the steps to check his work. He smiled at the result. He'd only missed his target by three inches, and he'd done some serious damage to the door. He tried the knob, but it didn't move. Deciding to move his shot between the door knob and the door frame, he went back to his position and lined up his shot.

The instant he fired, a pain like none he'd ever felt before ripped into his right thigh. The impact blew him off his feet, and he fell backwards down the steep steps, discharging another bullet. He lay at the bottom, air knocked out of him, his hands trying to staunch the blood draining from his leg wound. After a moment, his head cleared a bit, and he forced himself to his feet. Wincing and moaning, he dragged himself and his bloody leg up the stairs. He'd miscalculated on that last shot, but on the plus side he'd blown open the door.

Wanting to get to the helicopter for his rifle, he moved through the house, dripping blood over the spot where he'd left Baby Adalyn.

He yanked open the luggage compartment and pulled out the golf bag with his Remington rifle barrel covered with a fluffy warmer. He dug through the side pocket and got ammo and his gloves, then reached inside until his fingers found his night vision goggles. Armed, he stumbled back inside the house, and collapsed into a kitchen chair. After taking a moment, to catch his breath, he put down the rifle and gathered supplies. Duct tape, a roll of paper towels, a pair of scissors would do for a start. After he took care of Hobday, he'd come back and tend to his wound with more precision.

Supporting himself with the back of a wooden chair, he used the scissors to cut away his pants. With one leg exposed, he sat gingerly into the chair and while gritting his teeth, proceeded to cover the entry wound with thickly folded paper towels, then as he cursed from the pain, held it in place by wrapping duct tape tightly around it.

Once the job was done, he took a moment to recover, then got up, stumbled back to the sink and washed and scrubbed and rinsed, until all the blood was off his hands.

As he returned to his seat, his eyes darted towards the windows and the front door, scanning for signs that anyone was coming. The longer they didn't come back, the more likely it was that Babette and Olga had been too stupid to take care of him when they had the chance. He'd go after Babette and Olga later, after he'd taken care of Hobday. Maybe the two bitches still had all the kids. He'd deal with Hobday, find some doctor to stitch him up, then he'd contact the operative he'd hired to placed GPS tracker on their cars, and then he'd go after them. If he found them fast, he'd bring the kids back and still have a chance to follow through on his original plan. He'd just be off a few days, that's all.

Heartened by the prospect of how easy it would be to find Babette and Olga, the man focused on his next task. Killing Hobday, before Hobday could kill him. After double checking that the Remington was locked and loaded, he put the night vision goggles on his forehead and headed out the door.

It was closing in on eight o'clock, and the slow sunset was growing closer towards dark every second. As he trudged down the road, each step was more excruciating than the last. He tightened his jaw and forced himself forward, ignoring the desire to go back to the house and see if there was morphine in the basement. The certainly was supposed to be, but he wouldn't put it past Babette or Olga to have taken it with them, or to have already used it up. Knowing that pain beat getting surprised by Hobday, he continued his forward progress on the dirt road.

The shadows from the canopy of trees closed in on him.

He'd intended to stop at a spot about a mile before the house, where a bolder offered both protection and a clear shot of anyone coming up the road, but after only a quarter mile his dizziness made his stop and settle on a large incense cedar. He leaned against it, panting from the relief of taking some of the weight off his injured leg. He positioned his body and his rifle and pulled down his goggles, then peered up the road. He was ready to meet Hobday for the first time.

38   SABRINA

My body ached from sitting on the floor. For the last hour, I'd been working at a steady pace, building the mosaic the way I always did on a vertical surface: from the ground up. But, since the bulk of the image was higher up, there wasn't much to show for all my work.

And I was having trouble coming up with a design. I kept thinking about the image I'd made when I was a kid. The kidnapped children, and the kidnappers beside them. But all I had to go on was a picture of Baby Adalyn, which I kept having to go back behind the video camera to look at.

I was starting to stress about how Jack might react if I had nothing worth looking at in time for his next report, and I didn't want to upset him, not after he'd threatened Jeannette and her two boys.

I needed to summon my inner muse.

I snapped my finger. Of course.

I dug into the pockets of my jeans I found the pieces of vision stick.

And then something else occurred to me. *If the vision stick works, maybe you can save that poor child for real?*

I left the wall and walked behind the camera again, and this time instead of staring at Baby Adalyn's photo, I started to gnaw and chew on my stick.

As soon as I'd swallowed it, I went back in front of the camera and back to the wall, waiting for my vision to start. Nothing happened.

Frustrated, I felt into my pockets again. Maybe I needed more. When my fingertips touched something round and hard near the bottom, I pulled it out, thinking a chunk of the vision stick had come off. I gasped at the sight of the widowmaker, and had a sudden, horrible thought.

I laughed, like a crazy woman, for a second -- then caught myself. I couldn't do that. That would be wrong in so many ways. And besides, as much as I hated his guts, the truth was, until I could legally undo the ties that bind, he was my husband, and I'd made a promise. For better or worse.

Frustrated, I shoved the stupid seedpod, or whatever the heck it was, deep into my pocket and washed my hands under hot water, just as a precaution. Fuzziness blurred my vision, and I pulled off my outer shirt then tugged at the sports bra, trying to get some air on my perspiring skin. I picked up where I'd left off focusing on Baby Adalyn's shoes, but all I could think about was that damn wedding.

I'd had a handful of awkward and meaningless relationships with men, but when Jack appeared in my life it was the first time I was courted. He was too good to be true. Handsome, attentive, always buying me gifts and telling me how pretty I was. A few months into our relationship, I'd agreed to go with him to Vegas so he could test out his new BMW sports car. After we checked into our room, he persuaded me to 'have a little fun for a change,' encouraging me to go to the bar and have some drinks. I wasn't much of a drinker, but he insisted that I 'let my hair down for once.' So, I did.

I didn't remember much of anything after that first drink in the Casino bar, but I do remember waking up the next day, the sun burning bright as it was already noon. Jack came over to me in the bed, and gave me a deep kiss, as he smiled from ear to ear. "Well, good morning, Mrs. Bressler."

I remember feeling disoriented and thinking, when I could think, that Jack was making a joke. But then he showed me the wedding ring on my finger, a huge one-carat diamond that took my breath away.

He was hurt that I'd forgotten our nuptials, but after my initial embarrassment at blacking out for the most important event of my life, I started to question him about it. Wanting the details. Where had he been when he asked me? What had I said? What was my dress like? And more questions. Jack closed up, not interested in trying to remind me of something that obviously was not important enough for me to remember. He was hurt. So I dropped it.

Not imagining any reason why he'd make this shit up, I'd just accepted Jack's version of the truth, like a fool.

Finally, he stopped acting hurt and showed me the pictures and told me all about how it had happened. We were on the Gondola ride at the Venetian and, after kissing, I was the one that had confessed my love. He, apparently, admitted that he loved me too, and then went straight to the chapel and tied the knot.

I still couldn't believe it, until he showed me the pictures.

And even though I was pretending to be okay with the whole thing, I remember being pretty upset about having lost my whole engagement and wedding experience. But I didn't express how I felt. We'd driven back much of the way in silence, and I was thinking about asking him to take me to my apartment. I wanted to think things through before I committed to sleeping in the same bed as him every night. But he pleaded with me to let him show us our new home.

I relented, my heart starting to race as he passed the middle-class area where his condo had been and drove towards Sunset Hills.

"Why are we going here?" I asked.

"Just wait," he said with a grin.

And when he drove past a guard house and into a neighborhood of executive homes, then clicked open a three-car garage attached to a home with a Tuscan façade, he said, "Welcome home, Mrs. Bressler."

"How, is this possible?" I asked him as helped me out of the car.

"I sold the script," he said excitedly.

I had been so blown away by my new prosperity that I'd forgotten how I hadn't been thrilled when I'd first found out he was writing a movie script about the Fourth of July Kidnappings. He didn't mention this fact until after I'd told him everything I could remember about the event.

We almost broke up when I learned the truth, but he wooed me back with gifts and flowers. All the other men in my life were always just trying to have sex, or ask me for money, or get me to do their laundry. Jack was the first man who treated me special, like a lady...

So, as time passed, I stopped worrying about the script, telling myself that no one would buy it.

I mean, the story was ten years old, and had only been a big deal in Washington, where the kidnappings had occurred.

But I'd been wrong. Not only had the script sold, it had sold for enough to make Jack Bressler a seemingly wealthy man. So I got over myself and stopped being such a pill, and let him carry me over the threshold. I had a handsome and attentive husband, a big house, and fame and fortune on the horizon. What was there to complain about?

I opened my eyes as a shudder went through me. Maybe it was the vision stick, or maybe sense was finally seeping in. I'd never been on a gondola with him, I'd never told him I loved him, or suggested we get married. Just like he'd roofied me to get me out of Diversion and to wherever the hell I was now, he'd roofied me back then and set up the sham wedding.

Total fucking bastard, I thought.

A wave of fatigue washed over me, dragging me onto the floor. I lay on my side, unable to move, and gave into the urge to close my drooping eyelids. I seemed to leave my body as I watched myself convulse amongst the broken bits of tile, and saw myself drift into a different reality.

I peer out, listening to the whir of the camera. I'm somewhere, but I'm also nowhere. As I watch from above I see myself rising from the floor, moving about; crazed, frantic, intense. I see my hands and fingers moving rapidly over the wall – my canvas. I pick up brushes and pour paint into puddles on the floor and smear charcoal and pastels on the wall, and take fat markers and bring to life an image... I don't see what I'm creating. I'm seeing through someone else's eyes. I'm drawing what the other eyes are seeing ... They are me, I am them...

Caleb knew what had happened to the man who'd pleaded for his life. He'd heard the shots, and then no more sounds from the man. Footsteps on the cellar stairs told him where Sir was heading. Caleb whispered to the boy beside him, "I'll be right back. Quiet. Quiet as a mouse."

As he ran into the house, he saw the bag, and inside he could make out tiny hands reaching out to him. "Oh, man," he whispered at the sight of it. "I'll be right back."

Grateful [for the first time] that they had never fed him enough, and that he had such a slight frame, Caleb slid noiselessly across the wood floor, avoiding the loose boards he knew always creaked. He knew that Babette was lazy and that she kept a spare key to the cellar hidden. He went to the junk drawer and felt around till he found it. She thought she was clever, taping it to the back of the drawer. After tearing out the key, he closed the drawer with a slow, steady movement. His heart pumped so fast he heard the drumming of blood in his ears. Blowing out a slow breath, he inched his way to the open door of the basement, staying in the shadows, out of sight.

Down in the cellar he heard Sir grumbling to himself. He heard banging as if cabinets or drawers were being opened, or shut.

As he tiptoed the last few feet across the linoleum floor, he poised himself for action. Holding his breath, his fingers clasped around the door handle and he inched it closed with the patience of a snail. After taking in the smallest of breaths, he slipped the key into the lock, and trembling, but determined, fingers turned the key. He heard a gasp of alarm from the basement, then remembered to turn off the light. He hit the switch then ran, scooping up the bag with the heavy baby as Sir screamed and pounded on the door.

The baby cried as he pushed his way down the steps. His mind reeled. Sir had taken yet another victim, this time a mere baby. Was there nothing he wouldn't do? He put the heavy burden on the ground and called to the boy still crouched and hiding under the stairs: "We've got to go now." The boy hesitated, but then started to come. Caleb grabbed onto the child's emaciated wrist and helped pull him out. Out in the clearing, the light from the open door of the house reflected off the boy's face. His eyes were full of fear, but he was waiting for instructions. He was being a brave little fox.

"Help me," Caleb said, pointing to the bag with the crying baby. Together they lifted the bag, each of them taking one of the handles. "The car," Caleb said. They put the baby into the back seat of the old car, then Caleb told the little boy to climb in next to her.

Caleb's heart raced as he scanned for signs of Babette or Olga. He knew they'd be coming any second. "Try to get her to stop crying."

As Caleb climbed into the driver's seat, the little boy in the back seat started to speak in a soothing voice to the baby. Caleb managed to put the key into the slot by the wheel of the car, and when he turned it, the engine roared to life. Before, when he'd tried it, he couldn't get it to stay on – but this time, it did. "Yes," he said and pumped his fist into the air, and bounced excitedly in his seat. "Now what?" he asked himself. He stared at the stick in the middle of the car. It was in the P spot, but there were other letters as well. D, R, 1, 2 & 3. He tried to pull it to the R, deciding that D probably meant drive and R probably meant reverse, and since the car was facing the house, D wouldn't do. But he couldn't get the stick to move. "Come on," he said, his chest about to explode with anxiety. He swung his head around, fearing the wrath of Babette and Olga any second, and knowing that their anger would be nothing when compared to the fury of the man locked in the basement. He tried to calm himself, and called on the dark angel for help.

He closed his eyes and put his hand on the top of the nob. For the first time, he felt a little button. He pressed it, and it gave, and when he pulled back this time, the stick moved. But so did the car.

"Shit!"

He managed to stretch his legs until he got his foot on the pedal on the left. The car braked. Breathing hard, he kept the brake pedal down and tried again, this time watching as he eased off the brake. The car moved back slightly, then stopped. He moved his foot to the other pedal and pressed. The car bolted backwards. He understood. Left stop. Right go. His legs were so short that his butt almost hung off the edge of the seat, but as he applied consistent pressure on the correct pedal, the car began to move. He held onto the steering wheel, then called out to the little boy in the back. "Sit up and look out the window, tell me which way to go."

"I don't know what you mean?"

"Tell me to go straight or turn a little one way or the other. Left or right."

"I don't know left or right."

"Do you know where your heart is?"

"Yes."

"That's on your left side. Okay?"

"Okay."

Caleb stretched his body as best he could, and could kind of see where the trees were cleared and where the road was. The car moved towards it.

"Keep going straight," said the little boy.

Caleb's body ached, and his neck was sore from trying to twist his body so he could drive backwards, but it was working, and so far, no one had come running after them. When they'd been moving so long that he could no longer see the house, he let go of the gas, and put his foot on the brake. And took a moment to catch his breath.

The baby wasn't crying anymore. But the boy was sniffling. "You okay back there?"

"I'm afraid," said the little boy.

"How's the baby?"

"She's okay," he said.

Caleb played with the gear shift and the wheel, and decided that there had to be a better way. Little by little, switching from R to D, he managed to turn the car around so it was facing the road. It was dark, save for the light from the moon, and he couldn't see very well. He stretched back down and pressed the gas harder. He knew it wouldn't be much longer before he got to the gate. He saw the outlines of the old playground to his right and was staring at the large wooden structure with the deteriorated rope net hanging down from it when something moving fast caught the corner of his eye. He jerked the wheel and tried to slam on the brakes but his body slipped off the seat, causing his foot to get stuck on the gas. The car roared off the road, narrowly missing a tree, the dropped into a ditch. Caleb was thrown forward and he heard the little boy in the back slam against the rear of his seat, and the baby began to wail, and the engine died.

And for the first time in a long time, so did Caleb's hopes. The car was face down into ditch, butt poking out into the woods. "Are you alright?"

"Yeah, I think so."

"Baby?"

"I don't know. I can't get her to move."

Caleb scrambled into the back seat and looked in the bag. The baby wasn't crying anymore, and her eyes were closed. He felt her face, hoping for a pulse, a sign of life. It was weak, but it was there. Caleb let out a sigh of relief, and then he felt moisture on his hand, and wondered if it was raining outside, if he'd put a hole in the ceiling. Then he tasted salt on his tongue, and knew that he was crying for the first time in years. "I'm going to save you little baby, I promise. My angel will help us."

Then he said to the night, "Please dark angel, please help us."

39 BABETTE & OLGA

When Babette and Olga first heard the helicopter land, they met up with each other and headed back towards the house, ready to be chewed out for losing the boys.

But when they heard the gun go off, Babette pulled Olga back and they kept out of sight.

"If he could do that to him, then maybe he'll do that to us?" Babette said.

"If he wanted to kill us, he's had years to do that," Olga said.

"Yes, perhaps, but maybe now he wants to and before he didn't?"

Olga nodded at that reasoning. They remained hidden in the trees while they waited and watched.

They heard their master's voice screaming for them. "Babette, Olga, get me out of here."

Babette cocked her head at her sister, who was hard to see in the fading light. "He's been locked in the cellar?"

"Yes, it appears to be so, sister."

"You want to let him out?" Babette asked.

"No. Do you?"

"No."

"What do we do?" Olga wanted to know.

"I think we should leave."

"Okay sister. I think you're right."

From inside the house they heard Sir's shouting. "Olga, Babette, let me out of here now or you're both dead!"

Olga and Babette looked at each other, then towards the sounds of Sir shouting in the basement.

Olga took out her lighter and smiled.

"Got anything you need before we burn it to the ground?"

"No, not really, I can always buy more vodka," said Babette.

As they moved cautiously towards the back of the house, and the stacks of kindling kept there, Olga and Babette were so engrossed with their devious plan that they failed to see the three pairs of yellow eyes glinting at them from just beyond the tree line.

40   JACK BRESSLER

Jack was bored. They'd set everything up so the communications from the TV van only went one way. From him to them. He had the live cam focused on Sabrina, and they told him they didn't want to hear his report or see his ugly mug until exactly six o'clock. So he had to fart around, boring himself to death as he waited for his time to shine.

He wished he hadn't announced during his first report that he wouldn't bother Sabrina, that she needed to work alone. He wanted to see if she was even doing anything.

At four o'clock, he decided to get some beauty sleep. But before he lay down on the day bed in the living room, he noticed that there was a text on the phone used only by his benefactor. Knowing he hadn't exactly done as he was told, he almost didn't look at it. But he decided it would be something to do. After he'd told his benefactor that he had Sabrina in his custody, but needed a place to keep her safe where he couldn't be found, his benefactor, in typical fashion, had texted him an address.

He shared the address with no one from the television station, since he was already incommunicado with them, and was pleased to discover that the place was perfect for his needs. Out of the way, plenty of coverage in the trees, and a nice big room with smooth white walls for Sabrina's canvas.

But, some time after he'd made his first report, he received another text from his benefactor. And this one wasn't helpful.

Stop the live cam you idiot.

Jack recalled how much his face had burned with humiliation. He was sick of dealing with that anonymous prick.

For a while, the text disturbed Jack's calm, but soon his confidence returned. That mystery benefactor wasn't important anymore. He was about to make journalism history. All eyes in two countries would be on him. When it was all said and done, he wouldn't need his benefactor's help any more. The news media would be begging him to join their teams. He'd be a broadcaster again, set for life.

Jack had considered showing his disdain for the latest order by replying with a few choice words. But he didn't want the man to overreact and upset his production. After-all, unlike the rest of the world, his benefactor knew where he was. Instead, he decided to act as if he hadn't seen the message.

He had another beer and stretched out on the couch. Too bad there was no television, he mused. He closed his eyes and daydreamed instead, of accepting his new position as newscaster for a major market, praising him as he gleamed in black tie, acknowledging him for his innovative journalism.

He'd nodded off, and when he woke up, he decided to check on the cameraman.

Behind the house, hidden by the homes and the trees, the Channel 8 Newsvan had its engine humming and the big satellite dish all the way up. He knocked on the door and waited for Chubby to answer.

"Yeah?"

"I wanted to see what she's up to," Jack said. "Any eyes on that?"

"Sure, dude. I'm glad you're here. You can monitor the live feed while I get something to eat."

"Monitor?"

"Yeah. See that button?" he pointed to a button on the console next to a monitor the size of a birthday card. Jack nodded, then turned on the monitor. "Every fifteen minutes, the live feed automatically shuts off, and you got to give that button a good hard punch, within thirty seconds, or everything shuts off – and I'll have to back in there and reset everything."

"We don't want that," Jack said with a cocky grin.

"Yeah, we don't," said Chubby without a smile.

"You think you can handle this?" he added as he pointed to the button.

"I thought I could watch her," Jack complained as he stared at the empty monitor.

"Normally you could, but the monitor failed. But you can watch it on the live news. Here, let me turn it on for you. Not that there's anything to see. Last time I checked the media wasn't paying much attention to the live feed. She hasn't done anything interesting."

A light blinked on the faulty live cam monitor, and Chubby pushed him aside and slammed his fist on the button. The light went to green, then faded. "You got to keep an eye on that, man," he scolded. Jack wrinkled his nose as he caught the unpleasant stench of the man's body odor, and had to force down the urge to gag.

But then as the chubby cameraman departed and lumbered towards the house, Jack saw that they were showing his image on the current live news broadcast, and forgot all about the unpleasant odors in the van.

"Coming soon, the latest from the Ask Sabrina live cam, with our featured guest reporter, Jack Bressler," said the broadcaster from behind his desk. Above him there was a clip of him from his original report at the hidden location of the Ask Sabrina Live Cam.

"Man, do I look good, or what?" he said to himself as he lifted his chin and smoothed his hair.

They did a short replay of his earlier broadcast from the undisclosed location, when he'd first introduced what would be happening at the Ask Sabrina Live Cam, then the shots switched to the Live Cam, and Jack almost fell off his chair. Unlike what Chubby had described – a total snooze fest in the art department – she was going to town. Even as he watched her work, shapes were taking form, the images becoming clearer and clearer by the second. She moved like a madwoman on crack, just in time for his next report. He clapped his hands. "This is awesome, fucking awesome."

The live cam switched to a split screen showing a pair of talking heads, each one with their name and credentials showing underneath.

"It's truly a remarkable thing," said Stephanie Peller, from the Department of Media Studies at Vancouver, University. "Not only is Channel Eight making history by defying orders from both the Canadian and US Governments, they are also giving the public access to an unprecedented display. Have you seen what she's accomplished in the last hour? I'd say we are all witnessing what might be an authentic display of a psychic manifestation."

"I couldn't agree with you more, that it's astonishing, what we are witnessing," chimed in Charles Drunberry, Professor of Paranormal Studies, University of Ottawa. "And I for one, believe that his is nothing short of extraordinary. And that we are in fact witnessing a remarkable and most likely otherworldly feat. Especially when viewed against the other footage we have of Sabrina Cane."

There was a pause, as both talking heads waited. Drunberry piped up, "If we could take another look at the rain dance footage..."

Jack sat up in his seat, feeling taller and bigger than he'd ever felt. They were showing his report from Diversion, a report he hadn't yet seen. Where he'd single-handedly, and exclusively, captured Sabrina and the others making it rain.

The replay was all too short before the talking heads returned. They nodded, then the camera switched back to Sabrina on Live Cam. Jack watched for a while as Sabrina continued her remarkable pace. He focused on the picture, which was starting to come to life.

Charles Drunberry was having his say. "I know that all of Canada is hoping she's the real deal. That she can come up with an image that will help save Baby Adalyn. I wonder, do you think that object in the middle is supposed to represent Baby Adalyn?"

"It certainly appears to be a baby's face, but what is the baby lying in?" asked Stephanie Pellar.

"A crib?"

"I don't think so, looks more like a bag. And look at the hand that's holding one of the handles on the bag."

"You're right. I see what you mean. Do you think that's the hand of the kidnapper?"

"Well, if it is, that doesn't make any sense. I mean, look at how small that hand is."

"Maybe it's small as a metaphorical statement," suggested Charles Drunberry. His voice was nasal and his eyes focused up to his left as he thought about things. "To Sabrina, or perhaps to Baby Adalyn, if it's possible that she's indeed channeling the child's current experiences, then maybe the man is small-minded, or lacking in human kind-ness, thus the allegorical symbolism of a small hand."

"You might have something there, although my guess is that she's just building up layers and she'll be making that hand bigger later, most likely. It's truly riveting television, I'm sure Jack Bressler will be up for a Pulitzer for this piece," added Stephanie Pellar.

Both men nodded in agreement at that statement and Jack bounced in his chair, and almost came at the thought. The Pulitzer. No one would dare black-ball him after that.

"Well, I'm sure as the developing story continues, things will be revealed," Charles Drunberry said.

"Absolutely," agreed Stephanie Pellar, then she took a sip of her water. "What's she drawing now?"

Suddenly the Ask Sabrina Live Cam on the bottom of the horizontally split screen went away, and there were test bars, indicating technical problems. Both talking heads listened to their earsets.

Charles Drunberry said, "I guess we've lost the live broadcast for a moment or two."

"That's too bad, I hope it goes live again soon."

Jack was angry that these incompetents had fucked up, until he caught the flash of the blinking red light. He lunged towards it and pressed the button.

He pressed his palms to his eyes in relief when the Live Cam reappeared on the screen. He'd been that close to hav-ing it down for how long?

He sat back as the station just let the live cam run. Even the talking heads just watched. Next to them was the image of the baby in a duffle bag, which had become clearer with each stroke of her brush.

One of the two small hands holding the baby in the bag had become a person. Only it wasn't an adult. It was a child. Brilliant. Fucking brilliant. Since she had no idea who the culprits were, why not create a bunch of little kids as culprits? This would take the media by storm.

He felt himself grow a little hard with pride for her. She was his wife, after all. He adjusted his dick in his pants and tried to recall how long it had been.

He had a sudden urge to reward all her hard work with a little hard work of his own. Give her a little of his in and out magic; a soothing massage between her legs...

He knew that, given the current circumstances, she might not be too keen on that plan, but he had those pictures of her alleged real family – so he figured he'd be able to convince her.

Jack knew the smart thing to do would be to wait until after his report, after the six-o'clock news, but he was horny right now. Besides, she'd done enough for one day.

The talking heads had been saying things that Jack had missed, but the Sabrina shot still split the screen. He saw that a second child was coming to life. Shit. She was moving way too fast. If he didn't stop her quick, she'd be done, and there would be nothing more to watch.

He needed to milk his moment in the sun. He needed to keep her in the public eye all night, maybe into the next day.

It was in his best interest the longer she took to finish that mural.

The longer he was in the public eye, the better.

When Chubby returned to the van, Jack persuaded him to pre-record his six o'clock report.

Jack kept it short, five minutes, standing with the Channel 8 news van as his backdrop and making sure no trees could be seen in the camera lens. In his report, he waxed poetic about how remarkable his wife was, then went on to explain based on his experiences with her in the past that she could pass out at any point. "After one of her fugue states," he explained, "it's not uncommon for her to sleep, ten, sometimes twelve hours."

Jack watched as the camera sent the newly recorded broadcast via the satellite dish to the station. He knew from previous experience that the station would act like it was a live report, since the times were so close. With the show no longer an issue, he didn't need the cameraman for the rest of the night. Jack's dick twitched in anticipation. Jack thanked him for his fine work, then said, "let me get you another beer."

After lacing Chubby's next beer with one of his remaining Rohypnols, Jack delivered it, bottle cap off.

The newsman put it on the counter and didn't seem interested in drinking it right away, but Jack decided not to sweat it. He figured Chubby would get into his beer soon enough.

Jack marched back into the house and locked the front door. Then he sauntered into Sabrina's room, unable to stop grinning as he locked her door. After turning off the camera for the night, then wetting his lips in anticipation, he unbuckled his belt and stalked towards his wife, ready to redirect that manic energy of hers onto his cock.

41 SABRINA

My hands were covered in paint.

Someone was pulling me away from the wall.

As if coming out of a trance, I knew what was happening.

Jack was in the room with me, and he was trying to pull down my pants.

"Stop," I said, the words barely croaking out of me.

I managed to jerk out of his reach.

"Sabrina, honey, save it for Bubba," he said and pointed to his cock.

It was sticking out of his pants, waving at me like some sick joke.

"Jack, what the fuck? Get away from me."

"Sabrina, don't be a cow," he said. And he was on me, pushing me towards the bed.

"Stop it, you're hurting me."

But Jack didn't care. His eyes lit up, like that was what he wanted to do.

He let go of my arm to tug at my jeans, again.

I struggled, and screamed. "Stop it, stop" then shouted, "Rape. Rape!"

"You fucking bitch," Jack said as he shoved me onto the bed. "I'm going to fuck you up for doing that, you ungrateful whore."

I jerked my body violently, dislodging him then I scrambled to pull my pants back up over my hips even as I backed away on the bed. He had his belt in his hands, and he was slapping it menacingly against his thighs as he glared at me, cowering away from him.

My heart thumped as he stood up on the bed, then widened his stance so he wouldn't fall. He towered over me, raising the belt over his head.

"No, don't," I screamed as I covered my face and lunged out of the range of the belt, bracing myself for impact. But instead of the sharp sting of leather on flesh, there was a terrific booming noise and the sound of glass breaking.

I covered my head and slammed my body into the bed, closing my eyes shut as glass shards flew against my body, my arms, the bed. I heard the sound of a heavy body thumping to the floor. Then, I heard nothing, but the wind whistling in the trees outside the shattered window.

I couldn't process what had happened, but somehow I knew.

When I finally dared to peek, I couldn't stop the scream.

THE BILLIONAIRE'S SHAMAN

My estranged husband, Jack Bressler, was no longer looming over me, he was splayed out on the floor next to the bed. Half of his head missing.

I found most of the missing pieces as my eyes traveled to the ceiling and to my mural on the wall. By then, his body had toppled over like a bowling pin, and my chest was about to explode.

Self-preservation kicked in, as I realized that someone outside that window had just shot and killed Jack and I could be next. Desperate to get out of the line of fire, I flung myself onto the floor and, running on all fours, managed to get to the door. I spent too long trying to unlock it, then hurtled into the hallway and raced to the front door.

I tried to think. There was the other man, the cameraman, he was in the van. He could help me, we could drive away... Then I heard the van's engine race and heard desperate tires spinning in the dirt. "Oh, no, don't leave me," I cried. When I heard the next shot, I thought my chest would explode. I grabbed my heart and looked around wildly, trying to think of what I could do. A second later, wood groaned and metal tore as the van must have slammed into a tree.

"Oh, no, oh no," I moaned. The man with the gun was still out there, and the camera man wasn't going to be much help. I knew the shooter would be coming for me next. I bolted to the front door, and fumbled to open the lock. Then I ran outside and made a beeline for the side of the house farthest from where I'd heard the van crash. To my left, was a thick forest. I wanted to run into it, but I couldn't move. I was afraid to give away my position.

I stayed at the corner of the house, as my heart jackhammered in my chest. I closed my eyes, trying to listen for movement: the breaking of twigs, anything to give me a sense of the location of my threat.

When he grabbed me from behind, I screamed. But only for a split second because he'd expertly covered my mouth. I cried out in pain as he yanked my arm up behind my back and put the muzzle of cold steel against the base of my skull.

"One more noise like that and you're dead."

I gulped down my next scream and didn't fight or struggle as he dragged me away from the house, and pushed me into the woods. He brought me to a large car, which seemed to gleam in the moonlight, and shoved me into the back seat.

I didn't say anything. I didn't try to escape. I kept repeating the same words in my head. "Don't piss him off, don't piss him off, don't make him tie you up. Stay alive, until you get your chance to escape."

42 HARCOURT

When Harcourt, Mark and the FBI Agent zeroed in on the GPS location, Riggs pointed towards the accident.

"Jesus," Harcourt said, and he tried to get out of the backseat. But the door was locked.

"You're not getting out of this car," Riggs said, then she tossed her cell phone to Harcourt. "Call headquarters, it's HQ on my contacts."

"I thought you already did."

"They're standing by, just fucking call."

Harcourt nodded, but his chest was aching at the thought that Sabrina might be dead or injured in that wrecked van. He found HQ and called, explaining to the others that they'd found the target and there was an accident, and to send an ambulance and come right away.

After he hung up he peered out to where Mark and Riggs were walking around the newsvan. Harcourt saw Riggs' flashlight aim inside the front of the van, and flinched at the sight of a bloodied face buried in the steering wheel.

Riggs covered Mark as he pulled open the sliding door. Riggs cleared the inside of the van, then Mark checked behind her. Then they started towards the house.

Sirens blared and lights flashed, and within seconds the place was crawling with police.

Harcourt wanted to get out and help, but he wasn't dressed like a cop, he wasn't wearing a vest and he wouldn't be able to help Sabrina if he was dead.

Finally, Mark and Riggs appeared at this door and Riggs unlocked it. "She's not here," Mark said. Harcourt felt relief, knowing that at least they hadn't found her dead body.

"But there's something we think you should see."

A bright halogen light glared, illuminating bloody shoe prints which appeared to be running out of the house, and he knew that they were Sabrina's prints. He sucked in a breath, praying that the blood wasn't hers, and tried to be grateful that she'd been able to run. A deputy directed them away from the grim trail and Harcourt followed Mark and Riggs through a kitchen with signs that people had been recently eating. The stench of mustard and pepperocinis made Harcourt hold his breath.

They took him back through a hallway and into a room, which was also lit up by a Halogen light

"Stay on the plastic, please," said Riggs.

Harcourt just stared at the scene. The room was the same one he'd seen on the Ask Sabrina Live Cam. But it was no longer that same neat room. Instead of art supplies, on the floor was a body, head blown half off. Blood and brains were everywhere, including, he realized over much of the wall. "Fuck," he said. "Is that the reporter?"

"Yes, it's Jack alright," Mark said. "Harcourt, buddy, I hate to ask you, but doesn't that kid look, uh, familiar?"

"What the fuck are you talking about?" Mark was pointing to the mural, to a part that hadn't been obscured by the blood and guts, and as his eyes found the image, the image of a small child holding the bag. Harcourt's vision blurred and his knees buckled, and he stumbled backwards.

"Careful!" shouted Riggs, as she and Mark caught Harcourt before he fell against the halogen stand. "What the hell?"

"It's Cedric," Harcourt said pointing a shaky finger at the picture of the small boy. "Why, Sabrina, why?"

"Someone get that man a chair," barked Riggs. A moment later, Harcourt was seated at the back of the room on a chair brought in from the kitchen, and Riggs was up in his face. "Is that your kid? Why do you think she painted it? Is it because she knows you killed him, you son of a bitch?"

"Hey, lay off," Mark warned.

"I don't lay off child killers, and neither should you."

"For the fucking last time," Harcourt shouted. "I didn't kill my child."

"Yeah, then why did you have that skull?"

"I told you, I'd never seen it before the other night. Hobday put it there."

"Excuse me, ma'am," said an officer in the RCMP uniform.

"Yes, what do you want?" snapped Riggs.

"We got the preliminaries back on that skull and it's not his kid."

For a moment, her mouth hung open, but then her eyes narrowed again. "How many children have you murdered, you son of a bitch?"

"Fuck you," Harcourt said. And Mark took Riggs aside. They spoke for a moment and Riggs came back.

"I'm sorry, man, I know you're not the guy. I apologize for overreacting."

Harcourt stared at her, not sure if he believed her sudden change of heart.

He waved around to indicate the scene, as if that gave her a valid excuse for her behavior. Harcourt said. "I don't care what you think of me. I just want get out of here and find Sabrina."

As they discussed possibilities as to where she might be, and RCMP officer came inside, and directed his comments to Riggs, who despite being from another country, seemed to have rank at the crime scene. "Ma'am, we found more of those bloody footprints in the woods."

Harcourt and Mark and Riggs, followed the officer outside. They saw that there were already several officers standing ahead in a clearing. Harcourt's stomach lurched as he imagined what they might all be pointing their flashlights at. But, when they made it to the scene, the men were pointing their lights at something on the ground. It wasn't a body. It wasn't Sabrina. Harcourt's chest almost burst with relief. There was still a chance that he might get her back in one piece.

The men already at the scene, explained what they were looking out. Sabrina's shoe prints stopped near tire tracks on the ground. "She got in a car at this point," said one of the men.

"Do we know what kind of tire tracks?" Riggs asked.

"Not yet, but they are clearly from a large car, I'm guessing an SUV, and they are also relatively new, based on the tread."

Another detective came forward, and flipped a notepad over to find a note. "That suspect, Hobday, allegedly stole an Escalade earlier today. I think those tracks fit the vehicle."

Mark said, "So, we have a plate? I assume that's on the BOLO? Any sightings, yet?"

"I'll check."

The officer called Dispatch, relayed his question, then waited for a reply as everyone watched him.

He ended the radio call, then spoke to the others. "They just got word that the car had passed through the border, approximately twenty minutes ago."

"They let him through the border with a fucking hostage?" Riggs shouted.

The man shrugged. "Don't blame us, your US border patrol controls who gets into the United States, not us."

Riggs nodded, "And we don't know for certain whether she's a hostage or if she's working with Hobday."

Harcourt stiffened, and was about to rip her a good one for that last remark, but stopped when Mark's pressed his hand against his shoulder and whispered. "Cool it, buddy."

They went back to the house, and Harcourt and Mark hung out in the kitchen while Riggs made calls, updating authorities in the US. She came back to the kitchen. "Harcourt, I want you to have another look at the mural, you too Mark. I had one of them men, clean away some of the gore, so I'm hoping you might see something that will help us figure out what the hell is going on."

Harcourt, who'd not been able to take his eyes off the haunted look in his son's face, and barely registered the image of the two children holding a baby in a bag between them, and dark, angel wings stretched out above them, as if protecting them. He barely noticed the pair of evil eyes staring through a dark cloud on the scene. He barely registered any of it, because he couldn't take his eyes off his son's haunted face.

"See anything?" Riggs asked.

Harcourt let his eyes wander, and saw for the first time the details behind the three children. He saw the remains of a cargo net climber, a set of broken down set of monkey bars, and a tunnel crawl cast in shadow. A chill ran up his arms and down his legs. "I know where this is!"

Harcourt explained all about the abandoned military training camp near the Canadian border in the Washington wilderness that Peter Talbert had once tried to get him to purchase as a company asset. "He dragged me out there, thought it would be useful for executive training sessions and the like. I shut the idea down, and I'd never thought of the place again, but it would just like him to use it. The man, could never take no for an answer."

It took another twenty minutes before they could stage the plan of attack. Harcourt and Riggs and Mark would drive through the border and meet up with SWAT and FBI Agents mobilizing at a staging area close to where they hoped they'd find both Sabrina and Baby Adalyn.

43   SABRINA

When I came to, my first thought was where am I? But, then as if my brain knew better than to let me get distracted by forgetting, I instantly remembered where I was and who I was with and what had happened to me. My third thought was to not let Hobbledick know that I wasn't out anymore.

I made my eyes into tiny slits and by moving my head in micro-increments surreptitiously assessed my situation.

I was in that same big car, based on the strong new leather smell, and we were on the move – driving on what felt like paved road, maybe a highway somewhere. Even though it was dark outside, there was enough light coming off the dashboard for me to make out shapes inside the car. I could see my captor leaning forward at the wheel, as if he was looking for something. We were going at a slow speed, no more than five miles an hour. The headlights were on and as I looked ahead, I could tell we were on a mountain road, surrounded by forests and trees.

Great, I thought, and felt my pulse race.

We were in the middle of nowhere.

He's going to murder me and leave my body in a shallow grave, so animals will dig me up and eat the evidence.

This was no time to panic. Catastrophizing wouldn't help me. If I was to have any hope, I needed to keep my wits about me; I'd need to stay positive. I'd need to believe that I could get through this. That I could survive. Where there's life, there's hope. I chanted those words in my mind like a mantra until I fucking believed it.

He pulled off the road and came to a stop. My pulse raced, but I continued to pretend to be passed out. The trunk opened but I didn't risk peeking until I heard a metal snap, and when I did I saw that he had cut open a gate. It creaked as he opened it. A moment later he was back in the front seat, starting the car up again and putting it into gear. We drove through the gate and I knew right away that the road was unpaved and riddled with potholes. He drove slowly ahead for several miles. Then everything became dark and I saw that he'd turned off his headlights. We'd gone another mile or so, at an even slower pace, when there was a loud thump, and glass exploded in front of me.

"Fuck," Hobbledick shouted.

The car jerked to a sudden stop, throwing me out of my seat and onto the floor.

Hobday opened his door and came up firing into the trees.

Hoping that whoever was shooting at us was hoping to hit Hobday and not me, I braced myself, pushed open the door, then leapt out the car. I rolled away on the ground, dirt and stones [sticking to and] bouncing off my arms and face as I went. I got up and with the gun battle still behind me, raced towards the woods as fast as my feet could carry me.

A short while later, the gunfire stopped. I froze.

The woods were silent; not even a cricket chirped. All I could hear was my own heaving breath.

I looked around for better cover and started moving, slowly, towards a dark patch ahead. Then I heard it.

No. No. It couldn't be. I was hallucinating. But then I heard it again, louder and clearer, and I had no doubt. There was a baby nearby. A crying baby.

Trying my best not to make any noise, I ran towards the sound.

44 PETER TALBERT

Peter Talbert expected to miss his first shot, despite the night vision goggles, but figured he'd get him on the second or third shot. But he'd underestimated the effect of the wound in his leg. He had dozed off, exhausted from blood loss, and almost missed Hobday's approach. By the time he got the shot off, Hobday was close enough to him to do damage, so when the first shot simply shattered the windshield but didn't do any damage to his prey he had to deal with return fire. It splintered the tree he was taking cover behind and made it harder to get off a killing shot.

After several more exchanges, he could tell that Hobday was on the move, coming in for a kill shot of his own.

He decided to go for it. He might not be as good a shot as Hobday, but he was smarter.

When the next shot came, he yelled out like he'd been hit. Then immediately got on his belly and aimed the rifle up the path. When Hobday's next shot hit up by where his head had just been, he knew he'd fooled him. A moment later, Hobday's big body appeared like a bear's shadow and the man squeezed off two shots. Hobday's body jerked, then he fell backwards, and didn't move again.

After waiting long enough to make sure he wasn't being fooled, the man pushed himself back to his feet and cried out from the pain. The adrenaline must have masked the pain of throwing himself onto his injured leg, but now that the threat was behind him, he almost passed out from the pain. "Son of a bitch."

With Hobday down, it was time to take care of his leg.

He was about to go to the car and drive himself back to the cabin to hit the morphine, when he heard a sound out in the woods.

Someone was running.

Sabrina?

Who else.

Realizing that Hobday had done his bidding after all by bringing Sabrina Cane, he went over to the man. "Sorry about that, old boy."

Then he picked up Hobday's weapon and headed into the woods.

I thought I was losing my mind. But I kept moving towards the sound of a baby crying in the woods. When I reached a clearing that looked like an abandoned obstacle course for some military training camp, the baby's cries seemed to be magnified, as if in an echo chamber. Then I saw movement: a foot pulling back inside a giant sewer pipe, its metal reflecting moonlight, and I knew I'd found my source.

"Hello," I said, trying to keep my voice low as I inched closer to the pipe. "Who's here? Please come out. I'm not going to hurt you."

"I knew you'd come."

My hand flew to my chest and then to my mouth so I wouldn't scream. A child of twelve or thirteen stood behind me, staring up at me with giant eyes. His hair was wavy and thick and fell past his shoulders, but he was clearly a boy, and not a girl.

"What are you doing out here?" I asked, trying to keep my voice down and get him to do the same. "Hiding from Sir," said the boy.

The mention of another person reminded me that there was still someone out there. Someone with a gun. I heard the crack of branches breaking not far away. "Someone's coming. Protect the others," I said, "I'll lead him away."

"No, dark angel, I'll do it," he said.

At first I was shocked by what he'd called me, and then I realized he was serious as he started to move. I lunged after him and grabbed him. "No," I said and held onto him tight. "Shhhh."

As the footsteps got closer, a voice sang into the night. "Sabriiiiiiina, Sabrina Cane, come out come out, wherever you are."

My blood ran cold and I stopped breathing. Beside me I felt the boy stiffen and his hairs rise under my palm.

"Sabrina, Sabrina, Olly Olly Oxen Free Free Free. I'm not going to hurt you. Come out now…."

I moved my face so my mouth almost touched the boys ear. I could barely hear myself as I spoke. "He doesn't know you are here. It has to be me."

I felt him nod, and when I released his arm he didn't try to run.

After taking in a breath for courage, I bolted out of the clearing on tiptoed feet, and broke into a run, making extra noises with my hands and feet as I hoped to steer him away from the children.

For a while, it looked like I might get to the car, and then drive somewhere and call for help. But, when a shot rang out, hitting a tree a few yards to my right. I knew I wasn't going to make it.

"Stop, don't shoot, I surrender," I shouted.

There were no more shots. I turned around slowly, my heart beating a mile a minute and stared back into the moonlit woods until a man's shape appeared between two trees.

"Sabrina Cane, so very nice to meet you at last," he said as he hobbled towards me. His breathing was labored, reminding me painfully of Ellis. My eyes dropped to his injured leg, which had a strange bandage around it that glinted in the moonlight.

He waved his gun. "To the car."

I went in the direction indicated by the gun and when we got to the door, I stopped, not sure what to do. "Open the passenger door."

I did, and started to get inside. "No, you're driving," he said.

"Alright," I said, trying to keep my voice calm, trying to keep him calm.

He leaned against the door but kept the gun pointed at me as I moved around the front and got inside the driver's seat.

"Now, get in and start the car," he ordered. Then he grunted into his seat, the gun trained at me the whole time. I groped around for the key, but couldn't find it.

"What's taking you so long? I said drive." He was losing his temper.

"I'm sorry, I can't find the key."

"Turn on the fucking overhead," he snapped, jabbing his gun at the interior lighting console.

I felt around until a dome light came on, and I tried not to look at him or his gun as I renewed my efforts to search for the missing key.

"It's not here," I said, lifting my ass to check under my seat. "Maybe you're sitting on it?"

"Fuck it," the man said. "Help me back to the house."

I came around and helped him out of the car and, while he kept a tight grip on the gun, he put his arm around my shoulder sand used me like a crutch. After only a few minutes, I could make out the gleam of lights coming through the windows of a structure ahead. "You need a doctor," I said.

"Shut up."

When we got inside, he directed me to the kitchen table, and at gunpoint proceeded to instruct me as I washed up and boiled water, then, using a knife I'd sterilized with a lighter, he aimed the gun in my face until I got the bullet out of his leg.

After sterilizing the wound with vodka, he made me wrap the wound with paper towels and duct tape.

"Who are you?" I asked, after he'd seemed to calm down.

"Don't talk," he said. "Get me some water."

The pendant burned against my chest. And I remembered the widowmaker in my pocket. This was it. My chance.

"Of course," I said, with more excitement than I'd intended to. But the man was in too much pain to notice, I hoped.

I went to the overhead cabinet and found a glass, ducking my head to glance in his direction. He'd grown tired of holding the gun up, and it lay close to his fingers on the table, but his eyes were still open and I could tell he was watching me.

I filled the glass with water from the sink. But instead of bringing it right over, I pretended to stumble and let the glass slip out of my hand. It didn't break. "Sorry," I said and started to pretend to clean it up, turning my back to him as my left hand dug into my pocket and pulled the pod.

I put the unbroken glass on the counter, and reached for the paper towels to clean up the spilt water. "Leave it, bring me water."

"Okay," I said and took the glass back to the sink, and putting both hands out of his line of sight into the sink, I ran the water over the widowmaker, as I filled his glass again with water. I sniffed the air, hoping it wouldn't have a strong odor. It didn't. Then I regretted sniffing it, afraid I might inhale something deadly, so I held my breath until the water glass was filled.

Turning my face to sip in some air, I saw that my hands were shaking as I put the filled glass of water on the counter. I dropped the pod into the sink and turned the water on full blast as I tried to wash my hands.

"What's taking you so long?"

I wiped my hands on my pants, picked up the glass, and came over. "Sorry," I said as I placed it in front of him.

He lifted his glass and guzzled down the water. He dropped the glass hard on the table and wiped his mouth with the back of his hand. My heart hammered in my chest.

"I need you to go into that basement and go to the medicine cabinet and bring me the morphine and a syringe."

I blinked. Would morphine knock him out?

As instructed I went to the basement, turned on the light, and hunted around for a phone or another useful weapon, but there wasn't anything small enough to conceal.

"What's taking you so long? Get back here."

"I can't find the syringes," I said.

"On top, in a box," he yelled.

"Okay, I've got them."

With the whole box of syringes and two vials of morphine, I went back upstairs.

I was surprised to see him sitting up instead of slouched, and I was surprised to see a syringe, already filled with a light gold liquid sitting near his gun on the table.

"Put them on the table," he said, motioning to the bottles of morphine. I did.

"Now open a syringe, and hand it to me."

I did.

The second he had it, he put the needle into the drug and pulled back the lever, sucking in the drug. Then he shot himself in the leg, like an experienced junkie, and I watched his face relax.

After a while, his arms began to droop.

"Now come here," he said.

I hesitated as his fingers went on the syringe that was already filled when I'd come back upstairs.

"Give me your arm."

"No," I said, "What is it?"

He picked us his gun and aimed it at my chest. "It's going to make you sleep, so I can sleep and not worry about you trying to get away."

"But I'm afraid of needles."

"I said give me your arm."

Terrified that he'd shoot me if I didn't, I reluctantly gave him my arm. I turned away, praying that whatever it was wouldn't kill me, and winced when he stuck the needle in my arm.

"Now sit in that chair and duct tape yourself to the chair."

"What?" I said, already growing tired.

He threw me the duct tape, but when I tried to catch it, my hands weren't working and it hit me in the nose.

I didn't care, because a moment later, I was out.

"Fuck," Peter Talbert said as the sound of a car approaching broke through the silence only seconds after he'd watched the girl pass out. "Fuck, fuck, fuck," he said. He felt slow, dizzy… it had to be the morphine that was making his brain fuzzy. He regretted knocking the girl out. He could use her help now, getting to the helicopter, so he could fly away.

He tried to move her, to wake her up, but she was out.

"Shit," he cursed.

He forced himself to his feet. He'd get there on his own and get the hell out of dodge, while the getting was still good. He almost collapsed from the pain. In his fuzzy blur of agony, he had a vision. He could still have the grand finale, only instead of the children, he'd use Sabrina for the sacrifice.

"You, know Sabrina. It's a shame that the baby and the other kids got away, but I can still roast you, and the world knows about you so it will be almost as good."

Sabrina didn't respond.

"What, cat got your tongue?"

The car engine he thought he'd heard stopped and he wondered if he'd been imagining things. Maybe it was just a plane flying overhead?

No matter, there was no point in sticking around. Better get the fireworks started and head off into the sunset.

He checked his gun. He'd fired two at the pilot, and two into the door, then had switched to the rifle, so he still had two bullets left in his snub nose. He looked at the girl. He could put a bullet in her now and spare her the agony of being burned alive. But what would be the fun in that?

He wished again that he hadn't injected her with so much of the sleeping drug.

Unable to stop the grin so wide on his face that his jaws were starting to ache, he headed to the stove. After turning on the gas full blast, and shutting the window over the sink, he put the gun into the waist band of his trousers, and then looked for a walking stick. There was a broom leaning against the wall. He grabbed it, flipped it over so the bristles were up in the air, instead of down on the ground, and using it walking stick and lumbered out into the night, eyes peeled and ears listening for the sounds of any cars coming, as he made his way to the helicopter.

"Freeze, hands up, or I'll shoot!"

45 HARCOURT

They got there as soon as they could, but had to stop when they came across the abandoned SUV.

While the others stayed behind to search the area, Mark made Harcourt put on a vest, then he, Mark and Riggs headed down the road on foot in the direction the car had been going.

When they made it to the clearing, Harcourt said, "There, over there, going towards the helicopter."

Harcourt's sucked in air, fearful that Sabrina was already on the helicopter, that any second, he'd lose her again.

After motioning Harcourt to stay in the cover of the trees, Mark moved into the clearing, flanked by Riggs, both in a shooting stance.

Mark shouted, "Freeze, hands up, or I'll shoot!"

The man turned around slowly and Harcourt's face boiled with anger at the sight. "Peter fucking Talbert, you son of a bitch." But, Harcourt stayed put, the two professionals were handling the situation. Instead of staying low, he got up and moved trying to see inside the helicopter. Trying to see if Sabrina was inside it.

Peter had his hands up as he turned slowly around, but his hands were in fists as if he was holding something. He shouted in a clear voice. "If you care about the girl, don't threaten me."

"Where's the girl?" Riggs shouted.

"She's in the house, about to become BBQ," Peter said, as he dropped one of his arms but continued to hold something in his fist. "You shoot me and I fall, and then the bomb goes off. Poof. One less psychic in the world. Just like that."

"Wait," Harcourt said as he stepped into the clearing, positioning himself between Peter and the two officers of the law.

"What the fuck?" Mark shouted. "Get back!"

But, Harcourt held his position. Peter Talbert turned slowly around until he faced Harcourt. "As I live and breathe, if it isn't the wonder boy, Harcourt Raymondson himself. How the fuck are you old buddy, old pal?" His words dripped with sarcasm and bit into Harcourt's like the cold wind picking up all around them.

"What do you want?" Harcourt asked.

"Now, now, that is a good question. What do I want?"

Out of the corner of his eye, Harcourt saw Riggs and Mark inched closer, guns still trained on his former colleague.

Peter's face darkened. His voice loud and angry. "What I want is for those two idiots to drop their weapons and back the fuck off, or I swear I'll blow her up now!"

Mark and Riggs lowered their weapons but didn't let go.

"Drop them!"

Mark hesitated, then dropped his weapon, and Riggs did the same. Then they both started backing up.

"Peter, why are you doing this?"

"That's for me to know, and you to find out," he said with a smile, then moved towards the helicopter. "I'm going to get into my helicopter now and fly away. Try anything to stop me, and bye-bye Sabrina. But, if you let me go, then you can go in and save her. No harm, no foul."

Harcourt didn't believe it for a minute. As Peter Talbert struggled to get into the plane. Harcourt moved back into the shelter of the trees, then ran through them until he was lined up with the front door of the house. Behind him, he heard the small helicopter engine start and saw the leaves and dirt begin to blow under his feet as he bolted towards the house.

"Sabrina, Sabrina!" he shouted, once he was inside. Gas fumes permeated the air, telling him that there was no bomb or device. Peter had lied. Peter would just fire his gun at the house once he was airborne and blow he and Sabrina to smithereens.

As he rounded a wall he gasped at the sight of Sabrina slumped in a chair.

"No," he moaned.

He went to her side and tried to wake her up and pull her out of the chair. But, she was out like a light, and duct-taped to the chair.

Outside he heard the helicopter lifting off.

He hoisted Sabrina into his arms, chair and all, and while straining to keep his balance so they wouldn't topple on the way out he rushed towards the front door.

As soon as he made it to the steps, he heard Mark shout.

"Get away from the house!"

He didn't need to hear it twice, he was off and running, his arms burning from the strain of supporting the awkward load.

Above them, the helicopter circled. When Harcourt heard the first shot, he thought maybe Mark or Riggs had fired at the plane. If there was a second shot, he didn't hear it, because an explosion ripped through the clearing, deafening him, and he knew what was going to happen next. Turning around to protect her from the fall, he slammed onto his back, which knocked the wind out of him, then as soon as he was on the ground, he turned sideways and covered Sabrina, chair and all, with his body as best he could. The blast from the explosion slammed into them, searing hair of the back of his head, but didn't kill him.

"Sabrina, Sabrina," he said, not even able to hear his own words, as he scrambled to tear away the bonds of the duct tape.

Riggs knelt in beside him. Riggs took out a knife, switched open the steel and started to cut away at Sabrina's bonds. Lights of red and blue flashed all around him, as the rest of the team filled the scene. Riggs handed Harcourt her knife, then got up to concur with the others. Medics appeared and made him step aside as they attended to Sabrina. After a short while, one of the medics approached Harcourt where he'd been waiting on a stump. "Is she alright?" Harcourt shouted as his ears continued to ring.

"She's been drugged," said the medic, "out cold, but otherwise no serious damage that I can see."

Harcourt had to read the man's lips but it was enough to fill him with relief. "Thank God."

Then he thought of his friend. "Where's Mark?"

"Over here," said Mark who was letting a medic wrap his arm. "I got hit by house shrapnel."

"Will you two stop shouting?" shouted the medic.

"What?" Harcourt and Mark both said at the same time. Then they pointed to their ears.

"Where's Riggs?" Harcourt asked, after his hearing started to return and an army of FBI, Fire and Sheriff's officers filled up the scene.

"She went to the hospital with the children."

"The what?"

"Oh, didn't we tell you," said the medic. "They found two kids and Baby Adalyn. Alive." The young medics face was lit up with the excitement of it all. "And a dead dwarf over there in the woods, shot twice, once in the bag, and two old biddies ripped to shred by wild dogs or something back behind the house."

Mark and Harcourt exchanged surprised glances. The medic continued with a laugh. "Oh, yeah, they found a cop in the woods. Shot up pretty bad, from what I heard. Man, oh, man!"

"Dead?" Mark asked.

"Dead as a doornail."

After the medic proclaimed Harcourt fit to move, Harcourt checked on Sabrina who was still out, but the ambulance driver wasn't ready to leave yet. So, Mark and Harcourt made the rounds, staying out of the way of the firemen working hard to put out the blazing house, and the detectives working the crime scene, but they didn't get to see much, before the ambulance driver's whistle sent them running back.

Sabrina was already inside the back of the ambulance, and the man was getting ready to take her to the hospital. "I'm going with her, Mark," Harcourt announced as he started to climb inside. "That is unless you still plan to keep me in custody."

Mark slapped Harcourt's shoulder. "You go ahead. I'll stay here and help answer questions, try and keep you in the clear, for now." He winked.

They slammed the doors shut and Harcourt sat with the medic next to Sabrina. He held her hand as the ambulance put on its sirens and rolled away from the scene.

Harcourt had his ears examined and some superficial cuts treated while he waited at the hospital for Sabrina to wake up. With access to a working landline, he called Molly, who was back in Diversion, and told her to get a message to Maggie that Mark was fine and they'd all be home soon.

Then he went back to the waiting room to wait for Sabrina to come around. He thought about the impending vote, and he realized that he no longer gave a shit whether or not the board decided to vote him out on Wednesday. They'd change their tune and revoke the decision as soon as the word hit the press that Peter Talbert, the man who claimed Harcourt had stolen company money, was the man who'd kidnapped baby Adalyn. Peter's claims would lose all credibility. And Harcourt would be welcomed home with open arms.

Not that he cared.

Right now, all he cared about was making sure Sabrina was taken care of. He was resting his eyes in the chair by her hospital bed, when a nurse came in. "Mr. Raymondson? We have a call for you. Come this way, please."

Harcourt went to the nursing station and accepted the phone. "Hello, Raymondson here."

"What have you done to my sister?" said an angry voice on the other line.

"Sabrina?"

"Yes, Sabrina, who else?"

"Uh, she's here at the hospital."

"Oh my God, what happened, is she okay?"

"She's fine, but she's going to be out for a while."

"How long. Oh, my God, it's not a coma is it? Tell me she's not in a coma. Please."

"Not a coma, the doctor expects her to come to any time."

"Tell her to call me the moment she can speak."

Harcourt promised and after writing down her phone number on a hospital pad, he hung up and went back to the room.

"Hello," he said, when he saw that Sabrina had awoken. She had propped herself up and was looking around in bewilderment. When she turned and saw Harcourt's face, her eyes lit up just enough to make his chest squeeze with joy.

"I'm thirsty," she croaked and waved her hand at her throat.

He couldn't help but smile when he saw a flicker of recognition in her eyes.

He stood up, the edges of his mouth lifting as he leaned over her and grazed her soft cheek with his knuckle as he gazed into her soft brown eyes. "Hello, thirsty."

She smiled and he knew she was going to be okay.

He reached down and pulled her into an embrace. "I'm so glad I found you," he said.

There was a cough behind them. Harcourt straightened up and sniffed away the tear that almost came to his eye. "Yes," he said as man in a suit appeared in the room, flanked by Special Agent Riggs.

"May we speak to you, privately?"

Harcourt's alarm bells went off. Was he still a suspect? This was getting fucking old.

"We'd like you to speak to the kids," the man said.

THE BILLIONAIRE'S SHAMAN

"Oh, this is Special Agent Forbes with the Kidnapping Task force," Riggs said.

Harcourt shook his hand and relaxed. He'd forgotten that in addition to retrieving Baby Adalyn, during their rescue operation, they'd also apparently found two other children, also alive and expected to make a full recovery from their ordeal. He was happy for the children and their parents, but he didn't see what it had to do with him.

As Riggs and the other agent led him into the pediatric ward, Harcourt was surprised to see Mark waiting in front of a hospital room. Mark stood up as they approached, and Harcourt saw that his arm had been put in a cast. "Mark, how you doing buddy?"

"As well as can be expected," he said, and tried to smile, but there was something in the way he wouldn't quite look at Harcourt that made his stomach tighten.

Harcourt took a deep breath, ready to get whatever it was over with so he could hopefully get back to Sabrina's side. "So, where are these kids?" he asked, directing his comment to Forbes and Riggs.

"In here," said Mark, who opened the door, but stayed in the hallway.

Harcourt waited for Riggs to enter first, since she was a lady and he was raised to be a gentleman.

"You go ahead, I'll give you some time alone," she said.

Harcourt couldn't understand what the hell was going on, but he nodded and went inside. Behind him, someone reached in and closed the door.

His was in spacious room with two hospital beds and two patients. In the bed closest to the door was a young boy of twelve or thirteen. He sat cross-legged in the bed, a large book that looked like a medical tome in his lap, and he was staring at Harcourt with a grin on his face.

Harcourt's eyes traveled to the other bed, where a smaller looking child lay asleep, his back to them. All he could see was a thatch of black hair. For a second, Harcourt's breath caught in his throat; the strange child's head reminded him a lot of Cedric's. He shook it off. And directed his attentions back to the boy.

"Hello," Harcourt said, "I'm Harcourt Raymondson, what's your name, son?"

The boy put a finger on his chin and said in a clear, almost clinical voice. "I don't know my real name. But for a long time I've been going by Caleb."

Harcourt cocked his head at the boy's odd words, but only said, "Nice to meet you. What are you reading?"

His face lit up. "Anything I can find. Do you have a book?"

"No, but I'll see that you get some," Harcourt said, already warming to this odd child.

Silence fell in the room.

Harcourt decided to ask for the boy's help.

"Do you know why they asked me to come see you?" he whispered in a conspiratorial tone.

"I think they think you know Fox."

"Huh?" Harcourt said, thinking that perhaps the kid had a few eggs missing out of his dozen.

The boy pointed, then called out: "Fox, wake up."

Harcourt was about to stop the child from waking up, because he was clearly in need of rest, when the covers stirred. The little boy lifted his shoulder and rubbed his eyes, then turned around. "Caleb, what is it?"

Harcourt's heart slammed against his chest. This couldn't be happening. Cedric. NO. Cedric was dead. But he wasn't. His voice cracked. "Mark. Mark!" he shouted, and Mark rushed into the room followed by Riggs and Forbes. "Mark, tell me you see what I see, tell me I'm not going insane. Is that my boy?" His voice cracked as the child's eyes grew wide as he focused on Harcourt.

"Daddy?"

Harcourt's heart broke and repaired itself all in the same moment. Cedric's arms reached for his father and Harcourt hugged him until an alarm bell went off on one of the pieces of medical equipment, promoting Mark and the others had to drag him away from this son.

Over the next several hours, Harcourt's sense that he was having a dream or that he had finally dipped into insanity was challenged as the investigators and Agent Forbes, who was a child psychologist, helped to piece together some of the story.

Cedric remembered being dragged from his mother after leaving to go to the plane, and then he never saw her again. He had to live with the mean, ugly women, who told him his name was 'skinny brat,' even though he knew that was a lie.

Harcourt's anger for Peter mounted with the telling of how they'd treated his son and the other children. Caleb, who still didn't know his real name, said he'd been in that cabin for over ten years.

"Boys," said the nurse from the door. "You have a new visitor."

Sabrina was wheeled into the room. The hospital was clearly not ready to let her walk, even though she appeared to be fine. "Hi Caleb, hi Fox," she said to the two boys.

"Hi Angel," both boys said at the same time.

Harcourt went over to Sabrina and held her hands. "Cedric, this is Sabrina Cane. But not for long, I hope."

Sabrina looked up at Harcourt, eyebrows raised.

He leaned down and whispered in her ear. "Will you marry me? I want to know before I announce it to the kids."

Sabrina's heart slammed and clanged inside her, forcing her to grasp onto her chest. Beneath her trembling fingers, the amber pendant throbbed with heat. Had he just asked her to marry him?

She knew what she wanted to say, but could she even do it? She was already married, and hadn't had a chance to get the divorce. But then she remembered Jack was dead. She closed her eyes, saying a prayer and blessing for Jack's wicked soul, then opened her eyes as a calm sense of peace and tranquility ran through her.

She reached for her amber pendent and just to be sure, and felt its warm, pulsing agreement.

"Sabrina?" Harcourt's voice was laced with his need for her.

She turned her gaze up to the bravest man in the world she'd ever known, then mouthed the only word she could think of.

"Yes."

Epilogue

Harcourt

Harcourt watched with pride and a lump in his throat as his new family dashed around the temporary home in Victoria, British Colombia, trying to get everyone ready for the big day to come.

Sabrina, hurry up," Jeannette shouted up the stairs, as Sabrina climbed down the spiral staircase. Her head was wrapped in a silk, hiding the world's largest roller and she had her wedding dress draped over her arms inside a garment bag.

"Here, let me take that, I'm the Maid of Honor, you shouldn't have to carry that."

"Mama Sabby, let's go... I don't want to miss it. Hurry," Cedric said, jumping up and down excitedly. He wouldn't stop talking about the first ceremony.

"I'm coming, sugar, hold your horses," Sabrina said as she leaned down to pinch his cheek. Harcourt's heart filled as he saw her pinch his son's cheek. Cedric had blossomed since getting rescued, and there was a little bit of flesh on his face where there'd once been hollowed shadows. He'd put on just the right amount of weight. And his eyes had lost much of the haunted look. He gave Sabrina credit for helping him through it, and they were as close as if they were mother and son.

"You going to get married in that headdress?" Harcourt whispered into Sabrina's ear, unable to resist the friendly jab.

"Oh, you," she teased. "Would serve you serve you right, for allowing me to let my sister talk me into her doing my hair in the first place, instead of hiring a professional."

"You don't have to worry about her hair," Jeannette said, shoving Sabrina toward the door. "Just let her sit in the back with me and you keep Ellis and the kids occupied. I'll fix her hair up perfect. Come on, everyone, we've got to go. Where's Papa?"

As if his ears were burning, Ellis Hawkins wheeled out of the library. After making arrangements for Ellis to get his cancer treatments in Victoria, Harcourt had him moved into the new property which would be their home while the Diversion Mansion was rebuilt.

"Don't forget me," came a gruff, but smiling voice from the library, and Harcourt watched Sabrina's face light up at the sight of her father. The legendary jazz musician Ellis Hawkins, had at first resisted being taken in and moved out of his old house. But, after finding out that Harcourt had tracked down one of his old band members and that the man lived on Vancouver Island and wanted to jam, Ellis agreed to move out.

And not only Ellis. Sabrina had insisted on bringing over Jeannette and her two boys.

Cedric and Jerrod and Tyler had become instant brothers, and kept Jeannette and Sabrina on their toes. Caleb stayed more to himself, but Harcourt knew he looked out for the younger boys.

"Where's Caleb," Sabrina shouted as she completed her headcount.

"I'm here," said a quiet and gentle voice.

"Oh, great Caleb. Are you ready to meet the people from the Jenson foundation?"

Caleb face grew stern.

"I don't want them to call me Scott," he said.

"I understand, Caleb. I've already told them, that. But, they are human, and to them you are Scott Jenson, the boy they thought had been dead all these years. If they make a mistake and call you that, you have to understand – it's only because to them it's a miracle that you are here at all."

"I understand," Caleb said. "But, I still don't want them to call me Scott."

Sabrina and Harcourt both laughed.

"I'll be sure to remind them again before we meet them, all right, buddy? Harcourt said."

"All right."

Sabrina turned so she could wipe a tear from her eye, and felt Harcourt's hand squeeze her shoulder with reassurance. The decision to keep Caleb in their lives, to adopt him, and not to send him to some home for the socially challenged had never been in question for either of them, despite the protests of several psychologists and social workers connected to Caleb's case. They'd had some sleepless nights worrying about their choice, and what difficult times might lay ahead as Caleb was reintegrated into the real world, but they both knew that they'd get through whatever challenges presented themselves. And how ever difficult it might be for them, the whole experience had to be a million times harder for Caleb. Sabrina forced a smile back on her face and sparkle into her voice, before turning to Caleb again.

"Turn around, so I can inspect you. See how you look."

Caleb did a slow one-eighty in front of her.

"Very nice, but let me fix your tie," Sabrina said.

"Let, me," Harcourt said, intervening. "How a man ties his tie is something he should learn from his father."

Caleb's face lit up for just a moment, then became serious again. "You don't have to do this, you don't have to adopt me." Caleb said.

"I don't have to, but I'm going to. Now hold still Caleb Raymondson!"

Caleb's eyes glistened, as his father-to-be fixed his tie.

Sabrina heard Harcourt's voice crack as he turned his son-to-be around, smacked him on the behind and pushed him toward the other. "Go help your aunt with her little monsters."

Caleb's smile was wide and genuine for a moment as he headed toward Aunt Jeannette who was struggling to make Tyler and Jerrod presentable. Sabrina and Harcourt held hands as they watched Caleb approach. "May I help, Auntie Jeannette?" Caleb asked, all business again.

Jerrod and Tyler jostled with each other to be first in line to have Caleb fix their ties.

When Caleb inspected them both and nodded his head with approval, Harcourt cleared his throat. "Everyone ready for this momentous day?"

"Yeah," Jerrod shouted, then he punched Tyler in the ribs and the two boys started to chase each other around the room.

"I think you're trying to squeeze too much into one day, if you ask me. I mean," Jeannette said as she walked over to her sister and brother-in-law to be. "Certainly, too much for me, in one day," she counted off on her fingers as she spoke. "I'm supposed to be the Maid of Honor at my sister's wedding, then attend a reception hosted by baby Adalyn's parents, and then I get to watch my sister and my new brother-in-law get a medal for bravery from the Prime Minister, and then... we all get to watch a ceremony where Caleb becomes a member of the family and my sister becomes an honorary Canadian citizen. Am I forgetting anything?" Everyone laughed as Jeannette tried to catch her breath after spitting out all those words in one go.

"You forgot about your reward, Mommy," Tyler pointed out.

But, Harcourt knew she hadn't forgot her reward. Due to her announcement on television about where to find Sabrina, Jeannette was also going to receive a medal of honor, and a big fat check for her part in saving baby Adalyn. Harcourt knew that she hadn't forgotten that little bit of ceremony to come, because per Sabrina, Jeanette already had each penny spent.

Harcourt checked his watch and then rounded them up toward the door, herding them like sheep toward the waiting limousine, then turned as a car drove up. "Miss Molly," shouted Cedric and Jeannette's two boys.

Since moving to Victoria they'd seen a lot of Molly McCarthy. Cedric remembered his former babysitter, and she'd gone with them when they'd gone back to Diversion, because Cedric wanted to see the cottage. And even though both the mansion and the cottage were still burnt out shells, just visiting Molly's undamaged house and Dogwood Canyon again had done wonders for Cedric's state of mind.

Harcourt and Sabrina decided after that visit that they would rebuild the mansion and the cottage exactly as they were, and plans were already underway to make that happen.

Molly McCarthy hugged the boys, then gave Sabrina a kiss on the cheek.

"Thanks for inviting me," she said.

"What about me?" came a voice from down the hall. It was Ellis. Caleb hurried over to him. Caleb and Ellis had become very close friends. Caleb took charge of pushing the wheelchair.

Everyone followed Harcourt out onto the front steps of the house, and Caleb pushed Ellis's wheelchair toward the handicap ramp they'd had installed after his recent surgery. Thanks to Harcourt's endless funds, Ellis had been provided with a special medical treatment that had reversed the cancer and would extend his life for several more years. But, in a moment of enthusiasm for life, Ellis had managed to trip and brake his ankle, thus the need for a wheelchair.

As they moved toward the waiting vehicles, another car drove up. "There's Dr. Leibowitz," announced Caleb, as he kept a firm hold on the wheelchair so it wouldn't fly down the ramp. She waved to them from her sparkling vintage Jaguar convertible, prepared to join the caravan of cars headed to the ceremonies. The world-renown child psychologist, Dr. Helen Leibowitz, had done wonders with Caleb and Cedric, helping them deal with their traumatic experiences and easing their adjustment back to normal life. She'd also been the one medical professional in the group that supported Harcourt and Sabrina regarding their plans to adopt Caleb.

Caleb saw Dr. Leibowitz three times a week, to Cedric's one time a week. Cedric had adjusted fast. And save for the nightmares, and a case of the 'clingies,' he was almost the same happy child he used to be. And even Caleb was showing some signs of coming out of his shell. Sabrina and Harcourt understood that Caleb's recovery would be much more difficult, and that he might never fully recover. But, it didn't matter. They weren't going to leave him to deal with it on his own. And there was no doubt in Harcourt's mind that Caleb was a good kid with a good heart who cared for Cedric and would never hurt him.

And even though there might be challenges ahead, Harcourt wouldn't change a thing.

That thought made his stomach twist with guilt. That wasn't true. If he could turn back the clock, he would have seen Peter for what he was, and he'd never have let him get close enough to cause Sharon's murder.

But, then he looked at his bride to be, Sabrina. He loved her with all his heart. But, that didn't mean he had stopped loving his first wife. Sharon's voice seemed to rise in his head. She was saying, "It's okay, Harcourt. I want you to be happy, I want Cedric to have a new mom."

The memory of his wife, and the grief he still felt for her squeezed his chest hard, but he nodded his head. "Thank you," he said under his breath.

"Did you say something?" Sabrina asked.

"I said, let's get this show on the road," Harcourt called out for everyone to hear, as he waved everyone to the waiting transport. And guided his bride to be into the limousine.

She gave him a smile so sincere that it melted his heart. She loved him, and he loved her, and they were going to happy together for the rest of their lives.

He gave her a kiss, before letting her climb into the back with her sister for the first destination on their packed schedule for the day. The first activity was the private tea with baby Adalyn's parents.

As they made it to the gate of the estate, Harcourt saw that Mark and his family had finally arrived. They honked as they approached, and Mark waved and got in line with the rest of the caravan of cars.

As they drove past Mark, Harcourt noticed that Mark's daughter appeared to have a younger man sitting with her in the back seat.

Harcourt smirked at the sight, and made a mental note to give his best friend a serious ribbing about his daughter having a boyfriend. In his lap, Cedric settled in, burying his head into his father's chest as he closed his eyes. Harcourt squeezed his son tight.

He thought about Caleb, the boy that would soon be his legal son. Caleb had been offered a seat in the massive limo, but had insisted on going with Ellis in the handicap van. Harcourt turned his head around, to look behind and make sure, the van was still back there. At the sight of it, he relaxed.

Sometimes, he still couldn't believe what had happened. Cedric alive? Sabrina in his life? A new son in Caleb? He was so blessed.

No one could explain how Cedric had been spared, and with Peter Talbert gone, he couldn't ask the man that had to know what had happened. He'd stayed up with Sabrina for hours, trying to imagine what had gone down. Perhaps, Peter, who'd always been jealous of his wife and Harcourt's family, had somehow forced Sharon onto the plan, taken his son, but left the fireman's helmet, and convinced the pilot that it was okay to fly away – despite what had to have been Sharon's clear problems with her child being taken away. Or maybe, Sharon had been drugged and the pilot was in on it, thinking he was to be paid hansomely – but, then Peter had tricked him by planting the bomb on the plain and killing pilot and passenger.

Maybe, Peter had wanted to keep his son alive, just so he could tortue him later, by making him watch his son die for a second time.

They'd stopped trying to understand. Such evil was impossible to understand, Sabrina reminded him.

"What's important is that he's back in your life. It's a gift. A blessing."

Sabrina was right.

He'd been blessed.

Given another chance to be a both a husband and a father. Harcourt had no intentions of wasting that opportunity.

"Ouch, watch it you pulled my hair," Sabrina shouted from the back of the limo.

Cedric, who'd fallen asleep jolted awake, his body stiff with fear. "It's all right, son," Harcourt said as he stroked his son's skinny arms, trying to sooth him.

Cedric relaxed, and the fear wrinkles left his forehead. He smiled, then craned his neck to see what had caused the ruckus in the back seat.

"Sorry, princess," Jeannette snapped back at her sister. "Excuse me, for trying to make you beautiful."

In his lap, Cedric looked up at his father, a confused expression covering his face. "I thought Mama Sabby was an angel, not a princess?" he asked with those big eyes all curious.

"She's both, son, she's both...."

Peter Talbert declined the cup of tea, offered by the doctor's assistant. He'd changed his identity, changed his face, and even surgically altered his voice since going on the lam. He'd begun a new and profitable kidnapping operation, but it hadn't lasted for long. The mysterious illness had robbed him of his energy and strength, and he'd had to focus his attentions of getting well, which so far had not garnered much results.

The doctors couldn't tell him what was wrong, and no remedies or drugs they prescribed improved his condition in any way.

His mind went back to Seattle, and what had happened. He'd thought, he'd seen the house burst into flames, and he'd thought he'd at least burnt that stupid shaman bitch, but when he saw the news, he learned what had happened at the cabin after he'd flown away.

It was a huge story. He played a prominent role in the news, but the bigger story was all about the heroes: Harcourt and Sabrina and the two kids that supposedly helped save Baby Adalyn. Sabrina had fucking survived the fire in the house, and Caleb and Harcourt's brat, were all safe and sound. Worst of all, Harcourt was welcomed back to his company with open arms. He hadn't even managed to destroy the man's company, and the stock had rallied at the news that Harcourt Raymondson was coming back, but as a consultant only.

Just thinking about how everything had gone wrong, made him sick to his stomach, or maybe it was just his illness. He was nauseous most of the time.

Peter Talbert smiled to himself, recalling the bit of press he'd gotten in the business journals. The board of directors for Raymondson Industries had gone out there way to point all fingers at him, even as they apologized publicly to their stockholders for having been associated with Peter Talbert. But it wasn't the notoriety he wanted.

Another memory made him stretch his lips. Learning that that Babette and Olga had been eaten alive by wolves, that was priceless. He closed his eyes, as he tried to imagine the looks on their faces as the animals tore them apart. His smile broadened on his lips and he felt himself relaxing, and some of the pain in his body fading away, as he imagined their final moments.

"Mr. Reigrod? The doctor will see you now," came a voice.

At first, Peter Talbert kept his eyes closed. But, when she spoke the name a second time, his eyes shot opened as he remembered that he was Mr. Reigrod.

Peter Talbert followed the nurse and her clipboard back to the doctors' office to wait. The last time he'd seen the doctor he'd been sent off to have blood drawn, MRIs and several other tests to help diagnose his condition.

The doctor came in, shook his hand, then sat behind his desk and picked up a thick medical file, labeled, S. Reigrod. "I believe I've identified the cause of your current troubles," said the doctor.

Peter sat up. "What is it? Just tell me. I'm not paying you to beat around the bush."

The doctor turned a large medical book, which had been opened to a specific page and turned it so the patient could see. Peter had to rise in his chair since he was shorter than most men. The doctor also rose in his chair and pointed to a part of the page, where there was an illustration of a black seed pod.

"Your symptoms match Ziichetti poisoning, used primarily by African shamans and witchdoctors. It's also called the Widowmaker or the Widow Ball."

His mind raced back to that night in the cabin's kitchen and he recalled it now, although he hadn't thought anything of it at the time. He'd seen something like the ball shown in the medical book. A gnarled seed pod with spikes coming out of it. It had been lying in the bottom of the sink at the Washington cabin. He'd noticed it when he'd turned on the gas on the nearby stove. He'd thought nothing of it. Just more poor housekeeping on Babette and Olga's part – but, now it made sense. She'd got him water and she'd stayed at that sink for a long time. Sabrina Cane was a fucking shaman; she'd done that to him. "I don't get it," he said. "I remember when I was exposed, but that was months ago, it should be out of my system by now?"

"That's not how it works. It's a slow poison, but I'm sorry to say that it will kill you. Unless you can get the cure."

"Well, what the fuck is the cure?"

"I'm not even sure it exists, to be honest, but there are accounts that certain shamans have a ritual to cleanse the victim of the Widow Ball curse. That's obviously not the kind of medicine I practice, but I can put you in touch with some people who might know someone..."

Peter Talbert accepted the paper with the doctor's referrals, then headed outside into the dry heat, leaning hard on his cane to support his shaking legs. His driver stood by the car, smoking, but tossed his cigarette into the street when he caught sight of him, then ran to open his door. Peter slumped inside, then told his driver to take him to the pharmacy. This time, his doctor had ordered a larger quantity of the pain pills he needed. The effort of getting out of bed was bad enough. He had no desire to take another trip downtown just to get more pain pills.

As the driver moved through the throngs towards the dispensary, Peter Talbert pondered what he'd do next.

He'd find the right witchdoctors, he'd make them break the curse, and then he'd get back to work. The world hadn't seen the last of Peter Talbert. Not, if he could help it.

He ached from head to toe, and barely made it in and then out of the dispensary. After he settled himself back into the plush leather seat, his driver said, "Where to, Sir?"

Peter Talbert ignored his driver as they idled at the curb. With shaking hands, he poured whiskey into the crystal glass, took a deep gulp, then winced as he tried to swallow the harsh liquid down his swollen throat.

He should go back to his apartment and make plans to travel, to meet up with those who could break his curse. But, the idea of trapesing through some jungle to track down and force a bunch of witchdoctors to do his bidding made him incredibly tired. Why bother?

Despite how wrong his big plans had gone, he'd still managed to accomplish at least one goal.

They were moving forward with the movie. Yes, the emphasis, wasn't as much on him as it was about the stupid shaman and the brave little kids, but at least it was going to be made. And the true fans of evil would recognize the real star of the film. And the movie was destined to do well, thanks to his brilliant plan to kidnap Baby Adalyn. Already, he was more famous now than he'd ever be, again. He was number one on all the most wanted international criminal lists. What was there left for him to do? What new feat could he possibly accomplish?

And even if he could stop the Widow Ball curse from poisoning him, the damage already done to his body, was irreversible, per his doctor. He'd never be healthy again. He'd always have nerve damage and weakness. What was the point?

He was too tired, in too much pain.

"I'll take you home, sir," said the driver, as he moved into traffic.

As his limo drove through the colorful streets of Morocco, Peter Talbert with difficulty, opened the bottle of pain pills. He popped four pills into his mouth. They went down painfully, and he chased them with a long, deep pull from his glass.

He closed his eyes, welcoming the heat of the Maker's Mark as it warmed his chest. The pain reduced. He tipped the bottle over, resting it on his trembling lips, and put them all in his mouth, coughing and hacking as he struggled to swallow the rest of the pills.

"Are you alright, sir?" asked his driver

"I'm fine, you idiot," Peter snapped, or tried to snap, but his thoughts were already becoming unclear. He stared through the divider towards this driver.

"Where do you live?" he asked. Maybe it wasn't too late for one final act.

"In the south country, why?" asked his driver.

Peter fingered the gun in his pocket.

"Do you have any children?"

"No, sir," said his driver.

"Pity." Peter Talbert's body slumped in disappointment, and from the drugs. He poured himself another drink, spilling most of it on his pants. He let the glass tumble to the seat and drank from the bottle.

His mouth felt thick and he couldn't move his lips. "Is there a school?" he managed to say.

"What kind of school sir?" the driver asked.

He had his gun out and he saw that the driver's eyes had grown wide as they watched him from the rear-view mirror.

"The kind of school with bratty, little, children..." Peter Talbert tried to spit out the words, but they came out in an incomprehensible slur.

"Okay, Sir, I will take you there," said the driver.

Peter Talbert relaxed and closed his eyes, and blinked awake, sometime later as the car slowed and then stopped.

He peered through the windows, looking for a school full of children. But, he saw no children anywhere. Nor any buildings. The driver's door opened, and he waited for his driver to let him out. But, instead, he heard running feet.

"Come back!!" he tried to shout, but he could barely force enough air into his lungs. He unlocked his door and had to use all his strength just to push it open. He tried to get out and shoot his treacherous driver, but he stumbled and fell hard onto the dirt. He rolled over onto his back, gasping for breath, unable to move a muscle. For a long time, he lay on his back, looking up into the harsh and unforgiving sun. He had no idea if the pills would kill him, but he knew he would die from other forces if he couldn't get off the road. Animals would come and tear him apart, or perhaps robbers would end his pain, or maybe just heatstroke from the sun.

Peter Talbert liked to be in control.

He felt for the gun inside his pocket. It wasn't there.

With effort, he turned his head towards the car and the open door. Groaning, he struggled to turn over, and right himself and crawl back into the car. He'd get his gun and finish himself off on his own terms.

But, his muscles wouldn't obey his commands. He managed to turn over and get on his hands and knees, but before he could get to the door, the drugs overtook him, and he collapsed, arms splayed to his side, his mouth tasting dirt.

He laughed, as tears flowed, and he thought of the boy.

Caleb had been like a son to him. He'd done things for that child. Taught him how to read, kept him alive all those years, when he didn't have to. Somewhere in Canada in the next few days, Caleb would receive a medal for bravery. He'd been responsible for making that boy who he was.

They'd give him a reward for being such a good father, wouldn't they?

As fire and brimstone burned below him, and as he gazed across the endless depths of hell, he tasted a cool breeze blowing across his parched lips.

He slid into unconsciousness and gave in to the inevitable.

Maybe where he was going next wouldn't be so bad...

The End

MORE MIA CALDWELL BOOKS IN PRINT

Kidnapping the Billionaire's Baby
The Billionare's Triplets
The Billionaire's Triplets Matchmakers
Billioniare's Marriage Arrangment
Those Fabulous Joans Girls (Books 1, 2 & 3)
Scottish Billionaire's Baby
Aloha, Love
Billionaire's Baby Surprise
Hollywood Happily Ever After
Undercover Billionaire Boss

ABOUT THE AUTHOR

Mia Caldwell has been fantasizing about stories of "Happily-Ever-After" since she was a little girl, and now that she's all grown up her "Happily-Ever-After" stories have taken a steamier turn! After graduating from college Mia still wasn't quite sure what she wanted to do with her life. Bored with her day job as an Administrative Assistant for a non-profit, she started writing stories on the side and sharing them with her friends. They gave her the push she needed to share them with you!

She lives in New York with two rascally cats named Link and Zelda, eats too much chocolate and Chinese take-out, and goes on way too many blind dates. She's still waiting for Mr. Right, but in the meantime, she'll keep dreaming up the perfect man!

Sign up for Mia's newsletter and http://eepurl.com/biglo9

Connect with Mia and her fans on Facebook at https://www.facebook.com/authormiacaldwell/

Mia loves hearing from her fans. authormiacaldwell@gmail.com

Made in the USA
Charleston, SC
04 March 2017